THE ENERGETICS SERIES, BOOK 4

CARA AND THE HACKER

ELLEN BARD

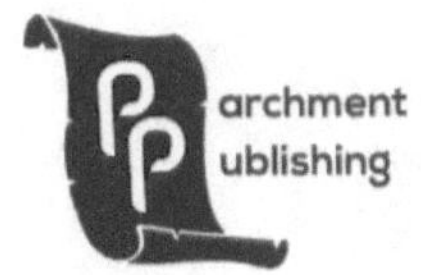

CARA AND THE HACKER

The Energetics Series: Book 4

Ellen Bard

ISBN-13: 978-0-9934394-8-3

Published by Parchment Publishing.
ParchmentPublishing.com

To every recovering perfectionist and control freak.

Let go a little.

Mess it up.

You're good enough just as you are.

The Chakras and their Energies

 **Muladhara:** The Root Chakra – Earth Element
The energy of nourishment and home, family and safety.

 **Svadisthana:** The Sacral Chakra – Water Element
Fluid and adaptable, the energy of movement and connection, of practical and physical creativity. The energy of pleasure, sexuality and sensation, and emotions.

 **Manipura:** The Navel Chakra – Fire Element
The energy of the individual; of confidence, of proactivity and of drive and passion. Playful and proud.

 **Anahata:** The Heart Chakra – Air Element
The energy of healing, and of balance, located in the middle of the body and the seven Chakras. The energy of love, of relationships, of devotion. Of compassion and empathy.

 **Vishudha:** The Throat Chakra – Ether (Space) Element
The energy of communication, of conceptual creativity, and of truth. Of expression, and of listening.

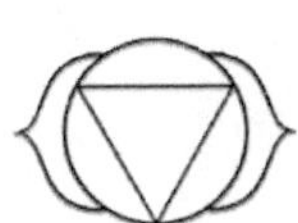 **Ajna:** The Third Eye – The Mind
The energy of imagination, of visualizations, and insight. Of clarity and wisdom. Of dreams and intuition.

 **Sahasara:** The Crown Chakra – None*
The purest of all the energies. Only experienced through the Grace of the Source (the energetics' name for the creator, the divine).

*Neither a dominant nor auxiliary Chakra for energetics

The Iskander Prophecy

(notes by Prof. Cuinn Ahern,
Ajna-Muladhara)

Dreamscape prophecy vision (C. Ahern):
Twelve energetics stand together against
unknown danger
Six male
Six female

(Only Blaize and Cuinn identified at the time of the first prophecy)

Damanea vision (Ajna Guild leader)
Need Protector, Creator, Healer,
Communicator, Warrior, Sage Archetypes.
Male and Female elements both

Does that mean we need two of each? A male and female Warrior, etc?

**Translation from Cappotian
(found in the notes of the Hermit,
Damir, deceased)**

Who is Iskander???

From the House of Iskander
When the Twelve shall gather

Each shall have a role
But on each the work will take a toll

Twelve bracelets will give them power
Activated by pairs or all at the final hour

The pair joined in the element of mind
Will fight tooth and nail but eventually find
Dreamscape defences must be breached
If their love be found and reached

The pair joined in the element of air
Will seek far and wide for something right there
Will locate puzzle pieces made of flesh and of bone
Then find heart-magic begins at home

The pair joined in the element of water
Will battle control that has to falter
Sacrifice made and offering given
Will help ensure both are truly living

The pair joined in the element of fire
Will uncover secrets, ancient and dire
Wild energy transmits, affects and enhances
Finds solutions and increases love's chances

????

Missing verses: Earth? Ether?

????

NB: Adam = Earth, Protector

Twelve bracelets, twelve stones
Together, not alone,

In pairs they will be
And only then will they see

Without the support of them all
The Circle, the Guilds - our race - shall fall.

Why Circle and not Circles?
If singular, major or minor?

As yet unidentified (Chakras = dominant or auxiliary)
Male (Manipura)
Male (Ether)
Female (Ether)
Female (Earth)

Missing: Sage (f), Communicator (f and m), Creator (m)

CHAPTER

1

Archer's feet pounded along the trail, while to his left, dusk enveloped the looming rust-brown metal towers that bled into the manicured lawns surrounding them. For Archer, Seattle's 'iron Stonehenge', aka the Gas Works Park, was a fascinating combination of humans' complexity: they destroyed and they created.

He changed his pace to cool down from his regular three-mile circuit. It was more dark than not, the silence of the usually busy park creating an illusion of intimacy between him and the woman coming through his Bluetooth headphones.

"Sorry Phoebe, I can't make it," Archer said. "I need to take over as lead coder on Whisper."

"I need you at this meeting. I only agreed to you taking on the project management because Whisper is so important to the future of the business, and you seemed keen," she said. "It's been a while since you were so excited about something."

Along with being best friends, Archer and Phoebe were, respectively, the CEO and COO of Disp@tch, the successful communications technologies business they had built together over the last couple of decades.

"I'm still excited. That's why I'm taking over the coding. It's just been a busy week, remember?"

A senior member of the management team had resigned this week due to family issues outside Disp@tch's control, leaving a pile of work undone, and there had been a potentially high-profile exposure issue where a teenage energetic had used their powers and had been caught on camera. Luckily, in this day and age it was easy to convince people that the real video was a fake, debunk the story, and ensure his race stayed hidden. But it took time.

Archer slowed the last few yards to where he'd locked up his mountain bike. He always used the same spot to secure it when he went for his much-needed run.

A prickle of discomfort ran across his shoulders, and he shrugged them a few times to dissipate the feeling, glancing around him to see if there was a source. He saw nothing out of the ordinary. He looked at the sky. Perhaps it was the threat of rain to come.

"It's critical you come," she persisted. "We need these investors. This opportunity has huge potential, but only if it gets funding. I need you there to present the technical aspects, and with a working demo. Arch, you handpicked the team for this. What's wrong with Indu's work?"

He stretched out his quads. "There are problems with the code, and it's easier for me to do it myself than have him fix it. Think of it like this: he's the equivalent of a state champion, I'm an Olympian. There's no comparison."

While he could almost hear her eyes rolling her side of the call, Archer was one of the best in his field, he had no doubts about that. And no, this was nothing at all to do with the fact his favorite thing was coding.

He had a sneaking suspicion that Phoebe enjoyed actually running the business a lot more than him these days.

"If you try and do it all yourself, you'll run out of energy. You need to take care of yourself, and using the team is part of that."

"I am using the team." He grabbed the sports drink he'd stashed in the down-tube bottle cage and drank.

"You need to stop trying to micro-manage every detail," she said. "Burnout is a thing, even for energetics."

"If you want the best demo, I have to be the one to develop it." It wasn't arrogance. It was fact. "Whisper will be a success because I've made the tech, not because I was at the meeting."

A rustle sounded in the scant trees behind him and he spun, his senses alert. A gull flew past him and his shoulders dropped. He shook his head, annoyed, rolling his neck. His unease likely stemmed more from guilt than from anything amiss in this tranquil park.

"How close is the team to finishing the demo?" Phoebe asked.

"Close," he said: only a partial fib. It was at least three quarters complete. Well. Half. Indu and his team had been working on it, but Archer had stopped them earlier that week, knowing he could finish it in much less time, with better results. However, it had been a busy week, and he hadn't gotten around to it. Yet.

He sighed. There'd been a time when he'd dreamed of being a historian. He'd stayed up late into the night as a child studying the myths of his people, the energetics of Atlantis, and how they intersected with the legends of humans. But that time was past. Day-to-day he had to be satisfied with places like this park, and while he loved its contrast of the natural world and industrial archaeology, it contained nothing like the mysteries of why his people had to leave their homeland many thousands of years ago.

He'd fallen into running Disp@tch—what had started as a fun coding project had become one of the largest communications businesses in the world. As well as providing various messaging apps and services for humans, it also provided a way of monitoring potential discovery by humans of the energetics race. As Disp@tch had become more successful, his parents had finally shown an interest in his work, and he'd become 'the business one' in his family, while his older sister was always 'the academic one'.

"Alright," said Phoebe. "I appreciate it. Can you show me a working demo by the end of the week?"

"No problem," he said, wincing as he worked out how many hours of overtime stood between him and Friday.

"Are you seeing anyone new?" Phoebe said, in the swift change of topic she was known for.

Archer pressed his eyes shut tight, a headache coming on. "I'm not dating anyone right now."

He unlocked his bike, then walked his empty drink over to the recycling can and dropped it in.

"I understand you don't love it. Believe me, I don't love parading myself with a random guy on my arm for the magazines either. But you haven't been on a date for weeks. Our public profiles are a core part of the business, and we agreed while we're both single we'd take advantage of the fact and keep generating PR and networking opportunities."

He turned the collar of his windbreaker up and walked back to the bike, where he leaned over to unlock it. This was a recurring argument. "You're a lot more photogenic than I—"

Before he finished his sentence, something hard slammed into his upper back; the breath knocked from him. The cellphone fell from his hand, and he lost an ear bud. He stumbled and tripped over the bike, landing in a tangle of limbs and metal.

"Archer?" Phoebe said, but he was thrusting himself away from the bike and springing to his feet, searching for the attack's origin.

Human or energetic? Random or targeted? Understand your opponent and you were more likely to beat them. Brains could beat brawn when combined with the sort of martial arts and energetic training he'd received.

He glimpsed a figure at the tree line, shrouded in morning mist, arm raised. A whirl of dirt rose from the ground in front of the figure and headed toward Archer.

Alright. That answered one question. An energetic, either a Muladhara, given the earth, or an Anahata, given the air. He glanced around, saw no-one else, and got ready to unleash his power.

"We need you. Kayla's having another episode."

Cara heard the words with a sinking heart, but jumped up from her desk and followed Ife through the corridors to the locked-down part of the Healing Center. Leeching could, and would, kill, eventually. Cara's job was to make sure that didn't happen.

As they ran, Ife apologized. "We wouldn't disturb you if we didn't need you, Cara. Sorry."

Cara served as General Manager of the Center, her role focusing on the smooth administration of both the Rehabilitation Center and the therapeutic section. She acted as a Healer in emergencies only, or she'd never have time to go home.

"It's been weeks, and I'm still not sure which side of the Center Kayla belongs on," Cara muttered as they bolted down another corridor, its smooth walls the healing green of Anahata Chakra.

Cara slammed her palm against each energetic ward and human-made biometric that they flew through. Security was a lot tighter in the Rehab section, and instances like this showed why.

Kayla had been a victim of a truly horrific act, her energy drained by another energetic. She had also been forced to leech from others, which had twisted her energy, and she trembled on the line between normal energetic and Rogue. Cara's team had been working with the girl to rehabilitate her, but she suffered terrible energetic and mental episodes, each more destructive than the last. Ife specialized in talking therapies, and possessed deep experience in integrating art therapy to help with expression of trauma, but the girl had yet to open up.

"She's trying to leech from Jason," Ife said, his long legs eating up the ground alongside Cara, concern visible in the way his delicate fingers wove through the air to illustrate his speech. He caught her glance and reassured her. "Thea's with him. He's not alone."

"Is he hurt?" Jason was the least experienced Healer in the Center.

He shook his head. "But the girl is a junkie. She should be clean by now, but she's not. Her energy is still twisted. I don't know if the block is coming from inside her, some kind of energetic residue we haven't picked up, or is something external."

"How could it be external?" Cara stopped for a moment outside the door to the girl's room. She pulled energy from the ether to fortify herself. A high-pitched scream came through the thick door. Something hammered against it from inside, and it shuddered. "Nothing should be able to get in or out of that room."

Cara gestured to Ife, who unlocked the door, opening it only enough for them both to slip quickly through, then closing it behind them and reactivating the locks.

Despite numerous wards, many of which Cara had woven personally, the room was in chaos. Kayla stared straight ahead, her dyed-blue hair lank around her shoulders. But she was one of the few points of stillness in the space, as items from the room whirled around her.

Energetics called these spaces Holding Rooms. Not cells. Never cells. Designed to be temporary, once the individual was no longer in danger of their energy distorting, they would take on a role that would help them atone, usually in one of the Guilds, using their energy for a purpose that served the race.

Kayla's room, like the others here, contained a bed, armchair, and desk with a wooden chair, and a private en suite bathroom.

Simple furniture, in natural materials, with clean lines, enchanted by Muladhara energy to be unbreakable.

They estimated Kayla's age at about nineteen or twenty, with energies of Ajna-Vishudha, though they hadn't been able to find out much about her life before an energetic on a walk had stumbled across her—broken, drained and left for dead in a small forest clearing near Vancouver.

The one thing they were certain of was the importance to her of art. She refused to talk about the events that had ended up with her lying beneath the trees, and in fact spoke rarely, but she *had* asked for art supplies. She barely ate, yet she completely covered every piece of paper given to her with sketches and drawings. Kayla had also taken to painting symbols on the white walls. Cara's hope was that it would prove a way for the girl to work through some of her trauma.

At the moment, Kayla clutched Jason by the upper arms. Her strength belied her wiry frame. Jason talked to her in a soothing voice, attempting to build a connection and talk her down, while the girl's art supplies blinked in and out of existence around them. Kayla had drawn a protective circle around them both in pastels—the intention held significance, not the material. Another Healer, Thea, her usually serious eyes wide, frantically worked on negating the magics the girl erected around herself and her captive. Flashes of light and color winked in and out around her stout body.

The girl was trying to take energy from Jason, and while he kept his voice steady, sweat beaded on his brow and his breath came in rapid bursts.

The chair disappeared from the desk, and reappeared the other side of the bed.

Cara's heart tripped, shocked to see this use of powers. Manipulating objects in space was a power some Vishudha energetics had, but usually those with more maturity and training than Kayla.

Though, as Cara took stock, it didn't look like she had control of the teleportation. Rather, it seemed to happen in reaction to the stress of the situation. Cara needed to stop this, and soon. With that little control, the girl could accidentally drain Jason in a heartbeat. *Oh, Source.* Cara rubbed her temple. This was getting out of hand, fast.

Was Kayla even aware of her actions?

"She's locked herself down, emotionally and mentally," Thea called. "She's drawing strength from her warding circle."

Cara nodded. Kayla didn't seem to have enough power to lock the Healer in place, keep Thea out of her circle, and leech, all at the same time. Thank the Source for that.

They were going to have to be more careful with her in the future.

Cara stepped into the chaos, and wrapped her own far, far greater power around the wards. Thea was very experienced, but Cara was the Center Manager. That made her more powerful.

Cara was Anahata-Manipura. She could have used her combat powers here, but that wasn't what Kayla needed.

Anahata was air and healing, but it was also the Chakra of love. And this girl was terrified. A black hole of self-hatred and agony.

Cara fed Anahata energy into the cracks in the circle the girl had drawn. Tiny threads of power crept into the minuscule fractures, widening them at a steady pace.

As she did, she stood as near to the girl's eye-line as possible. Kayla held Jason close, blocking her view of anyone else, but she could still hear.

A tense silence fell over the room. A stand-off.

Except it wasn't. Cara intended to distract the girl until her own magics worked their way into the circle. She wouldn't fail her patient.

"Kayla, release him." More blue energy edged through Kayla's barriers. Cara was nearly there. The girl must be tired. "This isn't the way. We can get you through this dependency and guide you so you can pull power from the ether again. Hurting others isn't the way to deal with your pain."

There was a flicker from the girl, her pale sea-foam eyes darting briefly to where Cara stood, and an almost imperceptible tightening of her mouth. The art supplies flickered in and out of existence in different parts of the room faster and faster—a pack of pencils moving from the bed to the nightstand to the bathroom door; a drawing shifting from the table, to the wall, to Cara's chest, where it drifted down to the floor.

The distraction was enough for Cara's energetic tendrils to push through. She shoved energy in and broke the circle. Stepping in quickly, she snapped a shot of sedating Anahata energy straight at the girl, who dropped her captive and fell to the ground. Cara got an arm under the girl before her head hit the floor, and Jason broke his fall with his arm.

"Clear this room out," Cara said, "And once she's down for the night, I want a meeting to review what happened. She shouldn't have been able to do this."

She laid Kayla gently on the bed. Standing, Cara turned to Ife. "I think we need to lock her powers down for the periods she's unattended."

Ife raised her eyebrows. "I thought we were treating her as a victim, rather than a Rogue?"

Cara swiped at her forehead with her wrist. "It won't be in any permanent way. But we can't have her do this again, whether or not she did it deliberately."

It took another thirty minutes to complete the ritual.

Cara yawned as she traipsed back to her office, passing through the various security points on autopilot, considering Kayla's case.

It had been a long day. The girl was unpredictable, and the route they usually took to rehabilitate those who weren't yet full Rogues didn't seem to be working, and Cara wasn't sure why.

Cara loved her job, and though she'd anchored her physical age to her early thirties, she had over 100 years of life experience, thirty of which were based in this Center. For twenty of them she had been running it, and during her time, she'd seen a lot of typical energetic health issues. This case both frustrated and intrigued her, and her usual approaches weren't producing results.

Perhaps she was getting stale. With their long lifespans, most energetics tried many roles and paths connected to their Chakras, in part to ensure the surrounding humans didn't notice their co-workers never aging. In their remote part of Vancouver Island, with no humans around the Rehab Center, it hadn't occurred to her to find a role elsewhere. She was good at her job, but was her job still good for her?

She stepped into her office and tried not to groan when she saw Ai lying on the sofa, her body on the cushions, her legs slung over the armrest, army surplus boots kicking against the side. Ai, an energetic girl whose parents had died, had somehow slipped through the cracks and had been placed into human foster care. 'Discovered' by Cara's dearest friend, Tierra, and her partner Fintan, Ai had missed out on the typical energetic upbringing, and was staying with Cara at the Center to learn more about Anahata, the energy they had in common.

The teen rolled off the seat and came to her feet. "I heard there was an issue with Kayla. Is she okay?"

Cara's forehead creased. She'd been trying to get Ai to take more of an interest in healing, but she had showed none so far, despite her sharp mind. How did she know about Kayla? Especially given that Kayla was currently on the rehab side, rather than the healing side? Cara wanted to keep her away from the Rogues, potential and actual, given Ai's traumatic history with them.

So where did this interest in Kayla come from? And why, exactly, did Ai care?

2

Archer's dominant energy was Vishudha, the element of sound, space and void, and combating the air attack coming toward him was as simple as creating a vacuum. The dirt fell to the ground, but the cloud masked the movements of his mysterious attacker, who had closed the distance between them. The dark-haired man raised a hand toward Archer, who jerked his shoulder back, avoiding the attempt to lay a hand on him. You never wanted an enemy energetic to touch you, as some could do significant damage with physical contact.

Archer's heartbeat pounded as he tensed, ready to move. Archer was lean and fit, and while he enjoyed martial arts, his Manipura training had been a long time ago. He had little to no experience of a true fight, a fight where the opponent wanted to cause lasting damage.

He fixed his gaze on the energetic as rain pooled at his nape, sliding uncomfortably down his back. So much for summer. His muscles were tired after the run, and stiffening, despite his expensive base layers. He needed a way out of this.

What was happening here? Who would want to attack him? Especially in the energetics' world? He had plenty of human competition, but the energetics race, a small group who lived peaceably and hidden alongside humans, had few conflicts between themselves. It was only Rogues, those whose energy had twisted, who were a danger to those around them, and he had no idea why one of them would openly attack him like this.

"Who are you? What do you want?" Archer asked. Maybe he could talk his way out of this. His greatest strength lay in his mind, not his body, as his Vishudha energies included the gifts of persuasion through his voice and words, as per his training in the archetype of a Communicator.

He still heard Phoebe frantically talking in his remaining earbud, but he ignored her.

Archer wasn't helpless physically, of course. But he underplayed that side of himself to the public, having settled into the role of the geek many years before. His wire-framed glasses with clear glass encouraged this impression. He hoped this assailant would also underestimate him. Archer had no illusions about fighting if he didn't have to. There was no shame in running from a fight you couldn't win, and Archer didn't take chances when the odds were against him.

The man ignored Archer's question, and lunged for him. He was definitely aiming for touch. Archer side-stepped quickly and, catching sight of a wooden bench to his right, he moved to put the bench between them. It wasn't much, but put him out of the other man's reach.

He had an odd look. He wore what Archer estimated to be a very expensive, tailored suit, dress shirt, and tie. Yet the jacket looked crumpled, the white shirt dirty at the collar. The man was unshaven, and had fixed his physical age in the mid-forties, unlike Archer's late thirties. He had the look of a feral, absent-minded professor.

There was a rumble, and the earth underneath Archer shifted. He began to sink. Shit. The earth energetic had created a kind of quicksand that clung to Archer's sneakers. He groped for the bench and twisted his body, freeing his feet and landing outside the patch the man had created.

More debris from the park swirled around Archer, slashing his face and exposed legs and arms. He needed to get gone. Drawing in power from the ether, he charged his Manipura, and released a wobbly, but effective oval of fire around his body that burned the debris to ash. He wiped a sweaty hand across his face, smearing the fine dark powder across a cheek.

He scanned the environment while trying to monitor his attacker. He needed to immobilize him long enough to get his bike and get gone. There were no other vehicles close by he could use. Phoebe's townhouse was a handful of blocks away and had plenty of wards to keep unwanted visitors like this one out. He could regroup and get help.

The rain was coming down harder, and puddles formed on the surrounding earth. A branch flew past him like an arrow. He dodged at the last minute, though it grazed his arm. He hissed in pain as his forearm stung. But the feel of the fiery burn gave him an idea. He turned his gaze up, looking at the awnings of a concession stand that stood empty and closed at this time of day, near where he had parked his bike. Water was pooling, dragging the plastic down, so it bulged. Archer could use that.

He needed to draw the man underneath, but another branch came towards him, narrowly missing his hip. Then another. Thankfully, the man's aim seemed off, his powers erratic. Archer moved backwards slowly, his hands raised.

"Look, I think you might have the wrong guy," he said, weaving a thread of his Vishudha energy into his voice in case some basic persuasion magic might work. "You should head home."

Blank eyes from the other man, and no response except for two branches thrown in quick succession. Archer was close to the concession stand, the other man following him carefully, almost robotically. Branches kept coming. Archer turned his body to the right to present less of a target, his left shoulder and hip closest to the assailant.

Without looking at it, Archer sent his Manipura energy into the water that had collected on the concession stand's awning, heating the liquid. Steam rose off the water as it boiled, thankfully going up and not drawing the attacker's attention.

Having heated the liquid, he then started to burn a hole in the awning.

But the next branch caught him in the gut, the broken, jagged end going through all three layers of clothing into left of his stomach. He screamed and bent over. Source, it hurt. Blood seeped from the wound, but Archer knew he didn't have time to tend it. He needed to get away, and now. He staggered back, drawing the attacker after him, until he was passing under the awning. As he did, Archer shoved his power into the plastic and blazed a hole in it, so the water, now boiling, drenched the man under it.

The man's shriek was louder than Archer's, and he dropped to the floor and rolled away from the water, panting and sobbing.

Archer felt a wash of shame that he'd used his powers to such negative ends before he drew in energy from the ether once more, knowing he had little left in him to get away.

He used ether to shift through space the few yards to his bike, an unusual power he liked to keep hidden, but given the other man's agonized cries, he didn't think he'd noticed. Archer dragged his bike from the pile of leaves that it had been thrown into, and eased himself onto the seat, the branch stabbing into him and causing him to almost faint for a moment. Shit. He couldn't ride like this.

With a swift movement, he pulled the branch out, the pain so intense he couldn't make a sound. He froze, then pushed ether into the wound and created a small stasis bubble, so it wouldn't change or get worse.

He knew he didn't have either the power or the energy to do that for long.

Getting on his bike, he pedaled for his life.

Elrian screamed, the pain of the boiling water excruciating. It took several seconds for his mind to free itself from his tortured body, until he could cut himself off from the sensations. He thrust both hands into the earth on either side of him, and drew on the cooling energy of the mud there, transferring the heat out of himself.

What in Nature's name had happened? He'd planned this so carefully. Watched the other man for days, understanding his routine. He'd painstakingly created a space nearby to try the remnant stone creation ritual again.

He lay limp on the now dry soil, trying desperately to draw energy from the ether. It was almost impossible for him now. His only access to his energies was through leeching on others, or from direct contact with the elements themselves, such as earth, for his Muladhara Chakra, or in the dreamscape for Ajna, the Chakra of the mind.

It limited him. The order that ruled his world was off kilter.

His lungs worked strenuously as his back pressed against the earth. He squeezed his eyes shut, trying to ground himself. He wasn't himself. Perhaps he had been wrong not to bring Dagon or Jowaki, his associates, with him. But working with a hired thug had nearly gotten him killed. Since then, Elrian's level of delegation had dwindled almost to nothing, uncertain who he could trust outside of Cassidy and Imogen. His skin crawled with a permanent sense of being hunted. Was he paranoid? Or perceptive?

He heaved himself to his feet, feeling brittle. He looked down at himself, clothes caked with dried mud, and shuddered. Unclean.

He'd crossed paths with a familiar energy more than once recently in the Pacific Northwest, and while twice it had felt like it could reasonably be a coincidence, the third and fourth times, he'd become concerned.

Concealing his tracks, he made efforts to weave new pathways from place to place rather than lead someone to his homes or boltholes.

He'd thought he'd escaped whoever, or whatever, it was. But had there been more at play? After all, the geeky CEO of a tech company had just outsmarted him. Had he known, somehow? Or had someone warned him?

He rolled his shoulders, aching all over. His limbs felt disjointed and seemed not to respond to his directions.

He had managed to snatch a taste of Archer's energies during their fight, which was a double-edged sword. Leeching from matched energies would have buoyed him up, but Archer wasn't a match. Elrian's body flushed with heat, presumably from the Manipura energy he'd taken from Archer, and the burns he thought he'd cooled with earth energy flared again. He shoved his energy against the alien energy he had taken, his body flashing hot, then cold, then hot. He broke out into a sweat.

How had Archer—a suit, a figurehead for other energetics to interact with—managed to best Elrian, centuries his senior both in magics and experience?

3

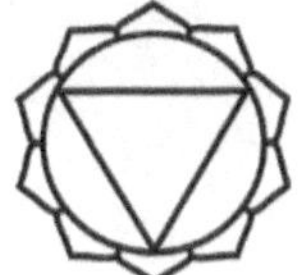

It wasn't even a mile to Phoebe's high-end condo, which, on the bike, Archer shouldn't even have noticed. With a gut wound, however, every push on the pedals brought additional torment. The stasis bubble held, but it didn't cover the entire site, and there were still places where he was aggravating the bleeding. His brain was so foggy, he couldn't quite work through what else to do. He pulled on his auxiliary chakra energy, Manipura, the energy of fire, as he went. Drawing on the vitality and willpower of Manipura, the spark of life, helped him avoid collapsing, despite being almost drained. It was harder than usual to pull from the ether.

He cauterized the ragged edges of the wound that had escaped the stasis bubble with a brief wash of fire, which caused new agony, but halted the bleeding while he wobbled on his bike to Phoebe's entrance.

He stumbled off the bike and dumped it where it lay. He'd buy another one if it got stolen. The doorman strode over, but exclaimed in worry when Archer looked him full in the face.

"Phoebe," Archer choked out. He didn't need to worry. Phoebe, clutching her cellphone, was pacing the lobby.

Catching sight of him, she ran over, her unusual blue-black hair with its white streak flying behind her.

"What the hell did you do this time, Arch?" She nodded to the doorman. "Help me get him upstairs."

"Do you need a doctor, ma'am?" he asked.

She shook her head. "No, thank you, Gordon. I believe I have supplies upstairs. I'll call you if there's anything we need."

Archer must have blacked out for a minute, as the next time he opened his eyes he was in Phoebe's luxurious penthouse, lying on her rich burgundy sofa, and there was no sign of Gordon.

Phoebe was muttering to herself as she cut off Archer's retro Tetris t-shirt. "I can't leave you alone for five minutes. You don't need a COO, you need a minder. Honestly, the things you'll do to get out of meetings."

Her touch was cool and competent, and he felt a great sense of relief to be in her hands. They'd worked together for decades, and she'd never let him down.

Phoebe was a tall, striking woman, and Archer had joked once her look was 'bohemian businesswoman', a mix of eclectic jewelry and accessories, usually combined with dark dresses and kitten heels. She had just returned from the office and was wearing a black, fitted jersey dress, with 50s makeup and a yellow polka-dot scarf in her hair. Their looks usually contrasted well, his own geek chic uniform of unnecessary glasses, brown cargo pants, button-down shirt and sweater combining with her appearance to demonstrate to the world their nerdy eccentricity. You could get away with a lot if you were 'quirky', they'd found.

Either way, she didn't look like your typical nurse, but he was grateful for her care.

"Thank you," he croaked. "It's probably not as bad as it looks."

She stopped and stared at him in disbelief. "Are you kidding me? I've called the emergency line. The chopper's coming. We're taking you to the Rehab Center on Vancouver Island. The bleeding's stopped but you have a bad internal wound. I've reinforced your stasis bubble, but we need to get you there before it disappears."

Archer jerked up in panic to disagree, or tried to. The movement sent a white blanket of pain across his system that concentrated his attention on the excruciating stomach wound. The last thing he heard as he lost consciousness once more was Phoebe asking what had happened.

Time passed. The loud rumble of a chopper brought him back to consciousness. He tried to move his body, but he was strapped to a flat surface, an IV going into the back of his hand. He was exhausted and had burned his fire energy to get himself to Phoebe. His head was so heavy that he could hardly lift it. He opened bleary eyes and saw a broad-shouldered man belted-in next to Phoebe. A gray and white husky lay next to the man, who was listening intently to Phoebe.

Archer groaned to get their attention, but the noise of the chopper was too loud. He flexed his fingers, and Phoebe caught sight of the motion, and put a pair of headphones and a mic on him.

The noise faded, and the man spoke. "Got yourself into a mess this time."

"Adam. What are you doing here?" Archer's vision was swimming, his brain a confused jumble. How did Adam, a Protector Archer knew through his work with the energetics, get here? Who was he hunting?

"I was on Elrian's trail," Adam said. "A burst of energy drew me to the area. Arrived after the fight. Threat assessment told me I needed back up before tackling him."

"Adam said you were lucky to get out without more damage," Phoebe said. "He tracked you because he could see from the blood trail that you were injured," Phoebe said. "He caught up with us just as the chopper arrived."

Elrian? Why was Adam tracking this Rogue? "What did he want with me?"

Adam's dark eyes were grim, and he rubbed a hand over rough stubble. The man was a mountain, his arms and shoulders thickly muscled. "Unclear."

Archer shook his head, or tried to. His vision swam. Adam was one of Disp@tch's key contacts in the Guilds. But he couldn't quite piece together why he would be here.

He couldn't get a grip on anything that was happening.

There was a muttered conversation between Adam and Phoebe, and a woman Archer thought might be a medic reached over and adjusted the line connected to the IV.

A calm, heavy feeling sucked Archer down into blissful unconsciousness.

Cara handled Ai's concern about Kayla. She wouldn't let Ai meet the unstable energetic any time soon. Her new ward was street-smart, but she was still learning about the world of her genetic family, the energetics, and her maturity needed a lot of development. Hopefully Ai had hundreds of years ahead of her to make her own mistakes, but for now, she was Cara's responsibility.

Cara met with the Senior Healers to discuss what had happened with Kayla, and they agreed on a new treatment plan, with greater security—one that would manage the strange hallucinations she was having until they could understand what was causing them.

Once Kayla rested, Cara would need to reassess her. She was missing something, she was sure of it.

Cara sat at her desk and rubbed gritty eyes with her left hand, rotating her stress balls in her right. This day had been a long one. Every time she'd tried to finish the last few critical tasks of the day, someone had popped in to ask her a 'quick question'. She'd tried to keep a smile on her face and support her staff, but she was at the end of her rope. She needed to rest and recharge.

Her office was a space designed to support her in that, despite her workload, and she adored it—lucky given how much time she spent in it. The room had more touches of the Châteauesque buildings the Center had been modeled on than some of its spaces. Oak paneling, floor-to-ceiling bookshelves on one wall. A large curved window with a window seat. Even a stone fireplace, though now it was summer and she hoped not to need it for a while.

Another knock at her door. Cara glanced towards it. "Come in."

It was Osana, her executive assistant. Loyal to a fault, and still working, despite the fact it was late. When Cara's gaze met Osana's friendly brown eyes, her smile softened and became real. "What can I do for you?"

The other woman bustled over and plucked the stress balls out of Cara's hand and put them on the large oak desk. "You can go home and get some sleep. We need you in good condition. All this work will still be here tomorrow."

Huh. That was unusually assertive for the warm Osana. Cara glanced at her reflection in the computer screen and winced. Alright. She did look pretty bad. She was sort of… fraying at the edges.

Cara shuffled the papers on her desk, and picked up her mug to take it to the kitchen, but Osana grabbed it and steered Cara out of the door, bundling her coat, scarf and hat into her arms as she did. "I'll wash that."

"You need to go home and rest too," Cara called back. Osana lived offsite with her wife.

"Don't worry about me. I'll come in a bit late tomorrow. You should too, though I know you won't. I know it's pointless saying this to you—again—but we can get in more help if you need it," Osana said.

Moments later, Cara was out in the cool night air, shrugging on her coat. She walked to her small house on the grounds. She was *so* ready for bed. There had been an increase in the number of energetics whose energies were twisting recently. Instead of the usual five to ten, she had nearly double that to handle in the Center, yet the same number of resources. While she probably needed to hire more people, she had hoped it was just a blip, an anomaly. Was it more than that? She'd spoken to a few of the other Healing Centers and they all had more Rogues than usual, with no apparent reason.

She sighed. Another problem to fix. As the Manager of the Center, she was its ambassador to the outside world, ensuring her team could get on with the amazing and important work they did unbothered by the ebb and flow of Guild politics.

She'd skip her usual thirty-minute training in the morning. Most days, to keep her auxiliary Chakra, Manipura, honed, she did a quick practice of some offensive and defensive skills with the energy of fire, combined with a brief run. Though recently, the frequency with which she'd skipped it to catch up on her sleep had increased. Was she leaning too much on Anahata? Out of balance with herself? She shook her head. She was tired. And had a right to be, given everything that was going on.

Her cell rang, and she pulled off the glove she'd drawn on moments before, digging around in her bag to answer it.

"It's Adam. We're flying in an emergency. I've told your people. I need you on it."

She blinked. Adam was her best friend's brother. She'd known him for decades. He was also a Protector working for the safety of the Guilds and their race, and had brought in a prisoner or wounded colleague now and then to her over the years. It was rare that he requested her personal involvement.

"What kind of guest?"

"A friendly. Gut injury." A pause, which wasn't like the quietly decisive Adam. Taciturn maybe, but never hesitant.

"What is it?" she asked.

"The friendly," Adam said. "Elrian attacked him. It's bad."

The tiredness fled her system. She spun on her heel and ran.

4

Cara went directly to the helipad, where several of her staff had already gathered a wheeled gurney and other medical equipment.

She scanned the skies until she caught the distant sound of blades cutting through the air. The *thump-thump-thump* got louder, and a staff member passed her ear protectors before it got close enough to land.

The chopper touched down, and her staff transformed into the efficient machine they were. Adam jumped out and helped unload a body strapped down for transport onto her team's gurney, his dog leaping down after him. Once the patient was secure, she ran alongside the gurney as they made their way along the paths to an emergency treatment room.

"Status?" she snapped out.

"Gut wound with stasis bubble," said Adam. "Sedated for transport."

She could see a medic from the chopper liaising with Thea, presumably filling her in on treatment details so far.

In the room they had prepared, she stood at the patient's head while her staff took care of his IV, cut off what remained of his clothes, which looked like sportswear, and washed the blood away so they could inspect his wound.

In the meantime, she centered herself, and once again drew energy. Always harder when she was tired, it took effort, and she knew she'd suffer for this the next day, but needs must.

She placed her hands gently on the man's head, his medium-length brown hair softer than it looked, and sent exploratory energy across his body, seeking abnormalities and aberrations. A couple of healed hairline fractures, one in an arm from childhood, and one in his tibia, which looked like an adult break. Scratches and bruises.

Energy levels dangerously low.

She swore. "He's been leeched from. It doesn't seem to have gone too far, but it's there."

The biggest wound, and the one they needed to address first, was the wound in the gut. It was concerningly deep, made by some kind of jagged object, and had caught the small intestine and punctured it. Shit. She probed the torn edges and found minute splinters of wood. This kind of injury had only a fifty percent chance of survival in a human facility. His odds were better as an energetic, but still not the odds Cara wanted.

The casting of the stasis bubble was fading, but the wound gave the impression of being created minutes ago rather than hours ago, as Adam had told her. If the patient had done this, he was a quick thinker.

She pushed energy into the area to reinforce the stasis for the moment until she could do more. Keeping a hand on the patient's head to continue monitoring his energies, she studied his body, looking for confirmation of her findings so far. It seemed more than one wooden projectile had caught him, but most of them had glanced off or hit him in less problematic areas.

"We have two priorities," she reported. "He has very little energy in reserve, and what he has, needs rebalancing. Thea, I want you on that. Second, the gut wound has torn through the small intestine and needs to be closed. I don't think we need a resection, but we can assess as we operate."

Her team bobbed their heads around her, attending to their various tasks. She jerked her head at Adam and a vaguely familiar female to get them out of the room, and got to work.

Several hours later Cara rested her back against the wall and rolled her head to stretch out her tight neck muscles. They had stabilized the patient. She couldn't spot any signs of infection, but he would need to be monitored closely for a while, and it was going to take time for him to recover.

Around her, staff secured, stored and disposed of the items they had used during surgery while she studied her latest case as a person, rather than a patient. Clothed in one of their gowns that he made look surprisingly good, he had the lean body type of a runner, with well-defined arms that had long, smooth muscles over the upper portion.

His mouth, relaxed in sleep, had a full lower lip, and a faint shadow under the skin indicated there would soon be stubble on his jaw and chin.

Those weren't the only shadows, however. His eyes were closed, but they had bluish smudges underneath them, showing he could really use the rest they were giving him. She had been surprised to see that they'd needed to remove glasses from him. No energetic needed them, so there was rarely a reason to wear them, and it made them stand out. In fact, the last time she'd met someone—

Oh.

Realization flooded through her, and the vague feeling of familiarity Cara had had on seeing the woman he'd come in with clicked into place. This was Archer Hampton, and the woman was the co-founder of Disp@tch, Phoebe Korr. One of his people had needed treatment at the Rehab Center the year before, and Archer, clearly used to being in charge, had tried to run the show. But this wasn't his boardroom. This was her clinic. *Her* domain. It had been a power struggle he was doomed to lose.

She washed up and walked out to update Phoebe and Adam.

Phoebe sat upright on a club chair in the well-appointed relatives room. She jumped up as soon as she saw Cara, hands clenching and unclenching. "How is he?"

"He'll be okay."

The other woman sagged in relief.

"As long as he follows our treatment instructions," Cara said, flatly. If anyone had control of the man inside that room, she suspected it was Phoebe, though it was unclear if they were lovers as well as business partners.

Phoebe grimaced. "Ah, yes. Sorry. I'll talk to him. I wasn't sure you'd remember us."

Cara tilted her head. She very much doubted that, yet Phoebe had been nothing but polite to Cara and her staff, unlike Archer.

She relented. "He's going to be okay. But it was a serious wound. How did it happen?"

"Fight with Elrian," said Adam, who took advantage of the low, boxy design of his club chair to relax, his legs stretched out and crossed at the ankles. Adam didn't waste energy.

"Yes, but why? Why was he attacking this guy?" A guy who had nothing to do with fighting and prophecies and healing, one who had chosen to operate in the human world, for financial profit and gain.

Phoebe held up open palms, shrugging helplessly. Adam's husky got up, padded to her and wound through her legs before returning to sit at Adam's feet.

"We'll ask him," said Adam. "Thank you for your care."

"Of course," said Cara. She would treat anyone, Rogue or regular energetic, nice person or arrogant jerk.

"At least he can't boss you around this time," said Phoebe, with a weak laugh.

Damn straight, he can't.

Although she might enjoy putting him in his place if he tried.

Archer groaned and tried to blink his eyes open. Where was he? Where was Phoebe? What had they been doing? He turned his neck.

Oh, Bright Source. Agony tore through him, and he grunted. His head fell back.

A cool, small hand touched his check, then his brow. It felt so good. Was it Phoebe?

"What's happening?" he ground out. "What's wrong with me?"

"You're being treated. Looks like your metabolism went through the pain management more quickly than most." It didn't sound like his friend. The voice was lighter and warmer than Phoebe's more melodious tones.

He sucked a breath in and cracked his eyes open the smallest possible amount. Bright. It was so bright in here.

He was in a room he didn't know, but not a human hospital. There were several people in the room. The woman at his bedside looked familiar, but he couldn't place her. Pain throbbed through his gut, and the lights in the room made his head ache. It was hard to focus with the pain pressing in on him, crushing his skull and tearing through his abdomen.

A male voice growled into a cell in the corner of the room, a large husky alert and watching Archer at the man's feet. Definitely an energetic place.

"…unclear why they targeted him," Adam said into the phone.

Pieces flooded back: his run, the attack, his flight to Phoebe.

"His injuries are severe. He needed help. I had to make a choice. Archer, not Elrian."

Archer's chest was tight. He tried to swallow and coughed, squeezing his eyes shut against the pain. The gentle hand lifted his head and put an ice chip to his lips. He sucked it gratefully, though he desperately wanted water to ease his parched throat.

An apologetic voice spoke. "Sorry. No water, in case we need to do more work on you. I'm going to put you under again in a moment."

He shook his head quickly. Too quickly. Everything spun, and he wanted to throw up. His stomach muscles cramped in anticipation and the pain shot through him like lightning. Source, this was tiring.

"Phoebe," he demanded, though her name came out weakly, not in the imperious way he'd been going for. A small sigh, tightly controlled, but definite, slipped from the woman beside him.

Darkness. He rested a moment, two, three; he wasn't sure.

"Archer, thank the light. You're badly injured. You need to do what Healer Cara tells you."

Cara. He knew that name. Didn't he? There was something he was missing, something to do with this place, the voice. He had a stray thought about honey.

"Do you know why he attacked you?" Adam said.

He shook his head again. He really didn't.

"Who?" he got out.

"A Rogue." Adam put a hand out to his dog, who rubbed his colossal head against it.

"A bad one. What have you got yourself tangled up in, Archer?" Phoebe asked. "Is this connected to one of your extracurricular projects? Have you been consorting with pirates again?"

Adam's head moved fractionally to the side. "Pirates?"

Phoebe rubbed her temples. "He goes treasure hunting. He's always getting into scrapes. Though never anything like this, and usually with humans, not energetics."

"I didn't...I haven't..."

A voice cut across him. "You can ask him later. Right now, he's in a lot of pain and needs to rest."

Archer bristled. He couldn't remember anyone but Phoebe interrupting him outside his family for the last decade. Apart from one.

Oh.

His eyes widened. Fuck the pain, he thought, and turned his head to see the owner of the voice, who he now had a strong suspicion he recognized.

"The sexy shrew!"

He was in the biggest energetic Healing and Rehabilitation Center in North America, on Vancouver island, off the west coast of Canada, a place he knew because he'd brought in a seriously injured employee for treatment before.

The treatment had gone great, the equipment and design of the Center incredible, but his interactions with this woman—who he remembered with a groan was both the head honcho of the place, and one of the top Healers in the region—had not.

She'd been bossy, opinionated, and really, really annoying.

"Archer!" Phoebe sounded aghast. "Behave!"

"If you mean we've met before, then yes. If you mean I'm the person in charge of this facility, then also yes." The woman's smile was sharp and fast, disappearing as quickly as it appeared on the heart-shaped face. "Welcome back, Mr. Hampton. I'm Cara, the Head Healer of this Rehabilitation Center, in charge of your care."

Dammit. Pain was wearing him down, and he struggled to think. He didn't have his usual filters in place. "Like hell you are."

He needed out of here, and into a facility where the gorgeous general manager didn't hate him and think he was a privileged jerk.

Whether he *was* one wasn't relevant.

He tried to rise out of the bed, but for the third time the pain tore through him. He attempted to pull energy, but he was empty, and trying to draw on the ether felt like mining diamonds with a Q-Tip.

Cara was busying herself at the IV that went into his arm. He groped for it with his other hand, but it was leaden, and she easily placed it back at his side as if he were a child. Not a hair moved out of place on her honey blonde bob.

"Stop." He swallowed, his mouth dry again. She twisted something, and he felt the disturbing sensation of cold liquid rushing into his veins. "You're not my Healer. Or my Doctor."

"Mr. Hampton, you need to rest now."

He shook his head, muzzy, the room wavering at the edges. He was losing focus. "You're pretty, but that doesn't mean you can boss me around."

"Oh Source." Phoebe stifled a horrified laugh. "Cara, I am so sorry. It's the pain and the drugs. He doesn't know what he's saying."

"Mmm hmm," Cara said, though it was distant.

She was bossy. And she was pretty. So pretty. But he needed to go home. He was good at words. He'd tell her. She'd let him.

"I have to leave. But you *are* pretty," he repeated. There. That was right, wasn't it? Those were the two things he needed to say.

He nodded slightly, with satisfaction, and laid his head back down.

Very pretty.

5

Cara's cheeks were pink as she watched Archer go back under, his face smoothing out into peaceful lines, though retaining its distinctive angular jawline.

She pressed the button to summon another of her staff members. "Prudence, can you monitor and review the drugs we're giving Mr. Hampton? His energies are more powerful than I realized, and we need to keep him sedated overnight so he can begin the healing process."

Prudence, sweet, competent and kind, was a specialist in pain management and anesthesia and would make sure that Archer got the rest he needed. In the meantime, Cara's annoyance with herself grew. She'd underestimated Archer, which wasn't like her. Had her personal feelings clouded her judgement?

If only she could put him under every time he got annoying. When he'd been here before, he wasn't even a relative of the patient she and her team had been looking after, just his boss, and he'd been difficult. He leveraged the charm of Vishudha to cajole or bribe her staff, and sometimes even the other patients, into doing whatever his employee wanted, whether or not it was what he needed. Archer had no idea about the healing arts.

Still, she thought grimly, he was a patient and needed her care. She finished in the room, handing him over to Prudence and others, and nodded a crisp goodbye to Phoebe.

"Adam, can you come to my office? I'd like a word."

He jerked his head in assent and followed her. She opened her office door to find Ai sprawled on her front, frowning in concentration, trying to create a puff of air that would blow out the candle she had lit, mercifully on the hearth of the fireplace.

"Ai, you should be asleep," Cara said. But Ai had already jumped up, awkwardly greeting Adam with a fist bump. Cara shot a narrow blast of air at the candle so Ai didn't set the office on fire, as the girl spun toward her.

"I heard Archer Hampton and Phoebe Korr were here," Ai said, almost bouncing in place, though it was the early hours of the morning. Cara was starting to suspect the girl had an energetic's sense for trouble. That, or the chopper had woken her up.

Cara sank into her office chair and massaged her temples. "Yes. Archer Hampton is a patient."

"They're famous! You know that, right? Are they really energetics?" The last words were muffled as Ai had her face in the long-suffering Argus's fur, her arms wrapped around his neck.

And that really said all you needed to about the pair. What energetics—who could live hundreds of years—in their right mind would court fame? Live in the public spotlight where they risked bringing attention to their race?

Cara gave up and buried her own head in her arms on the desk. Maybe everything would go away if she closed her eyes.

"Yes," Adam responded to Ai in the wake of Cara's silence.

"What happened?" Ai asked.

"Elrian attacked him," Adam said.

Dammit. Cara's head snapped up. That's what she got for dipping out of the conversation for a moment. She shot Adam a glare. There was no reason to tell the girl that.

Ai stiffened. "Why? What's he done? Why does Elrian want him?"

Adam held out his hands, palms up. "We don't know."

"Was Phoebe able to tell you anything on the ride over? Or Archer himself?" Cara asked. She slid her stress balls into her hand, and spun them, the repetitive movement comforting.

"No."

Sometimes she could do with Adam being a little less succinct.

"He won't come here, will he? Elrian?" Ai gripped her phone in one hand and stood, ready to bolt. Argus wound his way around her legs. She petted him absentmindedly, and her shoulders loosened.

"We're on an island, and a remote part of that island at that," Cara said. "We have both human and energetic defenses, and we have a small but strong contingent of Healers here with powerful magics and auxiliary energies of all kinds. Elrian's not going to try for Archer here. He's resting now, but when he's off sedation, we'll focus on understanding his connection to Elrian."

Ai was almost vibrating with anxiety.

"Cara's auxiliary is Manipura." Adam surprised Cara by speaking up. "Stick with her, kid. She'll keep an eye on you."

Huh. "Thanks."

A horrible thought struck her. "You don't think he's one of the six males in the prophecy?"

Adam cocked his head. Argus chuffed.

The prophecy, which had begun with her friend—and dreamwalker—Cuinn, spoke of a cataclysmic event that only the formation and banding together of six energetic couples could stop.

Elrian appeared to have been trying to prevent the couples from forming, but so far, three couples had been joined: Cuinn and his partner Blaize, who had in common the Chakra Ajna, associated with the element of the mind; Tierra, with her partner Fintan, associated with the element of air; and most lately, Nixie, Blaize's childhood friend, and Jeb, a senior Healer at the Guild, associated with the element of water.

Cuinn had also identified Cara and Adam as being part of the prophecy, but of the other four energetics involved, three were still a mystery, and one was a male who was hard to make out from the details of Nixie's sketch. Dark and handsome, was Nixie's joke, but Blaize and Cuinn hadn't found any more prophecy splinters in the dreamscape that would help them flesh out the details.

Cara was tense about it all. She knew her match wasn't Adam, the brother she'd never had: the idea of sex with him made her nauseous. She'd looked at the sketch of the mystery male, but hadn't felt anything. And she wasn't keen on the idea of being fated to fall in love, their world's future somehow depending on whether or not she clicked romantically with some guy she'd never met.

She groaned. Or a million times worse, someone like Archer.

"Not enough data at this time," Adam said.

She parked the thought. The Center took up her time and was her great love. She was helping with the prophecy where she could, but she had little time and attention to spare. She'd support her friends as much as she had time for, and would come immediately when there was an emergency, but she needed to keep the Center going too. And that in itself wasn't straightforward given the recent rise in Rogues and the fact they hadn't had an increase in staff to match.

Duty. Everything was about duty. Her duty to the Center, her duty to her friends, her duty to her race. And she was fine with that. Responsibilities guided her and helped to ensure she felt her life was meaningful. Being a Healer fulfilled her deeply. It was just that right now, she seemed to have conflicting duties. If she needed to grit her teeth and form a relationship with someone, she would, but he'd need to fit in alongside her obligations to her job, and ensure she still supported her friends. She sighed. Well, not all relationships needed to be as intense and romantic as those of her friends.

Adam stepped around her desk and took the stress balls out of her hand. He gave her a one-arm squeeze that also lifted her out of her seat.

"Everyone to bed," Adam said. "We reconvene tomorrow."

"Alright. Ai, no need for you to—" Cara began, but even as Ai opened her mouth to protest that she wanted to be there, Adam stopped her.

"Ai attends too. Also Phoebe and Archer."

Cara growled, and Adam raised an eyebrow. Argus made another chuffing sound that was almost a laugh. Dammit. She hadn't meant for that to come out. She'd intended to deal with the Archer issue like a reasonable adult. But this had been a long, long day.

"We're not going to tell them about the prophecy are we?" she said. "That feels more of a risk than is necessary. We have no idea what he's into."

"Agreed. But we need more info." He glanced at Ai, and opened the door, gesturing both of them out, while Argus nudged the back of her legs. "Ai, you're in, but silent. Watcher only. Got that?"

She nodded, eyes wide, and he slapped her on the back. "Good. Tomorrow, both of you, 0800 hours."

They trooped out of the door, Ai thoughtful, Cara bemused at being banished from her own office for the second time that night.

Ai slipped off to her room in the guest building, and Adam walked Cara across the wide open space between buildings to her house. Dawn was creeping over the horizon. None of them would get much sleep tonight.

"Ai's history with Elrian isn't stellar," Cara said. That was an understatement. Ai's friend, Indigo, had been leeched on, turned into a Rogue, then had tried to murder Blaize. Indigo had been killed in the ensuing battle. Ai herself had later been kidnapped and leeched on herself, though she'd been freed before too much damage had been done. Not only was she at the Center with Cara to learn, she was also there for her own healing, though Cara and her friends hadn't shared that with the teen. She'd been through enough. "And she has a fascination with Rogues that isn't healthy."

Adam nodded. "See you tomorrow."

Argus licked her knee, and she patted his warm head. Adam walked off, the dog trailing him, leaving her with one last command.

"Eat first."

6

Archer clawed his way into wakefulness, his eyes gummed up with sleep. There was a low hum of noise around him: the bleep of machines, the muted sounds of conversation from far away. He wasn't in his soundproofed, lightproofed bedroom, that was certain.

He scanned his body, which felt okay, though his middle was…missing. Startled, he put a light hand on his belly, and was relieved to find it was still there. Of course it was. He'd hardly be able to exist without his torso. However, bandages covered it.

He rubbed a hand over the light dusting of stubble on his face. As he inhaled, the unmistakable smell of antiseptic and cloves confirmed his whereabouts. He was in a healing center. What was he—

Something in him kicked awake, a spike of adrenaline.

Someone had tried to kill him.

He had experienced verbal attacks in the boardroom before, and as a prominent figure in the tech world, he had encountered multiple instances of online attacks, but no one had ever physically assaulted him.

Why would he be attacked? He frowned and massaged his temples, the dull throb of a headache nagging at him. It must be something business-related. With his high-profile status, wealth, and information and communication technology company, he was an influential figure with a reputation among both humans and energetics. He wasn't a contentious figure, and he and Phoebe worked hard to keep their business at the cutting edge, without using their powers to leapfrog ahead of the tech that humans came up with on their own.

Would they try again? Should he get a bodyguard? No. He'd hate that, being watched all the time, never being alone, never being free. Ramping up his self-defense classes, his running, his abilities to protect himself. That was the way forward.

He felt strange. Despite his attacker's efforts, he had stayed alive. He was wounded or he wouldn't be here, but he was in one piece. He had a peculiar feeling of invulnerability. His physical training, keeping himself in good condition, with alert reactions and a strong understanding of strategy and defensive actions, had helped him to come through a situation that could have killed him.

Hesitantly, he pulled energy from the ether. It wasn't easy, but more came through than had yesterday. He was no longer drained, but he wasn't yet well.

He looked around his room. It was spacious for a room of its type, with several visitor chairs, medical equipment, and a friendly but sparse feel. It even had a small couch and TV area. The benefit of a healing center was that it could be cleaned and sterilized energetically, so there was less need for the wipeable surfaces that came with a human hospital room. Still, he wondered how quickly he could get out of here. He had a business to run.

Speaking of which—he looked around. He never went anywhere without his cell, and a very limited number of places without his laptop. Phoebe had brought him to this place. She'd have left them somewhere close by for him, he was sure of it.

He shuffled himself up the bed to a sitting position. It was harder than expected. His body ached, but the pain he'd worried might come from his gut didn't appear.

Leaning back against the headboard, welcoming the rest it gave him, he scanned the room for his slim but powerful laptop and his sleek silver phone. He scowled as he saw no immediate sign of them.

Perhaps they were in a drawer for safekeeping.

His head spun as he dragged himself to the edge of the bed. He gripped it for support and took another minute, breathing harder.

He swung a leg over the side of the bed, and he felt the reverb of a dull twinge in his gut, as though he was feeling the sensation through layers of pillows. Alright. He probably needed to be careful. He concentrated, and his other leg followed the first. All he wanted was to inspect the drawers. He was sure Phoebe would have left his tech for him somewhere. It couldn't be far.

He leaned forward and rested a hand on the bedside table, using the other hand to pull out each drawer. Empty apart from some clothes.

He glanced down at himself, realizing he was naked. Well, apart from the sheet that was caught around his waist because of the twisting movement that opening the drawers had required.

Tech first, clothes second. He felt a lot more naked without his tech than he did without clothes.

Shit. Where was it? Anxiety bloomed in his chest. He sat, his hands supporting him on either side. Where else could she have put them? He tried to focus, seeing a nearby chest of drawers as another possibility. However, when he tried to stand, his legs wobbled, and he fell back onto the bed.

Right. Enough.

"Hello? I need help," he bellowed, projecting his voice at the door.

He waited a few moments, but nothing happened. He glared across the room at the drawers, as if willing them to come to him. They must be in there.

He hauled on his connection to the ether, hoping the trickle he managed to pull on would give him the strength to stay standing this time.

He gripped the headboard again, using it to steady himself as he drew himself slowly to his feet. He grit his teeth against the ache in his skull. Why was the light in here so damnably bright?

Once he felt stable, he took a step toward the chest of drawers—and promptly fell over. As he went down, the sheet, which had caught at his waist, came with him, and as it slid off the bed, the edges caught the jug of water on the bedside table, which fell to the floor, soaking both him and the sheet.

He yelled as ice cold water drenched him. The fall set the inside of his head on fire, and he had landed tailbone first on the tiled floor. He swore loudly and richly.

And then harder when he realized the door was open, and the haughty Center manager was standing there, her startling bronze eyes unflinching. He stopped swearing—out loud, anyway.

He set his shoulders and tried to look as dignified as possible. "I need my cell and laptop. Can you contact Phoebe Korr?"

She raised an eyebrow. "What is it you think you're doing out of bed, Mr. Hampton?"

"Finding my tech. I have important work to do, much of it time sensitive. So if you'll kindly get Phoebe, I can get on with things." He was going to ignore the fact he was on the floor. Naked.

Unfortunately, she didn't. She sighed and walked over to him. "Mr. Hampton, if you haven't noticed, you're sitting in a pile of wet sheets in the middle of the floor. You were badly injured, and you're only able to talk to me right now because we've pumped you full of painkillers."

She slipped a hand under his arm. "It's likely going to hurt, but push on the floor as much as you can. You're getting back into bed."

He wanted to resist, if only for form's sake, but even he realized it would be stupid to remain where he was.

He let her help him back into the bed, tried to ignore the dull burn of pain it caused, and didn't even wince when she put a foot on the wet sheet so it remained on the floor.

She used strong legs to help him back to a supine position—still naked. He wished for boxers, pants, anything that would cover him. There was no sign from her she'd noticed his state of undress, and by the time he was in a resting position again on the bed, he was so exhausted he couldn't muster up any embarrassment. It's not like energetics weren't fairly comfortable about being naked. But this situation wasn't about being nude. He was also vulnerable.

"Thank you," he said. He could allow for that. "Now get Phoebe, please. I need to work."

Cara handed him a blanket, then a hand on a hip, head cocked, simply stared at him. She ran her other hand, absentmindedly, over hair that already appeared in perfect condition. She was dressed simply, in a fitted navy dress that looked to be made of some kind of jersey material. She could have stepped from the medical environment to his business world in a moment.

After what felt like an eternity of scrutiny, his back prickling under the examination as he wondered what she saw, she pressed her lips together, and bent to scoop up the wet sheet, ensuring any water was mopped up.

"We're going to check your vitals, and then, if you're well enough, Phoebe, Adam and I are going to have a chat with you about what happened yesterday."

"Alright," Archer said, with some caution. "I'm not sure what other information I can tell you. But I'm open to that conversation. Just make sure Phoebe brings my tech with her."

Cara had dropped the sheet into a basket, turned to her cell and was typing a text message, presumably to alert Phoebe and Adam that he was awake. She glanced up. "No tech."

"I'm not asking," Archer said. Dammit, it really was hard to remain dignified when you'd been found on the floor, naked and wet.

"Let me repeat, you were badly injured yesterday. You need rest and care. Not work." There was no give in the woman. That dress might look touchable, but she was made of ice underneath it.

She pulled over a blood pressure machine and fastened the cuff to his upper arm.

"You don't use energy to check vitals here?" he asked, curious despite himself. He hadn't had a lot of contact with healer types, but he assumed they were all about magic and healing energies. He hadn't expected human technology. The cuff squeezed his arm tight. It was an unpleasant sensation, though it didn't hurt, not compared to the rest of him.

"We use whatever method is most appropriate for the task. I have no issue with blending human innovation with our healing experience. I could check your vitals with energy, but it's unnecessary, and it would take from my own supply, which I might need for an emergency at any moment." She narrowed her eyes as she examined the readings on the blood pressure cuff. She removed it from him and stuck a thermometer in his armpit.

"You understand the importance of tech as a tool, then," he continued. "I—"

A flicker of something that could almost have been amusement ran across her face. "Mr. Hampton. An affinity and pragmatism does not mean I'm going to hand you your laptop and cell."

Huh. Rarely did people catch him in the act of persuasion like that. He revised his assessment of her intelligence up. Again.

She turned to clean the thermometer and place it back in its position with the other monitoring equipment in the room. He lurched back up to a sitting position. His head was woozy, and he blinked to focus.

She bent down and opened a drawer under the bed, and pulled out a clean gown. She fastened it around him, just in time. The door opened, and Phoebe and Adam, Adam's dog, as well as a teenage goth, entered.

"Phoebe! I need my phone. And laptop," he said, trying to get in before Cara.

Phoebe rushed to his bedside. There were dark circles under her eyes. "Don't be an idiot, Arch. Do you have any idea how injured you are?"

He didn't. Why hadn't he asked? "What's the damage?"

"A foreign body impaled and perforated your duodenum, the first part of your small intestine," Cara said.

"A branch. It was a branch," Archer said.

"Right. There were wooden splinters that we had to remove before mending the tear. Infection is a major risk, and any sharp movements that you make have the potential to tear the wound open again."

Archer felt cold.

"You were also leeched from."

Anxiety pricked his chest. That sounded a lot more serious than he'd been expecting. "How long till I can leave?"

"A couple of weeks," Cara said.

Archer let out a bark of laughter. "That's not possible."

Phoebe stepped up to him and put her hand on his arm. "It is. Your job is to rest, but you can help Adam and his team catch the person who did this to you. Answer his questions, Arch, please. And stop pestering Cara for your tech."

Phoebe was one of only a few people who had no problem saying no to Archer. It was one reason they worked so well as a team, their genuineness with each other. She would never lie to him, or he to her.

"What about the deal?" he said.

"You need to trust me and the team," she said. "We'll manage, you get well. It's not a choice, Arch. You could have died. There's no point finishing the attacker's work for him."

Cara had swung between hot annoyance and barely concealed laughter at Archer. After Phoebe's pronouncement, he'd looked to Cara, not Phoebe, as if trying to pit his will against hers and change her mind.

Well, that was a battle he would lose. He was hardly the first disagreeable patient she'd had, or the first who hadn't believed he was truly sick.

Cara stood at the foot of his top-of-the-line, fully electric hospital bed, arms folded, and stared him down. Brown, densely-lashed eyes clouded with pain and frustration met hers. But the pain management techniques here were excellent, with both healing energies and human medical technology available to her to use. Her skills meant she knew he wasn't hurting *too* much.

He finally dropped his eyes.

Argus, Adam's husky, chuffed, and Cara reached a hand out to pet him. Adam moved closer.

"What happened? Details, please." Adam had a tablet and an electronic pen poised at the ready.

As Archer described what had happened, Cara ran an expert eye over his form, connecting the injuries to his story. There were the cuts and scrapes on arms and legs from the debris that the man had thrown at Archer. There was a bruise on his face, and a fine abrasion on his shoulder, where larger pieces had hit him. And there was the deep graze on his arm where the branch had come at him. He'd been lucky that hadn't gouged more of the flesh on his arm. They'd had to put a couple of stitches in it as it was.

The worst injury, however, was the gut wound. She'd had to work hard with her team to remove all the splinters, which had required her Anahata Chakra energy and taken a long time, during which they needed to ensure nothing entered the abdominal cavity that wasn't supposed to be there. Then they'd fixed the anatomical issues, the tears the branch had made in the different layers of his body. Staples for the intestine, then stitches for the muscle and skin layers. It had been a hard night.

Archer's attitude this morning certainly suggested he was back to his usual entitled self, but she'd put him on powerful painkillers instead of the sedative she'd have preferred, in order for him to be able to wake up and talk. She had objected, but Phoebe, who had a healthcare power of attorney for Archer, had agreed to Adam's request when he put it to her.

"Archer needs to be protected from this happening again. The sooner you talk to him, the sooner you can find the person who did this," Phoebe had said.

Cara checked her watch. This dose of painkillers was likely to wear off before the conversation ended, so she guessed he'd be a bit more amenable soon. Nature would do her work for her.

She'd check the dressings while she listened. She hated not being busy, which meant both hands and mind for her.

She frowned as she saw the sheet under him was still damp, then confirmed it with a quick touch. In everything that had happened, she'd missed it. Some of the water must have transferred from his body when she'd helped him back into bed, despite the dry blanket she'd laid over him.

"I'll change this," she murmured. Archer narrowed his eyes, but didn't protest as she deftly changed his sheet with him still in the bed, keeping his modesty intact. When it came to rolling him on his side to strip the current sheet and tuck the clean linen under him, the heat of his body surprised her. He had some Manipura, she remembered, and the fire of that always showed, though his balance of Chakras skewed much more toward his dominant Chakra.

"Why you?" Adam asked Archer. It wasn't the first time he'd asked, and Cara felt the frustration in the twitch of Archer's shoulder blades as she rolled him back into place. His body, while not Manipura battle-ready, was toned and in good condition.

"I don't know," Archer snarled. Evidence the pain meds were dwindling. "Why were you tracking him? Who is he? What else has he done?"

Good questions, Cara thought. She suspected he'd have asked them earlier if he hadn't been injured.

"He's a leech," Adam said. "Involved in several cases in the Pacific northwest."

Cara didn't look at Ai, who was perched on a visitor's chair. There was a lot more to the situation than that, but Cara agreed it wasn't the right time to share with Archer or Phoebe at this stage.

"He's killed before," she said briskly. "You were lucky."

Damn lucky. Elrian had killed a number of times now and had drained some of his victims. He'd kidnapped several others, and tortured them by leeching on them over a sustained period.

If Archer had had fur, it would have stood on end. "I used my wits, not luck, to get away. And why haven't you found him, if he's killed so many? What are the Protectors doing?"

Argus emitted a low, quiet growl, but Adam was impassive. Protectors, the archetype of Muladhara, were those trained in that energy, and the Guilds maintained a force who hunted Rogues. Adam was involved in this.

"He's dangerous." Adam's tone remained reasonable. Cara had rarely seen her friend riled.

"Don't be so cocky," Cara snapped at Archer, coming to Adam's defense. He might not be annoyed, but she was. "Now, do you have any more detail to add, or not? Because if not, you need to rest."

Adam stepped toward her and put his hand on her shoulder, though whether it was in comfort or to remind her to keep her temper, she wasn't sure.

She sucked in a breath, re-centering herself. With exhaustion weighing on her, she was more concerned about Archer than he was about himself. She tried not to show those kinds of emotions, because while she would never lie to a patient, experience had shown her that optimism and looking at the best-case scenario brought better healing results.

"If you have anything else to add, I'm happy to pass it on to Adam," Cara said, her voice professional and cool once more. "I'm sure he'll send you updates on the case when he has them."

Adam nodded.

"I have nothing to add right now," Archer said, his voice tight. "Thank you, Adam."

Adam inclined his head and exited the room, Argus loping after him. Ai stayed where she was. Cara would drag her out when she left, and hoped in the meantime the girl could keep her celebrity crush under control.

"This is Ai," she said. "She's involved in the case too."

Archer's eyebrows raised. "Alright."

There was a pause.

"Now," Archer said, turning his attention on Cara. "Can I please have my tech?"

Cara sighed. "We've been through this. You can once you're further down the healing path."

"I understood I was in the healing part of the Center, not the rehab part. Or do you treat all your guests as prisoners, denying them basic rights? Is that how you get your kicks, exercising your power over people who can't fight back?"

Ai gasped audibly behind her, and Cara's temper ignited. How dare he? How dare he criticize her running of the Center?

Her rational mind tried to point out the signs of stress and fatigue at the corners of his mouth and eyes, and his grip on his sheet, and remind her how much pain he must be in. Plus Ai was here, and Cara knew her role was to be a good influence.

However, as her mind told her that, her rusty Manipura Chakra, which apparently needed more of a focus on its property of discipline, and less of a focus on its fire, flashed to life.

"In point of fact, Mr. Hampton, Phoebe—who must, by the way, have the patience of a saint to work with you—shared with us that your work has a tendency to agitate you, and mentioned you have had issues with stress in the past." Cara tried to keep her voice even and cool, and ensure the flames inside her stayed there.

She caught Phoebe cringing out of the corner of her eye. Well, it was true, though Cara had made the final decision, and she would own that. "After discussing it with her, it is my decision as your Healer that tech will not help you get better. Rest will."

She cursed the man for provoking her. She'd seen him on the arms of many a model in the gossip magazines. How those women had tolerated him, she did not know. He must be a dreadful man to date, always considering himself right about everything.

"So unless you have any other questions, or you prefer to be cared for at another institution, I'll be back to check on you later." She raised an eyebrow at him in challenge.

He spluttered, and Phoebe stepped over to him. "Arch, please. This is the best care center in the area, and you're badly injured. Can't you just believe us for a change? We'll give you the evidence later, but for now, please, you need rest."

Source save her from such arrogant men, Cara thought. Phoebe shouldn't have to beg him.

"I have more important things to do than babysit spoiled rich guys. You're welcome to leave if you would prefer care elsewhere," Cara said. There was another muffled sound from Ai behind her. Cara felt a twinge of guilt, both for the example she was setting for Ai, and at the possibility the man might actually take her up on it. She'd promised Adam, after all, that she would look after Archer.

And, this was hardly going to help his stress levels.

Shit.

She stepped to the bed and unfolded her arms. "Look, you're probably in pretty bad pain, as what we've given you wears off. I'm going to administer your next dose, and we can talk again later when you're feeling better."

She moved his sheet carefully and checked his bandages. There was some bleeding, but it wasn't excessive.

Archer looked mutinous, and ready to argue further, but catching sight of the blood seeping under the dressings seemed to give him pause.

"I'll give you a moment with Phoebe while I get your medicine." Cara gestured to Ai to follow her out.

Once the door had closed, and they were outside, Ai let out a stifled laugh, her eyes round. "Cara!"

Cara forced herself to keep eye contact. "I've arranged for you to spend some time shadowing Osana this morning. You can head over there now while I finish up here."

"Uh, okay. See you later? I'd like to talk to you about Kayla."

Cara nodded, resigned, and Ai walked off. It didn't seem like Cara could put off a conversation about the young energetic for long.

Cara took a moment to herself to breathe before she went to grab Archer's next dose of pain medication from the storeroom and returned to his room.

She handed him the pills and watched him take them. He didn't look any happier, but when she asked, "May I?" and put her hand on his abdomen, close to, but not pressing on the wound, he grudgingly agreed.

She suspected the pinched look around his mouth and white knuckles were more to do with his pain than anything Phoebe had said.

She used her Anahata energy to soothe the area and drew a little of his pain into herself. She was a tiny bit impressed at his poker face, despite herself. He'd been in agony, and had barely let a hint of it show. Of course, that was stupid behavior, too. If he'd said, she'd have acted earlier.

Well, she wasn't a mind-reader. She could only help if she knew.

Feeling the heat of his muscled belly under her palm, she smoothed Anahata energy over the area, using it as a balm for his wounds and to soften the ragged edges of pain in his body.

Some of the tension left him, though the release was subtle. Satisfaction filled her. Being a Healer wasn't simply a job, it was an integral part of her being, and fulfilling her role met a deep-set need within her.

"Thank you," Archer said, though he said it as if his jaw was soldered shut.

She nodded. "Rest now."

Likewise, she needed to get some sleep. She'd head back to her room, shower, and indulge in a few minutes of her guilty pleasure, celebrity scandal and gossip magazines, then sleep.

Perhaps she'd search out stories on Archer. It was always better to know who you were dealing with. And if there was any chance of a girlfriend or an ex turning up, Cara would prefer to be prepared, so she could handle the situation appropriately. That was her job, after all.

She'd try not to feel too sorry for the likely many women who'd fallen in love with this supremely irritating man. He was handsome and smart, and had a charisma that some women found irresistible.

Not everyone had the wisdom to avoid him like the plague.

"I don't understand what you need to do to prevent this prophecy from coming to pass," Cassidy said. They sat together at the breakfast table in Elrian's home in the damp Pacific northwest forest. It had been his country house, though he'd lived mostly in Vancouver. Cuinn, who despite being his flesh and blood, he'd had to disown decades ago, had chased him from there recently, and Elrian and Cassidy had relocated here.

He circled his shoulders uncomfortably. There was a good reason Cassidy didn't understand. Every time he'd confided some of the more…unsavory details of the plan, she'd become furious with him, and he'd ended up having to blur her memory.

She knew he was working on something important, and that he was researching some of the deeper prophecies around their race's survival. All true. Elrian believed the human race was slowly eradicating energetics, and that unless humans were at the very least checked, energetics wouldn't survive the next century. Cassidy knew that Elrian was sick, and that the research had something to do with that. She loved him, and would go a long way to help him be well.

"You're helping, and that's what's important," he reassured her. Cassidy knew he was a researcher into the legends of their race, collecting and reviewing fragments of energetic documents when they were found.

But she wasn't aware of all the ways he used that information.

After centuries of life, money wasn't an issue. A long-lived race in a world of short-lived humans, energetics had for many years been able to leverage their longevity for resources. And resources, financial and otherwise, helped handle issues such as a lack of aging. Methods such as moving, coming back as a nephew or cousin, and in modern times, whispers of plastic surgery, along with the use of their magics, all helped keep their race hidden.

She poured tea for them both and sipped hers. Poised and cool, she was a highly intelligent woman. He loved her in his own way, though since the tragic and unnecessary death of his first wife, he managed the depth of emotion he invested in others.

What Cassidy didn't know about his plan was the minutiae, such as that the illness resulted from the research, rather than was its cause, and that his plan to help the energetics survive humans involved the necessary sacrifice of a small number of their own race to prevent them from stopping him from bringing his version of the future to pass. His prophecy research told him that if certain couples got together, it would give them the power they would need to thwart him, though he didn't know how—and luckily, they didn't seem to either.

Unsuccessful in stopping the first three of the six pairs, he had failed to kill that irresponsible water energetic Nixie on the Thai island, despite coming close to creating another remnant stone using her death. He'd seen Archer as an easy target, yet he'd eluded him too.

He didn't know all twelve of the energetics relevant to the prophecy yet. They were being revealed slowly in Cassidy's prophetic dreams.

He wondered if obscuring Cassidy's memory was affecting her ability to seek prophecy clearly. Or if it would eventually affect her long-term memory.

He kept her away from other energetics. Keeping house for him and nurturing their garden nourished her Muladhara chakra, and supporting him in his research sustained her Ajna chakra. The latter included her dreamwalking for him, and occasionally, for others who paid for her services. She built on her own education too, and by now had several degrees, and two Doctorates.

While he knew she was capable of a great deal more, he needed her with him. After all, she could do far more for their race supporting him than out in the world serving her own interests and needs.

"You don't seem to be getting better," Cassidy commented, the delicate skin on her forehead wrinkled. She put out a hand and rested it lightly on his. "Have you found anything in your research that suggests answers on how to cure your illness? I'm worried about you."

In the short term, only to leech from more energetics.

He hoped that if he and Imogen stopped Cuinn and his team of misguided do-gooders, and created the twelve remnant stones the prophecy had indicated they needed—though they still were unclear why they needed them, or how they would be used exactly—he would have access to almost unlimited power, and his need to leech would be a thing of the past. Leeching made him feel powerful, of course, but there was also a distasteful element to it.

He could admit to himself that he required it at the moment. It was a necessary inconvenience, although he could see it was taking a toll on him. He was struggling to pull power from the ether at all, and the periods he could go between his donors were getting shorter and shorter. The pressure was growing. The empty feeling inside him was ever-present. Even when he took energy, it was as though he couldn't replenish his chakras the way he used to in the past. He'd lost weight, and he was having more and more trouble hiding his cravings from his associates and Cassidy.

"Imogen was going to do some more research. I'll speak to her later to discuss her findings." He took a bite of toast, though it didn't sate his real hunger. He needed to work harder, he decided. Research more. There was a way through this.

Cassidy tensed and withdrew her hand. She busied herself with spreading jam on her bread. "I see."

Although Cassidy no longer held those memories, she'd retained a negative feeling about Imogen, despite the woman having been part of their lives for years.

If Cassidy knew the details of what he and Imogen were really doing, it would be more than negative. She wouldn't understand. He couldn't bear that. Couldn't bear to have her look at him with disgust.

Whilst he had been pleased with the damage he had left on Archer, he hadn't killed him.

His bad luck so far trying to eliminate the couples meant he needed to think differently. To consider the problem from another angle. He had begun the hard slog of translating and piecing together the Hermit's notes, to see if it would give him a different approach to try.

He also needed to identify all the individuals in the prophecy who were against what Imogen and he were trying to bring to pass. They knew three of the final six, Archer, that meathead Adam, and the Healer Cara, but they did not know who was in each pair. Cassidy's Ajna work hadn't shown them as yet.

In the short term, they needed to find out where Archer had been taken. Elrian had tapped his contacts in the northwest, energetic and human alike. There might not be that many true Rogues, but there were a lot more energetics happy to dabble in gray areas than the precious Guild leaders believed. Favors, charms, knowledge, art, all went a long way to convincing people to share what they considered harmless information.

Getting Archer's whereabouts was taking a little more work, but Elrian would find him eventually. Then he'd try something new.

7

"He's driving me crazy, Adam. He has money, for Source's sake, let me send him home with a private nurse."

Adam sprawled on the armchair in Cara's office, idly rubbing the head of Argus. "Can't. His connection to Elrian is still unknown. Staying here is as good as any protective custody."

Behind her desk, Cara threw up her hands in frustration and then grabbed her stress balls.

"Plus, we need more info on Kayla. You might connect something between the two. We might find out more about Elrian's plans." He turned serious eyes to hers. "I'm grateful, Cara."

"Gah, I know. You don't need to be," Cara said. And the man wasn't faking. Realistically, Archer needed another one, or even two weeks of bedrest.

But she was finding his presence a distraction. He was like a pebble in her shoe, persistent and difficult to forget about, despite all the things she was supposed to be doing.

In recent weeks she had felt a constant sense of strain, juggling her usual to-do list with the burdens of the prophecy, and her worry about her friends. Of course, that's why Archer would get to stay. She wouldn't leave her friends in the lurch, and the prophecy was more important than her dislike for the man.

Time to focus on that. She put the speakerphone on and dialed Tierra's number. She and Fintan were at Anahata Guild in Cairo, Egypt, where Tierra was recovering from an attack orchestrated by Elrian.

Caring Tierra, with her ready-smile and weakness for cake, was Cara's best friend. A woman who couldn't do enough for those she cared about, Cara had been thrilled to see the prophecy help Tierra and the Warrior, her long-time crush, Fintan, get together in recent months. Fintan's training and energies were in fire, and he was a great example of his archetype, Warrior, defending others with his skills. In his lifetime, he had been involved in many energetic and human skirmishes and conflicts as a fighter. Ever-protective of Tierra, he had learned to let her use her gifts to safeguard him in turn, albeit not with her physical strength. Cara thought they were perfect for each other.

Once Tierra and Fintan were on the line, Adam updated them on the situation at the Rehab Center.

"How are you feeling, Tierra?" Cara asked.

Tierra's warm voice came through loud and clear. "I'm mostly better. Aiko and Feng have been wonderful."

Argus gave a gruff bark, and Tierra laughed. "Hello, Argus."

The dog huffed through his nose and settled back. Cara knew how he felt. She'd been worried about her friend too, and it eased something in her chest to hear her voice. All of them had faced danger one way or the other, and it didn't look like that was over and done with yet.

"She's still healing," Fintan said. "We're taking it easy till she's one-hundred percent."

"Fintan keeps scolding me," Tierra said. "But really, all I've done is walk around the grounds, and spent time researching in the library with Feng."

Feng was the long-time head of the Archives at Anahata Guild, and one of the senior members. He was also one of Tierra's greatest fans.

"Hmm," Fintan said. "You know you can't hide things from me, especially now that the bracelets are helping me."

Adam sat forward in his chair and cocked his head. "Say more."

"We're finding the bracelets are giving us a strange sort of sensitivity to each other," Tierra said.

"I've never heard of that power in an energetic object. Are the bracelets somehow twinned?" Cara said. This was new. Nixie and Jeb had said their bracelets had given them more power, but that was when they were with each other and the bracelets were touching.

"I have a good sense of where she is and her health through the bracelet. And the same the other way. Not that I ever overdo it." Fintan said the last a little pointedly, but Tierra just chuckled. Cara could imagine her patting Fintan. Tierra would always put others first, rarely thinking of the cost to herself. Cara was glad she had Fintan to look out for her.

"Is it the same for Blaize and Cuinn, and Nixie and Jeb?" Adam asked.

"I don't know. I can check," Fintan said.

"Do that." Adam was rubbing his chin, eyes distracted.

"Have you spoken with any of the others in the last day or two?" Cara said.

"Cuinn and Blaize are focused on the remnant stones and Iskander. Nixie's attempting to translate the Hermit's notes. Apparently, it's horribly difficult," Tierra said. "She and Jeb are at Svadisthana Guild where Jeb's rebuilding his energies after he has repressed his Creator energy for so long."

Jeb and Nixie had been the most recent of the energetics pairs in the prophecy to get bracelets. It seemed the bracelets appeared close to the point at which a couple got together. The bracelets themselves were beautiful. Braided with four colors: the Chakras of both—their energy-in-common, and their other energy—plus white, the color of Source.

As another highly experienced Healer in the Guild, Cara had known Jeb for many decades. She'd seen the scars he'd taken from World War II, and how he'd retreated to the Guild. His work there had continued to contribute to their race, but she'd wondered about his own mental health.

Nixie, Blaize's cousin, was artistic, impulsive and incredibly loyal. As fluid as the water that was her element, she was able to change as the situation needed, yet could spend hours without distraction on the graphic art that was her day job, and loved Jeb with a joyous and unflinching attitude that had healed him in unexpected ways.

Cara had been uncertain that Nixie was a match for Jeb when she'd first heard about her, but her relationship with the previously somber Jeb had grounded Nixie and lightened her new partner's sometimes dark introspection.

Nixie and her Healer were good for each other.

"Have Blaize and Cuinn seen any of the last three energetics from the original prophecy in the dreamscape yet? And do we know who the unidentified male is?" Tierra said.

"Nope. Their identities are still hidden," replied Adam.

Once Blaize or Cuinn found a prophecy sliver that included a new member of the group in the dreamscape, they transferred it mind-to-mind to Nixie, who was also a talented sketch artist. She would draw the figure, and share it with the others. Sometimes the pictures had other clues that proved useful.

Their group was exploring all avenues and using all their talents to beat the horrible evil that was haunting them. They could do this.

"How are Ai's lessons going? She settling in?" Fintan asked. As the ones to first find Ai, he and Tierra had formed a strong connection.

"She's alright," Cara said. She hesitated. "She seems fascinated by the Rogues. She has a lot of questions about Kayla."

"Hmm," Tierra said. "It might be the girl's connection with Elrian. Ai might see an alternate self in Kayla. Ai was close to being one of Elrian's victims herself, after all."

Cara wanted to smack herself. Of course. She must be working too hard not to have seen that link. The girl's compulsion to understand Kayla might well be connected to her own experiences.

"We could use that. Kayla might share more intel with Ai if she also feels that link." Adam commented, shrewd gaze shifting to Cara.

She scrunched her nose. "Ai's so new to our world. I don't like the idea of her seeing what's happening with Kayla at this point. It's too dangerous." Ai was a teenager. They had a duty to care for her.

"Tierra? Fin?" Adam said. "Thoughts?"

A moment of silence passed.

"I don't know," Tierra said, slowly. "She's already involved in this whole thing, but she's with you exactly because we want her out of danger."

"Clue her in," Fintan said. "Tell her you need her help. She's a lot more street-smart than some of the more pampered energetic kids of her age. Who knows what secrets that poor girl Kayla has locked up in her head. If we have a chance to find out more, let's take it. But don't let Ai keep secrets."

It didn't feel like a great idea to Cara, but they all led on the decisions that were relevant to their expertise, and Adam was their strategist. Cara would keep a close eye on Ai, and if she felt there was any danger to her emotional or mental health, she'd remove her immediately.

"Did you discover anything amiss at the Guild?" Cara tried for nonchalance, but she had complex feelings about the Guild these days.

"Nothing yet," Tierra said.

Jeb was a Maven at the Guild, and had a feeling that something was off there. But so far, nothing.

"Aiko and Feng have gone out of their way to help us, and they're the only ones who know what we're doing. But everyone else has been helpful too." Fintan didn't sound thrilled about it, but Cara was relieved Aiko hadn't shown herself to be as controlling as some of the previous Anahata Guild Leaders—yet.

"Fintan's even finding he likes some of the Guild members," Tierra teased.

His recent visits to the Guild had been Fintan's first in many decades—despite it being his auxiliary Guild—due to some negative experiences in his training days. His relationship with Tierra had not only meant he'd come back to the Guild, but he was exploring his own Anahata again much more actively.

Cara understood his mixed feelings. On the one hand, she didn't trust the Guild fully herself, and had a tendency to keep them at a distance wherever possible. She liked to be in control of what happened at her Center, rather than let others change things from afar when they had no idea what things were like on the ground.

On the other hand, the Guild was her heart—literally, given the chakra it represented. Anahata was the chakra of air, the heart, healing. She sighed. She felt off-balance with worry about her friends. Tierra, who had been Cara's best friend for decades, had nearly died, and the amount of danger they were all in was unquantifiable. On top of the Rehab Center and the things Cara needed to handle day-to-day, she wasn't feeling her best.

Still, she'd do what she always did. Her duty.

Duty by friends, by the Center, by her Guild.

Mind you, she wasn't sure what the best way was to go about that right now. She respected Adam, she did, and he was the right person to lead overall, but it had been a while since someone had overruled her. Even the Guild left the Rehab Center managers alone.

"You need to take care too, Cara." Fintan's use of her name tuned her back into the conversation. A guilty pang went through her as she realized she'd missed the last few sentences.

"We're fine here," she said. "Given half of the Rehab Center is made to keep Rogues inside, we have pretty solid protection. Everyone's on high alert for issues."

"Has your intuition given you any hints?" Tierra asked her.

Interesting question. One of Anahata's gifts was the ability to sense issues through emotion. It was the 'gut feeling' humans talked about, an instinct about situations. However, Cara had had so much in her head recently she hadn't been listening to her heart.

"No," she admitted. She was twisting the spheres in her hand more roughly.

"Could it?" asked Adam. Argus padded over to Cara and licked her leg. She patted him with her free hand.

Cara rolled her neck, trying to ease the tension in it, and stopped the balls moving in her hand.

She lifted her hand from the warmth of Argus's neck, and placed it on her heart, pulling a sliver of energy. Gentle heat warmed her Anahata Chakra, and she listened at the intuitive level, trying to forget the analysis and logic she'd been leaning on, and hear what her instincts might have to say. Tremors of energy radiated through her, and she clutched the stress balls in her hand to stay grounded.

"Kayla," she said finally. "Something's off about the Kayla situation. We don't understand enough about what's happening to her. She's chaotic, flipping between different states. It's more than the typical aftereffects of what she's been through."

"Are you on it?" Adam asked.

She nodded, although a small voice inside her was yelling at the idea of piling yet another problem on her already over-stacked plate.

They finished up the call, and Adam and Argus left. She slumped in her office chair, then drew in a long breath. No time to mope.

She steeled herself, straightened her spine, and opened her email. At the top was one from Jeb. He informed her that Cara's Center had been chosen as one of four pilot centers for a confidential database project. The database would collect information on patients in the Center, such as name, power levels, location, health history, chakra details, issues with powers, what they could do with them, and so on. It would be of the highest confidentiality, with only the Center Managers of the places it was being trialed, along with a handful of people at Anahata Guild having access, so Cara would have to do all the collection of data from their various records, as well as the tedious data entry herself. She groaned.

She needed more work like she needed a hole in her head.

On top of that, Cara could read between the lines of the carefully written email to see it was going to be controversial, and a lot more work for Cara herself. It was one thing getting involved in the bigger issues of the energetic world because her friends were in danger. It was another entirely to get caught up in a bureaucratic battle.

She usually tried to keep the Guild as far from her business as possible. What would draw less attention, agreeing to be part of this trial or citing her current work levels as an excuse?

She needed to speak to Jeb directly about it, though it seemed that Maya, another senior Guild member, was the lead. Source knows when she would fit a call in to him, given the urgency of finding out what was happening with Kayla, keeping Ai out of trouble, getting Archer healed and out of the Center, and her actual job.

Her head ached, pressure building behind the temples.

She really hoped they worked out how to solve this prophecy before her head exploded.

8

Archer sat up in bed. Light streamed in through the tall windows, showing a bright summer's day. Though given the Center was on the south-west coast of Vancouver island, he doubted it was especially warm. He drummed his fingers as he considered ways to speed up his healing so he could get back to work.

It wasn't that he enjoyed his job. It was simply that he was the only one who could do it. Phoebe needed him, and he wouldn't let her down.

He'd lost count of the number of times people had told him to rest over the last couple of days. He was so over it. It was true, he still felt pretty lousy, but wasn't it better to distract himself by being useful? He wanted to work.

He couldn't imagine how much Phoebe must be struggling without him. In order for the new deal to succeed, he had to both work on the content and oversee the project itself. The stakes of the deal were high, and could impact the very direction their company took in the future.

Who knew what was happening without him to run things?

He tugged experimentally at the ether. If he could pull enough power, he might be able to energize himself to the extent they'd let him out.

He strained. It was like trying to suck up a thick shake through a tiny straw. His connection to what made the energetics who they were was damaged. Leeching affected people differently, as far as he knew, and it had hit him hard.

He slumped back against the headboard.

If he was honest with himself, he'd been struggling even before the attack. He'd been working 14-hour days for the last few weeks, having added bits here and there on the project into his regular schedule without considering there might be a need to delegate some things he was already doing.

He'd held on because he'd known once the project was done and the pilot shipped to Phoebe to demo it to the potential investors, he could go diving, his real love. It had kept him going, the light at the end of a long, dark, miserable tunnel. The possibility of heading off on his boat to explore another energetics archeological site.

But if he didn't get the demo done and make sure that Phoebe had what she needed, all their timelines would be pushed out, and he'd lose even the fragment of time he'd secured for his time off. Frustration built inside him, and he itched to do something, anything, that would get him out of here.

Cara entered the room, as self-possessed and classy as she was every day when she came in to check on him. No matter what other crisis she was juggling—and the employee gossip he'd overheard told him this was a healing center that was creaking at the seams—she never showed it. The only time he'd seen a flash of temper from her was when he'd criticized her running of her beloved Center.

"How are you today, Mr. Hampton?" she said.

He rolled his eyes. "My name, for the hundredth time, is Archer."

She was checking his vitals. "Progressing well."

He drew himself up in the bed. Dammit, he should have gotten dressed. He glanced down at the boxers and Rubik's cube t-shirt he wore, chosen because it was soft and comforting. He'd shower as soon as she left, and spend his days out of bed in future.

"I'm doing great!" He tried to project enthusiasm and, somehow, health. He could convince this woman to send him home. He'd spent years developing the charm of his Vishudha.

A twinge of pain went through his gut. Alright, he'd start by getting his tech. "You know what I think would help me get better?"

She sighed. "No. I need to talk to you."

"You don't even know what I—"

"No." Despite the word, her eyes were compassionate.

He deflated. He didn't have the energy to fight her today. Tomorrow, then. "Fine. What do we need to talk about?"

"Your attacker left traces of some kind of fungus in your wound, a poison. It wasn't obvious at first, and has taken us a few days to realize it was there." She finished noting his vitals on his chart, and perched on the bed next to him. Her eyes were compassionate.

Archer's facade of cheer dropped away as a ball of ice formed in his belly. "What does it mean? What is it doing?"

"From an energetic perspective, it seems to be having an impact on your connection between your chakras and your connection with the ether. In terms of your physical functioning, it's dampening your immune system and slowing your recovery."

His lips pressed together. His immune system hadn't been in tip-top working order for months, because of the amount of work and stress he'd been carrying. He ate as healthily as he could, and worked out, but psychologically, he'd been a mess for a while—that's what happened when you accidentally built a corporate empire to show your parents you were worth their notice.

However, sharing this would only add to Cara's view that he should be lying like a stick of wood doing nothing, and he suspected indicating he'd been on the edge of corporate burnout for months might not help his case that he should be sent home.

What he needed was solutions, not problems. "Alright. How do we address that?"

She raised an eyebrow. Had she been expecting drama? He didn't have time for that. If she told him what to do, he could control the situation.

"Now that we know it's there, we'll treat it, but it's even more important you rest, and keep the stress in your environment to a minimum."

He blew out a breath. So much for his escape plan. "Right now it feels more stressful not working than working."

She touched his shoulder lightly. "I see that. But when you talk about work, your pulse rate increases, and Phoebe indicated that work has been quite an intense environment recently. I can't take the chance. I can introduce you to a couple of the other recuperating energetics if you want some social time."

He really, really didn't. He wasn't sure if he could keep up his act more than for the healers and health workers who visited his room.

He wanted a nap.

"Thanks, but no. Tomorrow, maybe. Let me know what I can do to heal quicker."

Cara stood. "Sleep, eat, read, and take part in any treatment regimens or suggestions from the staff if you're able. Oh, and you can watch TV."

"Alright." The word stuck in his throat, but he forced it out with an attempt at a smile, and she left him.

He was officially over someone else being in charge of his life. No matter how pretty she was.

Time ticked by.

Archer's frustration grew. He stoked it, knowing it was better than the despondency it overlaid. He would get out of here. And soon.

He lay down. If necessary, he'd rest so hard today he'd make a dent in the bed.

A handful more minutes, and he got up again. He wasn't tired. Well, he was tired, but he wasn't ready to sleep. His brain was jittery, thinking about work, and making a to-do list for Phoebe. Surely she'd see they needed him back?

He stared out of the window. He knew the Center took up many acres of land, right up to the cliffs adjoining the sea, and he had a view of green spaces threaded through with gravel paths leading to other buildings and a forest in the distance.

He asked the nurse on duty about taking a shower. She wouldn't have it. "You can't get the bandages wet. We'll give you a sponge bath."

He tried to protest, to say it wasn't necessary, that he would be happy to use the extremely well-designed en suite, but she came back with a colleague, and with washcloths, towels, soap and water basins.

The next forty minutes were an awkward experience that changed his teenage sponge bath fantasies forever.

He spent it gritting his teeth and pretending to be somewhere else. Vulnerability again, he thought, as they soaped and wiped down his back. Being looked after wasn't something he enjoyed at the best of times, and neither were situations where he was out of control.

They left him resting on the couch, as he had flatly refused to get back into bed. Five times he had picked up and put down a Computer Weekly magazine that Phoebe had left him. He wasn't a reader. He hadn't realized quite the extent to which he relied on his devices for entertainment and distraction, as well as communication and work. Flicking through the TV channels hadn't been productive so far.

Two hours later, he was deep into watching a Korean drama, his mouth agape. The colorful performance from the cast took him through a love story that seemed to involve a girl finding out the boy she thought was her soulmate was actually her long-lost brother. Ouch.

When the door opened again, he didn't bother looking up, assuming it was food or the staff checking his vitals yet again. He was tired of the lack of privacy, tired of interruptions.

"It's not quite what I expected, but I'm relieved you're finally doing what you're told," came Phoebe's gentle voice.

Thrilled to see her, he still bristled at the idea he was obedient and bowing to others' wills. She walked to him and squeezed his shoulder, and he subsided, knowing how much she cared for him.

She was the sister he wished he'd had, and the best friend and colleague he could wish for. He could stop being such an ass for a moment with her, despite how grumpy he felt. After all, she'd taken a two-hour chopper ride to get here.

"What are you doing back?" he asked. He wasn't ready to show quite how euphoric he was at the distraction.

"Just wanted to check on you and reassure you that everything's under control." Phoebe said. She sat on the small armchair next to the couch and TV, resting her handbag on the low coffee table. "Don't stress about what's happening at Disp@tch. I've talked to Cara, and she says you need to be here at least another week, so I've delegated some things from both our plates, and picked up your critical tasks myself."

His heart sank. A week.

"I'm feeling better already," he lied. "I'm sure it won't take a week. Also, don't you have enough on right now?"

As well as her COO duties, Phoebe was dealing with a sick family member who lived in Seattle, and she visited often. He shuffled over to make room.

"You can sit here if you want," he said, trying to speak past a lump in his throat. He'd planned to leave everything in great working order so he could go on his diving trip with a clear conscience, and not leave Phoebe hanging high and dry. Instead, he'd gotten mixed up in something that was going to mess with their meticulous plans. Once he got back to work, it might be months before he could get things to a place where he could take the time off.

"We cover for each other when we're off," Phoebe shifted to perch next to him on the couch. "It's what we do. Anyway, your health isn't up for debate. You're here at least another week, and Cara gets to decide when you leave."

His mouth fell open. "Are you crazy? That woman thinks I'm an entitled prick. She'll keep me here if only to show she's the boss."

Phoebe's mouth quirked. "If she dislikes you that much, surely she's going to be trying to get rid of you, not keep you around? And what have you done to show her you're not an entitled prick?"

He started to protest, and she waved a hand. "It's not open for debate. I'm nixing further discussion."

That stopped him in his tracks. Over their years of working together, the two of them had developed a system of final noes, which they called nixing. It was a short-hand for them to express a powerful depth of feeling, and that they weren't going to be moved. There wasn't anyone else in the world he'd let have that kind of ability, but she'd saved his ass on a number of occasions by using it, and she deserved his loyalty. Plus, she was damn good at her job.

His fingers twisted in the soft gray-blue blanket he'd been using to keep warm. His shoulders sloped, and his emotions hit a new low. He wouldn't fight her.

Her voice softened, and she rested a hand on the blanket covering his leg. "See this as a good thing. A time to destress. And honestly, we still know nothing about why this guy attacked you. It could be dangerous for you out there. It gives Adam and the others time to find him and catch him. He hasn't picked up the trail yet, but he's working on it."

Archer had a twinge of guilt as he remembered Adam had stopped following Elrian to check on Archer. It was Archer's fault Adam hadn't already caught the Rogue. *Shit shit shit.*

"I'll stay here for the week. But for the love of Source, can I have my tech back?" he said, knowing the answer already.

She just looked at him, her eyebrows raised.

Shit.

"When do you think you can visit again?" He tried not to sound too desperate.

"I'll be back in a few days," she said, and the corners of her mouth twitched. She dropped a kiss on his forehead and left.

What on earth was he going to do with himself? He'd barely been here a few days, and he was going out of his mind with boredom.

A knock at the door interrupted his misery. A head popped into the room. It was the girl who'd been with Adam and Cara, Ai, her name was. What did she want? Were they sending teenagers to do his medical care now?

"Yeah?"

"Thought you might be bored, brought you this. You can watch them on the TV. The port's at the back." The girl shoved a data stick towards him. He frowned. Why was she bringing him anything? He was uncertain of her role in the Center. Was she an intern? Someone's kid sister? It wasn't unusual for Adherents, those who were in their first stage of training in a Chakra, to have real roles in the energetics world to develop skills. However, he hadn't seen the tattoo of a single line circling her upper arm that signified an Adherent. Which was unusual, now he thought about it. Most energetics started training in one of their Chakras in their mid to late teens. Perhaps she was younger than she looked.

"Thanks," he said, taking it from her. "Err, what is it?"

"A streamer playing some vintage video games." She flushed when he didn't say anything. "Thought you might find it fun."

He scratched his cheek. He didn't know what to say. It was a small kindness, but a thoughtful one.

Everyone had been perfectly nice to him here—well, apart from Cara—but he hadn't connected to anyone at a more personal level.

He perked up. "Thanks."

She nodded and fled the room.

Perhaps he'd make an ally.

Elrian sat at his desk in his spartan study. It was a place of work, he had no need of fripperies. He had been working for several days on the notes from Damir, the Hermit, while he waited for news from his network on Archer. Given the man was famous both in the human and energetic world, he didn't doubt he'd hear a whisper soon.

He paused. Hmm. Here was a writing about blocking a specific chakra of an individual and the connection between those chakras. Elrian had tried to do something similar to the girl Blaize's Ajna chakra when she had connected to the dreamscape unwarded, but it hadn't taken. He had thought it might prevent her from joining fully to her mate.

He'd thrown something very like it at Archer as he was getting away, fungus spores he'd added to the branches he'd thrown at the male. Was it working? At the very least, he'd be slower to heal. At best, it would kill him.

He frowned at a passage, his focus narrowing, and scribbled frantic notes. He consulted his dictionaries, checking the meaning of this word and that.

Several hours later, he called Imogen and put her on speakerphone.

"I found something," he said. He was jittery and wired, the thrill of the discovery warring with the fatigue that blanketed him. "I know why my blocking magics didn't work."

"Tell me, my love," Imogen said. He pressed his palms to his eyes in relief she was in a good mood. It was always hard to predict.

"The Guilds teach that if a chakra is blocked, it will impact the whole energy system in the body. Or, if the path between the dominant and auxiliary chakra is disabled or damaged, then that energetic will have trouble using or accessing their energy." He could hardly get the words out in his excitement. It wasn't often you discovered something that turned hundreds, or even thousands, of years of lore upside down.

"They don't simply teach it. It's factually correct. Anahata sees it in patients often," Imogen said. Her tone had cooled.

He sped up his delivery, trying to keep her attention. "Damir showed it doesn't have to be the case. There's a way round it."

"Hmm."

"It's possible to link each chakra to every other chakra, rather than have a main channel in a line between all seven. It can be a web, rather than a path. In that case, if you damage the path between two chakras, you can reroute through another part of the web."

There was a silence. Elrian hovered over the phone, waiting for her to say something. His jaw clenched. Could she see the implications?

"I see," she drawled. "This is interesting indeed. But why don't we know this? We have many cases a year. Why doesn't the energy simply reroute if this is possible?"

He'd spent time considering this, and the cases of the energetics who hadn't seemed affected by his castings. He'd pieced together different parts of the notes the Hermit had referenced and he thought he had it.

"Strangely, the Hermit's notes showed he found references in ancient texts that it happened all the time. But in the now, it takes a large push of energy to get through the web to activate it," he said. "Those opposing us have channeled surges of energy through themselves to fight us."

He hesitated. The next part was conjecture, not fact. "The bracelets they have. We don't understand them, or where they're getting them. I have a sense they're relevant somehow."

"So we don't know how to activate this so-called web?" she said.

"No," he admitted. "But Imogen, think about the impact on the race if we could find out how to make it happen. It would be a major Anahata breakthrough. We'd eliminate one of the biggest causes of sickness in our race."

"We're not here to make breakthroughs. Maybe if you find them, but it's not the priority. We're here to get power, to achieve our goals. Remember my love?" She was cold now. Cold and sharp, like an icicle. "Find where the final casting should take place, and do something about Archer. I take it you've failed to find out where he is?"

"Yes, but I will. Soon" Disappointment flooded him as she hung up.

He sat staring at the books and papers spread out on the desk. Were they still aligned in their goals? They both wanted power, certainly. Once he and Imogen had the power they deserved, they could rule the energetics and lead them back to the way they were in halcyon ancient times on Atlantis, their original home.

They would see the yoking of the human race, if not its extermination. And never again would an energetic have to sacrifice themselves for the sake of a human, like his wife had.

CHAPTER

9

"Still, no," Cara said. Did her lips almost twitch up in a smile? Archer thought so. He'd been in this room for four days now. Four long, techless days. Didn't they understand this was adding to his stress, not lessening it?

His time here was so boring that, somehow, he had begun to look forward to his quarrelsome visits from Cara. She came four times a day to check on his progress, and each time, he asked her two questions: 'Can I have my tech back?' and 'Can I leave yet?'

He'd started to ask in different ways. At first, he'd been surly, and then angry. And he'd taken that anger out on her. He'd raged. His usual grasp on his Vishudha, his ability to persuade, charm and use his voice and words, had been completely absent.

Let's face it. He'd been a dick.

She'd stayed cool and polite, which had fanned the flames as he tried to persuade her he was right.

Another night's sleep and he had changed his approach. He'd been polite. Then he'd tried writing the questions on paper and holding them up when she came near him. He'd put the questions under things he knew she'd lift, so she discovered them unexpectedly. He'd considered it a major win when he got any kind of emotional reaction, especially a stifled laugh, or a hand to her face to hide a smile. When her bronze eyes sparkled, they shone with a light he found almost hypnotizing.

The most recent gambit involved him writing the questions on the large windows in the room in petroleum jelly he'd begged from Prudence, then using his Manipura to heat a couple of carefully placed cups of water underneath the window so the steam rose and exposed the words. He was quite pleased with himself for thinking of that.

Cara fanned herself and opened a window. Cool, fresh air breathed through the room. "You're going to have to clean that off, you know."

"Worth it," he said and grinned. Coming up with new ways to ask had been a more fun way to spend the time than slumped on the bed, brooding and bored. And it distracted him from his anxiety about not being there for Phoebe and the team.

Cara finished her checks and stood next to the bed.

"Sit, please," he gestured grandly at the visitor's chair. "My reception room's being cleaned at the moment, but we can talk here."

She rolled her eyes. A good sign. Still, she sat.

Their initial meeting had colored his interactions with her. Months ago, he'd brought in one of his top team members, who'd been hit by a car crossing the road outside their head office building at night, after Archer had been working the team especially hard to meet a deadline, and Archer—still at work—had been called to the scene, and taken her to the nearest Center immediately.

In retrospect, he could see his guilt at the accident had caused him to be a little more protective than usual, and maybe, just maybe, he'd come on a bit strong. He and Cara hadn't had the best interactions. He'd seen her as bossy and power hungry. He'd questioned her methods, and in making sure that Indu had the best possible care he might have, perhaps, maybe, pissed Cara off. The last couple of days had shown him another side to her. She was both cool and fire, and unlike many people he met, human or energetic, she seemed entirely unconcerned with his fame and power.

Dealing in the world of human communications technologies, especially in social media, he met a lot of vacuous, shallow people. Cara, with her pragmatism and directness, was anything but.

"Are you *warming* to me?" he said, his eyes sliding to the windows, where the steam drifted out into the cool outside air. He felt a sudden need to charm her.

She stifled a groan at his admittedly terrible joke and shook her head. "How's your meditation practice?"

His brow wrinkled. "I'm sorry?"

"Meditation. To connect with the Source, ground you, and ensure you can focus when you use your Chakras."

"It's…alright," he said. He coughed and took a sip of water. He wasn't the best at dissembling.

"How much meditation have you done since you've been here?" Cara asked. She smoothed her skirt over her slender legs. She never wore heels, though her flats, while to his unpracticed eye looking comfortable, always seemed to include some tiny interesting detail, like the small silver bows on today's light blue shoes. She was an intriguing mixture, pragmatic and grounded in her healing, whilst exuding a sense of grace and ease. The latter was her air energy, he supposed. When most thought of Anahata, they thought of the Healers, because that was the major gift of that chakra. Many forgot it was also the Chakra of the element air. Some Anahata energetics could engage with the weather, create storms or even shape air. It was possible, though rare, for very powerful energetics of this type to propel or lift themselves using the element. He wondered what gifts other than healing she had.

"Not much," he said. Or, you know, none. He didn't enjoy meditation. It was sometimes a necessary evil for energetics, taught and practiced by all of them in varying amounts, but he had never taken to it. He'd done enough to progress through his Practitioner and Master level stages, and he had all three circlet-style tattoos to show for it. He'd never been interested in being a Maven, the teachers of their race. The thought of being responsible for an Adherent wasn't of interest to him.

Sitting still wasn't something he found enjoyable unless he was completely absorbed in a project. He'd used a standing desk for many years while coding, and had walking meetings.

He found it hard to clear his mind, and when he tried meditating, he would end up thinking about the next task on his list, and eventually he'd crack and go back to work.

Running worked for him, most of the time, as a way to handle stress.

Okay. *Some* of the time.

"Your cortisol levels are too high, and so is your blood pressure. As an energetic, these are things you should be able to regulate. These issues are draining some of your energy, and you need that energy to heal," Cara said. "I have a ritual I'd like us to do, and I'd like you to spend some time each morning and evening meditating."

Cara recrossed her legs and looked at him expectantly.

"I don't—how much meditation?" Five minutes in the morning and evening he could do. Ten, even.

"An hour each. We'll try the ritual later today, and see how you are. We might need to do that again tomorrow."

A cold lump settled in his belly. "I don't know if I can do that."

"If you want out of here and your tech back, you can," Cara said. Her face was back to that damned mask, implacable and set.

He ground his teeth together, holding himself back from snapping at her. Alright, he hated sitting still. Hated it. Even his holidays were hugely active. Sure, he did the meditation every energetic did, the stuff he *had* to do to keep himself healthy. He took a breath. Okay, perhaps he wasn't quite doing that, given what she said.

It's not like she was giving him a choice, though. She had the power here. To keep everyone happy, he needed her agreement to leave.

"Alright. Talk me through what I need to do for the ritual later," he said.

She walked him through the steps. Conscious of the need to keep her on his side, he didn't show on his face the discomfort that built inside him at the idea of sitting with his thoughts for an hour.

It wasn't an experience he was used to. Outside his family, who he avoided, the only person who dealt with him as directly and bluntly as Cara was Phoebe. Cara was strong, and he could sense the contained power within her. Her role demanded a lot from her. He hadn't seen the Rogue rehabilitation section of the Center, but a Rehab Center had some things in common with a Guild, in that the power of the person in charge was part of the protection of the Center and its ability to contain, rehabilitate and heal its inhabitants.

Ai cracked the door open and slid through. She'd been in a handful of times, and was a bright spot in his boring days.

Cara frowned. "Did you finish your reading already?"

"All done," Ai said. "I had more questions for Archer."

"I've been helping her with basic background about the Guilds," Archer said, as Cara turned a narrow-eyed stare on him. She glared at him for another few seconds before she returned a gentler gaze to Ai.

"He needs to do some healing work now. Go practice moving your energy around your body."

The teen's eyes shone, and she nodded eagerly.

"But do it within the protective circle we set up." Cara added hastily.

Archer stifled a chuckle. As one of the younger energetics alive, he still remembered his early experiments with energy. He'd set his physical age at around 35, but he'd been born in the 1950s. Growing up, his family of energetics had all been between 150 and 200 years old, apart from his sister. He'd been a surprise baby for his parents. Energetics weren't prolific in terms of having children, and in more recent times, he'd noticed even fewer births.

Estella, his sister, was over fifty years older than him, and had always drawn great admiration for her intelligence. She was a Vishudha-Ajna—the rocket scientist type, an academic focusing on Guild and human world research, her gifts all based in her mind. Smart she might be, but she had the emotional sensitivity of a rock.

Archer had grown up cared for, but isolated. He'd experimented with his energies a great deal on his own, and there were plenty of charred trees around his parents' complex in New England to show for it.

"Good luck," he called after Ai, as she went back out the way she came.

Cara turned her scowl back on him. "I'd rather you leave the girl's education to me."

Archer's jaw stiffened. "Why? She's bored, I'm bored. She's a bright kid, and I'm happy to answer questions for her about our world."

"I've designed a program for her to learn what she needs to," Cara said, her chin tilted up. "I have it under control."

"I can see why you're keeping her here," Archer said. "Anahata really fucked up by losing her."

Cara drew herself to her feet. "It was an error. An awful error, and the Guild is looking into why and how it happened."

He wondered what her relationship was to her Guild. She'd gone through the highest levels of training, and was both a Master in Anahata and a Maven, those who were allowed to formally take and train an Adherent. Ai didn't have the basic understanding of her energy that youngsters who had grown up in energetic families did. Hence this informal training, he presumed.

"Would you send her for schooling at the Guild?" he asked, curious.

"Right now, we have other priorities. She's safe here with me, and she can learn. What happens next, I don't know." She crossed her arms. "Prepare for your meditation. I'll be back in an hour to help you through your first attempt at the ritual. I have work to do in the meantime."

She left the room, and he sighed. He didn't like the idea of preparing for an hour long meditation ritual by meditating more. Pretty much anything sounded better.

He glanced at the windows. He'd clean them first.

Meditatively.

Cara tried not to stomp along the corridor. She'd left Archer to the end of her patient rounds, for some reason, and it had been a mistake. The man was infuriating.

She didn't like him manufacturing a friendship with Ai to distract himself while he was bored. He was a bad influence through and through, controlling and entitled. Ai had suffered enough abandonment in her life. She needed solid people around her. Archer wasn't a good role model.

She also wasn't sure that Ai was ready to be exposed to the level of casual privilege that Archer had. Few energetics worried about their finances, a byproduct of being a long-lived, magical race, but Archer's success had given him money and power beyond the reach of most. She'd seen him featured in the Forbes 400, one of the wealthiest men in America.

In addition, the gossip magazines she read showed a frivolous man who went to parties and galas with a new woman on his arm every time. Cara had a deep-seated need to help people. She couldn't see a man like Archer doing that. She wanted Ai to interact with energetics who would support her development and personal growth.

No, he wasn't to be trusted, and she didn't want him influencing Ai.

She decided to check in on Ai and changed direction to go to the accommodation block. She knocked at Ai's door and waited. Nothing. She frowned. Did Ai get distracted again? Had something or someone waylaid her, or had she found something more interesting on the way back to her rooms?

Cara cocked her head as a faint sound caught her attention. The second time she heard it she didn't have to strain, as the noise came through the door and echoed around the corridor. Uh oh.

She knocked once more, then slammed open the door, only to see Ai standing in the center of a protective circle—thank Source—fighting with a small but vicious cyclone.

Ai didn't seem to have anything inside the circle with her, which meant she was safe from debris, at least. But her clothes had ripped, and the shreds slapped at her hands and face, the fierce wind creating whips of the rags.

Ai fell to her knees as Cara entered, and lifted her head, her pleading gaze meeting Cara's. She was panting, the air inside the circle difficult to breathe. She opened her mouth, but whatever words she wanted to say were torn away.

Cara would have to break her circle and contain the wind, or Ai could suffer serious injuries. Cara threw up her arms and pulled energy. It was harder than usual, and she knew she needed to stop reminding herself about replenishing her own stores with meditation and do it, soon.

Later.

Ai had used chalk to draw her circle, and the elements were represented around the circle, the choices very Ai: a cactus for earth; one of her energetics textbooks for mind; a goose feather for air, no doubt collected from the grounds; a lighter for fire; a seashell for water and an old thermometer for ether, the hardest element to represent. Mercury was associated with the chakra, and this was one of the easiest representations.

The symbolic objects were on the circle boundary, and thus not caught in the maelstrom with Ai. If Cara could move the items off the border that surrounded Ai, she could break the protective magic. Then all she needed to do was to contain the storm.

Tears streaked Ai's face, and she dropped to the floor and huddled in a ball, her arms wrapped around her knees, her head ducked. Thin lines striped her flesh where her torn clothes had struck her.

Cara seized the Anahata energy inside her and molded it to her hands like gloves. Air energy to protect against air energy.

She kneeled next to the circle, and with a surge of effort, she grasped the item representing the lowest Chakra, Muladhara. The cactus was in a small pot, but weighed as much as a boulder. Cara tugged, trying to detach it from the circle, but it wouldn't budge.

"Relax your will around earth!" Cara shouted over the contained storm's noise. "Let me remove it!"

Ai's fists clenched, and her terrified eyes were wide. "Can't!" she mouthed.

"You can. You absolutely can," Cara told her. "We'll do this together. Focus on the plant, and earth. Let that element go. I'll keep the circle whole."

Ai slid a hand across the floor to touch the boundary where the cactus straddled it.

"Together," Cara said. Her heart beat out a fast tattoo, and she worked to show only a calm, encouraging expression while concern for the teen churned inside her.

With a jerk of her hand, Ai released the energetic bonds that held the cactus to the circle, and then pushed it away from the boundary with her fingers.

Cara slammed her palm against the energetic hole and pressed energy into the space as fast as she could. After a minute, the boundary felt robust again. She let out a breath.

"Water, now," she instructed a wild-looking Ai. Another bloody line appeared on the teen's cheek as a button ripped from her clothing and tore across her flesh.

Ai shifted position to move the shell. Again, Cara shoved energy into the gap the shell's lack of presence left.

The next, the lighter representing fire, was one of Cara's own energies, so it was easier to smooth the break in the protection.

The storm within threw Ai against her own boundary, still successfully keeping her energies contained, but the forces were increasing. Her dark hair was plastered across her face.

They needed to work faster. She gestured to the feather, and Ai stretched out a shaking hand across the floor and shoved at the feather. As Cara's strongest energy, she caught the feather and subsequent gap with less effort, and she nodded. "Next. Quickly," she said.

Ai rotated her arm to reach the thermometer, but her first attempt did nothing. The wind caught her and lifted her for a moment, smashing her into the other side of the circle. Sobbing, Ai crawled back across the small space, extending a trembling hand. It touched the object, and she squeezed her eyes shut as she unbound it from her circle.

This was harder to catch, and Cara wavered for a moment, the storm inside the circle making it swell, seeking the smallest gap from which to escape.

"One more," Cara shouted over the wind, smiling encouragingly at Ai.

Ai rolled to face the textbook and straightened her arm at the elbow. She stopped a few millimeters from the book, and looked back over a shoulder at Cara, who nodded emphatically. "We've got this. Trust me."

Ai flicked trembling fingers, and the last object detached from the barrier. Cara poured energy into the circle. When she was confident it was only her power holding the barrier, she took a shaky breath.

Ai was on the floor, her hands protecting her head, clothes fluttering as though they were independent entities.

Cara gritted her teeth. Time to face the storm.

She tapped into her Anahata, hands crossed over her heart, touching her air Chakra.

She stepped close to the circle, then in one smooth action, she pressed her face to the magic barrier, and breathed in.

The inhale was strong, steady, and infused with energy. It caught the tempest and defanged it, drawing it into her, so it raged within Cara's energetic body rather than around Ai's physical one.

Cara flickered her eyelids open for a millisecond to check Ai's limp body was still rising and falling with her own breath, before she concentrated on the magic battering her from the inside.

It clawed at her, and she wrestled with the raw power Ai had pulled from the ether and unleashed. Pain streaked through her in red smears, and she screamed even as she dissipated and equalized the pressure. Cara breathed it out again, harmless once more.

She sagged to the ground and reached out a hand to Ai, who gripped her hand back, crushing Cara's fingers. Cara could hear her whispered chant, "Thank you, thank you, thank you, I'm sorry, I'm sorry, I'm sorry."

10

It had been another long day. Cara thought wistfully of a full night's sleep, which still seemed a distant goal. Right now, she had a new teenage energetic to manage.

She and Ai sat together at Cara's dining table, eating a meal that Osana had brought them from the Center's dining hall. Despite the warmth of the room, Ai had a thick woolen blanket wrapped around her shoulders, her eyes downcast as she forked up mouthfuls of pasta. She would sleep in Cara's guest room tonight.

"I'm sorry," Ai muttered, so softly that Cara had to lean forward to catch it.

"Why are you sorry?" Cara asked, carefully.

"I couldn't control it," Ai said, still looking at her dinner. "I pulled too much and I couldn't control it."

"When did you know you'd pulled too much?" Cara said. She needed to understand where the issue lay. Was it overconfidence? A lack of control? A lack of understanding? An accident? Each scenario would need different handling. "Talk me through what happened."

Ai glanced up at Cara, guilt lacing her dark eyes. "I'm not sure. When I went back to my room, I was excited to practice. I've been talking to Archer a lot and he does such cool things in both the human and energetic worlds, it made me want to be better. I'd love to build something like he has one day."

Cara stiffened. "Being an energetic is about helping people and the wider world."

"He helps people," Ai said, eagerly. "Have you heard about the programs Disp@tch is running, bringing communications technology to low-income countries? Or the work he does for the energetics in North America?"

A PR stunt, Cara wanted to say, though she bit down on the words. Something about that blasted man had inspired Ai, and while he didn't deserve the admiration, she didn't want to dampen the girl's newfound motivation.

"Alright. What happened when you went to your room?"

"I set up the circle like you told me. I was careful," Ai said, moving her food around her plate. "I reached into the ether for Anahata energy. But somehow the connection opened too wide, and the energy came through in more of a rush than I expected. I tried to close the link, but too much had come through, and I panicked. I didn't know how to absorb it. Then you came in."

"Why do you think more energy came through than you wanted?" Cara said. It sounded like an accident, perhaps driven by over enthusiasm. Ai was still new to this, Cara reminded herself. Normally, a teen would have had more practice in these basics, and would have been learning theory from a young age, but Ai had been thrown into their world with none of that background. Cara had been trying to take over from the brief education Tierra and Fintan had given Ai, but perhaps she hadn't given the teen enough time. Cara rubbed her temples. There was never enough time.

"I don't know," Ai said. "I guess I'm just not that good."

"You're not that experienced," Cara corrected. "It's not the same thing. What would you do differently next time?"

There was a long silence. Cara had plenty of ideas she wanted to suggest, but even though she hadn't been an active Maven for a while, she knew it was better for learners to come up with ideas themselves where they could.

"More reading on how to pull only the amount of energy I need, I guess. And to talk about it some more," Ai said, eventually. "And maybe... you could be there when I try again? Give me suggestions?"

Cara nodded. "No problem."

Of course she would be there next time. She wasn't letting Ai try again without strong supervision, given what had happened. However, Ai asking for her help, versus being told she would be watched like a child, was likely to produce a much better outcome, no matter how much Cara wanted to coddle her and prevent her from doing anything dangerous until she was certain she would be okay. People learned from mistakes. Energy was dangerous, and Ai's experiences today would give her more respect for their world, which wasn't a bad thing.

Cara finished her food, while Ai pushed her food around her plate, her eyes downcast. She worried at her bottom lip with her teeth.

"Eat your food, not yourself," Cara said. "It's tastier."

Startled, Ai stopped. "Uh. Cara?"

"Yes? What's up?" Patience, Cara reminded herself. Patience. Cara wanted nothing more than a good night's sleep, but there was definitely something worrying Ai.

"What makes a Rogue?"

Cara frowned and pushed her hair back from her face. She hadn't expected that. "We don't know. It's something that we continue to research. It happens when someone's energy is twisted and wrong."

"I know that." Ai put her fork down impatiently and sat up in her chair. "But why does that happen? And what does it really mean, that their energy is twisted?"

"It's a shorthand way of saying their energy is being used in a negative way, rather than for their Chakra's purposes." Cara thought for a moment, trying to put it simply. "Take the energy you and I have, Anahata. What does the Chakra stand for?"

"Healing and love," Ai replied promptly.

"Yes. As well as balance, relationships, compassion, and empathy. And it's also the Chakra of air. So we can use the energy positively for those things, as well as using magics that involve drawing on the weather, or changing the composition of the air into different gases, or even moving objects or ourselves with air if we're strong."

"Those are the good things, right? What do Rogues do that makes them a Rogue?" Ai persisted.

"Some of the most obvious ways are using their energy to hurt others. For example, using Anahata to make someone sick, instead of healing them."

Ai's eyes widened. "Like what happened to Tierra on the island? Can you do that?"

"Probably. I've never tried," Cara said. There were the strongest provisions against that kind of energetic activity at the Guild. For good reason. "Using our power in a way that causes injury to people, property, or the environment would likely lead to being considered a Rogue. When discovered, they would be judged by senior members of their Guild, and sent to a Rehab Center."

"So it's nothing to do with the energetic themselves? Just their actions? Rogue is an energetics' fancy name for a criminal?" There was something off with Ai, and Cara wasn't sure what. Was there a specific reason she was asking these questions, or was it regular curiosity about the new world she was part of?

"Hmm. Not exactly. Behaviors are one side of the coin. But twisting energy can also be about their powers. The emotions associated with a Chakra can also turn to their darker side. Compassion and love can twist to hate. Forgiveness can turn to hurt and bitterness."

"Can it be seen from the outside?"

"Sometimes. Not always. There are times when energies might twist very slightly, but the energetic can readjust themselves, and their behavior never shows external signs."

Ai stood abruptly and took their dishes to the kitchen. Cara frowned after her. The teen was definitely behaving strangely.

Ai returned, but didn't sit back at the table. She stood, with her arms folded, as if ready to receive bad news. "How does it happen?"

"That, we don't really know," Cara admitted. "We can diagnose it. But we don't know what causes one person to twist and another not. We teach our people to avoid the behaviors that we've seen lead to it in the past. Our training at our Major and Minor Guilds is designed to help us with this. And it's why as part of formal training Adherents in a Chakra are paired with a Maven, who can keep an eye on their developing powers."

"Is it always the person's fault if they become a Rogue?" Ai said. Her teeth were back worrying her bottom lip. "Like Kayla. Is she a Rogue? She seems pretty messed up."

"Kayla is a tough case. She went through a bad time, and people did bad things to her. Her energy hasn't twisted, but she's at risk. She's here to get better." Though they still hadn't made the progress Cara had hoped for. They had tried several treatment options, and every time Cara thought they'd stabilized her, there would be an incident, though luckily none as intense as the situation where she'd leeched on Jason.

"I'd like to talk to her. I really think it would help me get to know her."

Cara's brow wrinkled. This was the opportunity that Adam had wanted her to look out for. Cara had plenty of misgivings, however. "Why?"

"I meant get to know Rogues better. And the dangers." Ai's words tumbled out.

"Rehab is no joke."

Ai looked down, and Cara relented.

"It is dangerous. But maybe you can talk to her and help us out."

Ai's head snapped up, her eyes narrowed. "How?"

"Kayla was exposed to Elrian, but she won't discuss him. If you talk to her, you might get her to open up."

"I could do that," Ai said, vibrating with enthusiasm.

"Only for short periods, and I'll be watching from outside. We'll debrief afterward, you and I, and discuss topics for the next session," Cara said. "You need to understand she's not stable. You can't let her touch you, for example."

"I know, I know. Archer told me some stories of Rogues. But Kayla isn't like them. She's young, like me. You said yourself that what happened wasn't her fault. She was a victim. I can help her."

"What does Archer know?" Cara said, stung. "He runs a business. He's not a healer."

"He employs some energetics who have been in rehab centers. Ex-Rogues, I guess. He said I could talk to them at some point."

Heat washed through Cara. How dare Archer offer that to Ai without checking with Cara. He had no right. She was an innocent in their world, a girl whose experience on the human streets had positioned her to think she was more worldly wise than she was. Encouraging her in her strange obsession with Rogues was not his place.

"No. Just no," Cara said, trying to keep her voice level. "Archer Hampton is here to get better, and then he will leave, and we won't have any further connection with him."

She hoped.

"Actually, he said he could give me a part-time job if I was interested, or even an internship once I know more about which of my energies I want to focus on."

Exhausted, Cara's temper blew. "Well, that's not going to happen. Even if he did follow up on that offer—which he won't, we're just distractions while he's bored—Cuinn, Tierra, Fintan and our friends can give you the background in energies you need before you study at a Guild. You don't need him, and neither do you have time for his job offers."

Ai folded her arms and pressed her lips together, setting her jaw. Cara ignored her and continued.

"And I don't want you visiting him anymore. He's a bad influence. You have your studies, and your administrative job. You have plenty to keep you busy."

"Thanks for dinner. I'm tired. I'm going to bed." Ai turned on her heel and walked down the hall to the guest bedroom, where she shut the door quietly.

Cara put her head on the table and groaned.

She hadn't handled that well. So much for all her training. Ai had come to the energetics with trust issues, having lived most of her life in foster homes and on the streets. She had a past none of them had yet delved into, giving the girl the time and space to share at her own pace. Her experience with Elrian had been a brutal introduction to the dark side of their race, and it made sense that she'd be interested in Kayla because of these experiences. Cara was grateful to Tierra for spotting the connection.

Cara needed to get some sleep. Exhaustion had eroded her control over her emotions. The last thing she wanted was to push Ai towards Archer by making him seem like forbidden fruit. Cara had messed up on some basic teen psychology there. She'd need to rescind her order in the morning, while trying to keep the girl as busy as possible so she had little time to spend with the man.

Archer was charismatic, even sexy. She accepted that. Source, dating a man like that must be a nightmare. He drew people to him, taking advantage of his geeky facade to seem harmless, but then used his damnable charm and attractiveness to get his own way without thinking about others' needs.

She needed to help get him well and out of here asap.

Archer was feeling worlds better, having gritted his teeth through another sponge bath, and dressed himself in clean clothes. He'd even moved from the bed to the couch, and was watching the video files from the data stick that the girl Ai had brought him. The guy on the screen was playing Sonic Caverns, which, after watching for a bit, Archer was amused to find was based on Crystal Caves, an obscure cult classic—a game he knew well, as he'd been part of the small design team who'd produced it many years before.

Despite her being the one to persuade him to agree to it, Cara had postponed the ritual till the next day, citing an emergency elsewhere in the center. She'd cautioned him to meditate in the meantime, and he'd tried, he really had. But he hated it and had turned to whatever distractions he could find.

A knock at the door, and Ai darted into the room. She nodded a greeting to him, then glanced at the screen he was watching. Her face lit up when she realized it was the stuff she had brought him. It didn't last, but he felt pleased to see a more positive expression on her face. She'd seemed so serious the few times he'd met her.

"Grab a seat." He gestured to the chair across from him. "Thanks for this. I'm enjoying it."

"Yeah? I love this girl and her take on the games. I play this one all the time. Do you know it?"

"I don't know this one, but I know the original," Archer said. He scooped up the remote and paused.

"There's an original? What is it?"

"It was called Crystal Caves, and it was pretty popular twenty years ago. I guess before you were born."

"Huh," she said. "I've never played games that weren't on a phone. I didn't have much access to tech…before." She waved a hand vaguely. Phoebe had got a bit of the girl's backstory from Adam and had passed it on, and he knew Ai's life previous to meeting Tierra and Fintan hadn't been a bed of roses.

"There are some key differences between the two games," he said. He left the statement hanging, and it wasn't long before she cracked and asked him what they were and why he thought they'd changed the design. They had an in-depth conversation about the game design decisions the Sonic Caverns people had made, both good and bad. Archer thought the Game User Interface—GUI— was better, along with the graphics, but that the game itself was a dumbed down version of their original.

"That's so cool," Ai said. "I'd love to play the original. I wonder if you can play it on a phone, and how much it is."

"I have access to a version of the original you can play on your cell if you're interested. I was the lead coder."

Ai's eyes grew wide. "Seriously? That would be way cool."

Archer wondered idly if the teen had any other words than cool for good, and not cool for bad. "No problem. If I had a device, I'd do it now, but it'll have to wait till Cara gives me permission."

"Yeah. I heard she said you couldn't use any tech."

Ai hesitated, as if dying to say something else. He quirked an eyebrow at her, encouraging her to go on.

"Did you do something? You're sick, right, recovering from Elrian's attack. You didn't do anything that would mean you…" a long pause "…should be on the other side of the Center?"

He gave a quick laugh. "No, nothing like that. Cara just doesn't have the same relationship with tech as me, and has the idea in her head it will set my recovery back."

Ai nodded, though she didn't look convinced. Probably someone from her generation would find it hard to imagine. She was as welded to her phone as he was to his. Cara, though, was an energetic who wasn't tech-centric in her Chakras, and had been born a lot earlier than Archer, despite her appearance.

"She's pretty rule-following," Ai said, uncertainly. "I guess she knows what's best."

Well, he wasn't going to touch that.

"My family didn't think video games were a good use of my time when I was growing up," he said. "They didn't have the same instincts with tech as me. They were all much older, and it was hard for them to connect with how quickly computers appeared and became important in the world."

"How did you persuade them differently?" Ai asked.

"Vishudha Chakra has an affinity with languages, one reason out archetype is called Communicator—and for me, part of that turned out to be coding languages. I showed my family how computers could help me learn and weren't the waste of time they thought. And those skills helped me to build Disp@tch. That, they understood."

At the mention of Disp@tch, Ai shifted in her seat, as though remembering who she was with. Archer was used to being treated like a celebrity—by humans at least, as energetics tended to be less susceptible to fame. It was power that made them take notice.

Archer had that, too, but he was young enough in energetic terms not to be deferred to by many.

"I should go. You need to rest," Ai said. She twisted her hands together in her lap. "If you want any more recordings, let me know."

Hastily, Archer held up a hand. "No need to leave. I'm resting now. I'm resting really hard. Look."

He gestured up and down his body, which was cocooned on the sofa, a pillow at his back. He was enjoying this interaction, and he didn't want her to leave. He understood what it was like to love tech and not have anyone to talk to about it.

And if she left, he'd have to go back to pretending to meditate.

"How are your lessons progressing with Cara?" he said.

"Alright." Ai shrugged. "She's pretty busy, but she finds time for me."

"The Center seems to keep her occupied," Archer agreed. "Does she have much of a personal life?"

He was just making conversation, he told himself. Keeping the girl here to keep him amused.

Ai tilted her head and frowned. "How do you mean?"

"Friends, family, relationships outside the Center, that kind of thing. Hobbies."

"Oh. I mean Adam, Tierra, Fintan, those guys are her friends. And the people who work here she's pretty friendly with. They think she walks on water."

"She seems to work hard. And what she does is important work," Archer said.

"I guess," Ai said, though she didn't appear convinced.

"Hobbies? No boyfriend?"

Ai snorted. "She doesn't have time for either of those. Though she has a stash of gossip magazines she doesn't think any of us know about. Other than that, she reads medical journals, energetic research papers on Anahata and other Chakras, that kind of stuff. And old stuff, ancient history."

"Gossip magazines?" Archer raised an eyebrow. What a delicious piece of information, and how incongruous with the serious and professional persona she presented day-to-day. And no lover. Which wasn't relevant to him personally, but it was always good to understand the people you were dealing with, especially when they had any kind of power over you.

He and Ai chatted more. She was cautious around him, physically keeping a distance, but she seemed to have lost the awe she'd come into the room with. He wondered how many positive experiences with adult males she'd had in her life.

She talked more about one of the energetics staying in the Rehab Center, a young woman called Kayla, who'd also been leeched on by Elrian. Ai seemed fascinated with the girl.

"Be careful," Archer said. "Remember what I told you about Rogues. They're unpredictable and there's a lot of variety within those who are named that. Some are truly evil, some just took a destructive path and can be rehabilitated."

"Can't everyone be rehabilitated?" Ai asked.

"Maybe," Archer said. He wasn't convinced. Some energetics, for whatever reason, were born with twisted energy, and got worse over time. He had no doubt Healers like Cara did good work, but some people were just broken. Though he employed several energetics who'd been through the Rehab Centers and were now fine in various roles in Disp@tch.

"Anyway, the Healers' work on sick or injured patients like me is important too. Clearly." He grinned and waved a hand at himself. "There's plenty of stuff to learn. It might be more interesting than you think."

She looked doubtful, and it struck him that Kayla was a living reminder of what could have happened to him. He'd been attacked and leeched from, and had gotten away. Kayla hadn't. A slight shiver went through him, and he slipped his hands in his pockets. Perhaps he should show more gratitude for his recovery, and moan less about being here. Some alternatives weren't fun to think about.

He was resting, though. Following instructions, despite his feelings on the matter.

He realized with a start that Ai was looking at him expectantly, and he tried to replay the conversation in his mind to see what she'd asked.

Nope, no idea.

"Sorry Ai, what was that?"

"Do you want to borrow my tablet for a bit? It has some games on. You already have access to cards and board games, they aren't banned, so that doesn't seem like something that would be a problem if I lent it to you for that."

Archer felt a giant weight fall from his shoulders. "Yes, that would be amazing."

He tried not to sound too eager. Relief was within his grasp.

"I'll turn the Wi-Fi off and you don't know the password anyway, so you can't use the network." Ai sounded like she was trying to convince herself.

He didn't want to spook her by saying anything, so he nodded. As if that would be an impediment to him getting online. He'd been cracking Wi-Fi networks for decades. Rooting the locked up commercial tablet so he could make it into a device from which he could pilot Disp@tch's platform would be a bit more difficult, but it would keep him occupied.

Ai disappeared and came back a while later with the tablet.

"Don't let Cara know," she said. "I don't want to get in more trouble. But cutting off your tech seems pretty heartless. She has no clue what it's like not to have access to it. She can be so strict."

Archer almost smiled at Ai's dismissal of Cara as old-fashioned. She wasn't wrong. But he'd seen Cara use very up-to-date human tech in her healing, so he didn't think it was that. Though it was true she wasn't as fused with her devices as most people in the 21st century.

She left the tablet with him, and joy bubbled up inside him with access to it. Cracking the Wi-Fi code and password took minutes, as they were using the unoriginal HealerAnahata4—Anahata being the fourth chakra.

He wouldn't think about what Phoebe might say if she found out, because she wouldn't find out. Tech was his lifeblood. It wasn't something that made him ill. And he'd do Cara's damn ritual—if she ever had time, that is. It wasn't his fault she'd postponed it, he thought righteously. He'd been ready.

He organized his space on the couch so he could hide the tablet under the cushions if anyone came in, and spent some time looking through what apps were loaded onto the device. In theory, the tablet was a walled garden; a closed platform where all applications had been pre-approved by the mobile device's service provider. However, there was always a weakness somewhere.

His browsing hit gold a while later. A social cooking app he'd kicked off his own platform for security loopholes was still available. The app had been so poorly programmed that rather than going through the proper APIs, it exposed some system level functions in order to read the user data.

The app's team had been lazy, and they'd only run the source code through an obfuscator which made the code confusing enough most wouldn't be able to make head nor tail of it.

Archer wasn't most people.

He began reading through the output, which most would consider gibberish. He drew on the tiniest surge of Vishudha energy, which came to him more easily than it had a few days ago. It enhanced his language abilities and made sifting through the supposedly meaningless characters clearer.

After an hour, his head ached. After two, his eyes were dry. He got up, gave himself a few moments to stretch his arms and hands—being careful of his abdomen—and had a glass of water. Then he got back to work.

He was used to marathon work sessions. Any coder worth his or her salt had completed many overnighters, running on pizza and coffee, to hit a deadline. Admittedly, he wasn't in the best shape, but his desperation and deep need to connect to the wider world through the internet was fierce.

Another hour, and he was in a sort of trance state. The characters streamed past his eyes like sand, while he looked for the information he needed, sifting through the information it provided him.

The sound of the door opening shocked him out of flow state with a jerk, and he stuffed the tablet into its hiding place while ensuring his body covered the movement.

He looked up to see who it was, heart jackhammering in his chest.

Cara.

He tried to avoid any micro-behaviors that would show guilt. She was trained to read people's feelings, and he'd prefer not to get Ai into trouble. He didn't so much worry about what Cara might do to him, but he'd also rather keep the device, especially as he was confident he could crack it, given time.

"Hi," he said, aiming for casual. Possibly too casual, given their usual antagonistic vibe, as her eyes narrowed in response.

"I'd like us to do the meditation ritual," Cara said. "Are you okay with doing it now?"

"Sure," he said. "I'm pretty sure I can fit you into my busy schedule."

Discomfort rolled over his back as he wondered if she could feel him trying to replicate the playful nonchalance he'd been interacting with her from before. He gestured at the television on the wall, trying to ensure he didn't glance to where the tablet was sitting under the cushions. "I can catch up with my new Korean friends in 'Spring in My Seoul' later today."

Her brow wrinkled for a second or two, and then she shook her head. "Alright. Have you done some meditation sessions since we talked?"

"A bit," he said.

A long stare from her followed, where he had to remind himself she didn't have Ajna as one of her Chakras, and thus couldn't read his increasingly guilty mind.

"We have a room here that we use for more complex healing rituals, but I think we're okay to do this in your room, unless you feel otherwise?"

He nodded. The more painless this was, the better. Fuss-free.

She talked him through preparing the space, which was simple as energetic rituals went. A protective circle, drawn in light-blue chalk, the color of Anahata's healing energy. In the circle there was a candle for focus, placed between a flat cushion for her, and a floor chair for him. The chair was flat with the floor, but had a back so he didn't have to rely on his abdominal muscles to sit.

"You need to bring your stress levels under control. We'll do this ritual together a couple of times to replenish your energy, and then your meditation practice twice a day should be enough," Cara said.

She was so serious. It made him want to poke at her, to make her laugh. She had a beautiful smile, but she rarely directed it at him. His eyebrows furrowed as he tried to imagine her reading the gossip mags Ai had claimed were her not-so-hidden pleasure.

She sat, folding her legs neatly underneath her. Archer followed, and winced as his sore stomach muscles contracted as he sat, and his knees groaned. This position had been very familiar to him when training, but spending a lot of time with humans meant he didn't practice some of the ways of the energetics as much as he used to.

They settled themselves on the floor, cross-legged, the candle between them.

Cara had already closed the blinds to more easily focus on the flickering light, and it brought out the warmth in her honey-blonde hair, and the amber sparkled in her eyes.

"Put one hand on your Anahata Chakra, and one on mine."

He reached out and put his right hand on her heart, and she covered it with her left. They did the same in reverse over his heart. He could feel the throb of her heart under his hand, and her pulse in the connection between their hands. Though touch was a common part of healing in their world, it was a stark change from their previous interactions. He had the fleeting thought he was glad he'd brushed his teeth, and then scowled at himself. She didn't care if his breath was fresh.

"Anahata is the Chakra of healing and balance."

"Okay," he said. He hoped the ritual would be quick. He didn't have time for bells and whistles.

"Balance within the aspects of ourselves: body, mind, and that which we call spirit. Balance within our six Chakras, and the seventh, Sahasara, the Chakra of the divine." Cara made strong eye contact as she talked, and Archer thought about how lovely her voice was to listen to. "Balance within our body, our health. Balance in terms of loving ourselves and loving others."

Something pinched inside Archer at those last words. He frowned for a moment, and she paused. Okay, so he still had some family issues, clearly, if those words caused that kind of spike in his feelings. Now that, she might sense.

Cara raised an eyebrow.

"Go on," Archer said. "I'm all good."

The last thing he wanted to do was go into a deep and personal discussion of how he'd felt alone as a kid and essentially created a billion dollar company as a way of showing his parents he was worthy of their love.

"Sure?" Cara said.

"Yes," Archer said. So long as there wasn't a quiz later.

"I want you to focus on the word balance," Cara said. "As you do, concentrate on the heart Chakra."

Archer frowned. "It's not one of my Chakras. I can't draw energy to it."

"Then it's lucky I didn't ask you to do that, isn't it?" Cara said, with a twinkle in her eye. "I'm going to be the one pulling Anahata energy, and feeding it into your system as if I was healing you. Then blend it with your own energy and sort of, hmm, smooth it through your system."

His head tilted as he tried to understand her.

"Just because it's not your dominant or auxiliary Chakra, it doesn't mean you can't nourish yourself. All Chakras, not only the ones that are active within us, require a minimum level of energy, or we get sick. The same with humans, who have no active Chakras," Cara continued.

He nodded. He thought he followed her logic. He had given little thought to the powers of a Healer, and how they worked, not since he went through the energetic basic education and training all his race did as children and youths.

"You're simply taking a more active part in the healing than you usually would. And this way, you may get a better feel for your own levels, and monitor yourself better in the future, so you can ensure you don't deplete yourself to the levels you are now." She still had a warm hand on his heart. It was small under his, and felt somehow precious. He resisted an unexpected urge to squeeze it.

"So I think of the concept of balance, I open to the healing energy you send into me, and try to level it out across my non-active Chakras," he said. "Is that a reasonable summary?"

"Yes."

"Then, by all means, let's try it."

She closed her eyes, and he did the same.

He brought the word 'balance' into his mind, anchored it, and let other thoughts drift away.

His mind was a stream, balance was a rock in that stream, and everything else was a leaf, floating past.

His hand over her heart tingled, and his Anahata Chakra seemed to suffuse with heat under her palm. They made a circuit where she fed her energy into him and he could feel it spreading out into his body. She drew the energy through him and out again, over and over. That way, he didn't take energy from her, but while her energy moved through his system, it healed like a gentle balm, nudging his body into rebalancing itself.

He concentrated on shaping and molding the energy inside himself, and sending it through the channel along which each of his Chakras was a node, all the time trying to keep 'balance' front of mind.

It was a sort of mental juggling, and was one reason energetics had a meditation practice. He grimaced. He had a short attention span, and it was possible that he'd been a little arrogant in not practicing for a while. The affinities around which he'd built his business empire came, if not easily to him, then with less effort than most. He spent little time practicing non-essential skills. His time was all accounted for.

He breathed in and out, using his breath to help him spread the energy out.

"Focus on your non-active Chakras, one at a time, starting at the bottom with Muladhara," Cara murmured. "Can you feel the Chakra, and see if you can sense the level of that energy?"

He took his attention down to the base of his coccyx, where Muladhara Chakra was situated. He could almost find it, but it was slippery, and hard to keep his attention on it long enough to explore it, like trying to hold water in his hands.

After some time, he could focus on what looked to his energetic gaze like a faint red glow.

"I see it, I think," he said. "It's weak."

"Feed some of my Anahata through it, and as you do, let your energies wash through it and enrich it," Cara said. "Remember, balance. Tell your body you will care for it better in the future. You will nourish it and sustain it. You won't let it get into this depleted state again. Muladhara is your foundation. The element of earth keeps you stable."

Archer's nose itched, and he longed to scratch it. He tried to focus on Cara's words, but his attention kept wandering. Source, meditation was hard.

He repeated the messages she'd told him to his body, but he was glad no one could see him.

After a few minutes, with his concentration drifting back and forth from his indistinct Muladhara, to his nose, to the warmth of Cara's hand, to well, anything else really, he realized with a jolt that his Muladhara was a little less faint. The red was purer, and it hummed with a low Lammmmmm sound.

"Good," Cara said, and Archer felt a disproportionate sense of pride. He shook himself. "Move up to Svadisthana, and do the same."

Archer moved his focus up to the next Chakra, connected to the element of water, a few fingers above Muladhara. They repeated the exercise, the orange Chakra becoming slowly more perceptible as he repeated the words Cara fed to him, about creativity, emotions, and pleasure. He tried not to fixate too much on the last as he forced himself to keep his eyes shut.

His Manipura, his auxiliary Chakra, already shone with a yellow light. His willpower had always been an asset, although he could see it wasn't at full strength. Had he been neglecting it?

"Give Manipura your focus and attention, and thank it for its support," Cara said.

He wrinkled his nose, glad she couldn't see. He concentrated on the Chakra, and reluctantly thanked it, feeling stupid. The Chakras weren't sentient, and he wasn't sure how this was helping.

There was a quick burst of bright yellow, and sparks filled his vision. There was a hard stab of something, not pain exactly, but sensation, as if something had flown apart inside him, then the pieces rebuilt themselves into a whole, but in a different way. It happened in a second, and his eyes snapped open and he reared back, breaking physical contact with Cara.

"What the hell?" he said, panting slightly.

Cara's eyes were wide, and she still had a hand over her heart, the other stretched out as if entreating him. She lowered both hands to her sides slowly, her face the picture of confusion.

"You felt it?" she asked, swallowing.

"My Manipura going crazy? Yeah. What did you do?"

She sucked in a deep breath. "Nothing unusual. Your Manipura must be unstable."

She got to her feet and stood looking down at him, hands on her hips. "You need to spend more time meditating. We'll give it a day, then continue with the ritual tomorrow. Your lower Chakras both seemed to respond well and improve. Do some of your Guild grounding exercises for Manipura, and rest."

"Can I go for a run?" he asked, knowing the answer but needing to ask anyway.

She rubbed her brow and suppressed—barely—a sigh. "Don't be idiotic. You could barely sit on the floor without pain in your abdominal musculature. How do you think running would affect that?"

He squirmed. She'd noticed that, then.

"Stay here. And for Source's sake, don't do anything stressful." She gave a final, pointed look at his gut, and then marched out of the room.

Archer waited a few minutes before he rose gingerly, and went over to the door, opening it and surveying the long empty corridor in either direction. Everything looked quiet.

He sat back on the sofa and slid his hand behind the cushions until his fingers found the cool, familiar surface of the tablet. He sighed in relief, and began to read.

Elrian played with the ring on his finger, rubbing the milky stone. One of his most precious possessions, the ring stored energy he had leeched for emergencies. So far, he'd stopped himself drawing on it, reasoning that there might come a life or death moment when he required it. But it called to him, a siren offering release.

Elrian wasn't feeling strong. Cassidy kept bringing him nourishing foods and asking how he was, if there was anything she could do. He'd snapped at her this morning.

He needed time alone.

He'd sent her on a spurious errand to get him some supplies for a casting, and she'd seemed pleased.

Was she pleased to help him, or pleased to get away?

No matter.

The Hermit had had a convoluted brain. He'd written notes in many languages, some of them extinct or unheard of in the modern human world. Elrian only had some of his notes, those that he and Imogen had stolen from the Hermit's home in the City of the Dead in Cairo when they'd killed him.

It was strange how he found it easier to follow the Hermit's logic now. Elrian was up to the task, though time was an issue. There had been a time when Elrian was a straight-line thinker. A man of black and white. These days, he had less trouble following the dots that a man like Damir had left, and it seemed to get easier each time he returned to study his notes.

The section he was working on was in a strange mix of both East and West Aramaic, which was making it slow going. He'd been drawn to the section because he'd spotted keywords around disabling Chakras.

What he'd found had been a series of experiments Damir had done on himself and several of his willing Adherents over hundreds of years. The man was a good example of an energetic who worked in gray areas—considered in good standing with the Guild, despite having broken away and doing unusual experiments in unorthodox ways.

He massaged his temples. The work was demanding and intense, and his body was struggling. The food and drink Cassidy brought him wasn't enough to satiate him.

He touched the ring again. He didn't have another energy donor at the moment, as he had agreed with Imogen he needed to lie low, so there was no possibility of refueling on the horizon. Every sip he took was gone for good.

A tremor went through him.

If he deciphered the Hermit's notes, he might find the answer to stopping Cuinn and his companions, and clear the way to access unlimited energy. Then the ring would be redundant.

Plus, Imogen was pressuring him for results. He loved her devotedly, passionately, but her words could flay him like a sharp knife. They hadn't found the right location to do their final spell, and he'd hoped the notes he was reading might point him in the right direction. Imogen had also reminded him that now three couples had joined, they would need to ensure two couples did not make their romantic connection to fulfill their side of the prophecy.

He didn't need reminding.

They also needed to make more remnant stones. So far, Imogen had made most of them. Elrian had come so close with Nixie, but he had misjudged the power of the storm that had chased him off.

Remnant stones were dangerous to create, and required the death of an energetic. Not only an energetic, but the right dominant chakra match. The ideal would be to create them from the deaths of those named in the prophecy, but any chakra match would do.

He'd give a lot for access to energy. His access to the ether was congested, and even when he visited it in his dreamscape, he couldn't bring any energy back. While he was there, he felt good, powerful, bathed in energy, but it didn't actualize in the material world when he returned.

The stone's smooth surface felt warm, like a lover's skin. It would be the work of a moment to draw on it, and he'd be stronger.

But, no.

He went back to his papers.

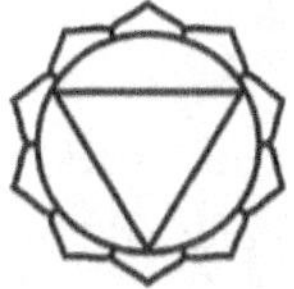

The next day Cara ran from one patient to another, trying to fit in her admin between crises. Something was up, and she didn't know what. Two additional Rogues had been admitted this past week alone, in addition to the already larger-than-usual population of Rogues they were holding.

In addition, patients weren't recovering as quickly as usual, their energies disrupted.

The incident with Archer had thrown her off her stride. She'd told him it was nothing unusual, but she'd lied. Something in her Manipura had reacted to his, and engaged with it in a curious way. It was as though her Manipura had reached out to his, even though it had been Anahata energy she had been using. Their energies had mingled somehow, before retreating into their own Chakras. It was on a long list of things she needed to check into. A list that seemed to keep getting bigger, no matter how quickly she completed the tasks on it.

She wanted to pop in on another of the long-term patients, Sophea, an Ajna energetic who'd become lost in the dreamscape and never returned to her body, and had been in a coma ever since. A rare situation, and a tragic one.

Despite her coma, the woman often reacted psychically to any strange happenings in the Center by restlessness or talking, despite being unconscious. She had even shared the occasional prophecy, though these were usually only obvious in retrospect.

Today, the woman seemed peaceful, and a quick scan of her Chakras didn't indicate any issues or unwanted psychic visitors, but Cara would get one of the Healers with Ajna as their auxiliary to check on her, just in case. Cara felt a particular responsibility for Sophea, as she had been Cuinn's Adherent when her mind had vanished into the ether, and Cuinn asked about her regularly, despite all they had going on.

Cara trudged back down the corridors to her office. The Center had been built in the late nineteenth century, using Châteauesque as the architectural style that was in vogue with many of the wealthy industrialists of the so-called 'Gilded Age' and could therefore be considered a private retreat for the very wealthy who might have 'nervous conditions'. The marble floors which she imagined had been hugely expensive at the time it had been built, had lasted, and the now-aged wood panelling brought a touch of the earth element inside. She loved the tall windows that let in air and light throughout the building.

As she walked up the shallow stone steps of her office turret, she considered how she was going to manage the extra number of Rogues and patients in the Center with her already limited resources. Energetics weren't a large race. There were only so many Healers, and part of Anahata Guild's role was to move them around to make the best use of them. But it appeared everyone wanted more Healers right now.

She passed by Osana's desk. "Any messages?"

"Maya's assistant called to check that you got her email about her special project," Osana said. "Do you have what you need for it? Can I help?"

Cara bit back a groan. "Yes, I do, and unfortunately, no, you can't. This one's with me."

Osana pursed her lips, and flicked her long, bronze curls over a shoulder. "You're telling that poor boy off for overwork, but what kind of example are you setting? You need to look after yourself, dear."

"That 'poor boy' is a billionaire, and arrived here in a private chopper. I don't think he needs your sympathy," Cara ground out, as she looked at the staff roster on the wall for the next week and considered where they might need extra cover. She tipped her head to one side. If Kayla was over her hallucinations, which Cara suspected she might be, then once she'd been checked over by an Anahata-Ajna Healer she'd require less close attention. That might free some resources up.

She was still studying the roster when Prudence flew in, glossy bob swinging around her petite face and gentle features. "Cara, can you help me? I still have one more patient to check on, and I have a date tonight, and my shift already ran over because of the new admissions today. I already canceled on her last week when Archer came in and we had the all-nighter. Can you check on them for me? I tried every other Healer. I brought her notes."

She turned mournful kitten eyes on Cara, who laughed despite herself. "Okay. Give me the notes and anything I need to know, and the timing that the check-in needs to happen and you can go. I'll cover you."

Prudence sagged in relief and grabbed a pen and a Post-it from Osana's desk and began scribbling.

Cara avoided Osana's raised eyebrow and slipped into her office before her assistant could admonish her further. Opening her email, she saw a reminder email from Maya—had the woman really needed to email *and* call?—as well as some documents from Cuinn that Cara had promised to look through for any references to the prophecy.

She sagged in her chair. She had so much to do. Taking a deep breath, she picked up the phone and called Jeb. They exchanged greetings, and she got to the point.

"I've talked to seven of the other Centers in North and South America. I wanted to see if our intuition that the Rogue population has experienced unusual levels of growth is true or not."

"Thank you, Cara, that helps a lot," Jeb said. "Things at the Guild are chaotic. What have you discovered?"

"They've all seen increases in their usual numbers in recent months, albeit small ones," Cara said grimly.

There was a brief silence. "Did anyone have any ideas about why?"

"No. And no-one realized others were experiencing similar increase. They're so small, no-one saw a pattern till now. I need to call more Centers, to find out how consistent the issue is, and if it's on other continents as well, but I wanted to update you." Cara picked up two stress balls and twirled them slowly in her hand, ensuring they didn't clink together.

"We need to understand if it's linked to the prophecy, or if it's a coincidence," Jeb said. "Or if we have an unrelated issue."

Cara was selfishly glad that she didn't work in the Guild. They were dealing with enough right now, and if this was a new concern, then Jeb's workload had just increased yet again.

"I'll gather more data," she said. She'd help in the ways she could, and try not to feel guilty about not doing more. "Speaking of which, I wanted to ask you about the database project, and how much of a priority it is. I'm drowning in work right now."

"It's important," Jeb said. Cara's heart sank. She'd been hoping for a different response.

"I understand it's about tracking people, especially troublemakers and Rogues. But why do we need the database to gather information on all our visitors? I feel uncomfortable about it," she admitted. "How does it fit with our ethos to Heal? Why are we collecting information in this way? It seems a human thing to do."

"I hope it will help us identify patterns with the Rogues in advance. Our record keeping is outdated, and this will enable us to understand our race better, so we can play the role Source wants us to, supporting the natural world with our energies."

Cara was still doubtful, but she trusted Jeb, so she'd leave it for now.

"How are you doing? How is the Center?" Jeb asked.

She told him about Kayla, Ai, and a sanitized version of Archer's recovery. Given all Jeb was dealing with, she didn't share her own bad feeling about the prophecy, and a sense that events were getting out of her control. She thrived on being in charge of her own destiny, and the idea that external events were making her lose her grip on that were…unsettling, at the least. She was trying to be pragmatic, she was, but she was living with a sense of discomfort underlying all her actions. Still, Jeb didn't need to deal with her stress and anxiety on top of his work.

But perhaps she could ask him about his own experiences.

"What was it like to meet Nixie? To have a relationship that is part of a prophecy?" She flushed and was glad she was on the phone so he couldn't see her. She was so busy, the idea of trying to fit in a relationship on top of everything else made her insides churn. Her life was organized and under control, and even though she had a lot to deal with, as long as she was in charge of her actions, she'd be fine.

But surely Source wouldn't do that to her, wouldn't give her more than she could handle.

"It was unexpected," Jeb said, wryly. "Nixie's the opposite of me in a lot of ways. And Source knows, I wasn't ready to leave the Guild."

Cara picked up a third stress ball, and added it to the two in her hand. The motion soothed her.

"How do you feel about it now?" she asked.

"She's the best thing that ever happened to me," he said.

"And what about the whole destiny thing?"

"I resisted it at first. And I believe I had a choice as to whether to have a relationship with Nixie or not—we always have free will. But Source gave me an opportunity to experience love, and live a bigger life," he said. "Mostly, I feel lucky."

The churning inside Cara increased, and her breathing accelerated.

"Thanks, Jeb. I'll let you know what else I find out. Stay in touch, and take care, both of you."

Jeb said goodbye, and she rang off. The conversation hadn't calmed her. Her foot tapped on the floor, jitters building inside her.

There was a rap at the door, and it opened to reveal Osana.

"What?" Cara said, more sharply than she meant to.

"You asked me to remind you to see Archer before the end of today, and I'm heading home soon," Osana said. "Uh, also—"

"Yes?"

Osana cocked her head and gestured at the space around Cara, her face carefully blank, though her eyes seemed a little wider than usual.

Cara frowned and looked to where Osana had pointed. She swallowed.

She had levitated her three stress balls, which spun around her head, rotating slowly.

The three balls thudded to the floor, closely followed by Cara's forehead on her desk.

"Shit."

Archer was on a roll. Ai had let him keep the tablet, and in-between nurse visits, he'd worked his way through the obfuscator's output and made the changes he needed to elevate his account to superuser, which had enabled him to completely root the device. He'd enjoyed the diversion. It stopped his skills getting rusty.

From the small sofa in his room in the Center, he accessed his usual Disp@tch account, and was able to use all the systems and programs he'd have access to on his own devices.

It was time to look at the progress of the project he'd left Phoebe with. She'd promised him it was under control, but he had his doubts.

It was worse, so much worse than he'd expected.

He stared down at the chart showing the project's current status, as compared to the project deadlines. Squeezing his eyes shut, he took a deep breath, muscles all over his body tightening as tension gripped his body. He felt the impact on his gut as a dull, faraway ache.

He opened his eyes, gripping the tablet in one hand, and navigated his way around the chart. According to which, almost nothing had been done.

Without him, Phoebe was well and truly stuffed. What the hell had his team been doing while he had been here? He hadn't expected them to be on time, but he had expected them to make *some* progress. Progress he could help with as soon as he got out of this damned place.

Heat washed through him, and his heart pounded. His body curled in on itself sharply, as if to protect him, and something gave way inside his abdomen.

His throat was tight, and he was sweating, though he wasn't sure the temperature in the room had changed. He was dizzy, and he had a sense of unreality.

Was he dreaming? Or having a nightmare? He massaged his temples, trying to ground himself.

He reached for his energies, and couldn't connect to them. He panted. The tablet dropped from numb fingers onto the bed.

Was he having a heart attack? Was this it?

Would he die here in this Center, having lived his life for other people?

12

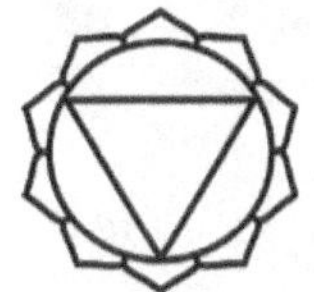

"Help," Archer croaked as Cara entered his room.

It took Cara moments of being with him to realize he was most likely having a panic attack. Ah, hell.

She'd warned him, she thought, even as she went over to him and crouched next to him.

"Archer, look at me."

His gaze darted all over the room, as if he was looking for an escape. Which would be natural, given what was happening to him.

"Do you have any pain in your arms?" she asked.

He shook his head.

"Have you been sick?"

Another shake.

"Pain in your chest?"

A nod.

"Is it a sharp pain?"

Another nod.

Okay, it was definitely looking like a panic attack. But had something specific set it off?

A wave of compassion flooded her. It was the first time she'd seen him truly vulnerable. For all the terrible injuries he'd come in with, he'd still been cracking jokes and arguing with her.

"Archer, you're having a panic attack. You're going to be okay."

His eyes were wide, pupils dilated and black, the brown of the iris almost lost.

"I want you to breathe with me. In through the nose and out through the mouth. Focus on me, and let everything else go."

He nodded, his body shaking, fists clenched at his sides.

"Breathe in and out, and as you breathe out, relax any muscle that you can."

He inhaled deeply, then as he let the breath out, one fist loosened slightly.

"I'm going to touch you. Is that okay? And then I'm going to help you with a little healing energy."

He nodded vigorously and clutched at one of her hands.

Alright, that hadn't been quite what she was expecting, but it worked.

"Keep breathing, in and out. In and out. Relax the muscles you can when you breathe out," she crooned. "Focus on the touch of our hands. Let everything else in the room, everything else in your brain, go."

She drew on her own energy, and sent tiny licks of it into him, each light touch of her magic designed to help him release the tension in his muscles. After their strange experience during the ritual, she kept her Manipura well away from him.

The feral look in his eyes dimmed, and his breathing slowly, so slowly, regulated. His body unknotted, and the tension in her own chest loosened.

She used a little of her magic to undo the catch at the window and open it. Fresh air wove through the room.

A panic attack wasn't serious in terms of health, but it indicated a bigger issue, and putting stress on his body at this moment had been exactly what she had been trying to avoid. Dammit, she was worried about the man, and was annoyed that she was worried. She was usually more objective about her patients.

The death grip he had on her hand slackened, till he was merely holding it.

She scanned his system with her energy to check his wounds. Her lips pressed together, as she found he'd jolted a couple of his internal stitches and they had torn. He would need a more thorough exam to understand if they needed to open him up again to repair them. In addition, his cortisol levels were through the roof. She would need to take a blood test to show him exactly what he had done to himself. Would hard data help convince him where her explanations hadn't?

"Can you lie on the sofa?" she asked.

His answer was to bring his legs up onto the seat, though he still wouldn't let go of her hand.

She swept a quick hand across the sofa in order to help him lie down, then froze when she touched something cold and flat.

She picked up a tablet.

"What the—" she bit the words off, recognizing that if she did what she wanted and roasted him for using a device when he'd agreed not to, it would likely make his symptoms worse, just as she'd got him to calm down.

She slid the tablet onto the floor, out of his sight. She'd deal with it later.

"You're going to be alright. You had a panic attack. It feels bad, but it's not serious in itself. I'm going to need to do some tests and scans to check on the rest of you."

She would get him onto the bed then sedate him. What the man needed right now was sleep.

And when he woke up?

It was time for a long talk with him about the implications of disobeying the Head Healer's instructions.

And he would not like it.

She went back to see Archer first thing the next morning, blood test results in hand.

She also had the tablet that she'd taken from his room the previous night. A device that she was confident she'd seen before.

Angry didn't even begin to describe how she felt. She had tried to keep her face neutral throughout the interactions she'd had that morning, but Osana had given her some funny looks, and the healer she'd spoken to at breakfast had cut their conversation short without giving a reason, so she wasn't entirely sure she'd succeeded.

She'd also avoided Ai, as she wanted to get the story from Archer first. And it was better she took her rage out on the adult male rather than the teenage girl.

She stood at his bedside, her arms folded. He'd glanced at the tablet in her hand when she'd come in and flinched. Well, good.

"You promised me you would stay away from technology," she said. "You didn't. And this is the result."

She placed the test results on his bed. "Your blood work shows your cortisol levels are well above normal range. Your non-active Chakras are also depleted, trying to fight the impact of this. When you had the panic attack yesterday, you set back your healing from your gut injuries by several days."

His shoulders slumped.

"Neither of us wants you here longer than you need to be, but you understand that I can't, in good conscience, send you home when you're this sick."

He couldn't meet her eyes. Damn right he should feel guilty.

"That's not all. Where did you get this tablet?"

"I can't tell you that," he said.

"You don't need to. I've seen it many times before. I know the scratches on it from where Ai dropped it when she was practicing with her energy in the courtyard. I know the tiny crack in the screen on the top left where she pushed it off the table by accident." Cara breathed in deep, trying to keep her emotions under control. She could feel her fire energy, something she usually kept deep inside, boiling inside her. "What I don't know is how you manipulated her into giving it to you. How could you take advantage of her like that?"

The man had the morals of a mushroom.

"I didn't ask her. She offered it to me," he said. Propped up against a pile of cushions, the covers were tucked under his arms, and he was picking at the soft gray blanket that covered the white sheets. The vulnerability in his posture clashed with the lightly muscled shoulders and wiry strength of his arms.

"You didn't need to take it. She's a kid. She has no idea of the impact of you having a device."

"Because you didn't tell me!" A voice burst from behind her. Cara held back a groan. Dealing with them individually would have been hard enough, but Ai overhearing her just now was all she needed.

"You treat me like a child," Ai continued. "It just seemed like another way of you trying to control people. You're so strict with everyone, and you set standards that are impossible to live up to. The guy was miserable."

Cara's chest and throat constricted. Was that how Ai thought of her? Cara had tried to look after her, tried to keep her safe, tried to take her responsibility to look after Ai and educate her seriously. Had she been too serious? Sheltered her too much? Surely the standards Cara set were for herself, not for those around her.

She turned and Ai stepped forward to the end of Archer's bed, stance belligerent, a mirror image of Cara's.

Archer let out what sounded like a groan. "It's alright, Ai, it was my fault. I shouldn't have taken it."

"Archer is a patient. There are rules set for patients that we all follow, for everyone's good." Cara said. "I treated you like every other adult here. I don't have to explain to every person the reasons for the various health decisions we make. They know we decide things to help people get better, not because we're tyrants."

There was a physical hurt inside Cara. She was doing her best. They had broken the rules, and somehow she was the one they had teamed up to attack.

"You can only work and learn here, and keep visiting Archer, if you follow the rules, Ai," Cara said. "Like everyone else."

"Please, Ai," Archer said. "I'd like you to visit. I've enjoyed talking to you."

Ai looked from one to the other, a flush high on her cheeks, her eyes flashing with anger and hurt and, Cara hoped, at least some guilt.

"Fine," Ai said, forcing the word out.

"Fine. Now I have work to do. Archer, I'll be back later to redo the ritual. Please rest as much as possible, and meditate as often as you feel up to it," Cara said. She wanted to get out of this room, which was full of disappointment, shame and regret. "Perhaps you can support each other by meditating together. Practice would help both of you."

She pivoted on her heel and left the room.

Elrian strode up and down the boundaries of his Haven, his safe space in the dreamscape. Cassidy, whose Haven had been linked to his for decades, since he had been her Maven and she his Adherent, stood with her arms crossed, watching him pace.

"I'm not sure why you need to find this Kayla, but I can probably help," she commented.

"How?" Elrian tried not to snap, but frustration bubbled out of him. Imogen's icy anger this morning had scared him. The energetic was already powerful beyond most due to what she'd been born with, her steely will, and, of course, her necklace. He loved her, would do anything for her, but sometimes it seemed difficult to convince her of that. He'd attempted to prove himself to her over and over. Would it ever be enough?

Elrian hadn't found Archer's location yet. The Disp@tch press release on the matter had stated only he was taking a sabbatical, and Phoebe Korr was stepping up to run the company. His sources had said Archer's location was top secret, limited only to Phoebe, and she was now surrounded by so many bodyguards that to attempt a kidnapping and extraction of information from her was a last resort.

Imogen had somehow created a sixth remnant stone, the stone he hadn't been able to create on the beach with Nixie. Elrian didn't even know who the victim had been.

He loved Imogen in a dark way that was the opposite of the way he'd loved his wife, and different again from his love for Cassidy, who he had brought up from a child.

But he needed Imogen just as much. Besides that, they needed each other to do the final ritual, whatever the steps leading up to it. Her necklace had the remnant stone that had started it all.

Their relationship was tempestuous. One moment she was sweet, kind, and full of the Anahata that was one of her energies, and the next she was mean, angry, and cutting.

She always apologized when she went too far. She loved him.

And one tremendous advantage of Imogen was that she would never ever be taken advantage of by humans the way that his wife had been. She could protect herself, and avoid the martyr's death his wife had suffered by working with their son, Cuinn, and others to help the humans during World War II. Going against his wishes, she'd traveled to Poland to work in a hospital with humans, and a bomb had fallen on the building in which she'd been working, killing her outright.

Her death had also been the death of his relationship with Cuinn. Without Cuinn's support, his wife would have listened to him and stayed out of human conflicts.

Let them wipe each other out.

Well, once he had the power of the remnant stones, he'd be able to help them with that.

Cassidy, a light, flowing dress covering her to below her knees, wrapped a scarf around her. She stood on a neat concrete path, a box hedge behind her. A Haven was designed by its owner, and Elrian liked clean lines, space, concrete and metal.

He hadn't been to Cassidy's Haven for a while. He wondered what it looked like these days.

No matter.

"You seem exhausted. And your energies are…" she hesitated, "in some disarray. Whatever you're working on, I hope Imogen or you find the answer soon. Could you tune into me as another member of your Minor Guild, with a similar energetic pattern? Would that help you reset?"

He scowled, pausing in his pacing. What did she mean by disarray? Could she tell he'd leeched on victims with different energies? Was there something he was showing externally? He'd have to wait until he was next with Imogen to check.

In the meantime, her suggestion wasn't a bad one. If he was leaking enough for Cassidy to realize, who knows what others might see.

He'd found Kayla once already in the dreamscape, but she'd got away, and he hadn't caught sight of her since. At the time, he'd indulged himself before gathering information, and that had been a mistake. The next time he found her, he'd understand where she was, and what she'd revealed to others, before taking her energy, and if necessary, killing her.

Prophecy shards he'd uncovered in the dreamscape had shown him that the girl represented a potential breach, that despite his efforts to keep her memories of her time with them scrubbed, she had retained dangerous knowledge she could pass on to their enemies.

Plus, she had gotten away. He felt a stab of hatred. Held in an out-building on his grounds, and despite being half-dead, she had escaped into the forests while he had been in Thailand chasing down Nixie.

That couldn't be left to stand. He had to show Imogen he could fix his mistakes.

He nodded brusquely. "Alright. Come here."

She stepped toward him. Within his Haven, he needed no specific ritual circle. The entire area had wards and protections such that it would be nigh impossible for an enemy to find, let alone breach. The whole Haven was his protective circle.

"Concentrate on both your energies," he said, and placed his palm on her forehead where Ajna Chakra was located, the fingers spreading onto her scalp. "Give me your energetic pattern to focus on."

Her Ajna glowed indigo, shining brightly. As the Chakra of the ether, the dreamscape, it was at its height here. His own Ajna wasn't in terrible shape whilst here. Being in the dreamscape relieved some of the gnawing emptiness caused by his inability to pull energy in the physical world. He smoothed and soothed his Ajna, coaxing it into a pattern that looked more like Cassidy's.

It was his Muladhara that was more the issue. He'd lost some of his ability to connect to his body and to have that physical presence and solidity that most earth energetics projected. Given that Muladhara and Ajna were at the top and the bottom of the energetic body, it could be a challenge for energetics with this mix to keep them in balance, but he'd let his destabilize.

Her Muladhara flared red at the base of her spine. He concentrated on it, and let her pattern fill his mind.

He put aside the flush of angry shame that he was reduced to relying on her to heal himself in this way, the energetic he'd trained as his Adherent.

He concentrated on the task.

Slowly, much too slowly, he brought both energies back up to a consistent gleam. The Ajna still surpassed the Muladhara, but the difference was less noticeable. And he felt better than he had in days. Since the last time he'd leeched, in fact.

Nauseous, he dropped his hand from her head, sick he might have leeched from Cassidy without meaning to.

"How do you feel?" he asked urgently.

She rested a hand on his shoulder. "I'm fine. And you? Did it help?"

"It did. Thank you." He sighed in relief. She seemed okay, no worse for wear.

"Do you feel well enough to seek the girl? You have her pattern, and you've been in her Haven previously, correct?" Cassidy said.

He nodded. "You can go back to the physical world. I'll take it from here."

If she went back, perhaps this time he wouldn't have to wipe her memory. He was worried she was losing time from his frequent need to excise parts of their life from her recollection. At first it had just been the time he'd meant to remove, and then she'd become more and more forgetful. He'd find her standing in the kitchen holding a glass, uncertain whether she was getting it out or putting it away. If he went on doing it too long, she would lose herself altogether.

It was another reason he needed to act fast.

She disappeared, and he drew in power from his Haven, putting protections around himself, then projected the girl Kayla's energetic pattern into the oily haze of the dreamscape outside his Haven and flung Ajna into it, the magic hitting the pattern then exploding out into a shower of spiral threads.

He would follow each one until he found the girl again.

Two days after Cara had reprimanded him so thoroughly, Archer decided he'd had enough. She had delegated his care to other Healers, and his daily litany of questions had been halted. Given their last interaction, it hadn't been a terrible idea to have had a break from each other, but he was over it.

He was healing from his injuries. He'd done the ritual again with another Healer, and had been meditating to reduce his stress levels, and he felt a great deal better.

His good behavior seemed to have been noticed, as he was checked on less, and Ai's visits weren't rationed. He'd enjoyed getting to know the girl, and had been relieved she hadn't held any ill-will regarding his actions with her tablet. She was smart and savvy, and while she had a lot to learn about their world, he could see her potential.

Now he was going to haul himself out of bed, and see the woman in control of his world. He didn't miss her, exactly, but his life had certainly been duller without their sparring matches.

He also really, really wanted his tech back. He'd had to suppress thoughts of what he had seen on the project management system in Disp@tch in order to bring his cortisol levels down, but Cara had also suggested to Phoebe that she not call him for a couple of days to help his stress management.

Whether it was a treatment or a punishment, he couldn't question her about what was going on.

If that project chart had accurately reflected their progress, he had truly screwed Phoebe. He should have been nearly finished at this point. He'd been relying on the fact that his team could get it done fast, with him at the helm doing most of the coding. In the past, he'd coded while sick, coded through the night, coded through holidays, coded without eating—he had never, ever thought he'd be in a situation where he'd be unable to complete the task.

He had dumped both his team and Phoebe in a mess.

He needed to speak to her asap to apologize at the very least, and see if there was any way possible he could help. If the project sank, and the investors went elsewhere, Phoebe would never forgive him—and he'd never forgive himself.

It was strange to leave the room where he'd been for so many days. He wasn't one hundred percent certain where Cara's office was, but he followed signs down the winding corridors to the administrative block.

Archer enjoyed the architecture of the Center. On his last visit, he'd seen how the rehabilitation half of the Châteauesque buildings had been updated to ensure that security was tight enough to hold some of the more dangerous members of their race. The healing side retained much of its older charm, however.

Reaching the administration area he discovered a veritable warren of rooms, which likely echoed hospitals all over the country. He found Cara's office by asking a harried looking administrator who barely glanced up at him before pointing down the hall to a staircase. He was glad he'd shaved and dressed. Well-practiced in projecting an aura of confidence and belonging, he was rarely questioned.

The staircase was in a polygonal turret, and he followed the stairs up to the top, with some effort, where he found an open space with an empty desk, and a door with 'Healer Cara McCarthy' inscribed on a plaque.

He didn't bother knocking. Taking a deep breath, he pulled his indignation and arguments together, ready to tell her exactly why he needed his tech back, and / or to be sent home, and threw open the door. Drawing on his sense of frustration and anger, he was ready to step the emotions up as needed.

As he did, there was a scream of frustration from the corner of the room, followed by three solid thuds into the wall.

He threw up his hands in a defensive gesture, shifting into a ready stance, and pulled on his Manipura energy, weak, but enough to call fire if needed.

Scanning the room in the next heartbeat, he realized to his shock that it had been the cool, calm and collected Cara who had let loose.

He turned to see what the projectiles had been and saw what looked like three Chinese stress balls on the floor.

Frowning, he stepped over to the wall and scrutinized it—and saw not just three dents, but many, and an interesting absence of pictures or breakables surrounding them.

Something welled up inside him as he turned back to Cara, who was looking at him, frozen in horror.

The thing in his belly grew and grew until he let out a guffaw that shook his entire body.

He laughed and laughed and laughed, real, true laughter, for the first time since he'd met Elrian in the park.

He laughed so hard he had to sit down on the chair placed opposite Cara's desk, the ridiculousness of the moment overwhelming even the discomfort of his abdomen aching from the movements.

Tears welled up in his eyes, and the laughter renewed itself every time he looked at Cara, half-risen in her seat and stuck in place, one hand covering her mouth and a deep flush across her face and chest.

Cara couldn't believe that she had nearly put a stress ball—alright, three stress balls—through one of her patients. She'd been working on the dreadful database project, trying to enter patient information into a system that, to her, seemed as buggy as hell, and she'd had it. The balls, which had over time become an extension of her hands, had flown across the room.

She wrinkled her nose. If she was truthful, she'd flung them at the wall. Hard. It was one of her few forms of stress relief, as the wall—and her assistant outside—could testify. Osana had been the one a few years ago to gently suggest they removed the framed photos from the wall, when she'd caught Cara sweeping up glass for the second time.

And the damned man was laughing at her! *Laughing!*

"You know you nearly had three ball-shaped holes through your body?" she said. She winced. She'd meant to apologize. But he was still laughing.

"You'd have healed me," he said, relaxing in her visitor chair like he owned the place, a broad smile still on that irritatingly handsome face. He wore cargo pants and yet another retro t-shirt, which meant nothing to her. "Nice office. I love the turret."

She tried not to splutter, falling back into her chair, her heart still hammering in her chest at the near miss.

He crossed his feet at the ankles, long legs stretched out. "So, what's got into you?"

She huffed. "A project I'm working on for the Guild. It's a new data entry system, and it's garbage."

He raised his eyebrows.

It was worse than garbage. The balls had gone into the wall just as she'd lost the data on a patient she had entered no less than seven times.

"Can I help?" He perked up. "I'm good with that kind of thing."

"No! No. It's a Guild matter."

He shrugged, but she could see disappointment and curiosity warring in his eyes. That was the last thing she needed.

Though she could not even begin to express how much she would have loved his help. In fact, she'd have loved to have just dumped the whole thing in his lap and walked out of the office.

The stupid system was supposed to have been audited already, but neither Maya nor Jeb was around right now to help her, though she'd called them both several times. There were also two other sites trialing it: the Singapore and the Bruges Rehab Centers. She would need to check the time zones and see if she could get hold of the Center Managers there to see if they could suggest any path that wasn't deleting the entire program from her system and sending all future emails from Jeb and Maya directly to her trash can. She gave a deep sigh.

"It's easy enough for me to help," Archer cajoled. "I'm already under a Non-Disclosure Agreement with all the Guilds because of the communications work we do for the Major and Minor Circles."

Cara frowned. She hadn't known Disp@tch did that. She was aware they did PR for energetics, and that the company was very successful in both the human and energetics worlds, but that sounded more organized—and, was a lot more responsibility—than she had been aware of. The Major Circle consisted of one leader from each of the six Major Guilds—in Anahata's case, Aiko, the Guild's leader, was also their Major Circle member. The Minor Circle was the same, but for the thirty Minor Guilds, like her own, Anahata-Manipura.

Essentially, the Circles were the energetics' government, as much as they had any.

She cocked her head. "What do you do for the Circles?"

He shrugged. "Clean up, mostly. Track and correlate reports that might relate to energetic issues. Keep ahead of and manage potential leaks about our existence. Either Phoebe or I meet with each Circle once a month by teleconference to discuss what's come up, and we have a direct line to Vishudha's leader as the point of contact at any time, day or night."

He didn't exactly say 'people a lot more important than you trust me', but he might as well have. It was essentially like meeting someone who had the personal phone number of the President of the United States, or Prime Minister of Canada. She sniffed loudly, though inside she was annoyed to find that she was impressed. And a bit taken aback. How did he fit all that in with the amount of socializing he seemed to do based on the photos in the magazines she read?

"Oh, and we provide their messaging and communications apps. Obviously. All encrypted to the highest standards." He leaned forward. "I mean, I've probably already seen whatever you're using. They often get us in to consult. It's basically like having Bill Gates to do your tech support."

She snorted audibly. "No. It's confidential. You're just bored."

"Damn straight I am!" He leaned cautiously back in his chair.

Yeah, she couldn't be dealing with this. Even if she got permission for him to help, he'd get bored after five minutes and wander off, leaving her with a worse mess.

"Was there something you wanted? I'm pretty busy, and I need to get back to work." She tried to get control of the conversation back. There was so much energy to the man. He was improving physically, she could see that.

"Yes. Can I leave yet?" he said.

"No."

"Can I get my tech back?"

"No."

He stood up and walked out without another word, her solid wooden door shutting behind him.

She slumped over and stretched out a hand to her stress balls, which floated back onto her palm.

And started to spin.

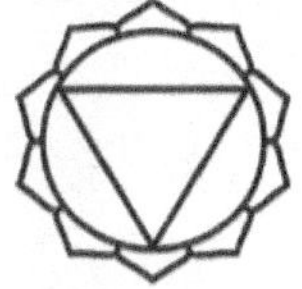

Several hours later, Cara had finished entering the current patients into the database. It had been a tough slog. The system crashed often, lost data, the interface was badly designed, and she didn't always have the information she was supposed to input at hand. What should have taken half an hour had taken much longer. She wished she could get Archer to check the system, but she would not introduce tech into his healing.

She wasn't at all certain about the entire project, and at some point, she'd need to talk to Jeb about it.

But not now.

She rubbed her hands over her face. Source, she was tired. She needed to head to bed earlier tonight, or she'd struggle to work effectively tomorrow.

Before then, however, she probably needed to visit Archer. She shrank in her chair, shoulders hunching, as she considered their last interaction. It hadn't gone great, and she should be setting a better example. She ground her teeth. Why did he get to her so much?

She was also uncomfortable at the thought she might have misjudged him. The activities he had talked about Disp@tch being involved in weren't anything she'd heard about before. While she read human gossip magazines, she avoided much involvement with the political and social world of the energetics outside of her friends. Was it possible Archer's persona in the human world differed from his persona in the energetics'? And if so, who was the real Archer?

He had offered to help. Which was kind. Though he was also bored, and knowing him she'd have found her screensaver changed to something ridiculous like Hawkeye if she'd let him near her computer.

She didn't love the fact he'd seen her lose her cool so badly. She hated to reveal that part of herself to others—one that only came out when she was really riled. She liked to project a responsible and steady image to those around her, a capable Center Manager and Healer who could handle anything.

Tools and techniques like her stress balls helped her to manage her auxiliary Chakra, her fire. She had a temper, but it took a long time to flare. She could get stressed, but it took a lot to make it happen.

There had been a lot happening for a while now.

She sighed. She should apologize and show him she was back to her cool and reliable self. Hopefully he wouldn't mention the incident to anyone else.

She walked to his room, knocked, and entered. He was on the sofa, watching a documentary on ancient antiquities. Huh. She hadn't expected that. She'd expected him to be a more typical cars-and-computer-games male.

He responded monosyllabically as she ran though the usual health-checks, his eyes fixed on the TV.

Her shoulders grew more and more tense as the silences grew longer between her questions and his answers.

Eventually, she got over her pride.

"I'm sorry about what you saw in my office. I actually love my job, things are just a lot busier than usual."

He glanced at her. "You seem pretty stressed."

"Yeah. We have a lot of guests on both sides of the Center, and I'm behind on admin and sleep."

"I think letting stress and anger out can be helpful. I don't have an issue with your Manipura. In fact you should let it out more often. It's a part of you as much as your healing powers." He sounded genuine, and she didn't know how to respond. Most people told her to chill when she got stressed.

Anyway, the idea that it might be healthy to let the stress out was exactly right for other people, but not for someone in her position.

"It's the opposite problem to mine, really," he said, dryly. "I'd love to have something to keep me busy."

She perched at the end of the sofa. "How's your pain?"

He narrowed his eyes, as if considering how honest to be. Eventually he shrugged. "A lot better, while still being present. I could do with distractions. It feels like it's been forever."

She gave him a tentative smile. "You're not the first in my care to feel that way. 'It is easier to find men who will volunteer to die than to find those who are—'"

"'—willing to endure pain with patience,'" Archer finished. "Caesar."

She gaped at him. She hadn't expected that.

"Uh. How did you…" she trailed off, realizing a bit late how rude it sounded.

His eyebrows shot up. "How do I know a Caesar quote?"

She flushed.

"I love history. I use vacation time to go wreck diving. I'll take a documentary over an action film any day, and I have an extensive collection of antiques."

"Sorry," she said. She couldn't believe she was apologizing again. It was uncomfortable to feel there was more to this man than she had thought. Usually she was better at reading people.

He shrugged. "In another life, I'd be a historical documentary maker. I make donations to museums where I can to support them, though it means I have to go to dreadful galas and dinners, and Phoebe always makes me take some woman with me to help Disp@tch's public profile."

He sighed. "My major interest is the history of our race."

"It is?" said Cara. Her mind was whirling, confused, unable to integrate this new information about Archer with her preconceptions. "In what way?"

Archer turned to her, more animated now. "I love the legends of our people, and the stories of us being greater, doing more for the planet and our race and people. The times when our magics were more."

"Aren't they just stories though?" Cara could see this might not be the most graceful response as quickly as she said it, but her brain was really not working properly at the moment.

"I think understanding our past better—which requires research and study as so much was lost—could help us regain powers we didn't even know we had."

Cara was less sure of that, but she'd already been rude enough. She wondered if she could harness this side of him and help him be less bored while she did it.

She tilted her head to the side and considered him. "Do you know a lot of stories about our past then? Legends of heroes and monsters, that kind of thing?"

He nodded. "My dominant energy means my language ability is strong, so I've been able to read a lot of our ancient texts from the different Guilds. My connections mean the Guilds will lend me books that are typically restricted."

"Do you know any that are suitable for kids?"

His eyebrows drew together, but he nodded. "Sure."

"Your health is improving, and I think you can increase your range of activities as long as they don't affect your stress levels."

He sat up straighter, but she cut his next predictable sentence off before he could begin. "No tech, and you can't leave. However, you can leave this room. Follow me."

He narrowed his eyes, but stood and did as she asked.

They walked through the corridors of the Healing Center, Cara checking in with her staff members as she went. Many of them had a smile and a kind word for Archer, pleased to see him up and about.

His charisma was clearly having an effect, and the staff seemed to have forgiven him for the impression he'd made on his first visit.

She opened a door to a light and airy room, full of bright colors and stuffed animals. She smiled at Jason, who nodded back, busy restocking the medicine cabinet in the corner of the room. There were also two children in the room, the only children on site at the moment.

One was lying in bed, and the other sat next to her.

BayBella, a dark, merry-eyed nine-year-old with black curls and skin a shade lighter than her hair, was here because some of her energies had manifested early, which had caused a kind of magical brain cancer.

Her dominant Chakra was Ajna, and unlike some of the Chakras where the powers might be more externally discernible, there had been no strong signs others could see, just a series of headaches that got worse and worse before her father, her sole surviving parent, brought the little girl to Cara.

Once they'd realized that the problem was that she was a prodigy, and her powers had manifested not only very young, but very strongly, it had been easy enough to stop things from going further, but harder to reverse the damage that the magic had already wreaked. She was easily distracted, and her energy levels were high. She had difficulty regulating her emotions. Her father visited as often as he could, but with three other children under eighteen at home in Portland, he couldn't be there all the time.

BayBella was acting out some kind of story to the quiet girl lying in the bed. Abi was six, and was here because she'd been caught in a magical accident. Her mother, a kind but scatterbrained Vishudha-Muladhara research scientist for her Minor Guild, had been working on an experiment in her workshop in their home's grounds in Sacramento, unaware that her husband and daughter had come home early.

Abi had come into the workshop as her mother had gone into the bathroom attached to the building, leaving the workshop door open.

Curious, the child had touched something—possibly several things—she shouldn't have, and chaos ensued. Her hearing had been damaged, and she'd stopped speaking.

While her hearing had come back, she hadn't yet started talking again. They were still uncertain if the problem was psychological or physiological. Although either one or both of Abi's parents traveled up from their home every weekend, during the week it tended to be just the two girls.

The two children had gotten on well from the start, and BayBella seemed to be good for little Abi.

"Hi girls, how are you both?" she asked.

BayBella nodded enthusiastically. "Good, Healer Cara!"

Abi smiled tentatively, her head remaining on the pillow. Cara came over and brushed out the little girl's blond hair, which was a tangled halo.

"What story were you telling Abi?" Cara asked BayBella.

"A story with dragons and unicorns and a teapot," BayBella said, gesturing emphatically and shaping her body into a teapot with the last word.

Cara caught Archer smothering a smile. Good.

"Girls, this is Archer. He knows many good stories. Would you like him to tell you one?"

Abi reached for BayBella's hand, and gave a tiny nod, in contrast to the other girl's infectious eagerness.

Cara gestured to Archer. "They're all yours. I'll come back in an hour. Don't overtire them, and remember all of you are healing."

She couldn't interpret the look Archer gave her, but he walked to the bed and sat in the seat opposite BayBella.

"Do you know what a pirate is?" he asked them both. "Because I have a great story about an energetic pirate with a human crew, and the Protector who captured her, many centuries ago, far, far away."

Cara smiled, and slipped out the door.

An hour later, she returned to the kids' room, her eyebrows rising at the sight of Ai, who had joined them. Jason also seemed to have been caught up, and the five of them were watching a video on Ai's phone, with a running commentary from Archer. It seemed to be about a dive where he'd recovered energetic artifacts.

She blew out a breath. The man couldn't—or wouldn't—follow instructions. Well, she supposed he couldn't do much harm on a phone, and the kids seemed to be enjoying the video and his reenactments of the fish that he'd seen on the dive. And Ai never let her cell out of her sight. She would hardly lend it to him, especially after the warning Cara had given her last time.

"Alright, time to rest everyone," she said.

There was a chorus of groans and protests from the kids, but Archer winked at them. "I'll be back, m'hearties."

Back in his room, he sat on his bed as she checked his vitals. They were steady.

She hesitated, then spoke. "Thanks for involving Ai. She hasn't seemed too interested in the Healing side of things, and anything that distracts her from her obsession with the Rehab side is useful."

"She's a good kid. I like her. She's sharp, and her views on game interface are interesting. She'll have career options in the human or energetic world when she's ready." He rolled his head and stretched out his neck, loosening his shoulders. "BayBella now, she's going to create a lot of mischief as she grows. I pity her parents. I'm exhausted after an hour. If I forgot to do one of the voices in a story, she told me off thoroughly, and then reminded me exactly what it should have sounded like, and made me repeat the section to her liking. She's a tyrant."

Cara couldn't help but smile at the thought of the tiny nine-year-old shaking a finger at Archer's tall figure. He hadn't done badly with the kids, it seemed. Though what had she expected?

Okay, she'd expected him to last five minutes and then slink back to his room.

Perhaps he wasn't such a poor role model for Ai after all, especially when compared to some of those she'd met in foster care and on the street. He had entertained three kids for an hour, despite his own health.

"You did a good job," she said. "Do you have children in your family?"

He shook his head. "No. I was the youngest in the group of energetics I lived with, by some years. They treated me like an adult for as long as I remember."

"What about your childhood?" Her childhood was far in the past, but she'd had the company of other kids. Her parents were both Healers, kind and wise, and they'd brought her up to be independent but care for others, just as they did.

Perhaps they'd given a little more energy to their patients rather than her, but she preferred to see that as them trusting her to look after herself. She'd run a little wild as a child, a creature of air and fire, and it had been as a teenager preparing to be an Adherent in Anahata Guild, when she had become grounded.

"I was included in topics the adults discussed. We lived in a remote area of northern Canada, and there weren't other energetic kids in the area. I was home schooled until fourteen, when I was accepted to Vishudha Guild, and they put me with teens a couple of years older. I kept to myself until I met Phoebe, whose interests aligned with mine."

He gazed out of the window, lost in his memories.

The beautiful and kind Phoebe. "Were you and she…were you ever together?"

He laughed. "No. We wouldn't have been a good match romantically. But in business, we do great."

"What did you do for fun as a child?" she asked. She tried to imagine the confident, charismatic man in front of her, a new woman on his arm at every gala dinner, with his own helicopter and goodness knows what else, as a gawky teen, coming into adolescence on his own in a community of adult energetics. And adult in their world could mean an age of over a hundred.

"Studied history," he replied promptly. "Like I said, I love it. I grew up looking for ways to enhance our powers, to bring our race back to the glory of the days of Atlantis."

Cara perched on the bed. "Atlantis disappeared thousands of years ago, and we don't really know how or why. There's no reason to believe we were truly great. I don't so much get the point of focusing on the past. There's enough to focus on in the present to help the world stay in balance while humans overtake more and more of nature."

"That's exactly why," he said, leaning toward her. "Our past hides secrets, I know it. Source gave us the role of guardians of its world, holding it in balance with our energies. But something's not right. We're not able to bring balance in this era. If we can understand our past, and why Atlantis fell, we could change that."

She frowned. "The reasons we're struggling to keep the balance now are human pollution, a lower birthrate of energetics than humans, and the Guilds squabbling. We don't need answers from the past to tell us that."

"I think there's more to it," he said, stubbornly. "That was what my next trip was for, diving in an area where they think there might be more energetic relics. I have a collection. We know what some of them do, some we don't."

Cara studied him as he talked. He'd grown animated, more excited than she'd seen him so far. She enjoyed seeing his fire in this, a passion she hadn't seen when they'd talked about his job.

So far, every interaction with Archer had proven her wrong about him.

She wasn't sure she liked it.

Every new facet revealed a new side of him. Sides that made him more complex, and more interesting.

She found she wanted to know more.

Archer woke a few hours later, after a nap. He was following Cara's instructions. He'd even meditated, for Source's sake.

Spending time with the kids had been fun. His energies meant he wasn't afraid of a bit of acting—after all, that's what most of his life was, pretending to enjoy the empire he'd built. BayBella was going to be a real charmer when she grew up, and heaven help any person she set her sights on. Abi, sweeter, quieter, had needed a gentler touch, and every time he'd coaxed a smile out of her it had felt like a win.

He'd enjoyed telling them stories. Talking about the legends and history of their race lit him up in a way nothing else did. He found it endlessly fascinating, tracing the patterns and path of their race's evolution, and how it intersected and crossed with humans. He had a store of tales that went far beyond the classic myths of their race.

As far as they understood, Atlantis had been a place where only energetics had lived. Human traders were met outside the ports of the island and their goods bartered for on boats. The mingling with the human race that had created the energetics' diversity of ethnicities had come later, after the great fall, and the exodus to Egypt and out from there.

But why Atlantis had fallen was a mystery.

Working toward solving that mystery was one of the few things that dulled the emptiness and dissatisfaction that he kept hidden about the rest of his life.

He stretched and yawned, sitting up and wandering to the window. He was glad that energetic Healing Centers had large rooms for patients. He gazed at the green outside, and considered asking to go out. His abdomen didn't hurt as much when he moved, and he felt calmer, more grounded. There was still a nagging worry about Phoebe and Disp@tch, but it was sinking in that he couldn't help much anyway in the state he was in.

He picked up the TV remote and eased down onto the sofa, trying to choose between the stuff Ai had brought him and Korean soap operas. He was starting to be fond of both.

A lump in the pocket of his pants dug into his hip, and his brows drew together. It's not like he had any possessions to put in a pocket.

He reached in and pulled out a phone. Baffled, he stared down at it. Then he glanced around guiltily, wondering if anyone was watching. He stood and walked to the window, leaning against the frame and facing out, so his back was to the door.

He rubbed a thumb over the phone, and it lit up. Turning it over in his hand, he recognized a sticker with the same symbol he'd seen on one of Ai's t-shirts. He groaned. They would be torn apart by Cara if she knew. Ai must have slipped it into his pocket as they were exiting the kids' room. How, he'd never know, as he hadn't felt a thing, but he guessed the kind of skills she'd learned living on the streets had meant her childhood had been very different from his own.

The cell had been left unlocked, and had the same software as the tablet. Having done it once, it wouldn't take him long to get back into his work system.

His shoulders hunched. He'd promised Cara he wouldn't, and she hadn't been wrong about the physical impact of his work. Dammit, he hated his job.

It was intriguing to him, and not a little endearing, that Cara seemed to be so passionate about hers. Yet she didn't seem to be driven by achievement, or fame, or power, or any of the things so many people wanted.

He brightened. He could help her out with her work, instead of burdening himself with his own. Stressballgate had indicated that whatever her secret project was, it had been built badly. The dents in her office wall could attest to that.

He could get in to the Center's system, poke around to find whatever the project was, and stealth-fix it so it wasn't such a pain for Cara. Plus, he never liked Anahata Guild, self-righteous as they were, and secrets were like catnip to him.

Hmm. Perhaps there was one more thing that blunted the ennui of his day-to-day. Maybe, perhaps, possibly, he liked the feeling that a little risk-taking brought him.

It took him a while to get in, but the smartphone was already on the Center's Wi-Fi, so not as long as getting into his own system had taken. But night had long fallen by the time he'd managed it, which was probably better, as she was less likely to be using the computer while he was poking around.

For fun, he started with her browser history, curious for some reason if what Ai had said was true about Cara's guilty pleasures.

Something in him wanted to know more about her. He'd loved that moment where she'd lost control in her office. It was so rare for her fire to shine through, and there was something enticing about it. He wanted to find other ways to coax that side of her out, he admitted to himself, wincing. Probably not the best thing to do to the Healer he needed to let him out of this place.

Her browser history included a website for readers where she'd logged several historical mysteries, many of which focused on ancient civilizations, such as Greece, Rome and Egypt. There was a big crossover in the documentaries he typically indulged in. He rubbed his chin, looking at the list. Interesting.

Then he hit gold. A bunch of celebrity gossip websites, with entertainment 'news'. And pictures. A lot of pictures. He scrolled through, grinning, and trying to fit this piece of the puzzle into the serious and work-focused Cara.

She was intriguing. He didn't know many people who seemed as dedicated to their jobs as she appeared to be. But it was good to know she had a lighter side. The work she was doing in the Center seemed intense, and the woman barely stopped.

He hit a picture and his eyebrows shot up. That was unexpected. It was a photo of him and... Layla? Laylee? A date that Phoebe had arranged for him to take to a Gala dinner for tech companies supporting charities. Laylu had been a human CEO of a start-up, and the friend of a friend of Phoebe. The two women had felt it would provide good publicity for both organizations, and indeed, it had made the gossip papers and the tech news. She'd been pleasant enough company.

The next two items in her history were also about him. Another photo, and an old profile piece on CNET. Interesting indeed. She'd been doing her research. He wasn't sure what to make of that.

He glanced at the time. Something to muse on later, not now when he might get caught red-handed with a contraband cell.

He looked at Cara's search history next, to see what he should be looking for, and what this so-called secret program was she needed to fix. People often googled an issue and so it was a good place to point hackers like himself toward holes in their system.

He hadn't got far when the door opened, and he slipped the cell back under a cushion, his heart thundering in his chest. He didn't hate the feeling. A little jolt of stress was as familiar to him as breathing.

It was Cara. He took pleasure in seeing that poise and composure and knowing parts of her she kept hidden, like the love of celebrity pictures and her stress ball explosions. He smiled at her, and she frowned at his expression, suspicion on her face.

She handed him a cell phone, and for a moment, he stared down at it, frozen.

"It's Phoebe," Cara said. "You seem a lot better, and she's going to keep the work talk to a minimum. But, Mr. Hampton, this is an experiment, and if you overdo it, it will be a while before we try it again."

She gave him a warning look.

He nodded.

"I'll be back in twenty minutes. Please try to contain the amount of trouble you cause in that time to a minimum."

She turned and walked out.

He watched her pert ass all the way out the door.

Just to make sure she'd gone, obviously.

15

Cara entered Kayla's room and studied the sleeping girl. They'd moved her to a secure, heavily warded room in the Healing Center, deciding finally that she didn't belong in the Rehab side. The girl was an innocent, no matter what the damage done to her made her do.

So far, they'd tried similar rituals to the one Cara had done with Archer, though with greater power levels, to mitigate the effects the leeching had had on the girl. Elrian's leeching had created a sucking energy drain within Kayla, such that her dominant and auxiliary Chakras had been reaching out blindly, seeking other sources of energy to replenish themselves. Cara had been trying to help the girl reconnect to the ether and to enable her to pull energy herself again, to control the desperate need to take energy from any place available.

Their progress hadn't been stellar. Kayla was still having occasional destructive hallucinations, for which they hadn't yet found a reason.

Kayla moved in her sleep, restless, her eyes fluttering under her closed lids. Cara frowned and stepped closer. The girl seemed to be muttering something, though Cara couldn't make it out the words very clearly.

"Help, please, help me. I'll do anything, just leave me alone, help, please." The words continued in a similar vein, the words mere whispers under Kayla's breath.

Was this a hallucination like the others? She had always seemed awake in previous episodes they'd caught. Cara's eyebrows drew closer together. Was it a nightmare? Her heart ached for the girl. Perhaps this was a reason the girl so often seemed tired, no matter how much sleep she had.

The whispers continued, agonizing in their desperation. A shiver went through Cara. She walked to the girl and placed a hand on her forehead. Perhaps she could help her sleep better for now.

Cara spun tendrils of her Anahata energy, and wove them into a featherlight net, then cast the net over the girl's head. It sank in, and Cara closed her eyes and slipped part of her consciousness into the net, trying to find the girl's nightmares and calm them.

What she found was certainly a nightmare, but not of the type she was expecting.

A presence, a dark shadow, was hooked into the girl's weak auxiliary Ajna, presumably through the dreamscape, though that wasn't a place Cara's energies could take her. But she didn't need to go there to see the impact of the actions.

Somehow, against all their understanding of leeching, the girl was being drained.

At a distance.

Cara snapped into action. The net she'd created to soothe became protection, as she shoved defensive Manipura energy into it. It lit up with the green of Anahata and the yellow of Manipura, and the shadow was starkly outlined against the bright lights. The indigo of the girl's Ajna was muddy, dark streaks through it like thickly thorned vines. Cara attacked the streaks, slicing with her Manipura, blending her healing and fire energies seamlessly.

The shadow reacted, slashing at Cara with those poisonous dark lines.

Kayla began to scream.

Archer promised Phoebe he was following the Healer's instructions, and that he was a lot better. He had ended up back at the window again. Yep. Definitely time to get some air.

"Do you want me to send you some of your dive planning research?" Phoebe offered. "I can email them over and ask Osana to print them."

"That would be great." He talked her through where to find the folder, and what he wanted. He wasn't entirely sure it would cheer him up to go back to planning a trip he didn't know when he'd be able to take, but it would be something.

While they were talking, a rock had formed in his stomach. She sounded her usual cheerful self, though slightly more harried than normal. Source knows she would be juggling a lot, handling all his work as well as hers, though she was a better delegator than him. She knew the strengths of the team around her, and how best to use them. He had a tendency to feel it was easier to do things himself.

"You needn't worry," she said. "I have things under control. Think of this as an opportunity for me to show you what I can do. Trust me. I can do this."

Whether or not they had an agreement to be genuine, unless she asked him directly, he wasn't keen to alert her to the fact he'd been in the Disp@tch system, but he had to ask. "How's the Whisper project going?"

"Good," she said. "Not easy, but we're making solid progress."

In his hospital room, Archer tilted his head to the side. Was she lying? Should he say something? It would be unprecedented in their relationship, a lie.

"We had some issues with the project management server though, so we've switched to a more basic way of tracking. I'll show you, give me a sec."

He was really puzzled now. He pulled the phone away from his ear, and looked down at the screen, waiting for the picture to appear.

A photo of a wall, with what looked like a tree of Post-its with words and arrows between the words showed up.

His whole body sagged in relief.

"A bit like the old days, eh?" she said. "I blurred the text because I don't want you spending the next two days pestering Cara to send me messages about the project, but rest assured we're making good progress and are on track for the meeting with the investors."

"What happened with the project management server?" he asked cautiously.

"Not sure. But the team didn't have time to fix the issue and do the work on the project, so I prioritized. They can fix the project management after this has shipped." She hesitated. "We miss you, Arch, don't think we don't, but we're getting it done. We can't build a business like ours around one person, no matter what kind of coding wizard you are. We're lucky to have you, I have no doubt about that—oh, and by the way, you're lucky to have me too—but the entire company can't come to a grinding halt because you're sick."

He didn't know what to feel. Relief, because the guilt had been tremendous, as Phoebe had wanted him to delegate the damned project in the first place but he'd missed coding so much he'd seen it as an opportunity to play and do something fun. If only it hadn't taken him so long to get around to it.

There was another feeling though, like a piece of grit inside him. He rubbed the heel of his hand on his sternum. Surely he didn't *want* to be needed?

"That's great. So everything's on track with the investors?" he asked.

"Yes. It's important we show them we can do this even with you out of the picture. They won't want to invest in a company where a key person being ill means everything falls apart," she said.

"Of course," he said, though the strange pangs in his chest didn't subside.

This was an opportunity. He would get to focus on planning his diving trip, while Phoebe took care of things. The pressure was off. The deal had been more important to Phoebe than him, anyway. It was her baby, an app that broadcast extracts of a user's life in real time, and a way to capture a new, younger market share.

He shuddered. The last thing he wanted was more customers. A bigger company. He wanted it all to go away.

So why was he feeling like trash?

"I'm glad you have it under control. I hated letting you down," he said.

"You won't let me down if you get healthy, and delegate this kind of stuff in the future. And if you let go of this project for now. You can't afford to get lost in this kind of work when you're healing from this level of injury," she said. "You know you have a tendency to go without food, sleep and goodness knows what else when you get absorbed in a project."

Perhaps this ache inside him was because coding was one of the few activities in his role he still found fun. Letting go of it felt symbolic in a way, that he'd truly lost himself in a job that he hated.

He sighed. "I know. Once again, I assure you, I. Am. Healing. I'm recovering, I'm doing what I'm told, and I'm being good. Thanks for holding down the fort."

They signed off, and he decided to return the phone to Cara as she hadn't appeared to take it back. He'd missed her when she didn't visit, even if she was only coming to check that he was doing what he was told.

As he wandered through the building, pleased that the pain in his abdomen was so much less tiring, he heard a long, terrible scream.

He turned towards the noise, glancing up and down the corridors, trying to work out where it was coming from. Should he help? He was no match for a Rogue at this moment, though they would surely be in the Rehab part of the Center, which Ai had told him was a separate building, with plenty of security.

That meant it must be this side of the Center.

Another scream, and a raised voice he recognized as Cara's.

He pinpointed the direction it was coming from, and ran.

Cara battled the energetic attacking her through Kayla's mind.

No wonder the girl hadn't been recovering.

Cara's tiredness burned away as she fell back on decades of dealing with Rogues and Leeches.

A commotion at the door distracted her for a moment, and her control slipped, the attacker tearing at the protection she was creating for the girl, a line of thorns like barbed wire catching Cara and rending her energies. Cara bit down on the agony.

She spun a second, stronger net, for defense and healing both. This one was larger, and ready to throw over Kayla's entire energetic body. Cara just needed to get rid of the parasite attached to her first.

She needed more power, more energy.

While to an outsider her body would appear to be standing motionless next to Kayla, her hand on the girl's forehead, inside their minds, the battle raged. Cara's fire was roused, and she had roared into action. She drew on that fire now, stoking it while she dodged the attacks the Leech, who she assumed was Elrian, threw out.

In the physical world, she felt more Manipura join hers, separate, but open to being directed by her. Surprise jolted her, but assuming it was another of the Healers, she wove it into her net, like differently shaded threads of yellow.

It was enough to give her the strength she needed.

After a few more seconds, she was ready. She breathed in deeply, pulled energy into both her Chakras, and detonated her fire at the same moment as wrenching Kayla back, the fire weakening the dark strands so she could break them, one last stab of Manipura splitting them apart. As the last thread fell away, she threw the net she'd made with the combined energy over Kayla's energetic being, which would protect her from further attacks.

The girl's clammy body stirred under her hand, and Cara left her mind to come back to the physical world.

Kayla blinked her pale eyes open, and stared up at the Healer.

"Has he gone?" Her voice trembled. She didn't move from her position on the bed, frozen in fear.

Cara glanced round the room, panting, and her heart stuttered when she saw it hadn't been another Healer in the room, but Archer, leaning against the wall.

She walked the few steps to the sink, splashing water over her face. Her eyes met Archer's, silently asking him, are you okay? He nodded, though he was pale and wan, and looked ready to collapse.

One thing at a time.

She took a moment to collect herself, then turned back to the girl sitting up on her bed. "Yes. He's gone. Was that Elrian?"

"Yes," the girl whispered.

"Why didn't you tell us he was attacking you?" Cara said. She had to work hard to control her voice, and not shout at the girl. Intellectually, she knew Kayla was a victim, but emotionally, she wished Kayla had let them know earlier, so they could have protected her.

"I wasn't sure if it was real." Kayla tried to hold back tears, until sobs engulfed her.

Cara came over and put her arms around her fragile form, and Kayla clung to her.

"It's okay," she soothed. "It's all going to be okay now."

Cara felt like she'd run around the island. She pressed the buzzer for attention while the girl cried.

One of the other Healers came in, and Cara explained the situation and detached the girl from her, with a promise to come back within a couple of hours and check on her.

Archer had stood quietly at the side of the room while all this went on, neither interrupting, nor seeking attention himself.

But she could see he'd overdone it.

"Come on," she said to him. "Put your arm over my shoulder. I'm taking you back to your room."

Much to her surprise, he complied, and they made their way unsteadily, the height difference making her support for him challenging, but this wasn't the first time she had done this.

In his room, she helped him gently to the bed, where he lay back with a sigh.

"Does anything hurt? More than usual?" she asked him. "I've never had a patient who relapses as often as you."

He gestured to his abdomen, and she sat on the edge of the bed and placed her hands on the area.

Her body hummed, and she drew on her healing energy once again.

She really needed to sleep.

Her power crept into his body, and she concentrated on finding the tiny tears and rips his activity had created. The damage was minimal, and it wasn't long before she'd got him back to the state she'd left him in before she'd handed him the call from Phoebe.

She withdrew her hands, but before she could stand, he'd caught one of them in his own larger ones. They were warm and dry, and perhaps because she was so drained, felt good. Really good. She'd seldom felt the touch of another in recent times. Instead of pulling away, she hesitated, enjoying the feel of her small hand being surrounded.

A moment, she thought. Just a moment, then she'd leave.

"I don't know why you find your work more interesting than me," Archer mumbled. "It's quite annoying."

Cara let out a humph of surprise.

"And you're so bossy and controlling," he continued, lightheaded. Perhaps he'd have a nap after all. "You can teach me how to like my work."

He pulled her closer to him and, eyes wide, she let him. She cocked her head as they studied each other, faces a few inches apart.

She put a hesitant hand up to his cheek.

He raised his head, and kissed her on the mouth, gentle and unassuming. Her lips were so soft, and his own lips tingled from the contact.

He waited until he felt the smallest return of the kiss from her, then lay back down, satisfied.

"We're going to go on a date," he said, as he drifted off, his eyes closing. "Yes. A date. That's what we'll do."

Soothed, he fell asleep with her scent wrapped around him like a blanket.

Cara walked out of Archer's room, bewildered, her cheeks hot.

What in Source's name had just happened?

"Oh no," she moaned. Had she kissed a patient? Someone under her care?

Her muscles clenched even as her heart gave a tiny skip.

She walked faster, needing the comfort of her office, her stress balls. She flew past Osana with a quick 'all good' to the other woman's surprised face and unasked question.

Shutting her door then leaning against it, her pulse pounded like she'd been in a race.

She grabbed the three stress balls from the desk, and reached into her drawer for a fourth, taking two in each hand.

Her eyes closed, she spun two balls furiously in each hand.

Somehow, that man had gotten under her skin. *Again.*

They'd been in a dangerous, adrenaline-filled situation, she reasoned. She knew the research that indicated external fear and excitement could be attributed inappropriately to a person you were with. That was all that had happened. Her body had responded to him helping her save Kayla with physical signs of exhilaration, and that had transferred to Archer when they'd gotten back to his room. She'd healed him, touched his warm, dry skin, and somehow she'd wanted to melt into him, and they'd kissed.

She shut her eyes briefly. She'd never done something so incredibly unprofessional before.

But he'd had the nerve to tell her they were going to date! She would have to put a stop to that as soon as possible. He couldn't boss her around like that. And just because she'd showed the smallest indication of kissing him back, did not mean he could take her going on a date with him as a given. He might have had a bunch of women fall at his feet at the slightest hint he was interested, but she was not those women. He might be sexy as hell, but she would have no problem resisting him. He might have eyes that combined the best of an endearing puppy and melting chocolate with emerald flecks, but she was more than able to refrain from falling for him.

Plus, Source knew, she had no time to date.

The best thing, she decided, as the stress balls rotated in her hands, a tiny vortex of air spinning above each one, was to heal him and remove him from the Center as soon as possible.

Let him be some other foolish woman's problem.

He would not be hers.

C H A P T E R

16

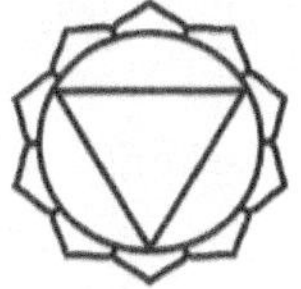

Archer waited for Cara's next visit with the anticipation and patience of a hunter. He had been tempted to go to her office that morning, but he'd waited, to rest and show he was doing what she'd told him to recover.

The events of the day before had set him back, but not in the same way as his previous reversals. He felt good. Better than good. He always felt better when he had a goal.

He had a new question to add to his previous two. And he intended to continue asking all three of them until he got yeses.

She entered and began checking his vitals with barely more than a murmured greeting. He grinned.

"Good morning, Florence Nightingale," he said. "I have three questions for you."

She looked up, startled. "Three?"

His grin sharpened, and her eyes widened as she caught his meaning. She flushed and continued with her checks.

"The answer to all three is no."

He was okay with that. He hadn't got where he was in business without being able to convert a no into an enthusiastic yes eventually.

"How do you feel after yesterday?" she asked. Her hands probed his abdomen, and he stilled as he felt her energy explore his insides. There was no discomfort, only a gentle but persistent ache.

"The pain is less. Moving doesn't hurt as much, and I have more energy."

"Can you tap the ether? What happens when you try to pull energy?" she asked.

He reached inside himself. And there, thank the Source, were his two energies, ready for him to use. The power shimmered as he took it inside him, shuddering in relief.

"When you helped yesterday, you accessed Manipura. That could have gone two ways: you could have hurt yourself a lot worse, or your desire to use your Manipura could have broken through whatever was blocking you. Thankfully, it seems to have been the latter." She glared at him. "But don't take that kind of risk again."

His grin widened, if possible. His face was going to split apart. It was a good day.

He looked down at her hands resting on his belly, and cocked his head. She had on a new piece of jewelry, a stunning piece that looked strangely familiar. The style was unusual, and it looked antique. It was a thick bracelet, with a striking blue-green sheen. There was a symbol on it, obscured by some kind of corrosion, almost as if the piece had been underwater for a long time.

"Can I look at your bracelet?" he asked. "It's amazing. How old is it?"

She frowned, then brought her wrist up so she could see it.

She froze. She seemed stricken, as if he'd given her terrible news.

"Are you alright?" He sat up, concerned.

She shook herself, and grasped the bracelet, tugging at it and turning it.

"The catch, where's the catch?" She fumbled at it, anxiety coming off her in waves.

"You want to take it off?" Who didn't remember how to take off their own bracelet? He didn't understand what was happening, but he didn't enjoy seeing her so distressed. He took her wrist and gently rotated the bracelet, trying to work out how to remove it. She stilled again, her gaze fixed to the jewelry as if it was a scorpion that could sting her at any moment.

Then she jerked her arm back, out of his grasp. "I need to go. I'll send another Healer to finish checking your vitals."

She fled from the room, Archer left to stare after her, exasperated and confused, and once again curious. What was it about that woman? She dangled mysteries like bait, then ran away.

The bracelet though, that was as much his area of expertise as hacking. He'd been diving sites for many years, looking for the ancient treasures of their race.

The jewelry around her wrist had looked frustratingly familiar, and he was determined to take a longer look.

Cara wasn't sure even her stress balls could help her now. She'd gone outside to the limestone cliffs, needing air, determined none of her staff or guests would see her like this.

As she strode up and down, the wind flowed around her, her dress flying around her legs.

She brought the bracelet up to her face to glare at it for the hundredth time. It wasn't coming off, she knew that. She'd tried several ways, including using her fire, before admitting defeat.

The others involved in the prophecy had had their bracelets appear before they got together with their lovers. So this seemed a terrifying sign that her life might be about to change.

On the other hand, this bracelet was nothing like those that Cuinn, Blaize, Tierra and the others had. Their bracelets were interwoven strands of colors that represented the energies of the couple. They were discreet, elegant and simple.

This—this was a thick metal band, that was almost primitive in design. Beautiful, but ancient, the stones that were set into it were a shimmering blue-green, and when they caught the light they were breathtaking. It was both stunning and alien.

She stared out over the cliffs to the sea far beyond. The day was gray, and clouds and fog combined in the distance so that the horizon was murky.

She took out her cell and dialed Cathair Cuinn. Cuinn himself answered, but put her on speaker with Blaize at Cara's request.

Cara had known Cuinn for decades, and was used to his analytical approach. A Professor at Vancouver University, he had deep expertise in Ajna, the mind, and was many hundreds of years old. Preferring intellectual to emotional connections, he could be stern, though he worked harder than many Cara knew. Since he'd begun receiving prophecy shards, he'd taken a leave of absence from his position at a University to understand their meaning.

He'd been persuaded to take on an Adherent, Blaize, a strong, tall woman who had trained as a Warrior, and was Nixie's cousin. Elrian had quickly realized she was part of the prophecy. After some stormy interactions, Blaize had been kidnapped by Indigo, an associate of Elrian's. After Blaize had been freed, she and Cuinn had seen they had more in common than they had understood, and that Source had been right to bring them together.

As more and more of her friends were implicated in the prophecy, events had snowballed. So much had happened, so much danger faced. She sighed. It wasn't Cuinn's fault.

There was no better man to talk to about the bracelet. He'd be able to help her take a logical approach. She knew it was the right thing to share information, yet it didn't feel easy to do.

"Something's happened." She swallowed. "I have a bracelet."

There was a silence on the other end.

"Alright," said Cuinn. "What are the colors? That might help us identify who it matches. Unless you have an idea already."

"There aren't any threads," Cara snapped, then catching herself, made a fist and took in a breath, calming herself. She threw out air, and fallen leaves danced.

"It's not like your bracelets," she said, trying again. "It's different. Older. I don't know what it is."

"Can we see?" said Blaize cautiously.

Cara shot a photo of her wrist and sent it to them.

"Do you know who the other males are in the prophecy? The unattached ones? Apart from Adam?" she asked.

"There are two we can't identify, as you know. One we still have nothing on, the other we've caught glimpses of, but not enough for a complete picture. In the prophecy shards, he's always surrounded by gloom, and his features are impossible to pick out," Cuinn replied. "We can send you the latest version of Nixie's drawing if you like, in case there's anything you can see we can't?"

Cara felt a jolt of anxiety stab through her. She loved Adam like a brother, but knew it would not be him. Was the most recent male that Nixie had drawn going to be her lover? Did she know him? If this was a bracelet that even had a match.

"Send it, please," said Cara. Why on earth didn't she have it already?

"Will do," said Blaize.

Was Archer one of the males in the prophecy? When she opened the email, would she recognize the tilt of his head, his sensuous mouth curved in that wickedly annoying smile?

He had no bracelet. She'd checked as she'd fled his room that morning. And she wasn't interested.

She kicked at the earth. Okay, okay, she *was* interested from a purely sexual point of view. The man looked good. But in every other way, he was exasperating, and his values were completely at odds with her own. His life was about creating a commercial business that made money, hers was about helping people.

There weren't any other males she was really engaged with in her life, unless you counted the staff of the Center, or others here to be healed or rehabilitated. None of them had made any more or less of an impression than the women she connected with, and she had never been attracted to women. Perhaps there was someone else out there who had a similar, strange bracelet, or perhaps the bracelet meant something completely different.

"Send as many photos of the bracelet as you can," Blaize said, "and we'll research it and try to understand it better. Maybe Cuinn can also find something in the ether that relates to it, a piece of prophecy we've missed."

"It could be Archer," Cuinn said.

Cara squeezed the phone in her hand. Her voice was as tight as her grip. "No bracelet."

"Okay. Keep an eye on him given Elrian attacked—ooff," Cuinn cut off halfway through the sentence. Cara mentally thanked Blaize.

"There's another thing," Cara said. "I discovered that Elrian was leeching on Kayla from a distance. He had accessed her dreamscape somehow."

Silence from the other end of the phone.

Perhaps she should have been less blunt.

Elrian was Cuinn's estranged father.

"Is she warded now?" Cuinn said, his tone emotionless.

"Yes," Cara said.

"Alright. That's new, and a concern. I'll warn those in the group with Ajna to update their dreamscape wards, just in case."

Cuinn quizzed her on the details, and then they went back to the bracelet, but they mostly went round in circles. They needed a lead of some kind to progress things. Cara's anxiety grew the more they talked around the issue.

When she finished the call, she blinked, considering herself in relation to the objects around her. Was she taller? Or had the trees got shorter? She looked down at the ground, which was further away than usual.

Ah.

In her agitation, she'd floated herself without realizing, just as she sometimes floated the stress balls.

She sighed, and dissipated the air currents holding her up, so she drifted down to the ground.

Time to get back to work.

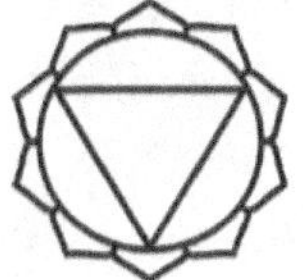

Cara didn't reappear that day, and though he asked the others who checked on him, including Ai, about her, they kindly but firmly directed his attention elsewhere.

The bracelet obsessed him. He couldn't get it out of his mind. It was hauntingly familiar, but he couldn't work out why or how he knew it.

Phoebe had couriered over research papers and some of his books, and he'd paged through them, trying to see if anything would jog his memory.

He thought it was energetic in design, but it didn't seem modern, and he didn't think Cara was the type who'd wear a deliberately corroded bracelet to make it seem older. Which meant it was old, or had been left somewhere to get that kind of damage.

Her reaction had also been mysterious. When he'd mentioned the bracelet to Ai, she'd gaped at him, told him she had to go, and run out of the room.

He slept badly that night, Cara and the bracelet on his mind.

When he woke, he decided he wasn't going to be given the run around again. He liked the ritual of asking Cara his questions, and he wouldn't be denied the next opportunity.

He got up early, showered, dressed and headed to Cara's office, avoiding any staff members he saw. He waited till Osana left her desk for coffee, and slipped into Cara's room.

Seeing him, she groaned. Actually groaned. He raised an eyebrow.

"Question time!" he said, beaming.

She put her head on the desk and he heard a muffled "No."

She lifted it again. "No tech. No going home yet."

"I have two more questions," he said, enjoying this interaction more than he expected.

"Will you go on a date with me?"

She leaned back in her chair and stared at him. "No."

Two of her stress balls levitated, but he snatched them out of the air and began to manipulate them himself. She scowled.

"Last question. Can I examine your bracelet?"

"No," she said flatly. "Go back to your room and rest."

"Only if you promise to come visit me later."

She sighed, and he sat on one of the visitor chairs, sprawling in an exaggeratedly relaxed fashion.

"Or I can rest here."

"Fine. Fine!" She shooed at him. "Now, go."

He grinned again, and got up. As he did, the cell on her desk pinged, and a message flashed up from someone called Tierra. He only caught a glimpse before she seized it and put it behind her back.

A bracelet?! Do you know who the guy is?

He sat back down, more alert this time. "Okay. What does that text mean? What's going on? Is that the Tierra who's Adam's sister?"

"Can't you let it go?"

"I'm bored. You have something on your wrist that reminds me of some kind of Atlantean treasure, and it looks like it's made from orichalcum."

She took her wrist slowly from behind her back and touched the bracelet.

"Well, it can't be that," she said. "Obviously. A friend gave it to me. I didn't realize it was a copy of an older piece."

"And you wouldn't be wearing a several-thousand-year-old bracelet around the Rehab Center," he said, observing her face, which paled. "That would be crazy."

Six stress balls hit the wall behind him like bullets.

"Mmmhmm…crazy," she said faintly.

Cara fetched herself and Archer glasses of water to buy her some time.

She'd checked the sketch that Blaize had sent, and Cara had ruefully agreed they were right. The gloom surrounding the figure made it impossible to tell anything at all about who he might be. The only clue was that he seemed to be within some sort of ancient ruins.

And it seemed Archer knew something about archaeology. So maybe…

Her mind raced, and she couldn't get her thoughts in order. Should she trust him with the complete story? Did he really recognize the bracelet?

"What do you know about the original?" she said, trying to be casual, as she put the water down. As far as she knew, none of the other bracelets had been historical artifacts, or at least, none of the experts consulted had recognized them.

"The symbol on it seems familiar," he said. "If you let me inspect it, I might be able to tell you. I wish I had the right books with me. I have a small library of texts in my apartment in Seattle."

"Of course you do," Cara muttered. She sighed and stuck out her arm.

He took it in his hands as if it was made of glass, and squinted at the symbol, coming so close she could feel his breath on the back of her hand. She tried not to squirm.

"It's small," he muttered. "A thick circle, but something at the top, where the circle overlaps… The corrosion obscures it, but I think it might be a snake eating itself."

"An ouroboros?" she asked. She knew the image, it was ancient, but she hadn't ever seen it connected to her race.

"I think so. I'd need to clean your bracelet up to see it properly. Or perhaps I can find the other place I've seen it and we can compare. I think it was put on artifacts which were used to counter something." He shot her a long look. "Strange that it's so corroded, if it's a copy."

She fidgeted, then gazed down at the strange bracelet on her wrist. She had reached her limit in terms of things happening, things to juggle, feelings to feel. She was kind of over this prophecy.

She gritted her teeth even as the thought slipped into her brain. Her rational brain smacked her on the head, and she stuffed the thought down.

She could deal with this, and she *would* deal with this.

"I'd be interested to know what the original bracelet was," she said, trying for casual. Archer's raised eyebrow and smirk indicated he wasn't buying a word of it, but he said nothing, and that would do for now. "If you have any info. I'm quite interested in ancient history."

That was true, at least. She'd be able to discuss the finer points of the Egyptian healing goddess Sekhmet, or some of the older Anahata texts that had survived from the period post-Atlantis. Not that there were many.

"No problem," he said. It felt like they were having two entirely different conversations, one spoken, and one very much unspoken, and Cara was worried about what she was accidentally saying without saying.

Source, her head hurt.

18

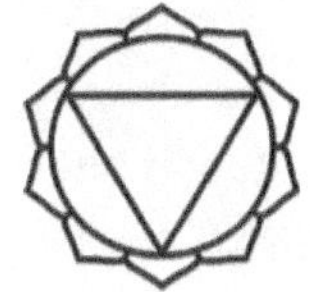

"I want to bring Archer in on the prophecy," Cara said, gazing at her computer screen where her friends looked back at her via a video call.

She had shown them the bracelet and explained Archer's reaction. Adam had agreed that anything Archer could find out would be useful.

Nixie sat in Jeb's lap on their screen. "What does your gut say, Cara? Go with that."

Cuinn, sitting next to Blaize in their little box at the top right of the screen, frowned. Cara caught Blaize's hand tightening, keeping him from saying anything. Logic was the basis for Cuinn's actions.

Cara would prefer to use both.

"Okay," Adam nodded. "Do it."

"Make sure he knows the importance of secrecy," Fintan said.

"Secrecy seems to be an important part of his work. I trust him," Cara said, and was surprised to find she did.

They all signed off.

She could admit to herself that she was relieved to be able to share things with someone, even if he was as annoying as Archer.

He'd come to see her again this morning to ask his questions, back down to three again now that she'd let him examine the bracelet. He was driving her crazy, yet she looked forward to being mad at him.

She groaned. How had he inserted himself into her life? And how could she be enjoying it?

Her computer pinged, and she read the email that dropped into her inbox.

Ice flooded her body. Oh, Source.

Anahata Guild were coming to inspect her Center.

She bit down on a scream.

It wasn't unusual, but this was the worst possible time for such an inspection, when she had so many things that could go wrong. She had too many guests in the Rehab side, and not enough staff. And the Rogues were tougher cases than they were used to, taking longer to get through to them, longer to support them to get well.

Should she send Ai away? Anahata were aware of her existence, but Tierra, Jeb and she had agreed that Cara would help her catch up on her education around their people before they sent her to the Guild.

Cara felt her jaw clench as she ground her teeth.

She needed to do something, to take some action. It was her way of feeling in control, she knew, but she might as well do something useful with the frustration.

She'd check in on Kayla. The girl was doing better since they'd realized what was causing her hallucinations and issues, but she still needed a lot of care.

She walked through the corridors, trying to imagine what the inspection team would see. An older building, kept in reasonable condition.

What might they find?

She opened the door to Kayla's room, concerned to see it was unlocked, and stopped dead when she saw Ai sitting on the bed with the other girl. Kayla's hand was on Ai's leg, and they seemed to be having an intense, almost intimate conversation.

"What are you doing in here, Ai?" Cara said, trying for calm. And how the hell had she got into the room? They had agreed Ai could see Kayla, but under supervision, with preparation and planning. Not like this.

Ai sprung away from Kayla, whose face shut down. What was going on here?

"I wanted to talk to Kayla about Elrian and Indigo," Ai said. "You said it was okay. I opened the door."

Indigo had been the person who had introduced Ai to Elrian, and who had died in the course of kidnapping and torturing Blaize. Ai had known her as a friend.

Looking at the body language of Ai and Kayla, Cara wondered if Ai had had stronger feelings for Indigo than those of friendship. Ai was someone who hadn't experienced a lot of love in her life.

"You're not allowed to be in here," Cara said. "You know that. How did you get past the wards?"

Ai shifted and folded her arms. "I used my power. I pushed and pushed until the door let me in. Anyway, you wanted me to talk to her."

"I helped," Kayla said.

Cara's chest tightened. That showed a brute force of power Ai shouldn't have been capable of. Perhaps she would have to step up the girl's training, and expose her to more exercises. They couldn't afford for Ai to have trouble controlling her energy. They'd decided that she needed a lot more education before she became an Adherent, but the downside of that was that her power wasn't bonded with anyone else, so someone stepping in if she lost control wouldn't be straightforward.

Another hour, another problem.

"Kayla says orichalcum is something Elrian's obsessed with," Ai said.

Cara's head snapped up.

"He calls it the lost element of Atlantis," Kayla said. Cara had to strain to hear. "He's been invading my Haven since I left, but that means I know some things about him, too. It's hard to hide everything in the dreamscape."

Cara shook her arm so her sleeve fell over her bracelet, although she'd told Ai about the bracelet already. She'd ask her later if she'd talked to Kayla about it, and Cara would also come back and talk to Kayla later. Maybe, just maybe, there'd be some answers rather than another mystery.

"Has he been back since we warded you?" Cara asked.

Kayla shook her head, the blue streak in her hair falling across her face. She looked younger than her years, more Ai's age now that she was calm.

"He's also obsessed with writings about soulmates and the Greeks," Kayla said.

"Maybe Cuinn can find out more?" Ai added.

Cara nodded. "Alright. Ai, call him and update him. Now let's leave Kayla to rest."

They left the room, and Cara pressed her hands on the door and shoved power into it, reigniting the wards with a great deal more energy than she'd used before. She'd need to get one of the staff to fix the human lock too, but the energetic lock she'd just put on the door would keep most out. Kayla wasn't in the Rehabilitation side anymore, but the locks were for her protection as much as anyone else's.

As soon as she stepped away from the door, Ai rushed to speak. "You said I should talk to her."

"Yes, but not by breaking down her door. Using your power like that was irresponsible." Cara was furious, but also conscious some of her feelings about other things were seething inside her mind. She couldn't take her growing stress out on the girl.

"The information's useful though, right?" Ai persisted.

Cara sighed. "Yes. But you're not on your own anymore, you're part of us, part of our team. When you put yourself in danger like that, or you disregard the rules of the Center, you create more work for me, as well as setting a poor example for the other staff and guests, who see you as my responsibility. You might not have been ready for that interaction. We should have talked about it, even played it through first."

Ai kicked at the ground, a mutinous expression on her face. "I've been taking care of myself for years."

Cara tried not to grind her teeth. She hadn't been in a parent type role for a long time. In fact, while she had been a Maven, she'd never had a child herself. She wasn't sure of the approach she should be taking here.

"Then you need to behave like an adult," she said, flatly. "And a member of the team. You know the danger we're facing. Your actions aren't only about you. Please, Ai."

Cara wasn't certain, but she thought tears gathered at the corners of Ai's eyes. Cara rubbed at her forehead. She wanted to lie down.

"Come on. Let's go have a cup of tea and you can tell me what else Kayla said. Then we can plan out our next steps." Cara relented and put an arm around Ai's shoulders.

She was ready for that cup of tea.

Archer fizzed with excitement. His frequent petitions to Cara had finally borne fruit, and after much negotiation and discussion with her and Phoebe, he'd been allowed his tech back. He'd given his word he wouldn't go into the work systems, and he'd only get updates on what was happening there from Phoebe. It would take willpower, but he'd stick to his word.

Luckily, Cara had provided him with a very good distraction.

Her bracelet was all he could think about. It had simply appeared, and her reaction to his questions was extremely odd. He'd love an in-depth look at the piece. He wished he had access to his books.

He'd pestered Phoebe to photograph sections of certain reference books, and he'd found what he was fairly sure was a drawing of the symbol, at least, though he hadn't found anything about the bracelet itself. The memory of whatever he'd read about it was an itch at the back of his mind, but he couldn't place it.

Eventually Phoebe had lost patience with his frequent texts, and had arranged to courier over some of his books. That would help.

He paced up and down his room, scowling, trying to pin down the memory. He wished he had those damn books already.

He picked up his tablet, and went through the material Phoebe had sent him, enlarging the pictures one by one.

Hours later, he stopped on one, a drawing of some ancient underwater ruins, which featured several bas reliefs. Was that the symbol on one of them?

He knew that style of architecture. An energetic friend of his had a piece from the underwater dig site the photos showed. He might even lend it to him, if Archer was prepared to give up some of his own pieces for a period.

One conversation later—difficult because his friend had haggled to swap the bas relief fragment with both a painting that Archer loved, and was going to miss, even if it was temporary, and a hefty donation to one of the friend's pet charities—Archer had persuaded his friend to send the fragment to the island so Archer could borrow it.

Sometimes, money was useful.

"You remember I'm trying to run a business here, right?" Phoebe said, when he called her again.

Guilt rippled through Archer's shoulders. "You're helping with my recovery."

"I hope you're not annoying that nice Cara," Phoebe commented. "She's decent, Arch."

"I'm not," he protested. "I'm helping her with…a thing."

"Hmm," Phoebe said, unconvinced. "Just remember, you still need her sign off to leave. You being bored like this is a good sign. You're almost back to your annoying, overzealous self."

It was his turn to humph.

"I have good news," Phoebe continued. "Indu—who, by the way, is actually a superb coder, good hire—identified that there's one module we do actually need you for in order to finish the demo, due to your inability to complete documentation or share knowledge effectively."

Archer squeezed his eyes shut as his stomach tightened. He knew it was true.

"However," Phoebe continued, "he got around the problem. We've faked that bit for the demo by putting fixed outputs into the prototype, which will show the investors what it's supposed to do without actually needing to do it, and it will be close enough to working that it's not going to be a problem on the business side. That's bought us the time we need until you get out of there and can mop it up by coding the real module."

Archer had that strange mix of feelings again. On the one hand, his stomach relaxed, as relief swept through him. He hadn't ruined all Phoebe's hard work by his arrogance. On the other hand, she'd done what she needed without him. And through a workaround he might not have come up with.

"Your team members aren't idiots, Arch," Phoebe said. "You picked some solid people, and they do you proud. You can let them off the leash a bit more often."

"They're a good team," he said, and they finished the conversation. He stared out of his window at the bleak sight of gray clouds above a turbulent sea in the distance. Was he so wrapped up in his own pride that he was blind to the fact they didn't need him for every milestone?

There was a knock on the door and it opened. He knew it was Ai, as she was the only person in this damned place who knocked. One of the many things that made it so frustrating to be stuck here was that there was no privacy, in body or space. People swanned in and out of his room at all hours, poking and prodding him and asking him how he felt.

He felt fine. Just fine. Ready to go home fine.

Still, the knock hadn't been in Ai's usual style, and the way she came through the door even less so. There were spots of color high in her cheeks, visible even on her darker skin.

He wasn't sure he had the energy for the teen right now. The thrill he'd felt about the bracelet and research had been punctured by the concept that perhaps his team didn't need him in the way he thought they did—and the corresponding confusion as to why that didn't feel like a relief.

"What's up?" he said.

"Cara being Cara," Ai said. "I was trying to help, trying to do a good thing, and I'm in trouble again. I'm always in trouble."

She paced as he looked on in bemusement. He didn't have a great deal of experience with angry teens.

"What did you do?" he asked cautiously.

She rolled her shoulders and shrugged them, the color in her cheeks heightening further.

"I went to visit a patient," she said.

He frowned. "That doesn't sound so bad."

"Right? Exactly."

Archer frowned. Cara was strict, but she was fair. "Ai, you didn't try and get into the rehab side of the Center, did you?"

She whipped her head from side to side, short hair swinging. "No!"

"Then what did you do?" he said. "Who did you visit?"

"I wanted to help her! I wanted to get more information. And I wanted to know about Indigo, and what happened to her. She was my friend. And Kayla's lonely. She doesn't have anyone to visit her."

Archer leaned in. "You went to see Kayla? She's in a secure room, isn't she?"

Ai ground her teeth obstinately. "She's not on the rehab side anymore. I pushed power into the door until the wards snapped. It hurt a bit, but it opened in the end, and I picked the human lock, that was easy. I just wanted to speak to her. Cara's annoyed because of her stupid orichalcum bracelet, but I don't know why. I think it'd be nice for her to have a boyfriend."

She stopped abruptly and put a hand over her mouth.

"The bracelet she was wearing today?"

"Yeah," Ai said, backing toward the door. Archer had to resist the urge to interrogate her. He knew it wouldn't net him the information any faster.

"It's orichalcum? Real orichalcum?" he said. "Do you even know what that is?"

"Kind of," she said, her shoulder at the door as she began edging it open. "It's real. Whatever it is. Pretty, but old."

For a teenager, old wasn't the same thing as it was to him. Ai favored shiny and new, and hadn't learned to appreciate that age could be a positive.

She'd slipped out the door before he could grill her more, but his curiosity fired up again. He'd known there was more to the bracelet than Cara let on.

The bas relief should come the next day, but he would also confront Cara about her bracelet.

He was determined to make her spill the secrets she was hiding.

He was going to help Cara, whether she knew it or not.

Elrian had found Kayla, and though the girl had shoved him out, the experience had gained him more knowledge than he'd expected.

She was in the same healing Center as Archer. Moreover, it was the Center run by Cara, the annoying friend of his niece, Tierra.

It had been Cara, while fighting him in the dreamscape, who had inadvertently given him the information about Archer's whereabouts, along with something unexpected.

On Cara's wrist, present even on her representation in the ether, had been a bracelet.

After he came out of the dreamwalk, despite some injuries to his psyche, he'd bolted for his books. His jubilance at the knowledge he had gained far outweighed any temporary damage. He paged through book after book, searching for the reference he remembered passing over.

"I don't understand what this bracelet is, or how it fits in with your work," Cassidy said, as she fussed over him. He hadn't told her he'd fought the woman wearing it, simply that it had been part of a prophecy shard he'd gathered in the ether.

"Our ancestors forged the bracelet in Atlantis," he said.

Her eyebrows shot up, and she sat down, putting an end to her fussing. Her hunger to learn had been a key personality trait from a very young age, and sharing knowledge had always been a good way to distract her.

"That's ten thousand years ago," she said, her tone reasonable. "How can it have survived?"

"Magic, and orichalcum," he said. "And a great deal of power. The bracelet has come and gone through history, and has been lost many times."

"What does it do?" she asked.

"That's somewhat unclear," he said. "There are many rumors, but it's hard to separate fact from fiction."

He rubbed his forehead. He was always tired these days. Tired and hollow, despite being surrounded by the biodiversity of the cool, moist forests of the area, with earth energy for the taking. Perhaps he'd been too quick to dismiss the damage the Healer had done. "It seems to be connected to the other stones, the other jewelry, but I don't understand why. There's a symbol on it that is important somehow. There's something in the description of it in the Hermit's notes which has been translated as a 'counter' in the past, which I think should be 'balance'."

He sighed in frustration. "But I don't know what it means. The man's notes are all over the place. It's like deciphering a secret code to understand what any of it means."

Cassidy placed a cool hand over his. "You're so pale."

He didn't need rest, he needed energy, but that wasn't a conversation he could have with her. He'd also found out something shocking about the stone Imogen wore around her neck. But he'd need to gather his thoughts before he had that conversation.

"I think I'm going to go for a drive," he said. "Perhaps visit a park. I need to spend some time replenishing my earth energies."

Cassidy cocked her head. "You can't do that on the property here?"

The house they lived in was huge, had its own gardens and woods, and was a perfect place for a Muladhara energetic to ground.

Indeed, had he been doing what he'd said, it would have been the perfect place.

"I need a change of scenery," he lied. "I want to walk a bit and think about the orichalcum and how it plays a part in my research."

"Do you think it will help you get better?" Cassidy asked. "The orichalcum? Could it heal you?"

"I don't know," he said. He turned the idea over in his head, considering. He did think that it would heal him, yes, but not in the way she thought. But perhaps there was merit in what she said. His bones ached, and the weight of centuries pressed down on him. He was wondering if his and Imogen's plan was truly one that would work. Perhaps there was another way to give the energetics power.

He was tired. It was tempting to just let this fight go, heal, and live out his life with Cassidy as his companion.

Pain wracked his body and he jerked without meaning to. His eyes closed for a moment while his muscles stiffened against the torment.

No. He was too close to his objective. Too close to putting the world to rights. And in this moment, what he needed was energy.

"I'll be back later. Have a good day, won't you."

She nodded, smoothed a hand over his hair that was already neat, and stepped back to let him pass.

He left the house, and went out to hunt.

19

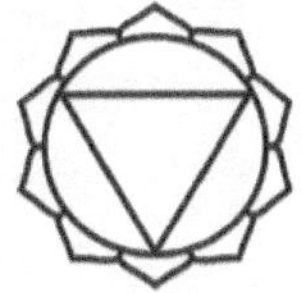

Cara decided she would take Archer for a walk. Show him a tiny fraction of the beautiful, if austere island, while she told him about the prophecy.

It wasn't at all because it gave her an excuse to wear a long-sleeved sweater that covered the strange piece of jewelry on her arm.

He also wore a sweater, olive cashmere that looked soft to the touch, with a casual button-down shirt underneath, a slim-cut racer jacket over the top, cargo pants and a black scarf. She suspected he'd have a t-shirt underneath it all however. She hadn't known him to be without some retro gaming symbol or saying on him as yet, though it had taken Ai to explain them.

The first few minutes they walked in silence along the winding stone path that led to the outside world. She nodded at the energetic at the gate that provided the last phase of security as she and Archer passed through it.

She didn't like to think of the Center as a prison in the way that humans had prisons. It was important to her that rehabilitation was the focus of the more dangerous guests—whether dangerous to themselves or others. It was true that sometimes there were those whose rehabilitation took a long time, or perhaps, might never be ready for release, but she never gave up on them.

Either way, security was important. Keeping the right people inside, keeping the wrong people out. What they did here was not for human knowledge. They had connections with some humans who delivered goods, or provided contracting services, but those humans thought the Center was some kind of elite addiction counseling center, and they accepted how remote the facility was because of that belief.

Vancouver Island was the size of Massachusetts, but its population was only ten percent of that state's, so it was the perfect location for an energetics facility. The nature that blanketed the island was perfect for her people to connect with their elements—it had a mountain range, plenty of coastline, fresh air, and a variety of flora and fauna.

Cara loved it.

They walked, but Archer stayed silent, which was unlike him. He hadn't even asked his questions today. She glanced at him. To her eyes, Archer was a lot better. Was he ready to go home? He was still walking with some tension in his gait. But he was improving. She opened her Anahata to get a sense of his feelings.

Pain, yes. But also a kind of excitement. Anticipation, perhaps? Did he think she was ready to let him leave?

She bit her lip. She shouldn't put it off any longer.

"I'm going to share with you information you'll have to keep confidential," she said.

He seemed to be fighting back a cheerful grin. "No problem."

She frowned. "This is serious stuff, Archer."

"Yes. Sorry."

She sighed. "Alright. A dear friend of mine, Cuinn, a very strong Ajna-Muladhara energetic, has been having prophetic dreams for a while. They involve a group of people defending our race against a dark evil. They also involve that group being paired up, male and female. So far they have been romantic couples."

She could hope, couldn't she, that it might not be like that for her.

He had stopped and was gaping at her. This clearly wasn't what he had expected.

"I'm one of the people who's been identified as part of the group."

"Wow," Archer said. "That's incredible. How can I help?"

"Archer!" She put a hand on his arm. "This is life or death stuff. People have died."

He stilled. "I'm sorry. Did you lose someone?"

"What? No." She was touched by his empathy. Again, she had underestimated him. "This doesn't frighten you?"

He stopped in his tracks and grabbed her wrist, his words coming urgently. "I have been searching for a chance my whole life to be something greater than what I am. To be like the energetics of Atlantis, with their powers, balancing the evils of the world with their actions. Fighting the good fight. Standing up for justice and truth. I will do whatever you need to help you do that."

She leaned back a little at the passion in his words. Not that they couldn't use his help, but this wasn't an adventure. Wasn't a story from one of his treasure hunting scuba trips. This was real. Horribly, terribly real. She sensed he meant well, but he might need a wake-up call.

"Thank you." She hesitated. The next bit she was uncomfortable thinking about, let alone sharing with another person. "Each of the energetics that was paired up, found a mysterious bracelet on their wrist."

His hand clenched for a second on her arm, then he lifted it up, and drew the cashmere back to reveal her new adornment.

She flushed. "There have been six energetics so far, three couples. None of the bracelets have looked like this. We don't know what it means."

Archer was looking at her. She couldn't interpret his expression.

"So mine may well not be connected to a romantic partner," she said. Her eyes slid to his bare wrists, and back to hers.

Something loosened in his posture. "It's real, isn't it? It's not a fake. The bracelet is true orichalcum, the rarest of elements. Few people have ever even seen orichalcum, let alone wear it every day. What you're wearing could be worth millions."

She swallowed. "We think so."

"I think I may be able to find out what your bracelet is. I've got something being delivered today that will help."

Her eyes narrowed. "What do you have coming? Did you tell anyone about the bracelet?"

"No, no." He rushed to reassure her. "I'll show you when it comes. It's under control."

She liked the pleasure and joy that he was exuding.

Should she tell him they thought he might be involved in the prophecy? That there was a possibility a bracelet might appear on his wrist?

Something twisted in her chest. No. Now wasn't the time. She'd hit him with enough information. She would give him a bit more background to the prophecies and what had happened with the first three couples, and then she'd let him be.

"Blaize was stalked and kidnapped by Indigo, who we later found out was working with Elrian." She hesitated. "Elrian is Cuinn's father."

Archer's mouth dropped open.

Cara shrugged. "They're estranged."

"Clearly," Archer muttered.

Cara spread her hands. "Blaize returned home safe. Indigo was killed, and Tierra, who has tracking as one of her Muladhara abilities, helped Fintan to trace her steps back to Vancouver, where they ran into Ai, who had had a narrow escape herself from Indigo, and was able to point them to a house she'd been living in."

"Poor kid," Archer said.

"Yes." Cara breathed in deep. "They found a drained body, a girl called Aimée Fortin, an energetic who had been attending a nearby University and had been abducted, and traces of another energetic. We later found out that Elrian was the other energetic, when he took Ai hostage, and offered her back as a swap for Blaize and Tierra."

Archer's eyebrows were practically at his hairline now.

"Tierra was captured in the fight, and Elrian disappeared. She made it back to us on her own, thankfully. It hit her hard, however."

"Of course," Archer murmured.

"By then, Blaize and Cuinn had joined, as well as Fintan and Tierra. But our understanding of the situation was still limited. Blaize took Tierra and Ai to where she grew up in Thailand, where Nixie and her family live, for some rest. Tierra got very sick, which is how Jeb, with all his healing expertise got involved." Cara's lips curved. "As I understand it, Nixie wanted to be involved even less than me. But Elrian had found a way to drain Tierra remotely, and to affect Jeb's control over his energy. It took time to fix it, and in the meantime Nixie tried to sacrifice herself to Elrian to save them. Jeb managed to get there before she was killed, and I think that might have been the clincher for Jeb and Nixie joining together."

She glanced at Archer. "But Elrian escaped. And you're up to date!"

They'd walked right to the sea, the salty air licking at them. She wrapped her arms around herself and stared out at the horizon while he absorbed it all.

The joy had settled, and he was more serious. "This is big, isn't it?"

She nodded.

"Big as in the future of our race, somehow. And we know little about how to stop it, what's going to happen, or even who's involved," he said.

She gave another nod, then scooped up a couple of spherical stones from the ground, rolling them in her hand. They clicked together with a pleasant soothing sound.

He stood for a moment, examining her, his lips pressed together. Dammit, what was the man thinking now?

"I think it's time for you to let me go home," he said, gently but firmly.

She opened her mouth to deny him, then realized he was no longer asking.

"Let me examine you, and then I'll decide. I'll check you over with Anahata energy, and then we'll run some blood work and other tests. If they're satisfactory, you can go. As long as you don't overdo it."

"Okay," he said.

"Even if we release you, it doesn't mean you're one hundred percent," she persisted. "You'll need to take it easy. Consider working from home."

"No problem," he said.

It would be a relief to have him out of her hair, she reasoned. This strange feeling wasn't loss, it was irritation that he was choosing now to be rational, finally, after causing her so much trouble.

Gah.

He was a distraction, and Source knew she didn't need that. She pushed aside the anxiety about the Anahata delegation for another time.

Ai needed more of her attention too. She hadn't been there enough for her, the Kayla incident showed that.

"You could scan me energetically now," Archer suggested. "There's plenty of air up here."

He took in a deep breath. "It smells amazing after being inside for so long."

"I love it here," she confessed. She studied him. "I should really wait till we're inside."

"Why?" he asked. "We're energetics. Nature is our domain. We function best in our element."

She couldn't disagree. She felt less tired than she had in days.

"We should sit down," she said. "Just in case."

They walked over to a mound of grass, and he took off his jacket and laid it down for them to sit on. She was reluctant to sit on the damp ground, but it put them in close proximity. She reminded herself that as a healer she had no issue with getting up close and personal with people. It wasn't, in fact, personal. And she needed to lay hands on him to check him.

She put the stones she'd been holding on the grass next to her.

He sat cross-legged, expectant.

She grounded herself, took a breath, and put her hands on his face.

His skin was warm under her palms, his stubble grazing her.

She drew on her energy, and sent it, seeking, inside him.

She threaded it through his system, checking the places that had been injured, like his gut, and humming with satisfaction as she saw the healthy tissues growing anew.

He was still beneath her touch, but she was irritated to find his presence was as infuriatingly *there* as ever. The man was just unable to fade into the background.

Her fingers increased their pressure a fraction as she realized she was picking up some emotional traces as well as physical ones. Guiltily, she went to withdraw, as it wasn't what she'd set out to do, but couldn't help but catch the echoes of some of his feelings— interest, fascination, eagerness, determination.

She pulled her energy out of him, and dropped her hands from his face. She'd better confess.

"I caught some of your emotions. My apologies. I'm more tired than I thought." She tried not to make it too big a deal. And it wasn't like she wasn't already aware he loved the history of their race. "You're really jazzed about the bracelet."

He contemplated her for a moment longer than felt comfortable, and ran a hand through his messy hair. "Sure. The bracelet."

They walked back to his room for the medical examination, both lost in their own thoughts. She found herself wondering, for a few indulgent moments, what it would have been like to have a bracelet like the others, with him having the twin. He'd probably drive her crazy, she thought, wistfully. She'd never have a moment's peace.

He grabbed her hand and squeezed it, and grinned that boyish, annoyingly charming grin he had. He let go before she had the chance to scold him.

"Don't worry," he said. "I'm on the team now. It's gonna be fine."

She rolled her eyes, yet even as she did, something inside her settled.

Maybe, just maybe, she believed him.

Archer couldn't believe that he finally had a chance to be a part of something meaningful. Cara had approved his discharge, but unexpectedly to them both, with no more restraints on what he could do with his time, he'd decided to stay a bit longer—bringing some of his tools to him. After all, the bas relief that he'd bargained for had already been on the way when she'd told him.

Early the next morning he got the call the chopper was arriving, and he ran outside, searching the sky. He heard it before he saw it, the low chop-chop of its rotors humming. Source, it was loud in the quiet of the island. He was used to helicopter noise, but somehow in the city it differed from this tranquil oasis.

He glanced around. He'd wanted the bas relief to be a surprise for Cara. The landing pad was clear of people or vehicles. There didn't appear to be any security around the concrete helipad, which was marked with the usual 'H'.

He stood well back, and waited. As it got close, hovering over the Rehab Center, he clamped his hands over his ears.

A yell got through the noise of the blades and he startled, turning behind him to see Cara running toward him, with three energetics behind her. He could see flickers of orange. Was she holding a shield while running? He squinted. In fact, she was holding a shield around all four energetics.

She screamed something at him, beckoning him wildly toward her, while the four of them stopped and arranged themselves in some sort of formation.

It dawned on Archer what was happening. *Oh, shit.*

He sprinted toward her, waving his hands.

The chopper was still hovering, but any minute it would begin to descend.

And she would blow it to bits.

"They're friendly!" he yelled as loudly as he could, his heart pounding. "Friendly! I know them! It's okay!"

Cara put a hand out, palm flat and facing the ground, and the three energetics with her all waited. Were they all pulling energy, ready to blast the chopper out of the sky? Shit.

He reached them, gasping, and stopped short of where he thought her shield was likely to be. "I know them, it's okay, they're not hostile, let them land."

"What the fuck are you doing?" Cara hissed at him. He wasn't sure he'd ever seen her so angry. "Why the hell didn't you tell anyone?"

He didn't really have a good answer. He'd told himself it was because he wanted it to be a surprise, but perhaps he was accustomed to doing whatever he wanted. He hadn't considered that they might think it was an attack.

The copter was still hovering. Cara gestured to one of the energetics with her, who spoke into a radio. "Tell them they can land."

"I'm sorry," Archer said, projecting his voice over the rotors. "I didn't think."

"There are procedures for getting approval for aircraft to land here. You don't get to go around those procedures. This place is heavily warded. We could have blown them out of the sky by accident." She had to shout over the noise. She'd dropped the shield, but hadn't told her team to stand down. Her gaze was on the helicopter as it landed.

They stood in silence, waiting for the chopper to still and disgorge its passengers and cargo.

Several people got out, and he realized something else that he needed to tell her, and fast. "Some of them are human."

She glared at him, then threw up her hands. There was a flash of orange, and he felt a pop as she dropped her shield. She jerked her head at the others, and they relaxed into postures that while alert, didn't look overtly hostile.

"Who are they?" she demanded as they watched a handful of people get out of the helicopter. One strode toward them while the others appeared to be getting a crate out of the cargo.

"Ah, it's materials to help with the—" he glanced at her colleagues "—puzzle we were talking about."

She narrowed her eyes. "Materials? What materials?"

"Art materials," he said. "Look, give me a bit of time to get it set up in my room, and I'll tell you all about it. Please?"

At her narrowed eyes, he tried to remind himself that he wasn't a naughty schoolboy but a man who ran a multinational company.

Her lips formed a thin line, and she gave him a reluctant nod as she walked away.

"I'll be in your room in two hours," she said, over her shoulder. "And Archer? This better be worth it."

Two hours later, Cara stood in his doorway, arms folded. She wasn't sure exactly what she was seeing. Artifacts and books were positioned in Archer's room, having been brought in by a team who had handled the art as delicately as if it were a sick patient. She groaned at the lack of sterilization. Source knew what germs they'd brought in. He was lucky she'd declared him healthy enough to leave, so she didn't need to worry about that, at least. Idly she waved a hand to activate the magics embedded into the room that would cleanse the room of pathogens.

Why was he still here?

He sat on the couch, a book to each side and one on his lap, frowning down at them, and occasionally picking one up to compare a drawing in one to a picture in another. This was the geek side of him, with a complete focus and drive on what he was doing. She could see why he'd tended to burn out if he put this level of intensity into everything he did.

She shook her head, and the movement caught his eye. He looked up and smiled hesitantly.

Yeah, he should be hesitant, she thought. "What is going on? I thought you were having more books delivered. Why are there bits of rock in my hospital?"

He stood up, the books falling to each side of him, and he scooped them up, muttering.

She stepped into the room. "Mr. Hampton, I'm sure you remember that as General Manager my magics are bound up with the Center. I'm the energetic cornerstone for the Source-blessed land the Healing Center is built on. I have the power to blast that 'copter out of the sky. This Center has wards, defences, you name it. You cannot bring in an outside air unit like that without telling us. We were a hairsbreadth away from someone activating the alarm, and all hell breaking loose."

He winced at the use of 'Mr.' "I did mention…"

She glared at him and he trailed off.

"Okay, okay, I'm sorry. I should have said it would be delivered by helicopter rather than courier. But I'd remembered a piece I'd seen that had the same symbol as your bracelet, and I wanted to bring it to you," he said, and gestured excitedly to a fragment of ancient looking-stone.

She blinked. "You…what?"

"The person who owns the piece agreed to lend it to me. Well, swap it for something else in my collection and a donation, but same same," he said.

"Archer, how old is that bit of stone?" she asked, slowly.

"Unclear, but several thousands of years, we think. More, probably. It's resistant to regular testing methods."

"It's worth some money then?" she asked.

His forehead wrinkled. "Sure. It's an item energetics don't want in the mainstream art market, which affects the value, but my friend paid about six hundred and fifty thousand dollars for it."

Cara gaped. "Shouldn't it be in a case or something?"

Feelings clashed inside her. On the one hand, the idea that they could move the prophecy forward through knowledge was powerful, but on the other hand, the casual privilege—even for an energetic— that Archer was displaying by getting that priceless artifact to the island by helicopter from Source knew where in less than twenty-four hours was mind-blowing. Money wasn't an issue for her, as with most energetics who'd been around more than a hundred years, but she hadn't amassed it like Archer clearly had.

"We wear gloves to touch it, yes, but the benefit of this being a hospital environment is that there's limited dust here."

Cara went over to the couch, sinking down, suddenly boneless. A book poked her ass and she shifted it aside, creating space for herself. She rubbed her forehead. She couldn't decide if she was pleased or angry or pissed or concerned. Or all of them.

Archer came over and perched on the arm of the sofa next to her. He tipped his head and studied her. "Come over to the artifact and we can look at the bracelet next to it. And if you don't mind, I'd love to take a photo of the bracelet so I can research while you're working."

She covered her wrist with her other hand protectively. She'd been busy that morning, keeping thoughts of the jewelry suppressed. Did she really want to understand it better?

She squeezed her wrist. She'd never shied away from difficult things before, she would not start now. She lifted her hand, and he grinned and stood, catching her arm and almost dragging her to the stone.

"Don't touch it, but let's put them next to each other and take a look," he said. He was almost bouncing. "Your bracelet seems so different from your description of the others, it must mean something."

She lifted her arm, keeping it a good foot away from the piece of rock. She examined the two pieces.

They knew her bracelet was made of orichalcum, an almost unheard of metal in the modern age, but something that was intricately linked to the energetics. It was magical in a way they didn't always understand.

The stone that Archer had brought to the Center was fascinating. Around five feet tall, shaped like a column it was decorated with obscure symbols.

"Where was this found?" she asked.

"In the Ionian sea," he said.

She raised her eyebrows. "Atlantis hunters?"

"Yes," he said.

She was surprised. "You buy into that? That we'll find it one day?"

"Of course," he said. "And when we do, we'll work out what happened to our ancestors."

"Seems to me we should leave well enough alone," she said. "A world-changing event like that, the destruction of most of a people and their culture, is something we'd do well to avoid."

She shuffled another pace away from the object, her mouth turned down in an unhappy moue.

He caught her hand. "No, it's the opposite. Knowledge isn't something to be feared. The more we know, the more we can avoid the same issues reoccurring."

She sighed. She didn't have the stamina for that argument, one that raged between energetics at the end of many a late night. "Alright, show me."

He dragged her wrist a bit closer and moved them to a different side of the artifact. Her breath caught in her throat.

Metal shimmered in the rock, metal that had somehow avoided the corrosion of the rest of the stone. The same circular symbol was marked out in the metal. This one looked much more like the Ouroboros, definitely a snake, rather than a dragon.

There was a flicker of green, and her bracelet sparked, like a low level electric shock. She jumped.

"What is it?" he asked, concern lacing his voice.

She frowned, and gazed down at her wrist. "Just static, I think. Okay, I'm convinced. Take your photos of the bracelet and find out what you can."

She hesitated. "And thank you."

Simply because he had money didn't mean he needed to spend it. They were in a life or death situation and she couldn't afford to turn down help because of pride. She wasn't alone in this. It affected her friends, too. She wouldn't risk them.

"I can give you what I know already," he said. "Seeing the two together confirms a few things for me."

She walked away from the object, and perched on the bed. "Okay."

"I think the bracelet is a sort of key." He paced. She scanned his body with a professional eye. He was moving fluidly, his rangy frame eating up the few meters in the room as he paced back and forth. "If we put it in the right place, it will act to unlock the site it's placed in."

"What place, and what site?" She wasn't loving this. It would be fine if she could take the damn thing off and hand it over, they could use the thing as a key wherever they liked, but the fact she'd have to be attached to it while they unlocked Source-knew-what wasn't sitting easily with her.

He glanced sideways at her. "We're not sure. It's connected to Source in some way, and there's likely more than one thing it unlocks. Think of it as a key to a magical machine."

She groaned. "That doesn't sound great. And where do you think this thing it unlocks is?"

He hesitated. "The site's underwater."

Cara stared at him. "I can't just up and leave the clinic on a jaunt. I have a job, responsibilities."

He came over and sat beside her. She rubbed her temples. He placed a hand on her forearm, away from the bracelet and squeezed gently. "I know it's a lot. But we can't get the bracelet off you as far as I understand. And I can get us there and back over the weekend. I have a private jet ready if we helicopter over to the mainland, and I already had a team set up for another diving trip who I've diverted to the area. We can join them there. I have thousands of hours of diving logged, you'll be quite safe with me and my team."

"Where is it?" she asked. Her head hurt. "I haven't dived for years. Archer, this is ridiculous. I can't just disappear."

"A long weekend, that's all. When have you allowed yourself more than a long lunch? You need to give yourself time to recharge," he ended, piously.

She let out a short laugh. "Where is it? Really?"

He cracked his knuckles and mumbled, "The Mediterranean sea."

She groaned. "You're barely recovered. What about your health?"

"Not only will I have you as my private physician, but the sea air will do me good." He grinned that boyish grin again, and something inside her responded, softening, then immediately tensed again. She needed to be firm.

"I have a Center to run. I have responsibilities," she said, standing. "We need to find another way to understand the bracelet."

His shoulders slumped.

"I need to go back to work. Let me know what else you find out, that doesn't involve weekend holidays to Europe."

She nodded and left the room. She wasn't going to think about him, or his crazy idea for the rest of the day.

She had enough on her plate.

20

Two days later, Cara, Ai and Archer boarded his private plane at Vancouver airport.

Archer was thrilled not only to be leaving the island behind, but to have a good reason to dive again.

"I can't believe this is happening," Cara muttered as they settled into the plush seats on the Cessna Citation business jet. "Adam really screwed me over."

"He was right to make you come. It's not like we can take the bracelet off your wrist. We'll be back at the Center by Monday, and it's in excellent hands," Archer said. "You have a great team. The Center runs like a well-oiled machine."

It was true. Once he'd got past their bickering, he'd been impressed at how she ran the place, blending the best of human and energetic medicine with modern management techniques. Her team adored her and were loyal to a fault.

He'd seen photos of all the bracelets now, and it was true hers was very different. The only commonality was that it had the color of

Anahata in a certain light, as orichalcum was a greenish metal. But there were no other colors plaited in like the other bracelets. He rolled a shoulder. The idea that she might be destined by prophecy for another man wasn't one he loved. He'd be quite fine if her bracelet meant something different. He hadn't asked her on a date for a while, but it wasn't something he'd forgotten. He was simply biding his time.

He wasn't entirely sure how Ai had ended up joining them, but she was almost bursting with excitement. She wiggled in her seat, her usual sulky teen demeanor gone.

"I can't believe we're going to Europe!" she said. They'd had to use Vishudha Guild to get her a passport at such short notice. "So, energetics really come from Atlantis? Where is it? I thought it was a myth."

"The myth has been meticulously cultivated for humans," Archer said. "We don't want them finding it before we do."

"Why did it disappear?"

"We don't know. All we know is that around ten thousand years ago something happened to the island, and it sank beneath the sea. Some energetics escaped, as well as those who'd been traveling at the time. But all the Guilds were on the island, so most of the leadership of our people disappeared. Those who were left rebuilt our civilization starting from Egypt, which is why Anahata Guild is there. The only Guild Leader who escaped was from Anahata, so they became the de facto leaders for a while until the other Guilds sorted themselves out," Archer said. He loved this stuff. He'd get lost for hours in the various private collections of books on the topic, as well as any Guild library that would let him in.

But it was the practical side of the research he adored. Diving, exploring, discovering artifacts. He worked with two teams, one for land explorations, and one for diving excursions, going after the relics of energetics' past. He'd amassed a comprehensive collection of both physical objects and knowledge.

Cara was paying as much attention as Ai, though she was still trying to pretend she didn't want to be here.

He spread out several documents on the small table between them. "Okay, gang. I have an idea of where we're going, but I'd like your opinions."

Cara's chin came up. He thought engaging her competitive spirit might help. He pointed to a photo. "Here's the detail on the bas relief I got access to, the one with the symbol that echoes Cara's bracelet."

He spread out several photocopied pages from energetic books, covered in his own notations. "The bas relief pointed me toward the right texts, and the point where we need to dive. We're going to use triangulation. The texts suggest we need to find two relevant features. The first is referenced as 'the dolphin on the snake'. The second is an old lighthouse. We can use both to triangulate to the dive site, which is where one of the temples of Atlantis was. It's not clear to me if it's a temple that was on the mainland of Atlantis or an islet that they used for other things, like a waystation, but either way, if we can find it, it would be a pretty big discovery."

Discovering Atlantis would be incredible. So it almost certainly wasn't that, but finding one of the solitary temples the energetics had built either contemporaneously or at a later date during their diaspora would be a huge find.

"But how does my bracelet fit in with this?" Cara asked.

"We've been looking at the bas relief as if it was a post or column, but actually it looks like more of a lintel." He turned the page and put it next to the photo of the piece of stone so she could see. "I'm more and more thinking it was part of some kind of machinery."

The next thing he was going to say sounded a bit crazy, but he had a hunch. A really big one. "I think they wrote the manual for the machine on the machine itself."

Cara cocked her head. "A machine? Wouldn't there be metal? What kind of machine? What is it for?"

She had him there. "I don't know."

She huffed. "This is a wild goose chase."

He grinned. He was on one of his planes with a woman he found very attractive, and a teenager he'd thought of as a friend, heading to explore a possible Atlantean site. There wasn't much she could do to bring his mood down. "Either way, I can provide you with a very luxurious pursuit. Champagne?"

She rolled her eyes, but he caught the faint smile. Yep. Definitely softening.

They slept on the plane, arriving many hours and two refueling stops later at Greece's Corfu international airport. There they took an SUV across the island to the harbor where his dive boat was moored. Conditions were forecast to be fair.

Their first task was finding the right place to dive, however. He thought he'd got a lock on it from the indicators on the machine, but he wasn't sure.

They piled out of the SUV at the Marina, and Cara stretched. Archer admired the lean lines of her body, and the way her hair fell about her face as she rolled her neck to get the cricks out.

It took them a while to walk between the still and silent boats, till they finally reached the floating pier to find The Adventure, his 34-meter motor yacht. He enjoyed the gentle movement of the wooden slats they stood on as the water rose and fell beneath them, and the warmth of the air as compared to the coolness of Vancouver they'd left behind.

"Hey boss," a voice called out.

Archer grinned. "Nahla."

The voice was attached to a lean black woman who wore loose shorts and a vest top. He strode over, jumped onto the boat, and hugged her.

"We thought you'd deserted us," Nahla said. "It's been almost a year since we joined you for your last crazy adventure."

"It's good to be back." He checked behind him. Ai and Cara were getting on the boat, Cara keeping a careful eye on the teen. His driver stowed the luggage in the cabins below, before waving and leaving them to it. "Thanks for being flexible, and coming to pick us up."

When Archer wasn't on *The Adventure*, Nahla and the crew continued using it to research and dive potential energetics sites, and luckily they'd been close enough to come and pick Archer up.

Archer luxuriated in the feel of the sea breeze. This was a place he felt truly free, work responsibilities paused, if only for a few days.

They were ready.

"Anchors aweigh," he called, and they set off to find another mystery of his people's past.

Cara was still uncertain how she had found herself in the middle of the Ionian sea with Archer, six thousand miles away from her beloved Center.

She might as well enjoy it, now she was here. She'd called Osana while she still had cell phone coverage and checked in, and all was fine.

Setting her shoulders, she took a breath of the beautiful sea air. She loved the coastal area around Vancouver Island, but she could appreciate the beauty of this very different sea. The weather was sunny and warm, there was a delightful breeze, and she was free of people asking her to solve problems. Her blue strappy sundress danced around her thighs.

She gazed at Archer, who was talking to Nahla, the boat's captain, a fit-looking woman with her hair in cornrows, and skin that reminded her of the blue-black depths of the sea. Her capable looking hands were busy with ropes, and there were laugh lines around her eyes.

Cara wasn't sure she really got Archer. He was an incorrigible flirt, a man who somehow was both a geek and charmed everyone around him. At the same time, he was a CEO of a tech company that served both humans and energetics, had money to burn, and was used to getting his own way in everything. She hadn't quite reconciled his seemingly contradictory aspects.

He strode to her, a spring in his step. He had on board shorts and a t-shirt—it said simply 'Levelled Up'—which he stripped off as he walked, dropping it on a bench. Did he seem lighter here? Happier?

"I could do with some sun," he said.

She examined his torso, looking at the scar across his abdomen with a professional eye.

"Like what you see?" he smirked.

She raised her eyes to the heavens and leaned in closer to his injury, prodding it gently.

He put his hands on his hips.

While she would admit this only to herself, she did like what she saw. His runner's body appealed to her. It was the kind of physique that was taken care of for practical reasons, rather than for show. She appreciated that. She wasn't a huge fan of exercise, but she kept herself in reasonable shape through her Warrior training, which she'd kept up since her Manipura Guild days. Mind you, during weeks like the last couple it was harder to fit into her schedule. Each Chakra had its own combat skills, so sometimes she trained alone, sometimes with others in the Center, practicing what she had learned decades before.

She liked his lean hardness, the subtle muscle of his arms. His lightly tanned skin fit in well with the Mediterranean, and with his brown eyes he could easily be from the area. He had an American accent, but that meant little with energetics, especially Vishudhas, who picked up languages, accents, and anything to do with voices more easily than most.

"Where did you grow up?" she asked. It came out of her mouth before she could stop it.

His eyebrows rose, but he answered readily enough. "California. On the coast. With a group of energetics who lived together in a quiet part of the state."

He sighed. "I've always loved the sea."

He did seem lighter. And she could feel it affecting her, too. She drew in the sea mist that flowed around her, regenerating her, as the yacht cut through the gentle waves. Her lungs expanded, and with an exhale, she let go a little more.

Maybe she didn't have to retain the professional distance she'd kept so far. She'd discharged him, and he officially wasn't her patient anymore. She could see him like a male, rather than someone she was treating.

She tapped a finger on her lower lip. Maybe she could consider herself on vacation. Indulge herself a little.

That bracelet wasn't going to run her life. She had choices. She had control.

She decided who she dated.

"Do you have a question for me today? Something to experiment with while we're on this little vacation?"

He frowned for a moment, then his expression cleared and his eyes widened.

"I might, at that," he murmured. "Lovely Cara, would you like to go on a date with me?"

She drew in a deep breath, and jumped. "Why, yes, Archer, I would. Where would you like to take me?"

A slow smile spread across his face. "I'm thinking the sea. A little adventure. Some swimming, perhaps."

"That sounds nice," she said. She stepped in closer to him and placed a hand on his biceps. It was defined, but not obnoxiously so. She thought she felt a reaction, but this still felt like she was stepping into the unknown.

The boat trip gave her the opportunity to contain any experience she might seek with Archer, to have a definite start and a definite end. She could enjoy this adventure and then go back to real life.

She heard footsteps, and retreated, finding herself smiling.

"So where are we going?" Ai questioned.

Archer, a delighted grin on his face, leaned back on the boat's rail and replied. "We're heading northwest, to the general location. We need to start by finding the lighthouse and the dolphin."

"Will you dive? Can I?" Ai said.

"We will, once we find the location, as it's likely to be underwater. We don't have time to teach you this time, but I can in the future, if you like. I'm a certified instructor."

Ai nodded, eyes wide. She was adapting to their world well, all in all. She'd certainly been thrown into the deep end. But it seemed like the skills Ai had learned to manage the foster care system, and then the danger of the streets, were serving her well. She was riding the rollercoaster they'd put her on with a levelheadedness that surprised

Cara. That was in part why she'd brought her along. Plus, Cara hadn't wanted to leave her with Kayla. For some reason the other girl was a temptation to Ai that was better left alone.

"If you want to understand more about how the boat works, you can ask Nahla. She's always happy to talk about her work," Archer said.

Ai nodded eagerly, and wandered off toward the captain. Ai seemed entranced by the whole experience. Cara reminded herself that they should do some energy practice later.

"Do you do this a lot?" Cara asked Archer, leaning next to him on the rail, but facing out toward the sea. Her hair whipped around her face, but she didn't care about the knots it would be in later. She was enjoying the wind, the briny atmosphere that was nourishing her Anahata energy in a way she hadn't experienced in a while. She relaxed her shoulders and tipped her head up, feeling the sun and breeze on her face as the boat cut through the water. It would be a good place for Ai to touch her Anahata.

He shrugged a shoulder. "When I can. It's difficult, being away from the business. I don't like to leave Phoebe up shit creek."

Cara frowned. "She seems to be good at her job, and managing okay. Not like she'd begrudge you a holiday now and then, if you do the same for her."

"Neither of us is great at taking time off," he admitted. "You're right, she loves her job."

She cocked her head. "And you don't?"

"It's okay."

Her frown deepened. "I don't get it. You seem obsessed with work."

He looked away. "It's important to me."

"But you don't enjoy it?" she persisted.

He turned so he was looking out at the ocean. He sighed. "Not really."

She put a hand over his on the guard rail. He'd deflated some from the energy and excitement he'd had when they'd been discussing the diving trip.

"Why do you do it then?" She asked, interested. She couldn't quite reconcile the energy and commitment he put into his job if he didn't feel passionate about it. Dedicated to her Healing Center, it took most of her energy, but she loved her work.

"It was fun at first. When Phoebe and I started, we were both studying at the Vishudha Major Guild, exploring communications and communications tech. We wanted to experiment with creating something that had usability built in from both a human and an energetic perspective. It was a research project." He turned his hand over and squeezed hers. She squeezed back, enjoying his warmth. "It got out of hand."

She raised her eyebrows. "You made a multi-billion dollar company because your research project 'got out of hand'?"

"Kinda," he said. "And I wanted to show them what I could do."

"Show who?"

He ran his free hand over his head and rubbed his nape.

"My parents. My older sister. The energetics I grew up with."

"Why?"

He tried to let go of her hand, but she held it tight.

"I grew up in a community of energetics who were mostly 150 to 200 years older than me. My sister, Estella, is fifty years older, and is quite a well-known academic." He shrugged. "She cast a long shadow. She did some pioneering work with Vishudha and physics and everyone in my community thought she was amazing. But she's not great with people."

Cara wrinkled her nose. "Doesn't sound great."

"I mean, she's not a bad person. She's just not exactly…emotionally intelligent. She's a forceful personality."

"What does she think of your business?"

His shoulders slumped. "She's an academic purist. She thinks I sold out."

Ugh, Cara thought, and shuffled along the guardrail so the line of her body pressed against his.

"My parents are proud, I think," he said.

Alright. That was a complicated personal history.

"Thanks for sharing," she said. "It sounds like a tough childhood."

"I never wanted for anything, and my parents and sister love me. They left me alone when I was a kid, and I was always treated as an adult, even when I was a child. The company I kept was all adults. It helped me grow up quickly," he said. Was he trying to convince himself? "But sometimes, I was lonely."

"You can love someone and still mess them up," she said. She freed her hand and wrapped her arm around him. He made a surprised noise but let her burrow into his side, leaning into her in turn.

"What about your family?" he asked.

"No great drama," she said. "They're still around, living their lives."

"Where are they? Do you see them much?"

"Not too often. They run a Healing Center in France. They're very committed to it. Plus, I've been around a while longer than you. As you live longer, you're more comfortable going for longer periods without seeing people and being okay. The fear of running out of time that haunts humans is less for us, I think."

That was mostly true. Her parents were kind and wise, but they tended to give all their energies to saving everyone else. They'd judged their only daughter fit to release into the world once she'd gone to study at Anahata Major Guild, and they had never seemed to worry about her since.

She didn't mind. Self-sufficient, her work kept her busy. She had Tierra and her family as close friends. They'd met when Tierra and Cuinn had moved to the town of Merrow in BC after Cuinn's falling out with his father. With few other energetics in the area, they'd visited the Healing Center looking for company, and the rest was history.

She knew many other energetics if she needed to be social, or when she was in the mood for dating, though the last wasn't often these days. Not since…hmm. She frowned. She couldn't actually remember.

"You okay?" he asked.

"Sure. I was just thinking it's been a while since I dated."

He raised his eyebrows and gave her a squeeze. "Oh really? I hope you haven't forgotten how."

Already pressed up against him, she turned the rest of her body toward him, and trailed a hand up and down his back. The heart Chakra loved touch, it was part of how they healed, and how they communicated. But she didn't remember the last time she'd let herself luxuriate in it this way with a man.

He gazed down at her, uncertain.

She tilted her face up, so he could feel her breath on his skin. "I don't think so. Perhaps you could check for me?"

She waited, and after several long seconds, where she wondered if she'd misjudged, he brought his lips to hers, and kissed her.

The kiss was long and lingering, the pressure light as a feather. She shut her eyes and shivered. She let a little of her air energy out to play, to sweep around them, ruffling his hair and dancing along his skin in places where her hands couldn't reach.

He stifled a surprised noise and she laughed.

Maybe this would be a good weekend after all.

21

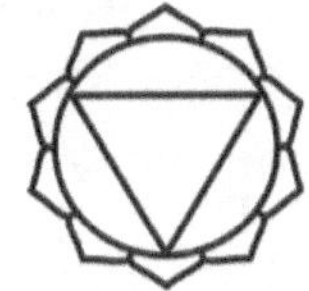

The small crew of the boat was alert and looking out for signs of the landmarks that Archer had identified. The first had been easy enough. Their research on the islands in the area had turned up the fact that the small island of Othoni was also known as 'Fidonsi'—Snake Island.

They'd spent several hours sailing around it, contemplating where and what a dolphin on the island might be. Finally they'd docked and Archer had decided they'd sleep and be up early in the morning ready to find it. He'd invited Cara to a late dinner in his cabin. His body hummed with excitement about her entering his space, and about them spending time alone.

His stateroom comprised three separate areas. A small bedroom where a large bed took up much of the room, his sheets a dark royal blue. Attached to that was a tiny head, including a shower and a sink, and finally, a space that he used as a living area and an office. He flicked on the stereo, picking Miles Davis's "Kind of Blue".

Cara raised her eyebrows when she saw the room. "You've been busy."

She wasn't wrong. He was ready to wine and dine Cara and give her the best at-sea date she'd ever had. He was thrilled to see she'd shown up in a cute white dress, covered in blue flowers, cut tight to the bodice with a neckline that was deeper than usual. He hoped it was a positive sign.

The kiss she'd given him earlier had been a surprise, but not an unwelcome one. He'd seen her warming to him, and he knew there was something that could be explored between them, but he wasn't sure she was ready, and he wasn't going to push, other than letting her know he was keen.

The kiss indicated she might be ready for more. But he would see how things unfolded, and his priority was building their out-of-bed relationship.

They sat down at the table, where their meal waited. It was the same as the others would eat in the mess, but he'd wanted privacy. Ai was eating with the crew, peppering them with questions, he had no doubt. The food they ate on the boat was high quality, he made sure of that, but not complicated. One member of the crew was ship's cook and steward in one, so they kept the meal plans simple.

"This looks delicious," Cara said.

"Italian seemed appropriate, given that's whose waters we're in. I often wonder how much we influenced that nation given the likelihood of Atlantis being in these waters," he said.

Cara took a forkful of the fragrant vegetable and cheese pasta dish.

"I was wondering," she said.

He cocked his head. "Yes?"

"You said you didn't enjoy working at Disp@tch. So if you could let it go, hand it over to Phoebe or others, what would you do?"

He sat back, his own forkful of food forgotten. He wasn't sure he'd been asked that before. Mind you, he wasn't usually as open about his dissatisfaction with his life.

He gestured around him. "This is what I love. Archeology, diving, uncovering our past. Like I said, I think that we as a race could do more in the world, that our legacy is to be greater than we currently are. I think there's something—or *things*—we're missing that we've lost as time has passed."

"Like what? And why? What evidence do you have?" Cara continued eating, and as she didn't appear to be arguing, but genuinely curious, he carried on.

"There are frustrating hints in the texts I've studied. I've gone right back to the earliest writings we can find. Languages come easily to me, so I can consult the originals in most cases."

Being a Vishudha energetic was handy in that way. His facility for programming languages was echoed by his proficiency for other languages, though there were some he didn't get on with, such as those that used the Cyrillic alphabet. He went back to eating as he talked, using his fork to emphasize points.

"I'd also love to shoot a documentary about some of the underwater wonders I've seen," he said. "For humans. The sense of peace that I find while diving is incredible, and I'd love to convey that to others. Plus, the wrecks and remains of cities or towns that have sunk put life into perspective, and I think both humans and energetics can use that reframing sometimes."

Cara arched an eyebrow.

"What, you don't think I have depth?" he said.

She shrugged.

Ouch.

He shrugged. "Gossip magazines don't exactly show my best side."

She blushed. He was tempted to tease her about it, but with some effort—more because he thought it was a cute little guilty pleasure rather than he thought there was anything bad about it—he refrained.

"People expect certain things of me," he said. "I live up to those. Phoebe and I have an agreement that we'll be seen in public at a set number of events per year. Taking a date with us guarantees publicity. It doesn't mean we're romantically connected."

She blushed harder. He watched, curious, as he finished his pasta. He'd have to compliment their chef later, it was good stuff. He put his fork down, watching as Cara did the same.

"This is an excellent date," she said, and got up from her chair. She walked around the table to him and took his hand, tugging him to his feet. "A little contained experience."

His brow knit, unsure. He forgot all that, however, when she tilted her chin towards him and snuck a hand around his neck, pulling him towards her.

Going with her motion, he let her draw him to her mouth. He groaned as she kissed him.

It wasn't the light kiss of earlier. She increased the pressure, and her tongue darted between his lips. He opened his mouth, and met her there. As he enjoyed her softness the dynamic trumpet of Miles Davis's "So What" wrapped around them.

He stroked a hand over her hair, then wrapped it around his fingers and used it to pry her away. A small sound of surprise escaped her, but she didn't protest. He was pleased to see she was breathing a little harder than normal. Source knew, his cock was responding.

"Shall we move to a more comfortable position?" he asked.

She laughed and they shifted to the next room. At the foot of the bed, she twisted and pushed him, so he fell back, grinning.

She landed on top of him, crouching like a cat, and dipped her head down to rain kisses on his neck. He ran his hands over her body as she did, liking the feel of her, that softness mixed with strength.

He felt a slight pain at his neck and realized she'd nipped him. She did it again. He growled and flipped her so he was on top. He didn't dislike the bite, but he wanted to return the action. His cock was hardening through the board shorts he was wearing, and he pressed his lower body against her.

She was panting. He scooted down her body and flipped up her dress. He poured his own kisses on her hips and smooth belly, gently biting the unprotected areas as he slid her underwear off.

She fisted his hair and pushed him down. Her skin was hot, and she smelled divine. He had no problem with laving her with his tongue, stretching up his arms, pinning her wrists to her sides. He buried his tongue in her delicate folds, licking and caressing her with his mouth.

She squirmed, but this time left him the control for longer, clearly liking what he was doing.

He'd realized what was happening now. He couldn't believe he hadn't seen it earlier, given their entire relationship looked like this. He dug his nails into her wrists, making her yelp. But the pain made her wetter, as his mouth could attest.

Both of them had Manipura as their auxiliary Chakra. They both ran their own empires, different though they might be. They were both used to being in control, and the bedroom was no different—and now it was his turn.

He felt the silken skin of her inner thighs press against his shoulders, keeping him in place, and he sped up slightly, and let go of one of her wrists. He added fingers to the stimulation he was providing, and she moaned, her hips moving in time with his actions.

She gasped, and her free hand grabbed his head, pressing him into her, and she came hard, underneath him.

He kept his fingers and mouth moving, his touch lighter, until she relaxed her legs and grip on his hair.

He sat up and slid his shorts off, his hand clenched around his cock. She looked amazing, her usual neat and tidy look disheveled, color bright on her cheeks, her skin almost glowing.

Her eyes were closed, as she—he hoped—enjoyed the afterglow of the orgasm they'd created for her. He watched her chest move up and down, holding himself back from plunging into her as his cock begged.

He was relishing this dance of control between them, and he couldn't wait to see what might come next. His partners tended to be reactive; they enjoyed their encounters, but expected him to lead.

She sat up. She stripped off her dress, and threw it to the floor in a move most unlike her. He wouldn't have been shocked if she'd got up, folded it and put it on a chair.

He grinned at her. There was an almost palpable sexual tension between them, an anticipation of what was to come.

"Stay right there." She crawled towards him. The power and strength in her body was erotic, and he did as she ordered—*requested*, he amended in his head—and watched with interest, and then delight as she placed her hands on his butt and drew his cock towards her face.

He directed it to her mouth, needing to be inside, but she stopped him with a palm on his hip.

"Wait," she said.

She moistened her lips in a gesture that had his cock throbbing, and used her mouth on him in the most heavenly ways.

The power in the room ricocheted between them as their Manipura energies wove around their bodies, flames shooting across burning hot skin, as the sexual energy built higher and higher.

They used the bed in creative ways, her on top, then him, rolling and flipping each other. It was exhilarating. He loved unraveling her usually immaculate demeanor, and getting to the woman beneath.

They each released a lick of their fire energy here and there, testing, probing for acceptance, for what was okay.

And right now, he was open to anything she wanted to try.

The sun had nearly risen as Cara stretched on the deck. She was delightfully stiff from her night with Archer, and she appreciated a less humid atmosphere than she was used to in Canada, warming and loosening her body.

Ai, leaning on the deck railing beside her, had her attention fixed on the blue sea around them. The Ionian sea lay between Italy and Greece. South of it was the Mediterranean, which led to Albania to the north and Egypt to the south—the latter being where the energetics had fled after Atlantis was destroyed. It was brighter than Cara had gotten used to, the sun yellower, with less of the greens of the forests and earth that were such an integral part of the landscape on Vancouver Island.

"What do you think of being at sea?" Cara asked Ai, who continued squinting into the binoculars she'd borrowed from the captain, who'd taken the girl under her wing.

"I love it!" Ai enthused. She pointed. "Look, there's some kind of flying fish over there."

Cara grinned, and borrowed the binoculars to look. The silvery fish jumped in and out of the water, the sun shimmering off their scales. They were incredible.

Cara handed the binoculars back, and gestured to the stairs that led inside. "Shall we get back to it?"

She was enjoying spending time with Archer, who was proving a lot more capable on the boat than she'd anticipated. He had an ease and familiarity with the sails and other technical looking stuff that she hadn't expected. She'd thought that Nahla would do all the work in her role as Captain, while Archer pretended he knew what he was doing and sat back. But it wasn't like that at all.

On the boat, Archer was still the same charismatic man, but his enthusiasm for knowledge was out in full force, this time in a more physical arena. He dodged around the boat like he'd been born there, no matter how much the deck rolled, and his comfortable rapport with the crew was on display as they carried out his orders.

He was so much more than she'd realized. She sighed. It was time to stop believing in what the magazines had shown about his playboy nature. Gossip rags were hardly the most reliable source.

She'd made the right decision to have a holiday fling with him, she thought smugly, thinking back to the night before. It had been fun, the control and power that had flowed between them. It had been a game between them, which of them was in charge at any point, and one she'd been surprised he'd been prepared to engage in. He'd had no problem letting her run the show, but had equally enjoyed wresting that control back from her.

She couldn't remember when she'd last had her mind taken off the responsibilities of the clinic. She'd been surprised at how good it felt to be free of that pressure, even for a day. Although the clinic could get in touch with her out here through the boat's radio, her cellphone didn't work, so she couldn't constantly check email as she might normally if she was with Tierra at Cathair Cuinn, where Tierra, Cuinn and Blaize lived.

An hour later, she was starting to get frustrated, as they still hadn't cracked the mystery of the dolphin.

"It makes no sense," muttered Cara. "Why would a dolphin be on the island?"

Archer studied the papers on the desk, frowning.

It was Ai who provided the answer. She squeaked, then, staring at her tablet, she drew something with a finger.

She held it up. Over the northeast of the island, where land jutted out, she'd zoomed in and outlined the shape of a dolphin's head around a small peninsula.

It fit.

22

Archer beamed. "You're right, Ai. We just need the lighthouse now."

"Wouldn't a lighthouse be marked on the map?" Ai asked.

"You'd think, but Archer seems to think it's pretty old," Nahla said. "Not been used for a very long time."

"How does it work, triangulation?" said Ai. "Trigonometry isn't a big feature of living on the street."

"If you take two points, like the lighthouse and the dolphin, wherever you stand in relationship to them, you can measure an angle." Here, Archer sketched two points, with a line coming from each, intersected between them. "But if you take a specific angle, like one-hundred degrees, then there are only two points within the zone we've identified that meet that criterion."

He put a point between the two points to its north and south, that shared as similar an angle as he could make, freehand.

"We're looking for an angle, that I think—I *hope*—will be in the lighthouse somewhere. Then a way to know which of the two points, North or South, we need to search."

They sailed on, scanning the sea around them for land. Finally, on an island so small it didn't appear on the map, there was a ruined building—one that looked like it might have been tall at one time, given the debris that had fallen onto the rocks and in some cases, into the sea. However large the island had been a few thousand years ago, now the ruins of the building took up most of the land.

Archer's heart lurched with hope. Could that be it? He clamped down on the emotion. It was too early for that. They would need to check it out—if it was, or had been, a lighthouse, it was in sore disrepair.

The boat became a hive of activity. The crew, who continued to move together like many parts of an organic whole, jumped into action and the ship's course changed to head toward what he hoped was what they were looking for.

It took another short while, but they were soon moored in the water near a tiny beach. Archer found himself joined on deck by Ai, Cara, Nahla and many of the crew as they gazed at the ruins.

"This is it," Archer said. "It has to be."

Cara nodded slowly. "Shall we check it out?"

Ai, Archer, Cara and Nahla took a dinghy to shore, jumped out and pulled the little boat onto the beach.

A short walk over sand, some rocks, and there on a jutting bulge of land stood the building. Whatever it was—or had been—it was in a terrible state, with vegetation creeping up the sides, and tangled vines ready to catch the feet of the unwary.

But it was the right shape.

"I thought a lighthouse would be cylindrical," Ai said.

Archer shook his head. "The notes I have indicate this one was rectangular, with an octagonal tower as the mid-section, and a square section at the very top that housed a furnace for nighttime illumination, and mirrors on the outside so the sun would reflect off it in the day."

"Wow," Ai breathed.

In front of them stood a construction made of light-colored stone. What remained was rectangular at the base, with what appeared to be the start of an octagonal tower on top. He couldn't see a square section, though plenty of stone had fallen in heaps around it.

"It must have been impressive," Nahla said.

"It would have been tall for a building of its time, that's for certain," Archer said. He paced around the outside, picking his way over scrub and chunks of cut rock half-buried in the ground. He'd asked Nahla to take photos so he could concentrate on finding any clues, but he couldn't stop himself snapping a few on his phone.

"Are we going in?" Cara said. She'd found an opening sunk into the ground, which meant stepping down to enter.

He wanted to—he really, really wanted to. But the structure was already mostly collapsed. How dangerous was it? He grimaced. What were the chances of keeping Cara and Ai out if he went in? Nahla, he trusted, she'd been on plenty of dangerous explorations with him. But the other two were new to this. He didn't think it was likely Cara would be left out at this point, given he'd dragged her halfway around the world for this. But he'd try.

"How about I go in and check it out first?" he suggested.

Cara cocked her head and looked at him for a moment, then turned back to the doorway, creating a Manipura light. She opened her hand and the light drifted through the entrance, banishing the gloom.

"We'll leave someone outside in case of an issue," Cara said. "But we'll take it in turns. Ai, as you're under my care, you're going to start outside—if it's safe, you can come in."

Ai parted her lips to protest then stopped as she caught sight of Cara's face, which was implacable. "Fine. As long as I can see it in a minute."

A shiver ran down Archer's back, and he couldn't decide if it was apprehension or excitement.

Cara disappeared through the entrance, and Archer stepped through after her, Nahla close behind. The area was large, with a staircase to one side.

"The staircase is big enough that they could have used a pack animal of some kind on those stairs to haul up fuel to the next floor," Archer commented absentmindedly, his eyes scanning the room to try to drink it all in.

"Where do we look first?" Cara asked. Archer sighed inwardly. The woman was always so pragmatic. Wasn't there room for a little wonder now and then? Still, he supposed she was right. He could come back here with his team and search for artifacts. Today, they were on the clock.

Archer was walking around the edges of the room, fingers running lightly over the stone. His research had indicated there was an inscription somewhere. Would it be visible to everyone? Or only energetics? He supposed that the ancients wouldn't want non-energetics finding the temple they were searching for.

He clambered over some fallen stones. One of them rocked underneath him and he heard a sharp intake of breath from Cara as he stumbled. He put out a hand and stabilized himself. "I'm fine."

Cara pursed her lips, but continued her own, more careful walk around the room.

Nahla stood watch.

"They're unlikely to be somewhere a human would see them, or recognize them. I want to search the room with energy," Archer said. "I'll use Reveal."

"Truth-seeking? I thought that was only for people," Cara said.

"It can be used on objects, if you develop the energy combinations and spend some time working on it," Archer said. "I've used it before at archeological sites when we're looking for something specific."

Nahla was frowning. "It takes a lot out of you though, no? I thought you were recently injured?"

Cara turned to face him full on. "Archer, what…"

"It'll be fine," he interrupted. He was already breathing in, pulling energy from the ether. It did take skill and intense concentration, as well as a lot of practice. He'd built the latter up over time, first at the Guild, then using Vishudha to search places where they'd never have found critical artifacts without it. His Reveal always had an edge of his Manipura to it, and in his mind he thought of it as a sword of truth, one that he wielded to cut away deceit, fakes or disguises.

He formed the blade in his mind, then put out his hands as if he was holding a broadsword, one hand at the bottom of the hilt, the other above.

He breathed in, and out.

Energy built in him, his body tingling. His throat Chakra, the seat of Vishudha, throbbed, and he felt choked, as if there was something he wasn't able to swallow down. Maintaining energy in this Chakra at this level took balance—too little and he wouldn't be able to use the sword, and too much and he might asphyxiate.

The sword formed in his hands. It shimmered, there but not there. He went to the door, and started at its right. He gently swiped the sword over the stone, the blade passing through without disturbing anything.

Nothing here.

He began a grid search, using the sword methodically to sweep each piece of stone in the walls. A few times, his energies wavered, and he had to hold for a moment, grounding himself. Archeology was for those with patience. Discoveries didn't come every day.

But oh, when they did, it was all worth it.

At the back of the room, in a small alcove, the sword hit resistance and he grit his teeth. Was this it?

He fed more energy into the sword and pushed it slowly, carefully over the area of resistance. Letters bled from the wall, forming an inscription.

Cara gasped.

Archer let go of the energy, and the sword disappeared. He panted and walked up to the letters on the wall, his head cocked to the side.

"It's Cappotian," he said. That was lucky.

"Can you read it?" Cara said, stepping up next to him.

He nodded, absentmindedly. He wasn't as fluent with human languages as many of Vishudha Guild, but the ancient language of the energetics was taught as part of the Guild's basic curriculum.

If you seek the Doorway
Find the animal that lives on land and water
Shine bright this light with Source
Alone,
Paired,
Combined.

"That's all it says?" Nahla said.

"It's all we need," Archer said, body still prickling, though whether it was from the energy he'd just pulled or excitement he wasn't sure. "It's a strange name for the temple though. Why the Doorway? All temples have doors, I'd imagine."

"A doorway to Source?" Cara said. "All a temple is, after all, is a way to connect to Source more directly, without the usual distractions."

Archer shrugged. "That works. We'll find it and see."

"You know what it means?" Cara said.

"I think so. We're looking for an angle, so between one and three numbers. From the verse, it looks like we have three. 'Alone' is easy, must be one Chakra, Sahasara, the Chakra of Source. So, a one. 'Paired' is also easy, I assume it's two. So that already gets us a long way. 'Combined', that's a bit more hit and miss. It could be three, for the three Chakras, it could be seven, for all Chakras combined, but my money is on four, as that's how many each bracelet has." He glanced at Cara's wrist. "Most of them, anyway. So an angle of 124 degrees is my bet, but it could also be 123 or 127."

"And the animal that lives on water and land?" Ai said from the doorway. "I tried my cell to find the answer but the signal here is lame."

"Given what we already know, it's—"

"A snake." Cara pursed her lips. "So the two points, the lighthouse and the dolphin rock on Snake island, along with us, make an angle. We have to move the boat to where the correct angle is, and dive there."

Archer tipped his chin to her in recognition. "What she said. But we need one more piece of information as there are two possible points that would match that criteria, one north, one south. Ideally we'd know which one so we don't have to try both. I need to check the rest of the building to find it."

He reactivated the sword of truth, and continued around the room. He found nothing else on this level. He walked toward the crumbling stairs, and Cara made a worried noise.

"Shall we take a break first?"

"We won't have time to come back today as we need to ensure you and Ai are back by morning," he said. He would pass the energies over every inch of stone he could find. He moved faster.

The going was harder on the second floor. Plenty of rubble covered the ground. He should probably create a light for this level, but doing that while he also held the sword wasn't something he wanted to bother with—and the sword itself let off a shimmering blue glow that lit the surrounding area.

His stomach throbbed. Not ideal. His energy use was pulling from his weakest point, his wound. Still, it wouldn't take him too long to finish here, then he could rest, or do whatever annoying ritual Cara would no doubt prescribe.

He picked his way over some fallen masonry so that he was effectively standing above the alcove below, albeit with a floor between him and it. He drew the sword through the air, and again hit resistance.

"I have it, I think." The shimmering blue light revealed a needle, its tip pointing upward. Alert, he stared intently at what he had revealed.

Then, holding the energy of the sword in place with one hand, he fished his cell out of his pants pocket with the other, and took a photo. He had an inkling what the clue might indicate, but he wanted to examine it more closely.

As he stepped over a particularly large piece of stone to reach the symbol, he heard a scream.

He jerked around, and his pants leg caught on the stone's jagged edge and he stumbled. He tensed the muscles in his abdomen automatically, and the wave of pain that swept through him bent him double. He tried to shake his leg free of the stone but he was caught, and he fell forward, one hand curved protectively around himself, and the other dropping the sword, which disappeared as soon as he stopped feeding it energy.

He landed with a crash, his side smashing into a stone that rested on the floor. Tears sprang to his eyes and his breath came harshly as he rolled—but there was no longer anything beneath him. He hadn't noticed the hole because he had been concentrating on the walls and the pool of light the sword cast. Darkness rushed up to meet him as he fell without even time to yell before he hit the ground with a sickening thud.

Cara's heart lurched for a moment as her senses were doubly assaulted by Ai screaming outside, and the sound of Archer falling. Her training kicked in.

"Nahla, go to Archer," she snapped, as she headed for the door of the lighthouse, blinking to stop the light from blinding her as she went in the direction of Ai's panicked noises.

She had to trust that Nahla would give whatever immediate first aid Archer needed, while she saw to Ai—the girl was younger, and was under Cara's care. Archer had been discharged as a patient, and if he was stupid enough to reinjure himself—she tensed at the thought, but shook it off.

Ai had backed up against the wall of the building, eyes wide, trembling. Cara scanned for the danger, ready but not seeing what was causing the teenager such distress. She followed Ai's terrified gaze and the pieces fell into place. A viper, hissing angrily, was a few feet in front of a frozen Ai.

Cara threw fire at the ground in front of Ai, separating her from the danger. The girl sobbed, her breathing hitching. Source, she was having a panic attack. Was she hurt?

The snake fled from the fire, and a small piece of tension left Cara. One danger down. She went to the girl.

"Have you been bitten?"

Tears streamed down Ai's face, her dark eyes blurred with them. She nodded, gesturing to her left leg, her breathing coming faster and faster. She'd begin hyperventilating if Cara didn't steady her.

Ai began to slide down the wall and Cara shot out a hand to stop her, pressing her back.

"No. Stay upright. We need to keep your leg below your heart until we've dealt with any venom. Can you do that for me?"

Ai nodded. Her teeth chattered, incongruous in the Greek sunshine.

Nahla appeared at the door of the lighthouse. "Archer fell from the second story and I don't know if he's broken anything or torn something inside. His abdomen seems to be a problem."

"Ai's been bitten by a snake. Do you have antivenom on the boat?" Cara said.

Nahla paused for only a moment before she recovered. "Yes. I'll radio in."

"Can you stay with Ai for a minute? Touch her shoulder, breathe slowly and deeply and try to get her to follow your lead. And don't let her sit down," Cara asked Nahla. She didn't wait to see if the woman would. She'd have to trust the woman Archer had chosen to captain his crew. Cara needed to triage, and she couldn't do that without information.

She re-entered the lighthouse, threw herself down next to Archer, and put her hands above his stomach. Her energy touched him lightly to discover what had happened.

Shit shit shit.

Nothing was torn inside—thank Source—but he'd stretched and damaged the tissues almost to breaking point, and the wound that had been healing so well had opened slightly. Not only that, he'd somehow managed to injure himself further. She ground her teeth, not sure whether annoyance or worry was at the top of her emotions in that moment.

Triage, Cara, triage.

His oblique was going to have a nasty bruise, but it wasn't torn, so she would leave healing his side for later.

His abdominal wound needed washing out, then she'd need to patch it. It wasn't bleeding much, not enough to be a problem.

He'd need time to heal, again, and she wanted to check him over with her human-made equipment.

He was coming back to the Healing Center—as a patient.

C H A P T E R

23

Cara sat at her desk in the Center, her body aching with tiredness, and stared down at the stupid bracelet on her wrist. All that, and she was no further in understanding why she had it, and why it differed from her friends' jewelry.

It had been a horrible journey back. They'd treated Ai on the boat with the antivenom, and she'd been fine, if shaken, though they were monitoring her.

Cara had sedated Archer to make the journey back as comfortable as possible for him, but she herself hadn't slept on the flight home, despite a very comfortable bed in the jet, spending the time berating herself for letting herself be persuaded to go. She'd talked with Adam on the flight. His genuine understanding had been hard to take. She'd been simultaneously mad at him for his part in making her go, and guilty because they'd brought nothing back for their efforts.

Mostly, she was infuriated with herself.

She'd let someone else be in control for the first time in a long time, and look what had happened. Ai got hurt, and one of her patients injured himself. She groaned. She should never have gone.

And now Archer was back in his room, his healing set back by a week.

A sharp rap at the door was followed by Osana entering her office.

"Anahata Guild have confirmed. They've sent over a formal notification that we're going to be audited. Apparently Maya's sent you a personal note."

For a moment, Cara gazed at Osana, uncomprehending. She shook her head, trying to get the cobwebs out of her brain. "What?"

"She and a team are coming to do an inspection. They've sent over the current checklists that Anahata have for Centers, and will send details of their itinerary later today. They're likely to be here within a couple of days."

Cara didn't even have the energy to snatch up her stress balls. She'd completely forgotten. She opened her email program, and sure enough, there was the note from Maya, who said the inspection was real, but while she was at the Center, she would also discuss how the database project was progressing. She signed off by saying she hoped Cara would demonstrate her worthiness for inclusion in the project, and that Anahata believed Cara to be someone who ran a model Center, and Maya looked forward to seeing it.

Cara squinted at the last words, unclear if there was an undertone she was missing.

Osana continued standing patiently in front of her.

"I can't believe the timing," Cara said. "Alright. Can you get the team together for a briefing as soon as possible? The inspection party could arrive any time in the next two or three days, and we need to work through the checklists to make sure we have everything in order. Excluding emergencies, ask people if they will cancel any leave they have in the next week."

Osana nodded. "No problem. I'll work through the lists and assign sections to the different team leaders to review and work on."

"That would be great, thank you," Cara responded, with some relief. An inspection from Anahata—something that only happened every five years—could have serious consequences if they failed any aspects. Anahata could remove her from her role, or any of her staff members, as they saw fit.

The Guild left the Centers alone, but reserved the right to check on them periodically. They funded them, wanting value for money in the way the Centers served the purposes of Anahata, and the population of energetics. "Anahata don't simply want us to pass. They want us to be a model Center. Tell the team they'll be here a while."

Osana left. Cara was grateful for her team. But Source, she didn't have the energy for this right now. Though there might have been times in her career when she'd have been proud to demonstrate her results and how well the team worked, at the moment she had bigger fish to fry.

She didn't *want* to test Anahata's database, or to be a model Center. There was no way the two weren't connected, either. It had only been four years since their last inspection.

She also didn't want Archer back in the Center, as a patient again. This time, she'd assigned others to look after him.

She wanted to be left alone to do her work. To run her Center, and to educate Ai in Anahata and the basics of their race and magic.

She wanted her crisis management to be back to just the odd flatlining patient or a Rogue causing trouble with out-of-control energy.

She sighed. She should be so lucky.

No matter. That was the job of a leader. She opened the documents from Anahata about the audit, and began to read.

"We have the opportunity to remove the threats of both Cara and Archer. I've arranged to be part of an inspection team going to the Center. You will join us." Imogen said over the phone to Elrian.

"You'll have to stay hidden until we plan how to remove them. Get to the island and as close to the Center as you can. We can take care of the escapee, Kayla, when we're there."

It was a good plan. Imogen would use her access to understand the defenses they had, and they would find a way to get rid of both parties. Kayla, however, was a small enough fish that taking her with them would be more useful than killing her. They still needed to make remnant stones. He'd have to persuade Imogen of that in person.

Timing was important. While he himself had been reenergized by his trip into nature to replenish his Earth Chakra—which had included leeching from a moderately strong energetic source—Cassidy had been showing more forgetfulness than usual. He had to admit, he was concerned. He knew it was a risk, given how often he had had to remove parts of her memory, but she seemed to ask troublesome questions more and more often. He excised her memories for her own good, as Imogen was clear what would need to happen to Cassidy should she find out what they were doing and decide not to work with them.

It was better this way. She helped him, as she always had, but didn't need to understand their full plan until it had been executed. Then she'd see he'd done the right thing.

But he worried about leaving her now, when he'd caught her staring into space for hours, distracted, or halfway through a task that remained unfinished until he prodded her. He should keep his visit to the island as short as possible.

"Is Cara keeping the database up to date?" he asked Imogen. "We'll likely need it."

"It seems so. I'll know more when I get there. I'll be in touch once we arrive."

Elrian sighed. Imogen rarely gave him a choice these days. Her cold rage when he disagreed with her on anything was disturbing, and he picked his moments for that.

"Yes, my love. I'll see you there."

24

Archer slouched in bed in the Healing Center, frustrated enough to want to throw his pillow across the room. He'd quite like Cara's stress balls right now, though he might fire them out the window. He gripped his tablet until his fingers turned white, then realized he'd better put it down before he broke it. He tossed it aside on the bed and put his chin on his hand, shoulders slumped forward, elbow on the hospital table.

It was himself he was mad at. When Phoebe had heard about his setback, she'd agreed with Cara and ordered him back to Vancouver Island in no uncertain terms.

He couldn't believe he'd put himself back in this hospital room—and ruined one of his favorite gamer t-shirts while he did it, an original Gabriel Knight print.

He hadn't been prepared to let go of his research materials, and thankfully, neither Cara nor Phoebe had told him no tech this time. He'd been switching between using his tablet and the research materials in the room, but he was finding it hard to concentrate, and the tech was being slow. The throbbing of his stomach reminded him what an idiot he was, and he had to admit it didn't feel great that Cara hadn't been in to see him that day. He leaned back on the bed to find a more comfortable position. It didn't work.

The time they'd shared on the boat had been special. He'd showed parts of himself he rarely revealed. She'd seemed genuinely interested. Had he been fooled by her role as a Healer, someone who asked questions of others as a matter of course?

Perhaps it was because he'd failed her. He'd found the coordinates, and then destroyed their chance of finding what they were searching for. Had he been conscious, he'd never have allowed them to bring him back without checking the coordinates. He'd have stayed on that boat, sick as he was, until they'd dived, even if he had to send others to make the discovery.

But he hadn't been.

If they'd had more time, if he hadn't injured himself, if he hadn't had to take Cara home, would he have found it? Whatever 'it' was?

He had been so close. Finally, a real chance, and he blew it.

He snatched up the tablet again, frustrated. He was trying to compile some code, and it was taking forever on the tablet. He was not in the mood to wait.

He hacked through the Wi-Fi of the hospital—Wi-Fi that sorely needed its security patches downloaded and updating—and used the CPU power of some of the network. No one would notice. He lost himself in work for a time, putting thoughts of the weekend's failures on hold. It felt good.

Finished, he was about to log out, but remembered Cara's database. He'd been distracted last time, but this time, he'd check it out. He narrowed his eyes, and rummaged around until he found it. It was the work of moments to crack Cara's password. He opened it up on his screen, and saw he could look up, amend, or enter new records. Curious, he entered his own name to see if he had an entry. It popped up, and he clicked on it.

At first, it seemed like any other medical record. His name and personal details, his injury, attached test results, and other standard questions he'd been asked. Fair enough, he thought.

He frowned when he saw it had his parents, and their parents—his lineage for several generations.

It also had his Major Guilds, Vishudha and Manipura, and his Minor Guild, Vishudha-Manipura. Each of these was clickable.

His frown deepened. What relevance did that have to his stay at the Healing Center? He clicked on his Major Guild, Vishudha.

Archer Hampton, Major Guild: Vishudha.

Special Abilities: Languages, Charisma and Persuasion.

Weakness or Limitations: Kinetic and Offensive magics, Pride.

He sat back, cold seeping through him. Had Cara said this was an Anahata Guild project? Who had access to this? He tapped on the tablet furiously, wishing for a proper keyboard, reviewing the security of the database. There were holes in it even the most inexperienced hacker could roll through.

He would never agree to this level of information being kept on him. Not only that, he didn't remember being asked. For Source's sake, he ran a comms company. He knew about information and storage.

He put the tablet to one side, his pulse hammering, and pressed the buzzer for attention. After some negotiation and waiting, Cara came in. She was back in her usual uniform of a smart, simple dress, this one light blue, that let her move easily but gave her a business-like look. The mussed hair and flushed cheeks of the boat were gone.

He turned the tablet toward her. "What have you done?"

She frowned and came closer, squinting at the device. It took her a moment to understand what he was showing her.

"How did you get into this?" she said, her eyes widening and her voice rising. She tried to grab the tablet from him but he pulled it out of reach.

"I took a look because I wanted to help. I thought it would be nice as I do this for the Guilds so often. The point is, it wasn't hard, which means you're holding information on me that I didn't authorize, and it's not secure," he said. "You haven't updated your

Wi-Fi security for months, even years, and the database has some key security loopholes."

"You signed the forms. You agreed to this," she said, her hands on her hips, but her gaze kept flickering from the tablet in his hands to his face, as if she found it hard to look at him. Good. So she should.

"I agreed to you keeping records relevant to my medical treatment!" he exploded. "Not detailing my every strength and weakness for my rivals to find. Why are you doing this?"

"It's a Guild project, like I told you. I'm in there, too. It's not personal. It's for the benefit of everyone," Cara said, her brow wrinkling, her palms face up.

"Of course it's personal! If you're in it, or your friends, you're exposing yourselves, too. You're in the middle of a crisis, for fuck's sake. Why would you leave yourself open like this while you're under attack?" Her, Ai, the other patients here, the other staff members. People he'd grown to care about, exposed in their vulnerabilities.

"It's irrelevant to the prophecy. It's a project for my Guild, part of my work."

He tried to breathe, to calm himself down. "This is the kind of information that in the wrong hands could be catastrophic. The Guild has gone too far. Who knows about it?"

"It's a new project, still in the pilot phase," she said. "Run by Anahata, being trialed at the Guild HQ in Cairo and two other Healing Centers. We track information on patients all the time. This is an extension of that."

He shook his head. "This isn't only for patients. This is built to collect information on every energetic. Why else would you have put in the staff members? Yourself?"

She shifted uneasily. "We work for Anahata. Besides, the Guild is hardly going to use it against people. We're the Guild of Healing, remember?"

"It's not like there's never been a Rogue with Anahata. And this kind of information is too dangerous to be held in one place like this," he said.

"No one's going to get it!" She threw her hands up and put them back on her hips. He could almost hear her teeth grinding. He barely noticed the way the material of her dress tightened as she moved, showing off the lines of her body.

"I'm an above average hacker," he said.

She huffed and rolled her eyes.

"But it wasn't hard to get in," he continued. "The database security was badly designed."

He took a deep breath, steadying himself. "I promise you, Cara, this is not a safe thing to do."

She scrubbed her face with her hands. "Archer. I'm sorry, but I don't have time for this. A team from Anahata is coming to inspect this facility any minute, and I have to make sure everything is in shape. The database is part of my job. All confidential information would be dangerous in the wrong hands, but we've never had an issue with that before. I need you to drop this. You're the one who hacked into a place he shouldn't have been. You invaded my privacy, and violated the Center's security. You're the one in the wrong here."

He opened his mouth to argue, but she turned on her heel and walked out. Something in his gut twisted, but he ignored it. She was wrong.

"Ask Adam what he thinks," he called after her, but without confidence she would hear him.

He put the tablet back on his lap and hurriedly tapped at the keys, in case she knew a way to block him when she got back to her computer. He went into his record again, and changed the strengths and weaknesses so they were no longer reflective or relevant. They'd stand up to a quick glance, and were coherent with his powers, but they didn't expose him. He hesitated a moment, then searched for Cara's record. He did the same to her strengths and weaknesses, amending her record in the same way he had done to his own, and then to Ai's.

He would protect those he cared for, even if they didn't know what was good for them.

Cara stood at the window in her office, gazing out at the sea beyond the Center. Her last conversation with Archer nagged at her. She had already tagged her tech people, such as they were, to update their Wi-Fi security. Maybe they did need to invest more in that area. Right now, she had two Anahata-Vishudha staff members who looked after all the tech of the Center as part of their work with other medical tech in the facility. Unsurprisingly, the Wi-Fi wasn't their priority, the life-saving machinery was. But perhaps she had been looking at it wrongly. The world was changing again. It could be easy to misjudge the pace of change when you lived for so long.

She moved her head, and her hair fell around her face. She frowned. She should have pinned it back. She was in her most formal work dress, practical, small heels, and had made her face up without over-doing it. She wanted to give the inspection team the picture of efficiency. A long-sleeved jacket covered her, including that damned bracelet.

A quick pain shot through her wrist, and she glanced down. What now? A static build up?

She pushed her sleeve up and studied it. Was it glowing? She stepped away from the window, alarmed. Should she call for help?

The pain increased, her wrist aching. The bracelet was definitely glowing, covered by a white sheen. Cara knew little about the qualities or characteristics of orichalcum. It was a legendary material, and despite her training and experience, she wasn't familiar with it. Another thing to put on her list, she thought. Sooner rather than later.

She gripped her wrist to ease the pain, but within a second the white light covered her whole body, and the discomfort turned into agony. She fell to her knees and closed her eyes against the brightness.

An array of emotions and images flashed through her mind.

Acceptance: The usual tension in her shoulders gone, her body loose. She sat curled up on a sofa, taking a plate of food from a man whose face was obscured, and laughing at a joke he'd made.

A blaze of white light. Her body burned, her head spun.

Balance: She walked along the cliffs, holding a man's warm hand. She wasn't on duty at the Center, and knew she had the day to spend with her lover. Tomorrow she'd go back to work, refreshed.

Another wave of light. Heat and dizziness rushed through her.

Release: The oft-crushing sense of responsibility she lived with every day had disappeared. The buck still stopped with her, but she shared her challenges with her top staff members and her partner, who she knew she could count on in every way.

A rush of white. Vertigo.

Liberation: She sat at the very same desk she now kneeled next to, but in different clothes, working through paperwork, a sense of satisfaction at a day well-lived. She would finish this next item then leave her desk, trusting another member of staff to handle things while she spent the evening with someone dear to her.

The white light was a blast this time, a cleansing, until she couldn't sense her own body, nothing but her hammering heartbeat to anchor her.

She concentrated on its throbbing, breathing until she could feel the air entering her body again. From her breath, from her pulse, she rebuilt her sense of self, until her vision cleared, and the flow faded.

She pressed her palms into the floor, still kneeling, fighting the onslaught of feelings she'd just experienced. She slowly opened her eyes.

What magic was this? Gingerly, she prodded the bracelet. None of the others had mentioned anything like this. And Cara had no Ajna, no ability to have visions. She pushed herself up from the floor, shaking, and staggered into her seat at her desk, staring at the familiar things around her, that she'd just seen in such a different context.

Those hadn't been from her past. They weren't the kinds of feelings she commonly felt. Her lips flattened. Alright, perhaps they weren't feelings she *ever* felt, not since she'd realized quite how responsible she needed to be for the Center, patients and staff.

What were they, then?

Despite the fleeting pain, there had been a peace and serenity along with each image and feeling, which suggested they weren't meant to cause lasting harm. Warnings? She rubbed her forehead. She didn't recognize herself in the visions, and that was disturbing in itself. Had it really been her she'd seen?

What would her life be like if she felt like that regularly?

A knock on the door. She screwed her eyes tight.

The delegation.

"Come in," she said, relaxing her face into a pleasant smile.

Osana slipped inside the room. "The inspection team have landed, and are on their way up from Victoria."

The team had traveled from Seattle by boat, arriving at Victoria, Vancouver Island's port. Osana had organized a car to pick them up and escort them to the Center. The plan was to make their trip as easy as possible and Cara was ready to curry favor in whatever way she needed in order to get this inspection over fast and successfully.

"Thank you."

"Can I do anything else?" asked Osana. She studied Cara, her eyes narrowing. "Are you alright? You look pale."

Cara shook her head. "I'm fine. Can you make sure security will let us know when they arrive?"

They'd likely be another few hours.

Sure enough, it was over three hours later when Osana came to get her. The car and team would have been through two security checks by the time the inspection team reached Cara. They would then go through another check at the entrance to the building, which Cara would then escort them through.

Despite the august nature of their guests, they couldn't skimp on the checks, as they were no doubt part of what the team were assessing.

Cara sighed. Having to watch her every move in the coming few days wasn't something she was looking forward to. She knew also that she'd need to focus more on her personal care given her role as General Manager of the Healing Center. She was already a strong energetic compared to many, and being the General Manager enhanced both her high level of natural power and her training. Control was central to this, because the power went both ways. Cara's power fed the Center—and she could also draw on the Center's power. If she didn't look after herself, she might impact the Center itself.

A handful of minutes after Cara arrived at the building entrance, a Toyota SUV pulled up, and disgorged three passengers before pulling away with a wave from the driver. Cara nodded her thanks before turning to greet her guests.

"Maya, welcome to the island."

Maya inclined her head. She was a tall, hard blonde, whose hair and jewelry glinted pale and sharp in the sunlight. Eyes cold, she gestured to the two women with her. "This is Auretta and Iris. We're looking forward to seeing how the Center is working."

Auretta was petite, pale and plump, with an air of disdain. Iris stood behind the other two, with dark skin and zig-zag cornrow braids, face mild.

Cara nodded. "Osana will take you to the rooms we have prepared for you, and then you can let me know how and when you want to start. When you're ready, I can introduce you to more of the team."

"Oh, there's no need for that." That icy smile again. "Make sure we have the codes and passes to access everything, and we'll do the inspection as we need to."

Cara tried to school her expression into blankness. The idea of Maya in particular wandering around at will wasn't comfortable, for all that Cara had nothing to hide. But this was the procedure. The Anahata Guild had free rein to examine the inner workings of one of their Centers at will. That didn't mean any Center Manager would welcome it.

"Okay, I can arrange that. Obviously we'll need you to respect patient needs, for example those who are recovering and who need quiet. Also the Rehabilitation area is secured, and protocol requires you have an escort." Touché, Cara thought. Maya could hardly argue if they stuck to and enforced the rules. And Cara had primed Ife— experienced, articulate and expressive—to take that role.

Auretta nodded. "That's alright. Send us the most junior member of staff who has clearance for that area of the Center."

Cara kept her face neutral though her heart sank. That was so *not* the plan. "I'll send someone to your rooms with the codes. Healing or rehab first?"

They chose the Healing half of the Center, which gave Cara time to prepare poor Jason to deal with Maya.

Handing the inspection team over to Osana, Cara raced over to the Rehab area, and gathered the handful of staff into the office. She was within one set of locks and magical wards, but there were plenty more woven into the walls of the building, into each door and window.

Equipped to handle about twenty-five Rogues, they had sixteen in-house. More than usual, but within their capabilities. Their aim was always to help Rogues to untwist their energies, like poor Kayla, and move them from the high security Rehab wing to a closed room in the Healing Center. There was a reason these places weren't prisons, despite the dark nature of what some of their guests had done. The energetic philosophy was that everyone could be redeemed, if they wanted to be.

Jason's baby blue eyes had widened when she'd requested he escort their guests, but he'd nodded readily, always willing to take on whatever was needed. "No problem."

She needed to trust him, she thought. Trust the work that she and the others had put into training Jason, who had only been with them six months, directly out of his Practitioner trial on his auxiliary Chakra. He was Anahata-Muladhara, steady and caring. She had to bite back the desire to fill his brain with instructions, to remind him of all the security protocols, to test his knowledge to check it before she let him be her representative of the Center.

He'd be okay. She couldn't let her fear, her need to control every situation, show. It wouldn't help him.

As she walked back towards her office, anxiety built. With every step, more feelings joined it, until she was drowning in an emotional backwash that was the antithesis of the vision she had experienced earlier.

She paused, took a long, slow breath. But her responsibilities, failures, everything she couldn't control piled up in her brain in a swirling mess.

Placing a hand on the cool wall, she tried to ground herself. But she flashed back on the look in Archer's eyes when he had accused her of betrayal about the Database. He had been appalled. Her stomach squeezed. There had been no acceptance there.

Pressing her palm harder into the wall, she tried logic. The hospital said they kept records on patients' personal data. And he'd signed that waiver. They just didn't say exactly *what* data.

Her stomach squirmed.

While she didn't know the details of the politics, one reason it was a confidential pilot was that not all the Guilds had agreed to it. Anahata was leading the project, but she'd heard Svadisthana in particular had argued strongly against it, probably because they were all free-wheeling artists who hated to be caged by rules of any kind.

That wasn't her problem, however. She'd agreed to collect the information and trial the database for her Guild. Everyone she was entering into it had agreed their data could be collected.

She was doing her duty.

Emotions built up inside her. She needed to release them.

She realized she was no longer touching the steadying wall, instead, her legs had brought her to the corridor where Archer's room was located. She nodded to herself, body aflame as if her emotions were becoming tangible. They would settle this. She would convince him she was right, and at least one of her difficult emotions would be gone.

She marched up to his door, knocked once, and went in.

He looked up from studying papers.

"Stop throwing your power around. This isn't your company. You're here as a guest of the Center. How dare you hack into our systems?"

"Hello to you, too. And it wasn't exactly difficult," he said, flatly.

"I could throw you out on your ass," she said, narrowing the mess of emotions to a righteous anger that flared hot. "It's only for poor, long-suffering Phoebe that I'm letting you stay."

He stood, wove his way through the papers, books—Source don't tell her there were more old rocks in the room, did he think this a museum?!—squaring up to her, and it was only her experience and eagle eye that saw him hunch slightly over his abdomen as he got up.

"So let me go. If you don't want me here, let me go." His eyes narrowed.

"You're injured. I can't let you go. You're not responsible enough to look after yourself. The minute you leave here you're probably going to accidentally walk off a cliff." She stepped into him. They were inches apart, him glowering, her glaring.

She would show him.

She lifted his shirt up, and his stomach muscles tensed. She sent a thread of energy into him to examine the wound. She didn't need to reach for the ether. Energy was bubbling inside her, eager to be used.

He was healing. If he had been anyone else, she'd have let them go. But he wasn't safe on his own. They needed to monitor him for another couple of days before she could even think about releasing him. "You need to be here."

"Oh, so I'm a prisoner now, am I?" he said. She could feel the heat of his belly where she held his shirt out of the way. The flush inside her built.

"Of course not! But you take risks, and you won't heal if you keep pushing yourself."

"Right now, you're the only one pushing me," he said.

She dropped his shirt.

"I'm trying to help you," he said. "Your bracelet is important. And I think it might also be dangerous."

"Don't change the subject," she said.

"Would you like to talk about us instead?" His tone had changed. Instead of fiery, it was silky. She wanted to wrap herself in it. Her body ached, but her brain was so muddled. So many feelings. So much fire. "I would. I'd like to talk about our time on the boat, where you weren't angry. Where sometimes you were soft, and sometimes you were commanding. We both wanted each other. Do you still want me, Cara?"

The hot anger inside her had transmuted. The churning in her stomach was lighter, fluttery. Yet she was still burning.

"Why haven't you been to see me?" He ran a solitary finger down the line of her arm.

She watched it, caught by the sensation that shivered out from his warm skin. "It was a holiday romance. A one-time thing. And you have other Healers looking after you. There was no need."

"No need? Hmm." When he lifted his finger and put his hand back down by his side, she grabbed it. The fire exploded.

"Goddamn it, yes, I want you. And it's bugging the hell out of me given everything we have going on." She closed the few inches between them, gripping his wrist like a tether, and kissed him, hard and demanding. He responded immediately.

There was an echo of the white light she had felt in the vision, like a flash going off. It was so fast she decided her over-active imagination had engineered it to give her an excuse to kiss him. Groaning, she quickly broke it off, and his eyebrows lifted.

"But you're trouble," she rasped, as much to herself as to him. "So much trouble."

"Too much trouble?" he asked.

She had no freaking idea.

Archer alternated between rest, meditating the way Cara had shown him, and research. He tried not to think about their argument about the database. She was wrong. He trusted her, and she had shared information that exposed him.

Was she contrary, naïve, or did she have such a blind loyalty to her Guild that she couldn't see the implications of what she was doing?

He paced around the artifact in his room, glowering at it. Books had piled up on his table and sofa, half of them marked in various places with paper. He was still trying to discover more about it, and the site.

Goddamn it, she'd shared information about herself as well, entering herself into the database as easily as she had him. Did she have no sense of self-preservation?

Then there was the minor matter of his pride. He didn't want to look too closely at that. Why should he care if she knew what his vulnerabilities were? She was a Healer. He had no qualms about that aspect of her. She'd never use that information against him, or think less of him.

Still, it felt uncomfortable. Sure, he knew everyone had strengths and weaknesses. But part of his public persona as a business executive was projecting strength and confidence. He didn't like showing the other side. He might feel not-good-enough, but others didn't need to know that. And she should know that. He was a 'younger' energetic, he had been born just after World War II, and some human conditioning always crept into their behaviors.

The fact he'd hacked into the database initially, well, it had been for good reasons. And lucky that he had.

Right?

He rolled his head, trying to release the tension there, before he went back to pacing. Then there was the trip that had started so well, and turned into a disaster. He'd been so certain, so sure he was right about the location. Yet they hadn't had the chance to find it. Because of him.

Maybe he should have gone without Cara first. But he'd been excited to share that aspect of his world with her, his love of the sea and diving. And he was proud of his team, the people he worked with. She'd seen him at his worst, he wanted her to see him at his best.

He rubbed his forehead. He'd been trying to show off, and had failed miserably.

Dammit, he needed to find that location. He wanted to redeem himself in her eyes.

He heard a short tap on the door, and Ai slipped in.

"Hey."

"How are you feeling?" she said.

He shrugged, then pulled a face at the pain. "I've been better. You?"

"I'm good." She bit her lip. "I wanted to see if you solved the puzzle."

"Puzzle?"

She gestured to his nightstand, where there was a sketch he'd drawn of the needle from the wall of the lighthouse. "We needed one more piece of info, right? So does that needle mean north or south?"

He picked up the paper and stared at it. "Needles used to be used as a sort of compass, as certain types of metal, like iron, are magnetic. We know our ancestors had technology way beyond other civilizations, so I would expect them to have discovered this. Which would mean, as the needle is pointing up, that it's most likely the north point."

"We have to go!" Ai's eyes shone.

"You know we can't." And if his tone came out somewhat bitter, he couldn't help it. "It'll be a long time before Cara trusts me with you again, and I'm still supposed to be resting."

"You seem a lot better," Ai said, eyes assessing him. "And Cara must want to know the answer too, she hates not finishing things."

He shrugged and changed the topic to video games. They spent an easy half hour talking, then Ai left.

Picking up the sketch once more, he considered his options. His gut told him he was right, but the only way to be certain was to go. To see for himself.

He was well enough to go, he knew he was. He'd done the work she wanted, he'd put himself back on the road to recovery.

He could find and dive the site, and bring her to it the next weekend. Or maybe the woman could take a bloody holiday. She worked like a demon.

He made up his mind.

Using his cell, he called his staff to arrange transport. Meeting a speedboat at the beach was likely to be the least noticeable. His staff could take the plans from there. That was what money was for, after all.

And Cara? He'd write her a note.

Perhaps one that she wouldn't find too quickly.

Elrian had arrived on the island before Imogen, but she had ordered him to meet with her that first evening. She got him through the external security gate without the guard there even noticing, but said it wasn't the time for him to penetrate further.

"I know we're on the right path," Imogen exalted. "When we arrived, my pendant reacted with a burst of power that nearly floored me. It's telling me this is our moment."

She was wired, her usual composed manner had all but disappeared under some kind of energetic hunger. She vibrated with magic.

Elrian sat on a boulder in a part of the grounds that was covered in shrubs and trees, providing a space for him to remain hidden. He had shucked off his shoes so he could bury his feet in the earth. He needed that connection right now to give him power, or Imogen might consume him without thinking. He barely recognized her. The feeling of emptiness inside him was ever-present, and a connection to one of his Chakra elements took the edge off. He knew, intellectually, that most people would consider them both to be Rogues, though he would argue with the definition of the term these days. He was envious that she didn't seem to feel the constant hunger that was eroding him.

She raised a hand, and with a quick pulse of power, destroyed a small rock on the ground a few feet away. Elrian's hands flew up to protect his face.

"My love, calm down. You'll attract attention before we're ready," he begged.

Imogen had control over her power such that she was able to be a Rogue hiding in plain sight at the Guild—when he realized the meaning of the name she'd chosen to use as her cover, it was hard to understand their stupidity in not seeing her—which had given them tremendous advantages. Losing that would be a blow.

She appeared so unpredictable, however, that he worried she would burn the identity she'd had for decades.

Her real identity, Imogen, had fallen into legend, now assumed dead, her dark acts stopped.

If only they knew.

"The work we have been doing has increased my power," she said. "I can feel it inside me, burning to get out. I want to use it. I *need* to use it. I could raze the place to the ground right now."

"Let's stick to your plan," he said. "Your position in Anahata Guild is useful. It gives us access to resources and information that are helping us decipher the prophecies. If you act precipitously, or you're discovered, we'll lose that opportunity."

Imogen had drawn up the shards of rock she had created into a cloud and was turning them. They spun faster and faster. A tiny tornado, barely the size of his hand, appeared in front of them. He swallowed. Imogen's magic, always stronger than most, had increased by leaps and bounds.

"If you spend the next twenty-four hours understanding their security, you can let me in just as you said. I'll do the work of dispatching Archer and Cara, and taking Kayla. It creates an alibi for you, and avoids suspicion."

The cyclone whirled. Was it growing? It was sweeping more particles up. If she released it, it could create a path of damage that would be hard to explain by natural means.

"Perhaps," Imogen said, "it's time we drew some attention."

Was her pendant glowing? Had she charged it before she came? It had power, he knew that, but she was always somewhat reticent to explain exactly what it was and how it operated. It needed to be fed, just as remnant stones had to be created by that burst of energy from an energetic's death.

"If we take out this couple, we can concentrate all our time and resources on discovering the location we need to take the remnant stones to once we have them—and hopefully how to use them. Your future access to Anahata's library could be vital," he said.

She pursed her lips. After a few tense moments, she opened her hand, palm up, and the rock fragments fell harmlessly to the ground. She was stunningly beautiful to him still. Stunning, but deadly.

He rose, slowly, and touched her cheek. "Be the dutiful Anahata Guild member. You're so much cleverer than them. Gather their secrets and tell me when you need me."

She nodded, though her eyes were on the far-off horizon.

"And when you do, I'll be ready," he said. "I will shake the very earth itself to do your bidding."

26

Ten minutes into the journey, Archer realized he had a problem.

"What the hell are you doing here?" he asked Ai. He couldn't believe it. How had he missed her sneaking aboard the boat? Her training must be going better than he'd known if she'd managed that. Although he'd been more focused on keeping himself to the shadows than looking out for someone doing the same.

"I heard you talking on the phone. I want to come," she said, her arms folded, face mutinous.

"How did you sneak out?" he asked. He had to raise his voice over the noise of the boat roaring beneath them.

"I told the staff I was going outside to check on you, and then I followed you to the coast. I used my energies to cloak myself. Anyway, Cara let me go on the last trip. It will be fine."

He groaned. He didn't think it would be, but he wanted this expedition to be as fast as possible, and going back might alert Cara and her team, and then he might never get away. Closing his eyes briefly, he sent up a prayer to Source that this didn't turn into the disaster he suspected it would be. "Okay."

Her eyebrows flew up. "Really? Great!"

"Cara's going to kill me," he muttered. And yet he wished she was with them.

"She's already mad at you," Ai said, matter-of-factly. "Not sure she can get any madder."

Archer rubbed his forehead. "Believe me, there's always the possibility of madder."

The tension in Cara's body grew as Maya and her team walked around the Center, making copious notes on tablets. Cara had tried to peer over their shoulders several times to see what they were typing, but with no success. The woman was unable to make a comment without some kind of undertone, and she was driving Cara crazy.

Her team member Auretta was almost as bad. She never stopped talking and had a sort of sympathetic concern that was almost as stressful as the disapproving silence. She'd ask a question, then nod and make a *hmmm* that implied she was so sorry that you were dealing with that, even when the question was as innocuous as what did they feed those who were healing.

Iris was the only one who seemed pleased to be there, and commented on the wild beauty of the grounds, and the organization of the Center that Cara had worked so hard to build. Cara was relieved by her presence, but had broken and gone to Archer's room twice to vent. He hadn't been there either time. She hadn't seen him all day. But she wanted to. She really did.

Still, he wasn't confined to his bed. She'd assumed he was out getting fresh air.

She went to see Sophea, their Ajna coma patient. She was restless. No wonder, given all that was happening.

But Cara knew her own agitation might be feeding this, given her role as cornerstone of the Center. Sophea was highly sensitive. Cara needed to self-soothe a little, meditate and re-center to make sure she didn't knock the Center off-balance while the inspection was in progress. She made a note to spend some of her evening grounding herself.

The third time she popped her head around Archer's door and he wasn't there, she went in. She stood at the center of the room and scanned it. Nothing had changed since the last two visits. He hadn't been back, and it had been hours. She didn't think he'd have the patience or stamina to be out for that long after his injury. Sure, he was nearly healed—again—but he wasn't ready for the outside world. And that was her professional opinion, nothing personal influencing that. Not that she wanted him around. He was a disaster.

She walked to the window to look outside and see if she might catch sight of him, when she saw the note addressed to her.

Cara,

I'm going to find the artifact. Once it's located, you can join me.

Archer.

She stood, blank-faced, staring. What the *hell* was he thinking?

She swiveled in place, as if he might be somewhere in the room she'd missed. The room was as empty as it had been last time she'd looked.

The man was an idiot. Barely healed, and he was off gallivanting in his private plane again? He had too much money, and not enough sense.

Ife stuck his head round the door.

"Oh, there you are," he said. "Have you seen Ai? She said she was stuck on working with the air element, and I said I'd help her, but I can't find her."

A horrible suspicion bloomed. Cara closed her eyes. Oh Source, please no. Surely, no.

"Have you checked her room?" she asked.

"No sign of her there either. I might have missed her, but I've been searching for a while. She's usually pretty reliable."

Cara opened her eyes. "Follow me."

She went directly to Ai's room, dreading what she might find. Perhaps she was wrong, and Ai had just gone for a walk. The girl was still finding her feet in their world, and it could be overwhelming. Perhaps she needed some time in nature to rebalance.

She knocked on Ai's door, with no reply. She pushed the door open, and caught sight of a note on the desk in Ai's sloping hand.

With Archer. All good! We're going to find the stone thing, then you can come activate it, so we're saving you some time. Will keep you posted!

Cara sank down on the bed. *How. Dare. He.* How dare he take Ai with him? She was under Cara's care, and he had no business inviting her along. That arrogant good-for-nothing. All that money and he assumed he could do what he liked with other people's lives.

So now she had a delegation of contemptuous middle management types wandering around her Center, upsetting her staff and guests, she'd lost a patient, and the young woman she was responsible for had run away.

She didn't have enough stress balls for this.

Alright. The audit team were handled for now. She had time to deal with Archer.

She picked up her cell, and called him first, but the phone was switched off, as was Ai's, though she left them both blistering messages.

She selected Phoebe from her contacts, dialed.

"Cara? Is everything okay?"

The story spilled out of Cara, along with rage, frustration and fear as to where Ai might be.

"So no, it's really, really not okay," she finished.

There was a pause from Phoebe. "Arch can be…difficult. But he's more responsible than you think. He wouldn't have invited Ai along without telling you. Is there a possibility Ai might have followed him and snuck aboard?"

Huh. There was more than a possibility, but it hadn't been something that had occurred to Cara. Ai had lived on the streets and in foster homes for most of her life. She was very independent. Cara sometimes forgot she wasn't like her peers in age. "It's possible, yes."

"Alright. Archer will take care of her, that I can promise you," Phoebe said.

"What does he know about looking after a teenager?" Cara said.

"For starters, they seem to have struck up a friendship," Phoebe replied. "Ai seems quite into games, and she's smart. But I think you've got Archer wrong. He's headstrong, true, and demanding, but he's a good man. A good energetic."

Cara snorted. "He spends his life being photographed for gossip magazines and at galas with a succession of hot women on his arm."

"He does, sometimes, though that's PR, he's not dating them. Neither of us enjoys that side of the business." Phoebe sounded amused. "I'm surprised you're aware of his public profile."

Cara flushed.

"Let me tell you some things about Archer. He and I founded Disp@tch from scratch, but when we started, we were researchers. As computers became more commonplace, Archer realized he had a real affinity with coding languages. We were looking at ways to monitor human communications for energetic exposure or activity." Phoebe paused.

Cara was listening, staring at Ai's small collection of possessions. Why did it matter so much to her what kind of a man Archer was? Why was this so important to her?

"We were hackers, basically. He loved what we did then, and I've never known anyone to work harder than him. It was such fun, in the beginning, almost a hobby," Phoebe said. "Then, we hit commercial gold, almost by accident. We created a secure messaging system—meant originally for energetics. We hated the idea of advertising, and privacy was critical, and our energetic users loved it—and ended up sharing it with their human friends. We'd built a business, and it was growing at a huge pace. To keep the privacy aspect for users, we began charging businesses to use it, and bang, by the late 2010s we were one of the first messaging apps out there, and very successful along with it."

"And Archer realized then that women would fall into his lap?" Cara said.

"You seem very focused on Archer's love life," Phoebe commented.

Busted.

"He's dated, certainly, but so far he hasn't found anyone he's wanted to share a home with," Phoebe continued. "And we made a deliberate choice to use that to the business's advantage. Being portrayed as the playboy-geek in the press humanizes him—and makes him seem less of a threat to our competition."

Another pause.

"Listen. There's something going on between you and Arch, I can see that. So I'm going to share some things I wouldn't normally."

Cara froze, and her flush deepened.

"Our work still takes up a lot of his energy, and in his spare time, such as it is, he's obsessed with the myths and legends of our people. It's what he loves, and I suspect one day he'll leave the business and make that his job. In the meantime, he doesn't think I can manage without him, and despite the fact that much of his passion for the business is to prove to his family he's as good as his sister—"

"Why?" Cara frowned.

"His family are all brilliant, but his sister is Estella Hampton." Phoebe said.

"The scientist who won the Nobel Prize in Physics?" That was quite the sibling to live up to.

"That's the one. His family love him, don't care what he does, but he has this need to prove himself worthy, and so he won't let go of developing the business," Phoebe continued. "He feels responsible for the people we employ, and for the work we do protecting energetics."

"Because he's controlling."

"He is. And because he cares, deeply. And if you don't mind me saying, that combination could apply to you, too, right?"

Cara's eyebrows rose. *Hmph.* Called out.

Who was Archer truly? He had been rude, entitled, but was that simply because he'd been hurt and stressed? Was who she had seen on the boat the real Archer? Or was the image the magazines shown correct, was he a controlling, flirtatious genius-geek who bedded a new woman every week?

She rubbed her forehead. She had used the image from the magazines to create distance between them. Believing that he was an entitled prick had made it easier not to fall for him.

"I know it's probably hard for you to believe, but the work we do at Disp@tch for energetics is as important to our race as the Healing Centers. Our systems mean we pick up on communications about the occasional Rogue or outed energetic quickly. Without it, in this age of videos in an instant, we'd never be able to stay in the shadows. And we're not ready—and perhaps never will be—to come out to humans." Phoebe sighed.

A headache throbbed at Cara's temples. Perhaps if she'd interacted with Archer differently, he would have told her what he was doing. Or if she'd built a stronger relationship with Ai, she wouldn't have gone off with him. She'd handled it wrong and now two people she cared about were off doing dangerous things, and she wasn't there to protect them.

An incredible noise assaulted her ears, and the ground shook. What the hell?

"What's happening?" Phoebe said. Her voice sounded far away.

"I don't know," Cara said, dizzy. "I need to find out. Something's happened, and I don't think it's good."

She hung up, dropped the phone into her pocket and shoved through the door, running toward what she thought just might have been an explosion.

Earth flew around Elrian as he strode through the Healing Center. He felt good in a way he hadn't for weeks, plunging his power into the ground and releasing it, shaking the foundations of the building.

The Healing Center wasn't his target, though. He was heading for the Rehabilitation Center. They needed to impact the group who were pitted against them in the prophecy, and Imogen had told him to do as he pleased. He was the distraction, while she went to kill Cara. He was going back for Kayla, and this time there would be no mistakes.

Chaos flew around him as he used Muladhara to send ripples through the earth, and concrete and bricks crumbled.

He reached the electronic and energetic gates of the Rehab Center. This should have proved a problem but Imogen had given him a key, along with the location.

He tapped in the code and swiped the key, and the door opened with a click. He stepped through, into the high security zone of the building.

The first Rogue he let out of her room was an older woman, whose Anja energy throbbed and pulsed, so he could almost see it. He'd been intending to simply let her out, but she was too tempting.

She stepped cautiously to the door, her head cocked. She put a foot over the threshold, and he gave in, grabbing her shoulder hard, and heaving with his energy. The power flew from her to him, as if into a vacuum, and his senses sharpened. As she sagged, he dropped her to the ground, and strode on.

Now so much power ran through him it seemed no fun to use the key he'd been given, so he threw his head back and roared, clenching then releasing his fists—and the magic he'd built up in them. The energy shot out of him, plunged into each doorframe, and shattered it. Eight doors blew open, smashing into each other and the corridor with a tremendous bang.

He stalked past the open doors, once or twice grabbing for an individual who came too close, and drawing energy from them. He no longer tried to match his own energies, finding it easier and easier to drain others. He was shaking, but the tremors going through him matched those he was shoving into the building.

Yet after walking through the entire wing, although he'd found sixteen Rogues, none of them was his target.

He strode back to the courtyard that joined the two sections, and entered the healing side of the Center. He finally found his target in a room with walls covered with sketches. She hadn't come to the door, huddled in her bed, her back up against the wall, her legs drawn up against her chest.

When their eyes met, she whimpered, recognizing him. He had no need to disguise himself, though Imogen would continue to hide her identity.

He closed the gap between himself and the girl, grabbing her by her shirt. He saw resignation in her eyes before she closed them. She was already beaten. She knew what was coming.

He centered himself, ready to drain her, then the movement of hands caught his eye. Her fingers repeatedly stroked her upper arms.

A memory caught at him, of a younger Cassidy doing something similar when she was anxious, or distressed.

He looked again at Kayla. She wasn't much like Cassidy physically, but something about her reminded him of the girl Cassidy had been; in the dark decades after his wife had been torn from him, when another, insignificant woman had left him with a child to bring up and mould as he wished.

Tears ran down Kayla's face as she waited, otherwise limp in his grasp, for pain or death.

He could deal either. Both. He had that power. He could rip the energy out of her fast, or he could savor it and pull it out of her a drop at a time. And either way, he could take a little, or everything.

A shudder ran through him at the idea of taking it all, his breath quickening. It would be so easy, and he would have so much.

But he didn't need it. He was still invigorated from taking from the Rogues he'd passed on the way in.

Perhaps this girl, this young woman who reminded him a little of Cassidy, could be helpful. A hostage or a shield. Perhaps he should wait a little longer to kill her. Anyway, he reasoned, that would give them the time to find out what she knew. If she truly had told the energetics he had come to hate anything critical about his and Imogen's plans.

He dragged her to her feet and she let out a helpless sob. He shook her and her eyes opened. He drew on his Ajna energy, infusing his words with control.

"Come."

27

Her Center was in chaos.

She sped toward the noise she had heard, adrenaline coursing through her. She pulled energy as she ran, preparing for…something. Anything.

Had a Rogue broken out? Or were they under attack?

Jason staggered toward her, bleeding from a cut on his arm. She stopped.

"What happened?"

His eyes stared, but didn't seem to see her. They were no longer innocent.

She put her hand on his chest, and let her Anahata flow into him, calming his sympathetic nervous system, and his shocky gaze steadied. She stopped before she normally would, conserving her energy. She didn't know what else might be needed.

"An explosion," he said. "The Center's under attack."

"Who by? What do they want?" Cara asked.

"I don't know. I saw a hooded figure use energy to attack Thea...
I was going to get help...but I'm not sure...I mean...I didn't know
where or who from—"

Cara nodded briskly. "Get out and call Adam. Go to Victoria to
our house there. Take anyone else injured with you, and get the
patients out. We're not equipped for a fight. I'll find what's
happening, I'm on my way to activate the defences, and hold them
until Adam can send reinforcements."

Victoria, the major town on the island, was a couple of hours'
drive away, but they had a smaller property there. Whatever
happened, they were going to need help.

He nodded and ran off.

She moved cautiously toward the first explosion she had heard.
Smoke drifted in her direction.

Was this Elrian? Surely he wouldn't attack a Healing Center. Was
he trying to free someone, or was this about the prophecy?

Or was it someone else? Her mind ran through the possibilities,
sorting through the Rogues and other energetics they had here. None
of them were highly dangerous. Dangerous, yes, but not *highly*
dangerous.

She threw a shield up around her as the noise of fighting and
destruction became louder.

She swallowed as she realized it was coming from the Rehab
wing.

Just who, exactly, was trying to break out who?

Archer floated through the water, kicking with his fins to direct
himself. He'd been searching the area in concentric circles, and was
on his third dive of the day. This should probably be the last, but
Source damn it, he was close, he knew it.

A shoal of fish swam past him, ignoring his presence. The
visibility hadn't been great, and although he'd seen rocks and rubble

on the sea bed that didn't seem natural, he hadn't found any structures.

The water pressed on his wet suit. At this depth it was cooler, despite the warm weather above. He checked the dive computer on his wrist. He needed to allow for the time to head back to the surface.

He'd expand his search one more time then head back up to the boat. He gave the okay sign, his thumb and finger together in a circle, to Nahla, his partner for this dive, and she returned it.

As he angled in another direction, he was surrounded by a shoal of tuna, their scales reflecting a silvery sapphire. Unbothered by his presence, they swam past him. He pressed on. After a few more minutes of inky blue, he caught sight of a large shadow. His breath echoed in his ears, the air tasting, as it should, of nothing, adding to the eerie experience. Could this be it?

He kicked his fins to move faster, and the shadow grew, finally turning into a looming structure.

This was it. The temple.

He swam around it slowly, fascinated. Accounting for underwater magnification, it was perhaps the size of a medium cathedral. It must have sunk into the sea somehow. Had that been natural, or had they submerged it on purpose? It was in remarkably good shape, either way, though he saw white coral on the sea floor in places, fish darting between them.

He checked in with Nahla, and gestured to an opening ahead. He wanted to go in and explore. He was looking for something that might connect to Cara's bracelet—where it could be used or placed—he wasn't sure exactly. He felt he'd know it if he saw it, though he had nothing to base that on. Just a feeling. But energetics knew their feelings were worth listening to.

He swam through the opening into a large room, his powerful flashlight showing the way, his heart a thundering soundtrack. There were many more openings that had probably been windows, though most were blocked. Rubble lay strewn on the floor, seaweed swaying between them and fish going about their business.

Several columns had fallen and settled in a mass of stone. He swam around them, trying to make sense of it all. What had been here? What had this looked like before it had vanished into the sea? And where could Cara's bracelet be placed?

He wished she was there with him, to share the wonder of discovery with her. He wanted her to experience how it felt to be in such a special place. To be so close to finding answers. They could use her bracelet together, and be another step forward.

Because this was incredible.

He swam through more openings, mostly what he thought had been doors, delighting in the exploration. Who had walked these halls before? What had they done here?

Finally, he came to a doorway that was larger than the rest, but mostly blocked. A huge door that looked like some kind of rusted metal hung from one hinge, partially obscuring the entrance. Next to that were large stones that could have fallen from the ceiling, but either way, the space left wasn't enough for him or Nahla to fit through.

He positioned himself so he could see through the gap, able to place his head and one shoulder in it, careful not to get stuck. This was the largest room yet, with carvings on the walls that he couldn't quite make out. He let his gaze wander, his heart beating fast. This was without question the most stunning find he'd ever made. Not that he could share it with the wider world, but perhaps it would show his parents all his efforts in this area had been worthwhile.

He frowned. Was there some kind of pattern on the floor? He tried to make it out, but silt obscured a lot of it. He pulled energy. There wasn't much he could do underwater, as he didn't have an affinity with Svadisthana, but perhaps… He concentrated, and created a small bubble of air, that he nudged to drift down to the floor. He moved it back and forth, and opened a space in the silt. By dragging the bubble around, and focusing his flashlight on it, he could make out the pattern, although it was hard to work out what it was in this way.

He checked his dive computer. Not long before he needed to start his ascent. Nahla would come seeking him soon.

He swept the floor with his bubble methodically, starting at the crumbling wall and moving his bubble from side to side, making careful use of the flashlight so as not to miss any light sources that might be present.

The first unusual marking on the floor he caught sight of was a circle. It was carved into the floor, but as he moved the silt away from it, it seemed to glow.

It wasn't large, perhaps the diameter of a watch face. He tried to expand his small air bubble so he could make out the whole thing at once. His body contracted at the effort. Unfortunately his dive computer didn't take account of this kind of thing.

The bubble increased its size infinitesimally slowly, with Archer on tenterhooks wanting to see what was there.

It definitely was glowing. Whatever this carving was, it had a purpose way beyond decoration. He squinted through the indigo darkness, trying to see the color. Was it red?

He continued sweeping, conscious of time. Another circle, perhaps orange? Everything was so murky down here. The glow of each carving helped, a little. The second carving wasn't parallel to the first, and he frowned, wondering what shape they would make.

Another circle, shining with a faint yellow glimmer. Then green, furthest away from his current position, the color seeming to flicker as he sent his air bubble over it. He was starting to have a suspicion about what he was seeing, though the why was still beyond him.

He could see it was a circle. A circle of…circles? He hit the next one, a blue ring. As he did his air bubble shivered, its outer surface rippling, and then seemed to get absorbed into the smaller circle, which flared blue, its faint gleam becoming a constant glow.

Archer could see it even without the air bubble, which was lucky.

But despite it sucking in his energy, it had told him what he was looking at.

An energetic circle. Six circles in a circle, representing all the Chakras, apart from Sahasara, the Chakra of Source.

Wait. He scrabbled to push his head further into the room, to get a better view, and, with some effort, created another air bubble. It was small, but he dragged it around the space between the six circles.

It didn't take long to hit it, especially as it was three times as big as the other circles. Although it didn't glow, he knew the color it would be when it did. The symbol of Source.

White. Perfect white.

He went over the floor again, widening his search to see if there was anything else there. This was it, he knew it, what he'd been looking for, but he couldn't see yet how Cara's bracelet fit or what they were supposed to do with it.

Another circle, expanding the area he had uncovered again. His forehead scrunched behind his mask. His time was almost up.

He saw it then, a little way beyond the green circle. A pillar, just as he'd thought. And a space in it where Cara's bracelet would fit perfectly. What was odd was the second shape carved inside the indentation. It was smaller, and he had to shine the flashlight onto it to see that it seemed to be a teardrop shape.

Something nudged him from behind and he jerked, hitting his arm painfully against the stone he was wedged against.

It was Nahla, and she was tapping the dive computer on her wrist and gesturing upwards. He nodded, and they started their slow ascent.

But he was elated. He'd done it. Found a temple of the ancients. He would bring Cara here. He would prove to her he was right to keep going, that he had finally found answers—finally found what they had been seeking.

C H A P T E R

28

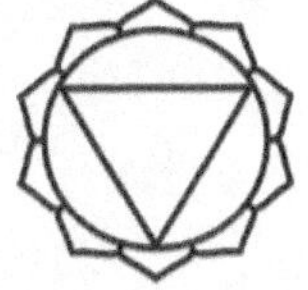

Cara burst into the courtyard that was between the Rehab and Healing sides of the Center—and ran straight into hell.

The heart of the Center she had dedicated herself to for decades, and nurtured and led, had been partly reduced to dust and rubble, while her people fought to protect it and themselves. Its tidy elegance had been turned to chaos.

It took Cara time to work out what was happening, given the blood, dirt and debris scattered throughout the yard. Ife and Thea were there, along with Iris, one of the representatives of Anahata Guild, all angled toward a fourth individual, whose face was hidden by folds of material.

Cara ran forward and spun her energy around her. World War II was a long time in the past, when she and some of her fellow energetics had joined the humans to fight, but she could still use what she had learned during that horrible period. She might not draw on them often, but she had a solid Manipura and fighting skills. Working with Rogues wasn't often dangerous, but it could be.

She threw up her shields, as familiar and reliable as an old friend. As she did, the mysterious figure attacked her with invisible darts made of air. So they had Anahata as one of their energies then. Useful to know.

Luckily Cara's shield was built of both Manipura and Anahata, which made Anahata one of the less effective attacks against her. The darts dissolved, her shields taking the hit, draining her energies a little.

The figure seemed to wear a dark-green hooded cloak common to Guild members of Anahata. Its movements seemed feminine, the hands that Cara could see fine and delicate. Surely this wasn't one of the three women who had come to inspect the Center? Two women, rather, as Iris was right out in front fighting.

Whoever they were, they were highly skilled, and very powerful. Even with four against one, the figure held its own.

A deafening noise exploded from the Rehab wing and her gut clenched. Oh Source. They were trying to break someone out. She needed to get past the person in the courtyard to protect the other wing. The Rogues in there were not ready to be released into the world.

Ife and Thea were strong, and if Iris was fighting with them, they could hold their own against one person, even if they were powerful. But even one Rogue being released could be a disaster.

"Imagine it's business as usual," she said, directing her voice to the three defenders' ears with a little air. "Just another patient, just another Rogue having a bad day."

A sharp nod from Ife. "Go."

"Without you, the Center's systems will fail," added Iris, who Cara could barely hear over the elements that were loose in the courtyard.

Cara dove toward the Rehab buildings, almost tripping on a flagstone that had been upended. Before she could get close, the figure attacking Ife and the others twisted away from them and toward her.

She frowned, but went with it.

"Change of plans," she panted. "Deal with the Rogues, I'll draw this one away. Once I've lost them, I'll go for the defences."

And with one blast of her power toward the figure, she ran.

"We have to go back down!" Archer gestured to the sea. "We need to find out more about the site and document it."

He paced back and forth on the deck, the wood warm and slightly rough under his bare feet. He had peeled his wetsuit down to his waist when he'd got back on deck, and he was enjoying the feel of the hot sun drying his body.

"You know we can't go back down today," Nahla pointed out. "We've done three dives already. At this depth we've hit the max, even with our energetic constitutions. Whatever is below will still be there tomorrow."

"But what was it?" Ai asked. "Can you tell us what was down there? Because right now you're sounding kinda out of it."

"A temple. One of the energetics' ancient temples," Archer said. "We have to get Cara here, ASAP."

Ai pursed her lips. "You'll have to go back and persuade her."

Archer sighed, knowing she was right.

He wanted Cara here. He'd found it. They could find out together what her bracelet was and what it did.

But he also wanted to go down again and explore the temple, mapping it out and documenting it. It was the find of the century for their people.

His heart was torn between two places.

"We'll send a couple of the crew down while we still have the light," suggested Nahla. "They can take cameras and document as much as possible. You can contact Cara and see if you can persuade her to come, and if she will, we can head back and meet her at the Marina."

"Fine," Archer groused. He didn't want others to explore the temple. He wanted to do it himself. This might be the most efficient way of approaching it, but it would pain him not to be the one down there.

Nahla went inside to brief her crew, and Ai, who was sitting on one of the wooden benches screwed down to the deck, her knees pulled up to her chest, cocked her head. "Cara might not want to come, you know. I wasn't kidding about needing to persuade her."

He frowned. "Of course she'll want to. This is the answer to her puzzle."

"We just left without telling her. She's not going to be happy. Plus, I've never seen an adult who works as much as she does. You already got her to leave her Center for a couple of days. You're never going to get her to leave again so soon." She went back to playing a game on her phone.

That wasn't a great thought, and the pit in his belly grew. As Archer went to shower, he considered how best to approach Cara. He wanted to call her, but maybe he should wait till he had some of the footage from the other divers. Now that he'd found something, she wouldn't mind the fact he'd had to disappear without telling her. He'd shown he was right. Plus, he wanted her there. That would count, wouldn't it?

Resigned he wasn't going back down again today, he stripped off his dive suit to his shorts, hanging it on the rail. He decided to call Phoebe to check on her. He blanched when he dug out his phone and saw the number of missed calls and texts. Finally he'd been able to distract himself from his tech, and the world wanted back in.

"Archer, finally. Where have you been? And is Ai with you?" Phoebe did not sound thrilled to hear from him.

"Uh, yeah. Did Cara tell you?"

"Of course she told me! She called me, frantic."

"Ai told me she left her a note…"

"I'm not sure the girl is even out of her teens, and either way, she's agreed to be under Cara's care. You should have called her."

"I'll text her when we get off this call." His stomach lurched as he said it though he couldn't quite tell why. He changed the subject, asking Phoebe how the demo was progressing.

"It's going great," Phoebe said in answer to his question. "I met with the investors over dinner last night, and we got on really well."

Huh. He'd always found it quite hard work to pitch projects to investors. "What did they think of the prototype?"

"I'm pretty sure they're going to go for it. The signs were good. Lots of engaged questions." Phoebe sounded more enthused than usual.

"You didn't mind dealing with them?"

"Mind? I *loved* it."

His brow wrinkled. She had? "Did they ask where I was?"

"I told them you'd been injured in a car accident, but would be right as rain soon. They seemed fine with it. More than fine. So you can relax, take the time you need to heal. I've got things handled," Phoebe said, her usual crisp efficiency returning.

They signed off the call, and Archer sent a quick text to Cara.

Ai is with me. She's fine. I'll call soon.

He waited a few moments to see if she'd reply. Nothing. He slipped his phone into his bag and went out onto the deck, choosing a quiet place on the starboard side no-one else was using. He heard the others chatting as they put on their dive gear.

Archer leaned on the rail, resting his forearms on the metal. Sea surrounded them, with land far off on the horizon. There were no people here, apart from those he'd chosen to be with.

Phoebe had given him some food for thought. He was pleased she'd got on well without him, of course, and that the business was in good hands.

Wasn't he?

If he was honest, he'd always thought of himself as the front man of the business, the one who could translate tech into business speak. He and Phoebe had fallen into those roles at the start—he was the technical expert, the brilliant coder, and when he wanted to, he could also use his Vishudha charisma to dazzle the external investors and clients.

Phoebe, as COO, was the person who'd set up their organizational structure, helped them grow. She ensured they had the right locations and equipment to work with, and that they employed the right people. She put the design touches on their products, liaising with marketing, and drawing on her creativity. She also helped inspire what they should actually create, coming up with ideas around communication that he then designed. She could code too, but he was better.

He was needed.

He rolled his shoulders, tension seeping in. Twenty-five years later, he was uncertain when they had last talked about their roles. They'd fallen naturally into what they were doing, and he'd thought they were both happy with them. Except…he hadn't been happy at all. Had she? He thought back on the last couple of years.

Had he been an idiot? Had he boxed himself into a corner, thinking he was essential, denying himself time with his hobby, when Phoebe was itching to step out of her own role, feeling equally boxed in? He sighed. Had ego got the better of him?

He and Phoebe were going to need to have a proper conversation about the future of the business, and be genuine with each other about what they really wanted.

He hung his head. He had thought he'd taken Phoebe into account when living his life, but perhaps in reality he hadn't thought outside his own unmet needs.

Thoughts of Cara followed. With more time away from the business, he'd be able to visit her, perhaps dive with her. He realized he was smiling. This site alone was going to take a long time to understand, even after they'd found how it connected to her bracelet. Then his stomach clenched as he thought about Ai's comment that Cara might not be interested in joining him.

Shit.

He really liked her.

The noises at the back of the boat had stopped, suggesting the others had gone down to explore. He itched to be with them.

He noticed a shadow on the floor, and glanced up to find Ai standing next to him, peering down at the water.

"What are we looking at?" she said.

His lips quirked. "Nothing. Just realizing I might be a bigger idiot than I thought."

She nodded sagely, turning to him. "Well, sure. About anything in particular?"

"You really think Cara won't come?" he said.

She pursed her lips. "We didn't exactly end the trip great last time. Dunno how much of a good time she had."

He thought of Cara in his cabin, laughing after sex, his hand stroking her thigh. He hoped she had had some fun when she'd been here. Yet she'd considered it a one-off.

"Do you remember how she was mad at you?" Ai continued. "The snake thing, the lighthouse, the torn stomach?"

He groaned and dropped his head to the rail, and put a hand up to massage his neck.

"Errr…" Ai took a step back, a shocked expression on her face.

"What?" He straightened abruptly. If there was danger to Ai, this time he would stop it.

Ai gestured to his wrist. "Um…"

"Words, Ai. Use your words," he said, and glanced down.

Oh fuck.

He stared down blankly at the bracelet on his wrist that he absolutely, one hundred percent knew had not been there a few minutes before.

Colored strands wrapped around each other: blue, yellow, green and white. He couldn't tell what it was made of, but there was no clasp. He tugged at it experimentally, but the material appeared strong.

Excitement fizzed inside him, then faded just as quickly, a cold bucket of water dousing the fireworks that had started.

Because two things occurred to him.

Source had gifted him a bracelet. He was truly part of this adventure, part of a group of energetics who appeared to have been tasked to save their race from a great evil. He had a destiny.

But this bracelet, with its clean lines and strong colors was nothing like Cara's.

His insides felt hollow. If he was prophesied to fall in love with someone with a matching bracelet—that person wasn't going to be Cara.

He swallowed.

"What are you going to do?" Ai asked. "Can I touch it? What's it made of? Why do you think it came?"

He shrugged, a numbness seeping over him. She poked and prodded at it, trying to get it off with no success. He let her, absorbed in his own thoughts.

He'd been given a chance at something incredible. He'd love to have Cara in his life, even if only as a friend. She was one of few people in his life, like Phoebe, who'd stand up to him, and tell him the truth.

He took out his cell and snapped a photo of his wrist, sending it to Cara, then Adam. The only text he included was a question mark.

He stared at the chat between himself and Cara for a while, willing her to read it and get back to him.

Nothing.

Cara, leaning against the wall of Archer's room, listened to the noise of her vibrating cell, and wished she had a different setting on the damn thing.

The cell had fallen from her pocket as she'd dashed into the room, telling herself it was coincidence she'd chosen to come here for a breather. Yet even as she scanned the empty space, there was a spike of disappointment that its usual inhabitant was still nowhere to be found.

She'd drawn the enemy away from where the Rogues were held, varying the distance between them, while still ensuring she—Cara had decided it had to be a she—stayed with her, and away from both her people or the Rogues.

Cara's wild dash hadn't uncovered any of her patients, thank Source, so it seemed that Jason had got them out of the building, or the enemy wasn't interested in them.

The attacker didn't seem to know the building well, which was a relief. She'd drawn them deeper into the warren of rooms and given herself a moment in this one to decide what the hell she was going to do.

Assuming Jason had done his job, Adam would know by now what was happening, and he'd be here as quickly as a chopper could bring him, with whoever he could muster.

When the enemy passed by the room, her plan was to give it a moment, then dash out the other way, and the chase would be on again. She'd keep their attention on her, and keep her people safe.

She also needed to activate the Center's defenses. There were three places that could be done, in a hidden nook off her office, and in two safe rooms, one the rehab side—she was unlikely to make it there—and one on the healing side of the building.

Now that, she might manage.

Crouching behind some of Archer's artifacts, she hoped the cell wouldn't vibrate again. Did she have time to grab it? She wavered, uncertain.

She scanned the books and priceless objects scattered around the room, wondering if there was anything that could help her. Her gaze rested on a dagger of sharp black stone on Archer's coffee table. She nodded grimly. It couldn't hurt to take it.

She took a breath, thinking of Archer and how he wanted to give her answers. Her mouth twisted. She wished he were here, dammit. The place she'd called home for the last thirty years of her life was collapsing around her, all that work to provide a safe place for her people to heal was being destroyed, yet she wanted him.

She couldn't imagine what kind of destruction was happening outside. She needed to get back out there. But a weapon would help.

She crouched, then leaped to grab the dagger, and scoop up the phone, wanting to get back to cover as soon as possible. Curse this room and all its memories of Archer. Her heart ached, and her Anahata swelled inside her sympathetically.

As she tried to snatch up the blade, the floor moved. An earthquake, here? The Center shuddered, the room trembling, floor shifting.

She didn't have time to puzzle over the how. She slipped, off-balance, somehow grabbing the dagger as she fell backwards. Her head connected with the bas relief, pain smashing into her. She threw her free hand back to protect herself, and her wrist banged into the stone. Shit. Cursing Archer for the mess in his room, she pulled her wrist to her chest protectively, activating her Anahata to heal the damage inside her.

The ground still rumbled, several artifacts being shaken off various surfaces in the room. One fell toward Cara, yet another of Archer's mysterious artifacts, and landed smack on top of her bracelet on the arm that she was trying to heal.

She bit back a scream.

She blinked and lay for a second, waiting for her head to stop spinning. She knew she'd been hurt more badly than she realized when the ceiling was replaced by a starlit sky. Her body vibrated, and energy burned through her, much more than she had pulled for her healing.

Her wrist throbbed, then the ache disappeared. The energy inside her built and built, and she massaged a temple groggily with the other hand, trying to stop it. What was happening? Her body tingled until tiny needles pricked her all over. She tried to sit up, but the device atop her was disproportionately heavy, weighing her down.

She couldn't move.

Stars surrounded her, their light blinding, the needles no longer tiny.

Fear chilled her. Was this a trap? She held back a scream as the energy both tried to press her down and drag her apart.

A flash of stars and agony, the room spinning faster and faster.

A moment later, the pain and pressure dissipated, only to be replaced by a warm weight on top of her.

She pried open her eyes.

"Archer? What in Source's name are you doing here?"

Archer sat up and rubbed his face.

He was hallucinating Cara. Right?

The sun had gone, the freshness of the sea breeze.

There was no shimmer of light on water, he was in a cool room, hidden in shadows. Colors were more muted.

He no longer felt the gentle movements of the boat, and the hard deck under him had been replaced by a soft body.

He stared down.

Cara.

Where was the boat? And Ai?

How the hell did he get here?

A moan came from beneath him. It really was Cara—and he was half sitting on her. He shifted his body, offered a hand to help her up. She put a finger to her lips and pointed to a spot behind the bed.

He frowned.

Wait, did the floor just move?

Oh gods, his artifacts. The room was in chaos. They lay around the room like fallen dominos. And Cara. Who was covered in dust. Shit. She looked dreadful, nothing like her usual calm, put-together, in control self. His heart raced. On hands—hand? Was there something wrong with her other hand?—and knees, she crawled to the point she'd indicated.

Okay. They seemed to be hiding.

He scrabbled over next to her.

"What's going on? How did you bring me here?" he hissed, keeping his voice low.

She stared, mouthing the word 'no'. Her pupils were pinpoints, and she was trembling. He squeezed his eyes shut.

Okay.

Regroup. Be logical. Work out what in Source's name was going on.

He'd been on the boat. Now, he wasn't. Cara had done something to transport him here, over thousands of miles—a power that hadn't been seen for centuries, that he'd thought was a myth. Whatever had happened, it was likely she'd expended a great deal of energy. She seemed shocky, and with no idea of what was facing them, he needed to be ready, though Source knew for what.

His heart pounded as he pulled energy. Scooting around to face Cara he took her face in his hands, his touch gentle. Her eyes seemed to gaze through him. In her right hand she clutched a familiar dagger, sharp and dangerous.

"Cara, look at me," he said. He kept his breath steady, trying to help her ground through his example. He'd never seen her so vulnerable.

Bad things were happening, and though he was desperate to know how Cara had brought him here, the priority was to understand the situation, and either capture whoever was doing this, or get themselves, and anyone else, the hell out of here till help could arrive.

He needed Cara here, not wherever she had gone in her head. He pulled a little Manipura, and really hoped he was doing the right thing as he placed his palm over Cara's belly button and pushed the smallest fraction of his fire towards her Manipura Chakra.

She let him.

For a brief second, their Chakras connected, their energies touching. He gasped at the intimacy, and drew back, physically and energetically. He didn't want to break the taboo of sharing energy, rather, he was using his to bring her back, to wake her up. To touch, not to merge.

Her gaze refocused, and she blinked.

It worked.

"I don't understand," she said, voice low. "Where did you come from?"

"I don't understand either," he said. He gestured around them. "But we can talk about that later. What's happening here? Why are you hiding? Is there some kind of attack? What do they want?"

She glanced around. "I'm not certain."

"Are you okay?"

She squeezed her eyes shut and exhaled as if to start again. "I'll be fine. There are at least two, maybe more. I drew one away from the courtyard, where some of the others were fighting. I need to get to the location where I can activate the core defenses, which will lock the Rehab Center down—Jason will have gotten in touch with Adam, so help is on the way. I think the attackers are trying to break a Rogue out, but when they saw me it was easy to draw them away. None of this makes sense."

At the edges of his hearing Archer caught a yell and a crash, as if something heavy had fallen to the floor and smashed.

"I need to get back out there. Can you fight?" Cara's words came out in a rush, but she seemed more herself. Alright.

She hesitated then grabbed his arm. "Wait. Did Ai come with you? Where is she? Is she okay?"

He placed a hand over hers and nodded, gesturing at the room which was otherwise empty apart from the two of them. "She's not here, so she's fine. She should be on the boat I just left, thousands of miles away. Safe."

He hoped to Source she was, but she wasn't in the room with them, so it seemed that only he had been dragged back to Canada. They'd need to check, but there was nothing they could do in the moment.

"I can fight. What's the plan?" he said.

"We need to hold out till Adam comes. In the meantime, we need to activate the shields. Once those are triggered, they will trap any energetics or humans who are within the perimeter of the Center where they stand, friend or foe. I'll need to add my power to the shields to keep them up."

He nodded.

"I suggest we both keep a Manipura shield up. Do you maintain your Guild training?" she asked. Yellow shimmers flickered around her as she created her shield while she talked.

He nodded again. "Good idea. We don't know what's out there."

"Yeah," she said. "Ready?"

He wasn't, but who would be? Less than five minutes ago he'd been on his boat, considering his discovery and his bracelet. Shit, the bracelet.

Okay, probably not the time.

He moved into a crouch, and gave Cara the ready sign. He didn't know how he came to be here, but he was glad he was. For her.

Elrian, still dragging the girl behind him, was heading back to Imogen. An attack came from his left, an attempt to lasso him with Manipura, but he brushed it off, and threw casual power at the man, knocking him back.

At the end of a narrow corridor he saw Imogen, two energetics trying to get through her shields. She appeared not to care, focused on her own progress, but he saw one draw back an arm as if to launch an arrow of power.

He a warning. She didn't acknowledge him. As he got closer, her pendant lit up with an odd green light, and the air turned hot, dry, and hard to breathe.

Imogen screamed, agony flashing over her face, fast then gone.

She set her face and straightened her spine, then flung out a hand. Power flowed out and smashed the walls ahead of her—as well as the two energetics, who were tossed against a side wall. The slender man slid down and rolled over, groaning, but the woman's body, had flown higher, and when she hit the ground it was with a snap, her neck at a ninety degree angle, dead.

Imogen stalked through a corridor of her own making toward a room close by on Elrian's right.

He frowned, relieved he'd been too far for the falling debris to harm him. The walls had come down like a house of cards, blowing a passage for her to walk through but leaving other walls intact. Yet she was untouched, despite the destruction. At least her hood still covered her face. He was concerned her identity could be revealed if she wasn't more careful.

He scrambled after her, shouting for her attention. Through the now destroyed walls he could glimpse the sky, which seemed to darken, wind whipping particles from the destruction through the corridor. He glanced up, and narrowed his eyes. This weather hadn't been predicted. Surely…Surely Imogen couldn't be affecting the climate to this extent? If so, this was a long way from the kind of localized impact on the natural environment that energetics usually were able to do.

He caught up with her, Kayla in tow, as she entered a room, where he saw Cara and Archer, the ones they had come for, huddled behind a bed, a shimmering Manipura shield surrounding them.

Imogen caught sight of Elrian and smiled fiercely. "My power is untold. I can create devastation. We have no need to be concerned about these peons twisting the prophecy against us. I can destroy them and this entire complex, perhaps this entire island, with a flick of my wrist, and salt the earth after."

Her silver-blonde hair fluttered around her face, though Elrian felt no breeze.

Elrian shivered. How had her power increased to this extent? Killing individual humans, and even energetics to progress their ideals was part of the greater good: the restoration of energetics to their rightful place at the top of the food chain. But he was an earth energetic, and the natural environment was something that all energetics drew strength from, and its protection and balance was their deepest purpose from Source. That was still part of him—the reason he was trying to fulfill the prophecy and restore the energetics to power was because of the damage humans were doing to the environment. If Imogen desecrated it in the same way, how was she different from them? Discomfort rippled through him.

Imogen laughed, and flicked power at the two, who sprang back, their shield protecting them and moving with them. Was she playing with them?

Elrian clenched a fist. First, they needed to deal with this situation. Once they were out of here he'd talk to Imogen and remind her of their plans. This rush of power she'd gained would settle, and they could refocus. She could control the power she gained.

They were closer than ever to their goal. He just needed to keep them on track.

Cara's shield held against the energy the woman had thrown against them, but only just. What in Source's name was happening?

Then an even greater shock. The woman's hood slid down, and revealed the face of Maya.

A member of the Anahata Guild leadership, was attacking them and destroying the Healing and Rehab Center.

Another burst of power from Maya, and Cara realized she didn't need to understand it right now. She needed to fight back.

She drew energy from the ether. Usually when she was in conflict with another energetic, it was someone in the Rehab Center, and her primary aim was to restrain without hurting.

That wasn't the case here.

Cara was a strong energetic. She had to be, to run the Center— and as the manager and lynchpin of the Center, she had more energy to draw on than most.

She sent a flurry of air projectiles toward Maya, whose shield recognized the familiar energy and let them through.

They smashed into her.

She should have staggered at least, even if she'd had a shield up, given the power Cara put into them, but the other energetic absorbed them as if they were nothing, the strange pendant around her neck glowing momentarily.

"Can you put up a void shield?" she yelled at Archer. "Her energy is too similar to mine, my attack's not working."

He nodded, absorbed in his own working.

Another energetic, a male, stepped through the doorway, yanking a passive Kayla behind him.

Shit. Cara recognized Cuinn's father, Elrian. They'd known he was involved, but it was a blast of cold air to come face to face with him after so many years. And he'd managed to get Kayla out of her room—a shudder ran through Cara as she wondered if any of the other Rehab energetics had been freed. Not all of them were as innocent as Kayla.

Archer's chin jerked as he released the magics he had woven. At first, she couldn't see what had changed, then Cara realized that the blade she'd been clutching had disappeared. She hadn't felt it move, it had just vanished from her hand. Archer must have shifted it with his ether. She peered around the stones they sheltered behind and saw Maya fling the dagger back across the room, smirking. Blood drops flew from it, so it must have pierced her body, but there were no visible wounds. It was as if nothing had happened.

What the hell *was* Maya?

Archer jerked beside her. "Fuck."

Cara hadn't had eyes on the path of the dagger, but Maya had catapulted it back at Archer, who hadn't avoided it completely. His arm was bleeding.

Also, he was barely dressed.

He finally tossed up the void shield.

"Better late than never," he gasped. "I thought that would work, sorry. What's going on? Isn't Maya an Anahata Guild member?"

Cara shook her head. "I don't know. We haven't managed to scratch her so far. And they have Kayla."

Cara grit her teeth. She'd have to try something different, less…direct. She pulled power and directed it to the air around Maya. Slowly, slowly, she drew oxygen molecules out of the air around the energetic, hoping Maya wouldn't notice. It should cause something like altitude sickness, and she would first become fatigued, then hopefully pass out.

"Keep her attention," Cara hissed to Archer.

Archer nodded and several bits of debris disappeared from the floor near them and reappeared over Maya's head, showering her with stone, wood and bits of furniture.

The damned woman waved a casual hand. They scattered without touching her.

Cara concentrated on directing oxygen out of the air around Maya's nose and mouth. Cara held her own breath, and waited for Maya to drop to the floor like the stones Archer had transported.

And waited.

Although only seconds had passed, Maya should have crumped to the ground. And she hadn't.

Desperate, Cara went back to a less subtle approach. Aiming away from Maya, Cara blasted several bits of furniture around the room into the smallest pieces she could create at speed. She then created a vortex—spinning the shards around Maya. While she knew the debris wouldn't touch the other energetic, it would blind her for a few moments.

"We need out of here," Cara whispered hoarsely. "Ideas?"

Archer blinked and tried to work out how the fuck he'd gotten into this situation.

He'd been on the boat in the Aegean sea, floating peacefully and basking in the glow of discovery.

Within a second, he was with Cara in the Center half a world away.

Now someone was trying to kill them.

He held the void shield up, protecting them from the worst of the attacks. He'd been shocked when the woman hadn't been affected by anything they'd thrown at her so far.

He scanned the room. This was beyond his training. He'd never imagined he'd feel sorry to have spent more time in the boardroom than a boxing ring.

His heart slammed into his throat as he got a better look at the man who had been standing slightly behind the bomb-proof energetic, with Kayla in front of him like a human shield.

He recognized him.

The energetic from the park. The man who had involved Archer in this mess in the first place. Archer's system, already on high alert, went into overdrive.

Brains over brawn, brains over brawn. Think. Think Archer, think.

He cataloged the furniture, the priceless weapons and artifacts he'd brought in, the medical equipment, a mix of energetic and human.

He caught sight of the oxygen regulator on the wall, with clear tubing hung coiled next to it.

Hospitals stored oxygen as a liquid in central tanks, then vaporized and distributed it to patients via an internal piping system. The system was stable, but opening a regulator too quickly could cause an explosion when combined with fuel and a spark.

It was risky and dangerous, but they might just be able to blow their way through a wall and escape.

"Crazy idea," he panted, still holding the void shield around them. He wasn't sure how much longer he could protect them with it, and there was no way he could do anything else while keeping it up.

She gestured impatiently.

"We smash the regulator off the wall, throw the bedding—and bed—at it, and light it up. Blast a hole in that wall and we'll make a run for it."

Her eyebrows rose, but she nodded, then her face twisted "We can't leave Kayla. She's practically a child."

He clenched his jaw. "We'll have to come back for her. Whoever this woman is, she's too powerful. We'll all die if we try and take Kayla with us."

"Maya. She's a Guild leader of Anahata. She was leading the inspection of the Center. But I don't understand why she's working with Elrian." Cara's gazed darted around the room, seeking answers, opportunities, escape. "We can surprise Elrian from the back and grab Kayla on our way out."

He shook his head. "I'm sorry, Cara. We need to tell the Guilds about her. We need to go."

Emotions bolted across her face.

"They want to keep her alive." As Archer said it, he prayed to Source it was true. "They haven't harmed her. They need her for something."

Cara nodded tightly. He could see the internal conflict, then he felt her pull power. She raised arms that had burst into flames. She looked incredible. She squeezed her fists and released tight balls of fire in the woman's direction, and he flickered the void shield to let them through.

The woman staggered very slightly, but yet again, no harm seemed to come to her. The man stood watching, hawk-eyed but silent. Archer wondered about his connection to the ether. He was gaunt. He had Kayla under his will, but perhaps he wasn't able to join in this fight.

A wave of energy burst from the woman back toward Cara. He'd gotten the void shield back up but whatever this casting was, it finally broke through.

Although not aimed at him, feelings leaked from it and Archer ducked his head. Shame, rejection. An isolation spell, with undertones of energy harmonics. A strange choice, and one which would have needed preparation. Cara recoiled then shook it off, seemingly untouched.

However, the energetic seemed to have put enough energy into it that she needed to draw more to cast again, and Cara pivoted. As she did, she used a blade of white hot heat to cut the regulator valve off the wall, and threw flammable debris in its direction. A spark provided the third side of the fire triangle—oxygen, fuel, heat. The wall exploded.

Archer and Cara, prepared, and crouching behind their limited shelter, were able to shield, but Maya, the guy, and Kayla were all thrown to the ground. Large pieces of wall landed on Maya, who had been closest to the explosion. Thank Source, Archer thought, surely that will slow her down.

"Go!" Cara yelled.

He launched himself toward the hole, a layer of gray dust on his shoulders, then realized that Cara was trying to grab Kayla despite her earlier agreement not to.

Shit.

The old guy, still calm, though lying on the floor, shook his head, and a ripple of power shot from him across the floor, a mini earthquake that shook free debris. Cara screamed.

"I don't think so."

Horrified, Archer grabbed Cara around the waist, and realized a couple of her fingers had been crushed between a wall and a piece of stone that had been tossed across the room. Blood streamed. Cara was pale from shock and the dust.

He dragged her through the hole, out the door of the second room, and plowed deeper into the Center.

"We need to leave."

Cara, cradling her hand, shook her head. "No, I need to activate the defenses. Source knows how many evacuated or escaped, but I need to lock down any remaining people to protect them and others. We have to get to the safe room. It's one of the places I can trigger them."

"Look at you," he said, through gritted teeth. "You're in no fit state to do anything."

"I've numbed it. I need you to follow me. Once we're safe, and the defenses are activated, we can treat our injuries and wait for help to arrive."

With an unpleasant shock, he remembered she knew the area, had more fighting skills than him, and despite her injury, was thinking clearly enough to work out how to save more of the Rehab Center.

It was a novel feeling for him, the dawning realization that someone else was better positioned to be in charge. He shifted awkwardly.

He followed her through a wasteland of noise and explosions and falling masonry. She darted into a maintenance closet after a few minutes, and pushed aside a set of lockers that were lighter than they should be.

Her right hand pushed power into a light switch, while a hidden panel shot out a laser that took a biometric reading of her eye.

"Energetic and human, the best of both." She smiled weakly.

A light came on automatically, and after they entered the hidden room he slammed the fortified door behind them. Cara limped to a console, and lifted a plastic cover that was hiding a panel that she placed her hand over.

"I need to feed the defenses with a little of both of my energies to raise them."

He stood behind her and put a hand around her waist, holding her up.

A moment passed, and a shudder of power went through him. Something had changed. He tried to access his energies and couldn't use them.

She had done it.

She grabbed a headset hanging on the wall, put it on and pressed a button. They waited. Time ticked past.

He heard Adam's voice over the other end. "Report."

"In the safe room, Healing Center side. Maya, the leader of the Anahata inspection team, is destroying the building. She has Elrian with her and they've taken Kayla."

"Already on our way. Be there in fifteen. Hold fast."

Cara signed off then sagged in relief. Archer gently removed the headset, and went to set up a cot he'd spotted folded up in a corner.

He helped her over to it, and propped her up on some cushions, making sure her damaged hand was above her heart, though Cara was still keeping the full extent of her injuries hidden from him. Blood oozed, and even he could tell it was bad.

"Who's the patient now? You better hope I'm not as strict as my last Healer," he said, grimacing at his terrible joke.

She tried a wan smile, and he glanced around the stark, windowless room. She needed water and some kind of dressing on her fingers. Plus he should check them both for any other wounds as injuries could be hidden by shock.

He left Cara on the cot while he dug out a first aid kid and a couple of bottles of water. The space was small, with capacity for perhaps four people to fit comfortably, a few more if they were prepared to squish up. It was bare apart from the communications equipment she had used, shelves that held emergency supplies, and the cots and bedding.

Sitting back down next to her, his pulse increased when he saw how pale she was.

"Show me the hand," he said gently.

She grit her teeth, and he wondered if she'd refuse. But she peeled it away from her top where she'd been pressing it. He stifled a gasp.

The fingers on her left hand were a mess, and the tip of her middle finger was gone. She clearly had channeled some energy to the area as the blood was seeping out much more slowly than he'd expect for a traumatic injury like that.

He glanced up. She was looking at his face, not her fingers. There was a weariness there, an exhaustion. Her world was crashing down around her. This place was her heart and soul. His heart ached for her.

One problem at a time.

"Okay, where are the painkillers?"

He wished he had Anahata energy to take some of the pain away. She took the painkillers he found willingly enough, which would help save some of her energy. She was likely the only person who could access her energy with the defenses up.

He cleaned her hand under her instruction, and bandaged up the middle finger with the missing tip. Then he checked them both over for any other injuries they'd missed.

She had the worst of it.

Finally, he positioned himself on the floor next to her cot, having dimmed the already low lighting. "Rest now."

All they could do now was wait. Had fifteen minutes already passed? Still, they didn't know who, or what, was out there.

The emergency defenses would guard what was left of the place, and he and Cara were as safe as they could be in the situation.

Her eyes flickered closed, and her breathing, while shallow, steadied. He hoped she slept.

He would guard her till help came. He would protect this beautiful, fierce, smart woman with his life. There was nowhere he would rather be.

"Turns out, I love you," he whispered in the darkness. "So you better stay alive."

31

Archer lay next to Cara, his thoughts thick as mud.

True to his word, Adam's team hadn't been far away. By the time they arrived, there was no trace of Elrian, Kayla, Auretta or Maya, just a swathe of destruction. Only two of those on the rehab side of the Center had escaped, plus Kayla, but two more had died. Archer's heavy heart lightened slightly when he learned BayBella and Abi had escaped unharmed. All other patients and staff had been evacuated to the safe house in Victoria—full to bursting—without mishap, except one. Thea's neck had broken when she was thrown against a wall by an intruder. Iris, the third member of the inspection team who had helped protect those in the Center, had been sent back to be heavily debriefed at Anahata Guild.

Adam had ordered Archer and Cara to rest after he'd taken a brief inventory of the place and checked them over for injuries. As well as her finger, Cara had a couple of nasty gashes, and bumps and bruises all over. Archer had escaped anything major, barring the minor knife wound he'd received from Maya.

Archer had taken Cara to her apartment on the grounds, which was unaffected. He didn't have much time to admire her personal touches around the place, taking off the worst of her bloodied clothes and lying her down. He had had just enough energy to shower, then pulled on a gray terrycloth bathrobe he'd found that must swamp her.

The Center had been attacked.

Cara was injured and likely had lost her middle finger down to the first knuckle. Healers could fix things, but they couldn't regrow them.

His own recovery had taken yet another hit, and he would need more rest. However, being stuck on the island no longer gave him pause. It had been a shock the day before to realize the feelings he had for Cara had turned into love, but it wasn't exactly a good time to bring that up with her. He had a bracelet, but it differed from hers. He didn't know what that meant, but again, considering Cara's world had just fallen apart, the bracelet was the least of her concerns. He would handle this with care to ensure she didn't push him away, and his way of doing that would be to wait for a better time. A much, much later time.

If only he hadn't gone away, he could have helped her with the fighting earlier. Or if he'd just taken her with him, she wouldn't have been there, and wouldn't have been hurt. But she'd never have gone, and the casualties without her would have been so much worse.

Yet he still felt he could have, should have, done things differently.

He slept fitfully, until she stirred, groggy, next to him. His heart squeezed at the lost look in her eyes.

"What's happening?" she asked.

He hesitated only for a moment, knowing reminding her of the battle and its impact would hurt her. But he updated her on what he knew, while ensuring she drank some water.

"And Ai is fine," he finished. "She's safe on the boat with the crew, and they're going to teach her how to dive. She knows there was an attack, though not the extent of it."

Cara nodded. Her eyes were dull, and he worried about her.

"How are you feeling?"

She blinked. "Not great. Can you help me up so I can view the damage? And I need to talk to Adam."

He wasn't sure that was the best thing for her to do, but she'd already started drawing back the covers.

All her movements were lethargic, like her whole body had become three times heavier. Activating the energetic defenses, and holding them with her magic until help arrived, would have drained her, especially after the battle with Maya. Plus a colleague—perhaps a friend—had died.

It was a slow process to help her rise, wash and dress. By the end, she was shaking from the effort. He made her a cup of tea and she nibbled on some fruit and yoghurt.

"You're sure you want to go out?" he asked, though he knew what the answer would be. At least it would give them the chance to see another Healer.

She nodded, and wobbled toward the door. He jumped up and took her arm, hampered by taking care he didn't touch her finger, or show her the bracelet he was now wearing.

That bracelet was his hope and his future. When she was ready, he'd discuss it with her. Till then, he'd take her lead, and hope against hope the shock she was feeling didn't cause her to take any action that might damage her—or them.

Cara stared, her heart tight, misery flooding her. Her life's work had been destroyed around her, and the devastation that had been left was incredible. Swathes of buildings had been wrecked. Two Rogues had escaped, two were dead. She felt for them as strongly and sadly as she would for any patient. She never gave up on a Rogue.

And Thea. Cara swallowed down the bile that rose in her throat.

They stopped at Archer's old room. The Atlantean relics were smashed, including the object that had fallen on her wrist when

Archer had appeared. She still wasn't sure what had happened. Had her bracelet revived some kind of ancient magic?

Her own injuries she was ignoring. The worst was on her non-dominant hand, so there was that. She was practical and experienced enough to know she'd get used to it, find ways around it.

But her feelings about it? Those, she'd work through later.

And then there was Archer. She'd seen his bracelet, no matter that he'd been trying to hide it all morning.

"Archer?" She turned to him. He was grieving, she could see that easily enough. She wondered how much the destroyed artifacts had been worth. A great deal, she suspected. Though the money, despite her initial thoughts about him, hadn't seemed to interest him as much as the adventure and mysteries.

She wondered if he still felt the same now.

She touched his arm.

He met her gaze. "How can I help?"

Pulling back his sleeve, she uncovered his bracelet. He didn't react.

"Adam says there are no other bracelets in play that we know of. And the colors, if not the style, are a match to mine. I think it's the twin. But I don't think that means what we thought."

He cocked his head, puzzled.

"Source must know I'm not ready for a relationship right now," she continued. And given that at this moment she felt like the worst person in the world, she couldn't, wouldn't, ask anyone else to be with her. For all she knew, too much proximity to her would mean they might die too. "So I propose that we participate in the prophecy as a pair, but not a couple. We commit to do what we need to as friends."

"Whatever it takes?" he asked.

She couldn't decipher his expression. She expected he'd been as dismayed by the bracelet as she was, and that's why he'd been hiding it. But they needed to face this, and work with it as best they could.

"Whatever it takes."

32

"Maya is a Rogue." Adam lounged in one of the dining hall chairs, his husky, Argus, at his feet. Those involved in the prophecy were meeting to assess the situation and consider the way forward. This room had been chosen as it hadn't seen the same devastation as some.

Archer rubbed his forehead. "I think we knew that, Adam."

"Yes, but she's also not Maya."

Now Archer was baffled. He liked Adam, he did. However, his concise speaking style could be frustrating if you didn't have the right context, and Archer was too tired to puzzle it out.

Several of Cara's friends—those who also lived in the province of British Columbia—had joined them on Vancouver Island to help, and they were taking a break from their work to share updates.

Archer had been amazed at how quickly Adam had brought them together to help, informing them of what was happening almost in real time.

Fintan and Adam both had positions in Guild security, and were working with their teams to review the physical and energetic evidence that had been left, tracing Maya and Elrian's destructive paths through the Center.

Aiko, head of Anahata Guild, had been informed, and was working with Jeb and Nixie to manage the impact of such a senior Guild member betraying them all. So far, it didn't look like anyone else apart from Auretta was involved—but no stone would be left unturned. Security was being tightened, and anything Maya had worked on was being checked. It wasn't going to be a fast process, so Jeb and Nixie would stay in Egypt, and had video-conferenced into the discussion.

Blaize and Cuinn were on site, interviewing those who'd seen Elrian and Maya to reconstruct what had happened from eyewitness accounts. They would cross-check this with any prophecy shards they had gathered from dreamwalking, and see if they could understand the bigger picture.

And Tierra, grounded and loving, was working side-by-side with her best friend Cara to clear up the wreckage left behind.

"Who is Maya, Adam?" As Adam's sister, Tierra must know his idiosyncrasies well, so Archer left her to pry the information out.

"Her real name is Imogen."

"Wait…" Cuinn said. "As in…"

"Yes," Adam said.

Archer was ready to throw something at Adam, then a memory tickled him. An energetic story he'd come across in older records, of a female Anahata-Ajna Rogue who'd joined the humans in their abhorrent practice of slavery, humans and energetics alike, and created her own private empire in the Caribbean a couple of hundred years ago. Seeking power, she'd sought out energetic artifacts, and tried them out on her hapless captives.

She had been stopped, but it had taken several of the Guilds working together to manage it, and many lives had been lost.

"I thought Imogen Kent had been killed," Archer said, swallowing.

"Apparently not," Adam said. "Maya's use of power yesterday showed the same distinct signature we saw with Kent, albeit with something extra."

"So Maya…" Cara said, slowly, "is actually Imogen Kent, an energetic who's a fable for our people to show how our power, when used in the wrong way, corrupts."

Argus gave a low rumble, and Adam nodded. "But somehow, even more powerful."

"I always knew Maya—Imogen—was unbalanced," Fintan said. Tierra leaned a head on his shoulder.

"How can we trust the Guilds now?" Cara asked. "Imogen was a Maven at Anahata, she taught students. She'd worked her way up to lead her Minor Guild Anahata-Ajna, and was part of the Minor Circle. Part of our governance."

Archer couldn't imagine how betrayed Cara must feel.

"We have to tell them what's happened," Cuinn said. "But we only work with people we trust to solve the prophecy. People outside the leadership structure of the Major and Minor Circles, or without connections to the Guilds. We're careful about what we share."

"Does that include Aiko?" Cara asked.

Jeb's voice came from the laptop on the table. "I trust her, but I'm going to be careful. She appears to be genuinely devastated at Maya—that is, Imogen's—betrayal, but clearly, we've been wrong before."

Archer wasn't sure this discussion would help them. They couldn't trust the Guilds, period. He could see Nixie and Blaize, who were also relatively young energetics, agreed with him.

Perhaps because of their age, some of the others had too much trust in the Guilds; most energetics served some time in their Guild on top of their early training in their two Chakras.

"We need to be careful about assuming that because Imogen was evil that others are in on this," Cuinn said. "This is likely to be a one-off."

"If we don't tell the Guilds, in fact, let everyone know, how will people protect themselves?" Tierra said.

Archer wanted to get back to the underwater artifact. He'd spent every moment when he wasn't focused on Cara, researching—well, what research he could do with the books that had survived, as he still didn't have his personal laptop. "We need to explore the Doorway temple."

Cuinn rubbed his nose. "There's no question it's important. But we don't know why or how."

"We have bigger issues at the moment," Adam said.

"The temple could be the key to the wider mystery," said Archer, trying to keep the frustration out of his voice. "It shows all the elements, and pictures of the bracelets, for Source's sake. We have to get back there."

He prowled the room, unable to keep still.

"It's underwater," Cuinn said, not unreasonably. He stood, posture upright and occasionally reached out to touch Blaize's hand. Did he even realize how often he did it?

"We will explore it further. But we have to prioritize. If it's been there millennia, it will wait a little longer," Cuinn said.

"Kayla's missing, Arch," Cara murmured. She sat in a chair, her elbows on the table. "We let her be taken. Our priority is getting her back."

Tierra squeezed her hand.

Archer felt sick. Of course a person was more important than the discovery he'd made, yet he couldn't help but think the bigger picture might save more people. Maya, or Imogen, rather, had been powerful to a level none of them had ever seen before, and there had to be something fueling that. Where was the power coming from? Right now, they didn't have the strength to fight her. They needed to power up somehow, and he had a feeling that the underwater temple might help.

"Besides," said Blaize. "We don't have a full set of bracelets. Who knows if it would work with what we have."

The temple still warranted exploring, even if she was right. They were missing two sets of two bracelets, the ones with Muladhara and Vishudha in common, respectively. They'd thought that Adam would have a bracelet, and since he didn't have Vishudha as an energy, he had to be one of the Muladhara couple. *Pair*, Archer amended.

He'd been told there were three energetics Blaize and Cuinn's prophecy dreamwalks hadn't yet identified—well, two now, as he appeared to be one of those three—and one for whom they had a drawing, but none of the others recognized.

"Can I get the sketch of the male you don't know?" Archer said. "In case I recognize him? Send it to Phoebe, too. Might as well cast the net wide."

Blaize nodded and pulled out her cell.

Archer glanced over at Cara. Her usual vibrant energies were muffled. She'd been working despite her injury, and they hadn't had a chance to talk much since that morning.

"We don't know where this Imogen and Elrian are. For all we know, they could still be on the island," continued Blaize. "Adam and Tee have tried tracking spells, but they've either gone, or have some serious cloaking abilities."

"What if they come back?" Cara said. "What do we do then?"

Archer shivered. He wasn't in a hurry to face Imogen again without a lot more firepower.

Nobody replied for a while. Not a great sign. Argus growled from his spot at Adam's feet.

"Connect with your elements," Adam said. "Stay ready."

"We need to understand what happened here and why," said Fintan. "We have two powerful Rogues on the loose, at least one of whom we already know has been leeching energetics. Both are beyond the levels of power a typical Rogue has, and we don't understand why or how. Archer, your underwater temple sounds critical, but we don't know how to use it, and our priority has to be here until we've made more progress. We need to keep the bracelets together."

Archer let himself slump back into his chair.

He couldn't help but think it was the wrong decision.

A ninety-minute drive from the ruined Center, Elrian had found Imogen, Auretta and himself a quiet but richly appointed house on the island. It belonged to a local celebrity who, according to the couple who took care of the housekeeping year round, wasn't due to visit for another three months.

Elrian had clouded the couple's minds, and sent them to their cottage on the grounds none the wiser about their visitors—having ensured dinner had been cooked, and the house was stocked with food and everything their group could need.

The gnawing sense of something missing inside him had been satiated slightly by the chaos they had caused at the Center, and his opportunity to draw energy from the energetics around them. He was calmer than he had been for weeks.

He wasn't sure what had brought him to take Kayla with them rather than drain her, only that his Ajna had indicated she might be important, and it was something to do with Cassidy. And he wouldn't take chances with Cassidy. She met a heart-need for him in a way that Imogen didn't, perhaps couldn't. Cassidy was stable, reliable and wise, and he had to trust she would weather his continued mind adjustments.

Still, it would end soon, surely. Imogen had revealed herself, and they had been close to success the day before. He wished she hadn't burned her identity as Maya, as it was decades of investment down the drain, but there was nothing to be done about that now. He had to be practical.

Cara and that pampered millionaire Archer had had to run and hide rather than stand up against Imogen. It had been a moment to savor.

He and Imogen sat at the dinner table, laid out with silver and china for a three course meal. Kayla was upstairs, guarded by Auretta. She wasn't necessary for this strategy discussion.

"We were so close," Imogen exulted. "My power was vast. There were moments when I was filled with so much I could barely contain it. You must find out why, and how I can keep hold of that power in future. It was a shame those two rats shut themselves up in their little cage."

"It was too risky to stay once their backup started arriving," Elrian commented, cutting his meat. He sawed off jagged strips, stuffing them into his mouth. His hunger was still present, though dulled, and he would fill it in every way he could. There was a sharper edge to him these days, a rawness. "We need to make more remnant stones, that has to be as important as disrupting the prophecy. Without them, we won't be able to complete the final stages."

Imogen pursed her lips. "The database has proved useful to target people, but we need to go wider once we've finished our work here on the island. We can run the algorithm on the data you pulled from the trial populations to source others who fit our criteria, then find them. The Pacific Northwest is on high alert now. It's not a good place for us anymore."

She took a dainty bite of her meat and chewed.

Elrian felt a twist in his abdomen. This area had been his home for many years, and Cassidy had lived here for most of her life. It was an almost mystical place, with the green of river valleys, rainforests, and snow-capped mountains—perfect for anyone with earth as part of their Chakras. He'd moved here to monitor his son, Cuinn, to be close enough to him for a revenge when the opportunity came, but it had become home as much as his beloved Ireland was when his wife had been alive.

Would he need to make Cassidy move? Could he convince Imogen Cassidy still knew nothing and leave her here? He wanted only brief contact between the two females. They were different parts of his life, though the cross-contamination was becoming harder to prevent.

He shifted uneasily as Imogen's actions from the day before replayed through his brain. Property damage he had no issue with, and he was at peace with acceptable losses of energetics in their quest for the greater good. The humans needed to be removed.

But Imogen had gone further than that. She'd damaged the natural world. Trees, stones, the earth, the flora and fauna around the Center—she'd seemed to delight in all kinds of destruction. It would cause an imbalance, the very thing Source put energetics on the planet to work against, and the spark that had caused Elrian to decide the humans should be eliminated in the first place. If he and Maya were as bad as humans, what then their quest?

"The power did seem intense," he said, wondering how to pick his way through this minefield. "It appeared to spill over to the flora and fauna."

"Briefly, yes," she said. "But everything will recover in time."

He extended her a strained smile. "This time. But as you become more powerful, my love, your control needs to increase in proportion."

She waved a hand. "My control is fine. It was a show of power to ensure our success. Fear is a potent motivator."

Now that was something he knew well.

"It's nothing to concern yourself about. When we go back to kill Archer and Cara, I will ensure the power is focused on them, nothing else."

Elrian raised his eyebrows. "Archer is likely to have gone, given his security team and position."

"The girl won't leave her precious Center until it's reduced to rubble. Which I am happy to arrange. She's wounded, in body and mind, and it's our best chance to kill her before she's reassigned. Or perhaps simply disfiguring her will be enough to put the boy off and stop them coming together as a couple."

"Others will be there. They won't be alone."

"We can use that to our advantage. On the off-chance that Archer is still there, the woman he works with, Phoebe, may be there too, and she's the most recent member of the prophecy identified in your dreamwalks, correct?"

He nodded. "I don't know who her partner is though."

She shrugged, and took a bird-like sip of wine. "One is enough. Plus, Adam may be there."

Elrian cocked his head. "I thought we were avoiding him unless we had to take him out. His role as a Protector means he's going to be much harder to defeat."

He rubbed at the fine linen napkin next to his plate. Imogen seemed wild somehow, despite her veneer of civilization. Unpredictable. Her control seemed tenuous, and she was ready to take chances he thought they'd agreed against.

"They won't be able to hold against me. I'll drain that girl you took from the Center, and they will fall one by one in front of me."

His heart stuttered. Images of Kayla flashed through his mind, puzzlingly, superimposing her face over Cassidy's. He shook the visuals away. Was this confusion between the two women his Ajna trying to tell him something?

Dizziness flooded him.

Was Imogen a threat to Cassidy?

Either way, he knew he couldn't kill Kayla.

"I saw we have a need for her." He tried to keep his voice normal, but it cracked on the last word. "In a dreamwalk."

Luckily Imogen, usually so perceptive, didn't appear to notice his lie. She was barely listening to him. "Auretta, then. At this point, you and I are enough. We don't need anyone else. There'll be time enough later to recruit more to our cause. By that time, they won't be able to stay away."

He nodded weakly.

"In the meantime, let us go use one of the ignorant human's bedrooms." She reached out a hand and cupped his cheek. "Their aesthetic taste is poor, but the fabrics are expensive and pleasantly tactile. Come."

She had barely touched her food, while he could eat the same again.

Obediently, he followed her up the main staircase to the master bedroom.

33

A knock sounded on Cara's open door, and she startled. She'd been staring out of the window, holding books she had picked up that had fallen to the floor in her office. Part of the great clear up effort. Though it seemed like all her efforts were designed to send everyone, and everything away. Every person's file she sent off made her realize it could be a long time before her Center, her home, her work—her world—was operational again.

If it ever was.

Archer had tried to talk to her several times about the bracelets, the database and his underwater discovery. But she was at capacity. She'd already deleted him from the database, despite the potential consequences from Anahata Guild. She agreed with him that there was something strange about it, but she needed to talk to Jeb before she did more. If there was a real issue, Aiko would delete the database from Anahata.

She couldn't think about the fact she—or that bloody bracelet—had transported Archer thousands of miles to her.

She couldn't think about the fact that Maya—Imogen, rather—and Elrian might still be close by.

She couldn't think about the fact her finger was permanently damaged.

Her stress balls lay abandoned on the desk in her office. She was way beyond them.

A tear leaked from her eye and she swiped at it angrily. Crying was inefficient. Of course it was important to process feelings, that was core to Anahata training, but there were better ways.

She turned, and saw Tierra.

"Cara, love." Tierra closed the few steps between them and caught her in her warm arms.

It felt so good. Cara let herself lay her head on her best friend's shoulder for just a second before she pulled away.

"Sit down," Tierra ordered, and cleared off the sofa to give them room. "Talk to me."

Cara collapsed on the sofa. She felt so drained. Proactively offering information was beyond her. "What do you want to know?"

"When did you last rest?" Tierra put a hand over Cara's.

Cara shrugged. "I took a few hours' sleep early this morning."

"And what are you thinking? What are you feeling right now?"

Another tear crept down Cara's cheek, and she used a shoulder to erase it. "Everything is in ashes, Tee. What am I supposed to feel?"

"There is no supposed to, you know that. You feel what you feel. But those emotions can help us to point to what's happening inside you, and what might be a helpful reaction from you." Tierra gave her hands a squeeze. "So tell me."

"Exhausted. Ashamed. Guilty. Angry. Regret. Betrayed." And a whole bunch more, but that was enough baring her emotional soul for the moment. "I was responsible for the people here, the buildings, their safety, and I let this happen. I let the land I was sworn to protect get damaged. I let Anahata in to inspect us, and the Guild betrayed us. Thea is dead. Others are wounded. Kayla was taken."

"Ashes," Cara repeated, dully. "This facility is my heart. I invested myself fully. I made it work. And now…it's gone. And so I feel that destruction inside. What's left of me? I failed."

"I'm not an Anahata expert, but with your energetic link to the Center, might there be some blowback affecting you after the attack? A physical, mental and emotional impact?" Tierra stroked Cara's hand. "You might not realize how connected you are to the environment, and Maya—Imogen—took from nature itself. As a conduit to power, nature may have pulled on you right back."

"Maybe," Cara said. "Or maybe I'm not the right person to be in charge of a Center if I can't handle what happened."

"That sounds so hard," Tierra said, and shifted closer to Cara and put her arm around her friend. "What would you say if it was me saying this to you?"

Cara's brow creased. Ugh, her friend was so wise, it was annoying. "That you need time to rest."

Tierra petted her back. "And I'd add a few other things. You did your best, but what happened was unprecedented. That it wasn't the Guild that betrayed you, but Imogen. And you need to take care of your most basic needs, rest, food, hydration, and somewhere to do these things that feels safe."

"My apartment isn't safe anymore," Cara said.

"Alright. So based on all that, what's the best action right now for you to be your best self?"

"Eat something and rest—and when there's time, take a few days away from here." But she hated that. "Yet I'm still responsible for the facility, Tee. I can't just walk away. Someone needs to manage the clear up efforts."

"And after you've done the initial review, is there someone in your team who could take that on? Or someone who could come and bring fresh spirit to support the team? You've invested so much in training those you work with, they're some of the best in the world."

They really were. She was proud of them, and they'd come through this well. They were shocked, of course, and some were injured and out of action, but they didn't share the crushing weight of responsibility Cara felt. And several of them had gotten away before the attack so weren't suffering the same effects as Cara. Perhaps they were better equipped to manage things for a few days while Cara stepped away. "I don't know."

Tierra put an arm around her and squeezed gently. "Will you let me in?"

Cara shrugged. Tierra took it for consent, as Cara felt a trickle of energy creep through her hand and wash through her body.

Strange though, it didn't feel like Tierra's usual energy. Cara had heard about how all Tierra's Chakras were activated, but feeling it was quite a different thing. While Tierra was using her native Anahata, there was a…fullness to the energy, a completeness, that Cara had never experienced.

"Your energies are both very low," Tierra said, voice soft. "I'll heal some of the pain, take it from you, but you're going to need time to re-balance. Your body is in a type of shock."

While Cara didn't deserve Tierra's kindness, it helped, physically at least. Some of the nagging pain in her finger—what was left of it—subsided, and many of the aches and pains in her body lessened.

The emotional pain though, that remained.

Tierra changed tack. "How's Archer?"

Cara's shoulders sagged. Source, another thing she'd messed up. "I told him even though we have matching bracelets, given all that's happened, we should be friends and work as a pair rather than a couple."

Tierra raised her eyebrows. "You did? And how does that feel now?"

Cara buried her face in her hands. "He's…something to me. Or he was. I just don't have the emotional resources to engage with it right now. And maybe I've burned that down too."

At the thought, her stomach clenched, and more tears crept down her cheeks. "Ah, Source."

"How did he react?"

"He didn't say much," she admitted from behind her hands.

He'd shown a careful neutrality, in fact. Hadn't shown a vested interest either way, though he'd said he'd work with her on it. Which, when she explored it in her mind, didn't feel great. Perhaps he hadn't needed her little speech. Or had been relieved.

"Did he make demands? Indicate you needed to invest emotional resources?" Tierra pulled out a tissue from her bag and handed it over.

Cara took it and used it to wipe her cheeks. "No. Actually, he said 'whatever it takes.'"

"So you didn't ask him what he thought, just presented him with the solution you thought you wanted, and he agreed to do whatever you needed?"

Cara tried not to wail and nodded. Ugh. She had. It's what she always did. Had she done the wrong thing? But either way, it's not like he'd protested. Despite the exceptional sex she'd thought they'd had, and the connection they'd made on the boat.

"Well, there might be one small upside of this horrible situation with the Center," Tierra said, slowly. "Didn't you say the main reason for not dating Archer was that your life was working so well? Now your life is…a tiny bit less perfect…maybe it's worth giving him a chance?"

Cara buried her face back in her hands.

She'd invested everything into her job, never imagining it could all come tumbling down around her like this. And what was left? The people. Her friends, the relationships she'd built over decades, or longer.

Tierra was right. She didn't have much left to lose.

So why, exactly, was she pushing Archer away? And how was she going to convince him to see it her way?

Archer was worried about Cara. She'd sustained a serious injury, but didn't seem to want to talk about it. This Center was out of commission for the foreseeable future. For now, all those who had been staying in the Center, on either side, were in the process of being transported to other facilities. How did Cara feel about that?

He called Ai and Nahla for an update. The water was blue and glorious behind them as they crowded together into the picture.

"We're mapping the site out for you," Nahla said. "By the time you get back we'll have a better idea of what's down there. But we're deliberately trying not to activate anything, given that we don't know the consequences."

"Nahla's teaching me to dive," Ai added, excitedly. "I love it."

"That's great," Archer said. While they'd told her what had happened, they'd played down the seriousness of it. The girl had had enough trauma, and should be safe enough in the middle of the ocean.

"I had an idea, too," Ai said. "I think Nixie could help us use the temple."

"How?" Archer's interest was piqued.

"Her energies include the ability to create an air bubble underwater. I think she may be able to push the water out of the temple so we could stand in it as if it was above ground. She can do really cool stuff with water. I saw her do it when Blaize, Tierra and I visited her in Thailand, and Tierra was sick."

Archer felt a thrill shiver through him. "Can you speak to her? Ask her if it's possible? I understand she and Jeb are visiting Anahata."

"Sure, I'll text her. Tee says things are pretty crazy there. But she's usually pretty good about getting back to me fast." She grinned at him. "And it's not like we don't have plenty of room on the boat."

Archer gave her a smile, acknowledging her effort to lift his mood. He must look as tired as he felt. Source, he wanted to be on that boat with them. But he also wanted to be with Cara.

He hung up, and headed back to his destroyed room.

He was engaged in the slow process of photographing and packing every shred, piece or chunk of artifact into separate, bubble-wrapped containers, hoping against hope that someone might be able to restore at least some of them in the future. While he wasn't the best person to do this work, the Center wasn't yet cleared for others to visit.

Phoebe appeared in the door. She studied him with a long look, then strode across the floor to engulf him in a fierce hug. He squeezed back.

She stepped back. "I hear you've been playing hero."

He shrugged uncomfortably. "Not on purpose."

"I'm glad. I like Cara. And I like you. You're one of my favorite people in fact. So I'd prefer it if you stayed in one piece." She sighed. "So talk me through it. What in the name of wishes and wanting has been happening here?"

He'd already checked with the group that he could be open with Phoebe. He filled her in on the discovery of the temple, his shocking transportation to Victoria Island, the attack, the rescue.

She perched on the ruins of the sofa, while he continued to sort through the rubble to see what else he could rescue. Busying his hands helped him process what he was saying.

She listened carefully. Too carefully. "And Cara?"

He tried for nonchalance, hoping she wouldn't notice the flush creeping up his neck. "She's not doing great, but she's okay. She's with Tierra right now."

"That's not what I meant. I've seen the bracelets that Cuinn and Blaize, Fintan and Tierra, and now you seem to have. And Cara has one too, though it's a lot more stylish than the others. Plus, I've seen the sparks between you both. I can put two and two together."

"Cara and I made a pact to be friends and work together for the prophecy as a pair, not a couple," he said. "She's not interested in a romantic relationship."

Phoebe stared at him. She seemed out of place in this trashed room, her pristine appearance at odds with the debris around her.

"You're an idiot."

"Excuse me?" He blinked.

"Love is a universal need. If you have a shot at a relationship, with someone you care about who cares about you, and is clearly endorsed by Source, then take it." She lifted an eyebrow. "Why on earth would you go along with what she said without at least discussing it? Don't you remember what it's like to run a company that's not doing well? The responsibility? The preoccupation? We had our days like that, and it was nothing compared to what she's going through."

"She said she wasn't ready for a relationship," he said.

"Did you tell her how you feel? And, as an aside, did she say that just after she'd experienced a huge trauma?"

"Well, no, and yes." Why hadn't he discussed it? She'd seemed resolute, but it was true he hadn't asked her why. Was it about him? About her? He'd always respect another person's wishes in a relationship, of course, but maybe he shouldn't have gone along with it without any kind of debate.

He frowned. Had he given in too easily? Should he have fought for her?

It didn't matter. He couldn't undo it.

Phoebe walked over to him and faced him. "Archer, are you happy at Disp@tch?"

"What?" Archer rubbed his neck. What was he supposed to say to that? Everyone hated their job at times, right?

"I'm fine."

"Fine," Phoebe repeated.

"No-one loves everything about their work, right?"

"Actually, I kind of do. I love making deals, trouble-shooting, setting strategy and moving us closer to our vision."

"Huh. Sounds like you love the CEO and the COO roles."

Phoebe hesitated. "It's more that it feels like I've been doing both for a while. The CEO is supposed to make the strategic choices, focus on growth, and the brand. The COO role is supposed to make it happen. But Whisper and our potential investors are strategic. Really, you should have been all over it."

"I was. I am." he protested.

"The coding. That's not what a CEO does." Another pause. "If you want to take a break from running Disp@tch, I'm happy to take over. I can promote my number two to the COO role in the short-term and see how it works out."

"Huh." Archer was stunned. "You don't want to work with me any more?"

"I do! Of course I do. But I want to work with the Archer of ten years ago, the passionate, enthusiastic energetic. These days you seem to avoid half your role, and the other half stresses you out so much you have panic attacks."

Archer grimaced.

"Sorry." Phoebe's tone was gentle. "I love you, and I want you to be happy. If you want to go help with this prophecy for a while, I can hold the fort here. But I also love working with you, and I love being COO. But in that case, I need the whole you back."

Well. Shit.

"Anyway, something to think about." Phoebe gestured to the books he was holding. He passed them to her and she packed them painstakingly into a box.

She changed the subject, and she filled him in on gossip from work, and how she was. His mood lifting as they chatted as friends, not co-workers.

"There's something else that's bugging me. While all this has been happening, Cara was given a database to implement as a trial, and I don't like it."

Phoebe arched an eyebrow, and he explained. "I don't think it's a great idea to collect the kind of information they're logging. It exposes people. She was asked to input energetics' locations, power levels, strengths, weaknesses—it just seems ripe for misuse. We're not humans, with their government. The Guilds don't—or shouldn't—police. It's not their role. It's a slippery slope, this kind of information collection."

Phoebe tilted her head to one side as she considered. "Perhaps. I can see both sides."

"Very you," Archer teased.

She inclined her head. "Indeed. As I understand it, all the Guilds discussed it, and Aiko agreed Anahata would trial the database. This isn't an Imogen issue specifically, is it? But we should absolutely offer to work on their security. Log the issues with it and you can send a White Hat report to Aiko at Anahata. We know we can trust her. We have clearance with them anyway; you'd be doing them a favor. This is a database that needs to be protected."

She reached into her capacious but sleek tote bag and took out a slim, dark-gray laptop. "Also, you seem bored."

She passed it to him. "Have at it. See what's happening to the data."

Archer stared at her, then at the laptop, then he let out a whoop.

"Have I ever told you you're my favorite co-founder?"

She chuckled. "Sit down and rest. I'm going to check in with the others and see who else needs help while you do that. I'll be back later."

He nodded absently, opened up the laptop and used his fingerprint to get in. They had biometric access to each others' devices in case of an emergency. It had saved them numerous times in the past.

He spent a happy hour repeating his previous work of getting into the database and poking around. It wasn't the kind of thing he got to do much these days and he enjoyed the novelty, getting lost in someone else's—shoddy, in his opinion—code.

Hmm. He leaned in. What was this? A bizarre routine that made no sense. It didn't seem to relate to what the system was supposed to be doing. He followed it into a rabbit hole of subfunctions.

Understanding dawned, and the concern that had been just a seed blossomed into a full grown tree. There was a hidden daemon in the code, one that was sending information outward.

He used some tricks to capture and analyze the frames of traffic, to narrow it down to a specific IP address range. As expected, it was in Egypt, and matched Anahata Guild's location. But he wanted more. He needed to know exactly to whom this information was going, who was collecting it through this secret channel.

As if he didn't know.

He ran a scan on the network communications and he found he was in luck—one terminal was online and connected to the backdoor he'd found in the software. For someone with his skill and experience it was trivial to throw together a quick and dirty reverse proxy and trap the traffic from the remote machine, tricking it into thinking it was still connected to the server.

That's when his luck struck a second time. Exploring the remote computer for vulnerabilities, he found that a maintenance port had been left open to enable remote connections by the Anahata IT Helpdesk. And by sending a query to that same maintenance port, he received back the name assigned to that terminal.

A shiver ran down his spine: the name was clear. MAYA_OFFICE_DESKTOP.

The idea that this woman, who had left such an incredible trail of destruction behind her, had access to personal and vulnerable information about so many energetics left him cold.

He put disparate pieces together. That weird attack that had targeted Cara when they were escaping from Imogen and Elrian had seemed strangely specific, and yet completely unsuited to either himself or Cara. Their choice of attack suggested they had gotten their information from the database after he had changed their real vulnerabilities to protect them both.

If he hadn't—a chill ran up his spine—it would have incapacitated or even killed Cara.

He swallowed.

They could have killed her.

He needed to tell her, tell Adam, tell them all about the true danger this database posed. And he needed to do it now.

34

To Cara's pleasure, Phoebe had come to help her. The two women were outside, clearing the area near the front doors of the Healing Center so items could be brought in and out. They had hired a couple of dumpsters, weaving a little illusion magic and claiming renovation work to the companies who brought them, and she and Phoebe were gathering the debris, then sorting it into either trash or items to save.

Phoebe was taking a call, roving around the grounds so her discussion didn't bother Cara.

Phoebe wore ballet flats, a scarf around her unusual two-toned hair, well-cut jeans and a teal sweater that flattered her slender curves. Her clothes were feminine but eclectic, with a necklace of orange stones around her neck, and Cara admired her strong sense of style. Phoebe's long fingers were expressive, and made Cara flash a glance at her own maimed hand. Even when they'd been whole, her hands had been made for work. Work that currently didn't exist. Cara tossed the next chunk of stone into the dumpster with somewhat more force than necessary. Tierra had helped with the pain, but her hand would never be the same.

Adam had learned through the local police that Auretta's body had been discovered in a house ninety minutes away, and he, Tierra and Fintan had gone to see if they could track the path Elrian and Imogen had taken from there.

Blaize had gone back to the mainland to the other side of Vancouver, in order to consult some texts. Only Phoebe, Archer, Cara and Cuinn remained of their group, with a few of the Healers here packing their possessions in order to move to another posting. It was quiet.

Phoebe came back over, forehead creased. "Something happen?"

"Nothing new." Cara used her power to toss more debris into the dumpster. At least it wasn't raining, though summer seemed to have taken a break. "Had Vishudha Guild already moved to New York when you and Archer were doing your training?" Cara felt a pang of…something. She was hungry for more information about Archer's life, even though not only had that ship sailed, she'd been the one to launch it to sea.

"Yes, it was well-established there by then. He and I found we had a common interest in the emerging field of computers, and thoughts on how communications might change globally over time—and what that might mean for keeping our race hidden." She huffed. "We had no idea what the world would look like in ten years, let alone twenty-five. But there were a lot of late nights discussing it, with a lot of wine."

"You founded the company in the early 2000s—how have you and Archer managed to hide the fact you don't age from the public?" Cara had paused her work, looking at the other female, who Cara's eye judged to have set her age in her mid-thirties, by human standards.

Phoebe laughed. "Yes, that's been a challenge. We were able to start our age then, saying we founded the company as students, rather than our real ages at the time."

"Both of you look in your thirties. Even with the most generous math you should be in your mid-forties in human terms."

"It's part of the reason we've both done PR with the Hollywood crowd," Phoebe said. "People don't question them as much when they look younger than their age. We've spread rumors we both have had plastic surgery, and that we're vain about our appearances. Luckily the tech crowd is big on the so-called 'longevity movement', so when we do interviews we drop mentions of this or that anti-aging treatment we're doing."

"You're crazy famous. How're you managing your exit plan with that level of scrutiny?"

"It's going to be tough. We never meant to become public figures, believe me." Phoebe sighed. Then she shot Cara a mischievous look. "Or did you think Archer enjoyed being in the gossip magazines?"

Cara's cheeks skipped pink and went directly to red. She spun around to pick up a piece of rock the traditional way while Phoebe laughed.

Cara found she liked the other woman. She'd expected her to swan in and out of the building much like Archer had appeared to at first, and be focused on her business rather than other people. But in fact, she was practical and down to earth, despite her sense of style, and had no problem chipping in.

Phoebe eyed her as she used ether to lift a larger piece of rubble up and over into the dumpster. "Archer's not who the magazines make him out to be, you know."

Cara rolled her shoulders, and turned her back, using a broom to sweep debris into a pile then flashing a quick flame through it to turn it to dust. "I've started to realize that."

Pain shot through her wrist, fast and acute, and she dropped the broom and clutched at it, moving the bracelet up her arm to see what she'd done. But there was nothing.

"Are you okay?" Phoebe said, moving closer, concern on her face.

"I think so, something happened with my wrist. It was probably nothing—" Another fierce prickle shot through her, right where the bracelet was.

"Your bracelet?"

Cara nodded, eyes narrowing as she stared down at the strange stones. She wanted to rip it off, this thing she had no control over and no choice about wearing. But it wasn't going anywhere.

"Didn't your friend Tierra say that there was some kind of connection they were discovering between, er, linked bracelets?" Phoebe said, her voice tentative. "And yours is somehow linked to Archer?"

Cara's eyebrows shot up. She hadn't thought of that. Was the pain a message from him? Or from Source about him?

What if he was hurt?

She fled to where she'd seen him last, cataloguing his books and artifacts for shipping.

Archer was already standing as Cara flew through his door, Phoebe hot on her heels. He'd been about to find Cara—or any of the team—to discuss the database. They couldn't have that kind of information used by Imogen.

But something else was wrong, he could see it in the women's faces. "Everything okay?"

Cara's gaze darted around the room, then she met his eyes.

"Something's wrong," she said.

"Are you alright?" Phoebe asked. "Cara's bracelet pinged her. We thought it might be to do with you."

He saw something pass over Cara's face, so fast he almost missed it, and his heart sank a little lower. He forced cheer into his voice. "I'm okay. Just a bit dusty. I was actually about to come—"

"Something is wrong. I have a bad feeling. The Anahata kind." Cara went to his window and looked out, scouring the landscape.

She pulled out her phone and began texting. Phoebe and Archer exchanged glances, and he sat back down. Cara had shown she wasn't someone prone to over-dramatizing. "Alright, not good. What else do you feel?"

She shook her head, fingers flying across her small phone keys. "I'm telling the others. Only Cuinn's still here, but we need Tierra, Adam and Fintan back here, ASAP."

He could tell them all about the database then. "Let Phoebe or I do that so you can connect with the feeling more. Perhaps get more information."

She shoved the phone back in her pocket. "Already done."

Her eyes closed, and he saw the shimmer of Anahata around her. Her bracelet seemed to grow more lustrous. Did he imagine his own bracelet warming in response?

"It's Imogen. She's coming for us." Eyes wide, she looked like she wanted to flee. "We can't stand against her, Archer. She's too powerful. We need to evacuate everyone who's left."

A shiver ran down his back. "There's more of us here now who understand what's happening, and we know more about what we're up against. We'll have to work together."

"I can't. *We* can't. You saw what happened last time." She gestured at the chaos in the surrounding room. "I couldn't protect us."

"What about the defenses?"

"They're not fully renewed yet." Cara's face was bereft of hope.

"You're not alone, and you have decades of experience working with and managing Rogue powers. As for your friends, many of us are trained to Master level."

He could admit to himself he wasn't keen to face that bleak well of power again, but running wasn't an option. And this was what he'd wanted, to be involved in a real prophecy like those of their ancestors, at the front lines of saving their race from danger.

Yet he caught sight of the bandages covering Cara's middle finger, the top section gone, as she got her phone back out to text, and wondered—would he sacrifice her to have that adventure?

But he already knew the answer.

35

Think, think.

Where should they go? Where could they make a stand that would put the fewest people in danger? Out of the Center. Somewhere with better access to the elements and fewer innocents.

"Follow me," she flung over her shoulder as she headed out the door.

Cara sprinted along the corridors. The brief flash she'd had of Imogen when she'd tuned into the heart-feeling had been coming from the north. There were few protections on the Healing Center now, barely enough to keep curious humans away, and certainly not enough to keep energetics as powerful as Imogen and Elrian out.

Cara was tempted to evacuate, to run, but there was a chance Kayla would be with them, and Cara wasn't prepared to miss it if there was. Ai would never forgive her if she did. Cara's last text had been to Cuinn to get everyone else out through the front gate, and Adam, Fintan and Tierra were on their way.

She wasn't sure about Phoebe joining them, but it was too late to worry about that. The woman ran like a greyhound. Something was nagging her about the bracelets, something that had caught at her brain from Phoebe's comments.

A few hundred feet from the partially destroyed buildings southeast and behind them, they stood on the windy limestone cliffs. Rain had begun to drizzle around them. The sea lay to their southwest, and from the northeast came three figures. A male and a female with a smaller, thinner female who appeared bound in some way to the male.

Cara huffed out a breath. The gamble had paid off.

So far.

"Archer, give me your hand." She shot out her left hand to him, and he put out his right. Their palms met, and she straightened her wrist so her bracelet touched his. She had an echo of her vision, the warmth of the hand offering her balance.

A rush of power shot through her, and his gasp told her something similar had happened to him.

"What can I do?" Phoebe said, catching on that something had changed.

"Protect Kayla and get her away if you see any chance at all. But don't risk yourself more than you need. Last time we couldn't stand against one of them, let alone both."

There was a scream, though whether it was from anger or delight Cara had no idea. But there was madness at its heart.

Cara lost sight of Phoebe as an intense gust of wind hit them, and she and Archer staggered back, their hands breaking apart. A rush of debris flayed her skin with splinters and sharp pieces of stone. Imogen was enhancing the natural weather along the cliffs.

The power the bracelets had raised remained, however. Cara could feel it wrapping around her, smooth and bewitching, enhancing what she could normally draw upon.

Another gust, and her feet slipped, and she slid along the ground. She glanced at the direction she was moving and her gut froze. Imogen was pushing her toward the cliff.

Archer's shoes briefly lost contact with the ground before he scrambled for purchase and steadied. Swearing as he realized Cara was being pushed toward the cliffside, he drew on his energy to teleport a rock over Imogen. It was a panic move, as he didn't have enough of that ability to move anything very heavy, but it glanced off her shoulder as it fell, and she turned her attention to him.

He heaved a sigh of relief as Cara stopped sliding toward danger, until that wind picked him up, smashing him into a tree. Dazed, he heaved himself upright, his head pounding. It had given Cara time to get away from the cliff, and she was sprinting toward him, shouting, but he wasn't able to work out what she was saying. He ducked behind the tree, and used his energies to explore those of the bracelet. Something vibrated through him, as if a string had been plucked against his wrist. The power was there. But he had no idea how best to use it.

So much was happening. Screaming, debris flying, then the air chilled around him and his teeth chattered. He used Manipura to wash heat through himself and keep his body warm.

He snuck a look around the trunk of the sturdy, mature Douglas fir he was using for cover. Cara was only a little way from him, protecting herself as she fled from the flat open area to the wooded area he had ended up in. Elrian was still close to Kayla, while Imogen stalked toward Cara, a smirk on her face, as if she knew victory was inevitable, and she was toying with them until then.

The bracelet vibrated again, trying to get his attention. The power. What could he do with the power? How could he use it to save them? To save Cara?

She skidded into him, and they huddled behind the tree. He flung up an ether shield with a sense of déjà vu.

"We need to distract them both for Phoebe to get Kayla," Cara panted. "Imogen is using a lot of air, and air fans fire. I'm going to surround them with a flame wall and use it to cut whatever bonds Elrian is trapping Kayla with. Holding them on the cliff top where it's stone underneath them will also protect the forest. Source knows what damage she might do otherwise."

Archer started to protest, not wanting her to put herself in more danger. Then he saw her, really saw her. She glowed with energy, her posture loose-limbed and ready for action. Her dash to him hadn't winded her. She'd drawn on her Warrior training easily, and her face was set in lines of grim determination.

She wasn't someone he needed to protect.

This wasn't a situation where he needed to be in control.

He didn't need to preserve his ego here.

The revelation hit him like a smack in the face, thoughts racing through him at a million miles an hour.

He always wanted to be in control. Even when he said he didn't. He wanted to control the narrative—personal, professional, and even, with Disp@tch—influence both the energetics and human races. His heart stuttered as he realized what an ass he'd been.

It wasn't like Cara didn't also have a need for control—and that was why their time in bed had been so mutually satisfying, as they'd let that control swing between them. But in real life, they'd both tried the control part, without relaxing at times to let the other lead. There'd been no balance. No compromise.

He was going to change that now.

"Touch the bracelets again, and tap into the energy it generates. Draw on me, on *us*, and tell me what you need," he said as he relaxed and opened himself to the bracelet.

Elrian watched in shock as Cara, drawing on power far greater than he'd ever expected, stepped forward and set the world on fire.

He was already shielded, but hadn't bothered with Kayla, and he lost her in the firestorm, the bond between them stretching then dissipating. He looked around, but the flames were higher than his head. She'd gone.

He heard an ululation, and the ground beneath him shook. Tremors of power spread from where he'd last seen Imogen. A loud crack sounded to his right, and above the fire he saw a branch break off one of the magnificent trees. His gut contracted, and not from the empty hunger that had gnawed at him for months. These trees were hundreds of years old.

Something was wrong. Imogen's power was affecting the natural world around them, in spite of their discussion. He tapped into the earth, using Muladhara to understand better what was happening. Animals were fleeing the area, but many small creatures were being somehow absorbed into Imogen's power. Dying.

If she continued like this, she could destroy all the life on the island. Or a great deal more.

She was no longer acting as an energetic, for the good of Source. Their aims were for nothing if she focused only on her own power. Was she out of control?

Or worse still, was she completely *in* control?

Cara's flames were keeping Imogen and him contained, but not Imogen's power.

He believed they could take Cara and Archer this time. Kill one, and seize the other to use to create a remnant stone.

But at the cost of the island? At the cost of what Source had tasked them with? That had never been their agenda. They were removing the humans because they destroyed the environment, they left scars on the flora and fauna around them that would take thousands of years to heal. Humans like those who had bombed the human hospital his wife had helped in during the War in Poland. Like those who had killed her.

Despite the heat of the flames, ice pooled at the bottom of his spine.

His connection to the earth was weak, shaky, and he couldn't tell if it was because of him, or what Imogen was doing.

He had to make a choice.

He could do nothing, and let Imogen end the prophecy here and now by killing one of the pair and capturing the other. They'd come away with another remnant stone and be closer to their goal.

But that would be at the expense of this beautiful environment around them. The trees. The cliffs. The plants. The animals. They'd all end up drained.

And he'd be just as bad as the humans who had murdered his wife.

He closed his eyes and kneeled on one knee, plunging a hand into the ground, the one that wore the ring he had kept so dear. The ring that could not be replaced.

And with every ounce of power he had, he siphoned.

Cara's flames held, but the earth shook around her. Whatever Archer or the bracelets had done, it had boosted her power. She'd never felt anything like it, but it was proving hard to maintain control, as wind whipped her hair around her face.

She wrapped her fire around herself like a cloak, grit her teeth, and ran toward Imogen. She used Anahata to boost her speed, hoping to blur and camouflage. Her move wasn't exactly out of the Manipura-Anahata playbook, but that's what she was counting on.

As she got close to the ring of fire, she picked up a change in the vibrations in the earth beneath her. Shit, was she going to be too late? She pushed herself harder, faster.

She hit the wall of fire, protected by the shields she'd made from the same fire, and dove through.

Surrounding herself with a wall of hardened air, she smashed into Imogen's legs, knocking her clean across the clearing. Grimly, Cara heard one of Imogen's bones break, and her scream of pain. The tremors calmed momentarily.

Cara had knocked Imogen out of the circle of fire, so she released it, and pushing herself up from the floor where she'd landed, she was puzzled to see Elrian with his hand in the earth. Was he gearing up for another attack? Before she could act, power radiated from him in a burst, and Cara pressed her hands to her head as she felt an agonizing shock run through her connection to the ether.

He'd taken the destructive power that Imogen had been using and turned it in on himself.

He slumped to the ground. Unconscious, or dead? She couldn't tell.

Imogen had dragged herself over to him. Cara started toward them, but Imogen grabbed onto Elrian's hair, smacked her breastbone.

And she disappeared.

36

They met in the cafeteria the next day.

Somber, Cara looked at her new friends, while they waited for the others to file in.

Archer sat with his business partner, deep in conversation. During the fight, Phoebe had used her powers to mask her presence, and had had a shield around both herself and Kayla before the firestorm had happened. Once the bond between Elrian and Kayla had been broken, she'd gotten the girl away as planned. Kayla, would first be debriefed by Adam, as they were still unsure why Elrian had gone to such lengths to take her. Adam believed there was more information she had to give them.

Then, she would be sent to a secure location far from any of those identified as part of the prophecy or Anahata Guild. She would be taken care of in a new environment, and receive counseling. Cara hoped she would recover.

Adam had arrived soon after Imogen had disappeared, and he and his team had spent the night combing the island physically and magically for any signs that Imogen might still be there. But she was gone.

Cuinn, Blaize, Fintan and Tierra were in the Center, and Jeb and Nixie were on a video call.

Adam nodded to Cara to start.

"We got lucky," she said flatly. "For some reason Elrian turned against Imogen. We damaged her, but without that, I don't think even the combination of Archer, Phoebe and I could have defeated her."

"She has some kind of magical artifact," Archer said. "Something like the transportation device that brought me from the boat to here. It got them out of there."

"Without Kayla, however, so there's that." Cara held Phoebe's gaze for a moment. "Thank you. We owe you."

"Pfft," Phoebe snorted, and waved away the thanks.

"Do you think Imogen has a bracelet like Cara's?" Blaize asked, with a frown.

"I didn't see one. I think whatever it was was on her chest. So a brooch, necklace, or something small enough to pin to her clothes," Archer answered.

"Or a ring she activated by striking her fingers against her chest," Fintan said glumly. "A lot of possibilities."

"I'm going to keep researching options," Archer said. "Whatever she has, the technology to create it went down with Atlantis, so it has to be pretty unique."

"The bracelets we have are from Source. Surely she couldn't have one?" Tierra said.

"Unless she stole it," Fintan said.

"Her power is unprecedented," Cuinn said. "Elrian's not the biggest problem, after all. It's her. But why did he turn on her? And what will she do to him for stopping her?"

Cara caught the squeeze that Blaize gave Cuinn's hand as he mentioned his estranged father. He glanced at her. "It's okay. He made his bed. I suppose I have some complicated feelings learning he's finally done something decent for a change."

With that, Blaize wrapped her arms around him. "Even addicts can care about something greater than themselves in extreme circumstances."

"I don't know why he did what he did, but our bracelets helped stop her." Cara said. "We touched them with intent and somehow my power was enhanced."

"Did Cara take power from you, Archer?" Cuinn said, his eyebrows raised.

Archer shook his head. "It didn't feel that way. I wasn't drained. More as if I was an amplifier."

"Similar to what happened between Fintan and me," said Tierra.

"I felt the power could have gone in either direction, too," Archer continued. "I could have been the focus, or Cara could have been. Though I don't know whether we could both have used it simultaneously."

Interesting, Cara thought. He'd made a choice to cede control of the power to her. She hadn't realized that.

Would she have ceded control to him if she'd been in his place? She rolled her shoulders, trying to remove a twinge of discomfort. She'd like to think she would, if she felt he was in a better place to use the magic successfully. But…she wasn't certain.

She could admit she liked to be in control. That she liked to make sure she managed all the details, especially when she was best placed to get them right. Which, in a purely practical way, was fairly often. But she could also admit that delegation had never been her best skill, let alone giving up control when she was in the middle of something she was good at.

She fiddled with her stress balls in her pocket. He'd trusted her when his life was on the line. Yet she wouldn't go on a single date with him, despite having feelings for him and being given the opportunity by Source itself. Alright, maybe her control issues were a little…out of control.

"More experimentation to be done by those with pairs of bracelets," Cuinn said. "Please share your data with Blaize and me on anything you discover."

"What's next?" Tierra said.

"At this point, we've only told what we know to the six energetics in the Major Circle and the heads of the Major Guilds, plus what's been shared with Anahata, and Cuinn's discussions of his prophecy shards with Ajna. It's time to alert the Minor Guilds as well, above and beyond what little we've shared so far," Adam said. "Imogen and Elrian are too dangerous to keep secret. This needs to be out in the open."

A ripple went around the room, comments varying depending on the kinds of relationship each person had with their Guilds. Argus got up and wound his way around each energetic's feet. Cara hugged him close when he came to her, and he carefully licked her cheek.

"They could have destroyed the island," Phoebe said, softly. "I felt it. Creatures and plants were dying."

"Not just the island," said Cuinn. "I've been studying the site of the battle, and the draining she was doing could have removed Source's energy from as wide an area as she had power for—and she has a great deal of power."

"So we're going to leave the problem to the Guilds? Because Imogen *was* the Guild, remember?" asked Fintan, a twist to his mouth.

Adam looked at him. "No. We tell everyone. We don't let the Guilds hide it."

"We have to follow up the leads we have," said Cuinn. "Search for Elrian and Imogen. Find out about the Atlantean temple site Archer discovered. Prophecy walk to find who else is involved. We believe there are twelve energetics involved, and we have nine identified at this point. It's becoming clear that we need the other three, as the bracelets are something that could make a big difference in this fight. We don't have enough information about them. We can't force connections either, they're gifted by Source."

Archer's head jerked up, eyes widening. The clash with Maya had distracted him from sharing what he'd discovered. "We need to destroy the database that Cara was working on."

Jeb's eyebrows rose. "How does that connect with this?"

Cara blushed, heat flushing through her body. She wasn't supposed to have told Archer about the project. She really hoped

Archer had a good reason for mentioning it, given that Jeb might never trust her again after this.

"The database is a collection of information that Imogen has direct access to, and could and probably has, targeted energetics with. I hacked it to replace Cara's and my stated weaknesses with fake vulnerabilities—and guess what Imogen tried to target on that first attack?"

That explained that mysterious-yet-specific magic from Imogen as Cara and Archer had been escaping. Cara's mouth opened slightly, but she didn't know what to say. On the one hand, he'd done it behind her back, against the rules; on the other, his actions had saved her life.

"I deleted you," she said, quietly. "After you were so upset about being included. I took you out. It's probably why she didn't target your weaknesses, fake or otherwise."

They stared at each other.

Archer closed his eyes, tension washing out of him. She'd protected him after all. Chosen him over her Guild. Archer let out a shaky, hopeful breath.

"So Imogen used the project as another way to find victims." Jeb was pale. "I need to tell Aiko. Phoebe, Archer, let's discuss how your company can help remove the possibility of remote access or vulnerabilities."

Phoebe nodded. "We can do that."

The group broke into smaller chats, working on plans and strategy, discussing options. Archer went to Cuinn, and switched Nixie and Jeb over to a tablet so the four of them could talk, balancing the device against a wall.

"I think the underwater ruins are important somehow," Archer said. "They're ancient—I can't even imagine how ancient. And I have some ideas about what the temple's for, and maybe even how it might be used, though it's not clear to me what it would do once activated. Cuinn, given your understanding of our race's history, and your dreamwalking abilities, perhaps you could come with us and dive the site?"

Cuinn raised an eyebrow, one corner of his mouth quirking. "I can't dive."

"Huh," Archer said, the lilt in his voice giving away his surprise. He shifted on his perch at the edge of the table.

"Even with hundreds of years of life, one doesn't get round to everything, Archer," Cuinn said, his voice a little dry.

Nixie smirked. "Well, Blaize grew up on an island. For someone without water as an element, she swims like a fish."

"High praise," Jeb murmured.

"Actually, that brings me to you, Nixie," Archer said.

She cocked her head, her bright eyes curious. "Yeah?"

"Ai told me you might be able to hold an air bubble underwater so we can study the ruins properly. Will you come on the boat, too?"

"Ah, so that's what her last message meant. Her texting leaves out so many letters it can be hard to make out. But a diving trip with my bestie? Sure!" Nixie's eyes gleamed. "Who else is joining?"

"There's a guy called Dylan Soliman who I've known of for years, and I've worked with a couple of times. His art and recreations of archeology—human and energetic—are incredible. I don't have a strong connection with him, maybe you could ask around? He would be ideal for this. We could do with someone with more of a specialty in this area."

"Sure," Nixie nodded. "I'll connect with some others from Svadisthana and make sure his reputation is deserved."

Archer had already done a full background check on him to see if he'd be as suitable as he suspected. Dylan was a respected yet free-spirited artist-archeologist energetic whose Chakras were Svadisthana-Ether. He even had a background in architecture. Getting him on board would give them professional help where Archer could only provide that of a hobbyist. Plus, if Archer was honest, the few times they'd met, he'd been able to geek out pretty hard when talking to him. Archer had been reading the man's books since he was a kid. But the fanboying would definitely be kept in check, for everyone's sake.

Still, he'd have time on the boat to ask a lot of questions…

He squirmed guiltily as they discussed a plan, agreeing to confirm how quickly they could convene on the boat—perhaps two boats given the numbers.

His gaze roamed over the wreckage of the building, and he caught Cara's eye as she smiled back at him, though it didn't seem to reach her eyes.

He was finally leaving the Center, and this time, he wouldn't be back. There was very little to come back to. It would take them time to get the facility back up and running, even if Anahata chose to invest in it, given what was happening in their world. If he ever got injured again or had a relapse, he would go somewhere else.

His chest tightened. Leaving the Center meant leaving Cara.

He loved her. Watching her fight Imogen had been both one of the proudest and most terrifying moments of his life. But she had been clear she didn't feel the same, and even though he thought there was a chance that he could push his way through some of that resistance, it didn't feel fair to her, given how vulnerable she was. Her life had been smashed around her, and only she could decide how to rebuild it.

Whether or not he was part of it would be up to her.

37

Cara was boxing up the last of the papers in her office when Archer came in the next day. She assessed him professionally, pleased to see he was moving well, and there was color in his cheeks. He hadn't been the easiest of patients, but she had got him close to full health, despite all the setbacks.

She glanced at her hand, then quickly curled the fingers into her palm, hiding the bandage that hid how much shorter one finger was than the others.

"Quick update." He leaned on the wall next to the door.

"More bad news?" She tried to keep her tone light, but clearly didn't manage it, as he blinked, then hurried on.

"Not bad. Not exactly good—neutral, really. I tracked the backdoor programming in the database back to someone I've come across before. There was an identifier in a comment in the code that gave me a name."

Cara perked up. "Can we find them? See what they know?"

Archer's mouth flattened out. "They've disappeared, and haven't been seen for several days. Adam's looking, but not hopeful. Imogen may have tidied her up as a loose end, or she may be in hiding. But Jeb says the internal investigation at Anahata showed that Imogen signed off on an invoice to the coder recently, so this is the last piece of evidence to show she had a second darker purpose for what the database could be used for. The evidence has helped convince the Major Guild members we need on our side."

"I guess that's good," Cara said. She tried for cheery and competent, something of the woman she'd been a month or two ago, but everything took so much effort. That foggy haze still dampened her emotions. She had formally broken her bond with the Center, but it would take her time to recover.

He stepped closer to her, though the desk was still between them. There were no chairs left in the room, they'd already been repurposed elsewhere. "I'm also here to say goodbye."

Her insides didn't just swirl, they did a full-on somersault. Her throat ached, and she struggled to breathe. She squeezed her eyes closed briefly.

"Right, of course. You're going back to the boat? And Blaize and Nixie will join you?"

He nodded. "Among others. The underwater ruins, whatever they are, are another lead to pull on for the team. Phoebe's going to take over as CEO of Disp@tch for a while."

She smiled weakly. "You're a full part of this now, eh?"

His chestnut eyes shifted for a micro-second to her bracelet, then came back to meet hers. "Yes."

And yet, she thought, with a startled realization, she—who had been involved from the start—was not.

She had considered this saving the world business something she could do on the side, while focusing on her job.

Had rejected Source's gift of a bracelet, love, and an opportunity to contribute to their entire race because it wasn't practical.

Because she was *busy*.

She groaned.

And it had taken her world to come crashing down around her—quite literally—for her to realize what she had almost missed.

How special this man—this infernal, infuriating, intriguing man—was to her.

How she—*oh, Source*—loved him.

"Are you okay?" Archer said, reaching across a hand to cup her elbow.

She hid her face in her hands and let out a muffled, "Not really."

He came around the desk to grasp her other elbow, gently using them to tug her hands away from her face.

Flushed, she couldn't look him in the eye.

"Can I help?"

Gah, no.

"Maybe." She stared at his superior thyroid notch, that little gap at the bottom of the throat she always found so appealing.

She had to be brave.

Sensible.

Grown up.

She had no job to speak of. No ties to hold her here. There was no Center left here to be the cornerstone for.

Her friends, and, apparently the energetic race, needed her.

She just hoped this man still did.

"Did you mean what you said in the panic room?"

He stilled, frozen. Oh Source, please let him know what she meant. If she had to explain she would be mortified. Surely there was only so much adulting in relationships one needed to do.

"I did," he said.

She didn't sag in his arms, but she lifted her head to finally meet his gaze.

"Would you like me to say it again?" he breathed.

She'd been in control for decades, and it was well past time she tried ceding it.

"I would."

A slow grin crept across his face.

"Cara McCarthy. I've fallen delightfully, disturbingly, and distractingly in love with you. Are you by any chance free this weekend?"

She didn't have much more to pack. She had handed over all her patients. Adam and his Protectors were searching the rubble and the island for anything their group had missed. Even Aiko, as her head of Guild, had suggested she take a break and support the efforts of the prophecy.

There wasn't much for her to do here apart from mourn.

Whereas with Archer…

She tilted her head and offered up her mouth, parting her lips slightly as her breath came a little faster.

She was ready to put herself in his hands. Something uncoiled in her chest as she had the thought.

His gaze raked her face, hot, searching, for just a moment, and then his mouth crashed down on hers.

As he kissed her, tension melted from her. He bit gently at her lower lip, and his scent and the tiny pain broke through her mental haze, giving her a peace and clarity she hadn't felt in days. She was hyperalert to the touch, feel, scent, sounds of him.

The bracelet on her wrist hummed with energy.

She slid an arm around his waist and responded to his greedy kisses with a mixture of relief and enthusiasm. Air currents danced around them, despite the fact the windows were closed. She let her element caress him just as she did with her hands, his skin warm and smooth.

Then the spot behind her bellybutton, the site of Manipura Chakra, began to radiate. Energy rippled inside her, and an imbalance she hadn't known was there righted itself.

His hands, which had been stroking her arms and back, stilled. He broke the kiss, his breath coming with the slightest of hitches.

"Did you feel anything just then?" He squeezed his eyes shut briefly and shoved back the few strands of hair that had fallen forward during their kiss.

She raised an eyebrow.

"I didn't mean because…." He gestured towards their mouths and flushed. "Did you feel anything inside your abdomen?"

He shook his head, frustrated, and groaned. "Okay, this sounds weird. Forget it. Let's go back to doing that thing. Before I stopped us doing that thing. Which I was an idiot to do. Because I really want us to do that thing."

She put a hand on her belly. "Here? At Manipura?"

"Yes! Yes. There. So you did? Please say you did."

She had. Her Manipura Chakra had slipped out of alignment so fractionally, and over such a long period, she had barely noticed it. Physician heal thyself, she thought ruefully.

Well, she had. Or more importantly, she had opened up to the possibility of someone else helping her with it.

"Funnily enough, I've been told I need a holiday from being in charge for a while. Turns out, Source seems to agree."

His melted chocolate eyes stared down at her, and he nodded slowly.

"I guess Source thinks we can balance each other. Very Goldilocks."

She frowned until she got it. "Ahhh. Not too little, not too much control for either of us."

"Just the right amount," he said, "at the right time."

She grinned. "Exactly. Now, let's get back to doing that thing."

"I think I can handle taking charge," Archer raised his eyebrows up and down at Cara. "Until you want to take it back. For a while, anyway."

He loved the idea that with Cara, they could take that in turns. That neither of them needed to be the strong one, but they could have each other's backs and lead at different times. That control could ebb and flow between them.

"Wanna come hang out and relax on my boat?"

He slid his hands up her arms, clasping them behind her back and pulling her into his chest. She felt so right there. She fit just under his chin. He kissed the top of her head.

She leaned back to look him in the eye. "You're taking my advice? Stepping back from the stress of running Disp@tch?"

He nodded. "Someone told me it was spiking my cortisol levels. Apparently, Phoebe agrees. Plus, I believe I have other things to do."

He caught her left hand, and tugged it up to uncover her bracelet. Then he clasped his right forearm over hers, their bracelets touching.

A shimmer of energy went through him from head to toe. A rightness. It was as if the ether was offering them more power than the usual amount he was able to pull. He closed his eyes and let his body bathe in it for a moment, the energy curling and wrapping around them both.

"The prophecy is mostly upside for me, apart from that pesky end-of-our-race stuff," he commented, as the power caressed him. "There are plenty of relics and energetic history to explore, which might help with the documentary I'm planning at some point. Oh, and there's also an incredible woman involved, who's smart, interesting and very, very capable."

Her cheeks heated.

"I can still consult, and code, and do the things I love, without the management stress." And for some reason, now that he'd faced down Elrian and Imogen, his need to prove himself to his parents had fallen away.

Perspective, he thought. It was a wonderful thing.

Cara stepped away from him, and put the last of the papers on the table into the box.

She picked up her bag, and hesitated a moment, her hand hovering over the stress balls which lay on the table. He tilted his head, waiting.

She shrugged, and pulled her hand back. Empty.

Elrian sat on the porch, wrapped in a blanket and drinking the matcha tea Cassidy had made him. She waited behind him, uncertain. The power he had taken into him on the island had nearly killed him, and he was cold all the time. Cold and empty.

And he no longer had the fallback of his ring.

Imogen's identity as Maya was finished. She'd had little choice after she had revealed herself on Vancouver Island but to not return to the Guild. Cassidy already knew her, of course, but as Imogen, and he'd deliberately kept the two women apart in the past. That would no longer be possible.

However, Maya had left chaos in the Guild, that could only be to their advantage. Aiko was going to need to get her house in order before she was able to properly aid the energetics in the prophecy.

"I should kill you," Imogen said to Elrian. Her words were cool, but her eyes showed a fire that wanted to burn him alive.

At this point, he wasn't sure how much he cared about living or dying.

"You were draining the earth. Taking the energy Source has tasked us with protecting. You would have left the island barren if I hadn't stopped you." He gulped, reliving the horror. "An action as bad as the humans."

The bone that had broken in her leg was healing, and she sat on another wooden chair with the leg up and splinted, while her Anahata energy worked to mend the break. She shrugged. "I needed it to destroy Cara and Archer. But you stopped me. And so, yet again, we failed. Four of the six pairs have bracelets, and we have only two more chances to stop them from succeeding."

Cassidy had her hand to her mouth. "What is going on?"

Imogen glanced at her and narrowed her eyes. "You're still keeping her in the dark? Removing her memories?"

He nodded, shoulders hunching as Cassidy turned horrified eyes on him.

"Yes."

And he'd have to do it again after this conversation. With Imogen in the house, Cassidy would be exposed to their plans more and more often. He only hoped it didn't affect her magics and other parts of her memory too much. Some part of him, the part that still had wishes that weren't to do with the plan, wanted to protect her from Imogen. After the island, his love for Imogen remained, but he trusted her restraint less. There was something about the necklace that was *wrong*.

Were their goals still aligned?

He still needed energy to achieve his goals. He hungered for the hit of energy taken from another. His ability to pull from the ether was barely a drizzle at this point.

"Send her away," Imogen spat. "She's a liability, even more than you."

He breathed in deeply, as if the oxygen would compensate for the lack of energy inside him.

"I need her to help me seek the last two energetics involved in the prophecy. While it's likely Adam and Phoebe are the next couple, there are still two energetics we can't see. Cassidy is one of the strongest Ajna energetics I know." *Just like her brother*, he thought.

"No more failure," Imogen said. Her back was ramrod straight. Her eyes stared ahead, though at what, he didn't know. "We find them and destroy them. There is no longer a need for subtlety. My links to the Guild are gone, but we have connections to those who support our aims throughout the Guilds. It's time to enlist them. It's time for war."

Cassidy stepped back from the table, looking at Imogen as if she were a poisonous snake.

He nodded. "As long as the natural environment is respected as Source wishes, I am yours, lady, for whatever you need."

He turned to Cassidy. "Come here, love."

She recoiled, eyes, as always before he took this action, full of hurt and betrayal. He knew, however, it would be gone momentarily. She wouldn't remember their conversation, would believe Imogen was a house guest, here to help Elrian with his research. Innocent research that Cassidy would help with. He exhaled, and reached out to take Cassidy's hand.

She let him, but didn't draw closer. Her other hand had moved from her mouth to her throat.

"Father, what have you done?"

CARA AND THE HACKER

EPILOGUE

Archer looked across the second boat he had procured for the expedition, that would join the one already anchored close to the relics site. He was wearing his new favorite t-shirt, which said 'St. George's Rare Books' a reference to the bookstore owned by Gabriel Knight in his favorite game.

A gift from his favorite woman, to replace the shirt he'd destroyed in the lighthouse.

Their hand-picked group of energetics would likely stay out at sea for several days, and needed more berths than his other boat contained. He was looking forward to seeing how Ai's diving skills had progressed.

Cara sat deep in conversation with Blaize and Nixie in the ship's bow, while Cuinn stood talking to Dylan, the nomadic archeologist-artist.

Tierra and Fintan would join Jeb at Anahata Guild, badly hit by the fallout from Imogen's actions, and under fire from the other Guilds. They would work with Aiko—carefully.

Imogen in her current incarnation was terrifying. No individual energetic could stand up to her, and Cuinn had shared his worry that even with a group of them they might not be able to contain her power.

Cuinn felt understanding the prophecy better would help them understand how to beat her, and he and Blaize would continue their work on that while on the boat.

While Archer understood better what was at stake, having seen Imogen and Elrian's magic at work, he couldn't help the excitement that bubbled within him. He had an opportunity few energetics in this era had been exposed to, the possibility of understanding more about why his race had lost their homeland of Atlantis.

They had the latest equipment on board, and a team that had literally been prophesied to save the world.

Cara laughed, and his gaze snagged on her. Her shimmering honey-blonde hair rippled around her face, and she frowned briefly, before glancing toward him. He smiled as her bronze eyes met his. Her lips curved upward.

And let's not forget, he had this smart, focused, incredible woman.

A woman who Source had given him a chance to love, and who made his heart sing.

His grin widened. "Cast off, crew. It's time to put to sea."

A woman he was literally going to sail off into the sunset with.

The End

Glossary

Adherent—Once an energetic is taken on by a Maven, they are called an Adherent as they train for their Chakra trial. As part of the ritual when they bond with their Maven, they receive one thin black band around the top of their arm (left arm for females, right arm for males).

Ajna—The Third Eye Chakra, associated with the element of the Mind and the color indigo. The energy of imagination, of visualizations, and insight. Of clarity and wisdom. Of dreams and intuition.

Anahata—The Heart Chakra, associated with the element of the Air and the color green. The energy of healing, and of balance, located in the middle of the body, and the middle of the seven Chakras. The energy of love, of relationships, of devotion. Of compassion and empathy.

Archetypes—There are six energetic Archetypes, one for each of the first six Chakras. See **Protector, Creator, Healer, Communicator,**

Warrior, **Sage**. Each has a symbol associated with it and specific magics.

Auxiliary Chakra—Energetics have two Chakras activated in them, that is, energy they can draw upon and use as power. Their auxiliary Chakra is the weaker of the two.

Chakra Trial—When an energetic wants to move up a power level, they are trained for several years by a Maven, and then tested by a Chakra trial (e.g. From Adherent to Practitioner, or Practitioner to Master).

Communicator—The Communicator may be someone who is able to express themselves persuasively, with an ability for languages and communication. Their affinity with the element of space (ether) means they are able to manipulate their own and others' auras, and can use astrology to predict the future. Strong Vishudha energetics may be able to stop time in their locale, and can use the etheric plane to astrally-project or very rarely, physically travel between locations.

Creator—The Creator may be someone who generates many ideas, or has access to fertility or sex magics. Their affinity with the water element means they are able to draw on aspects of the weather, particularly rain and storms, and are at home in bodies of water. They are likely to be able to use creativity to influence others—for example, music, art, or writing. Strong Svadisthana energetics are highly imaginative, and charismatic, and may inspire others in turn. They have a strong affinity for pleasure, and an intuition about what will bring fulfilment and joy to others.

Dormant—When an energetic is born, their energies are Dormant. At birth, their strongest (dominant) Chakra is almost always identifiable and they are given a name linked to this (e.g. Blaize's dominant Chakra is Manipura, linked to fire).

Dominant Chakra—Energetics have two Chakras activated in them, that is, energy they can draw upon and use as power. Their dominant Chakra is the stronger of the two.

Dreamscape—see Ether

Dreamwalker—An Ajna energetic who can go into the dreamscape and gather prophecy.

Ether—Also known as the dreamscape, where Ajna energetics can create their Haven and use Ajna to search for prophecy shards or do other activities related to their energy. The ether is also the place where raw energy is drawn from by energetics, so all energetics have some kind of internal connection to it.

Guild Leader—The energetic who is the leader of either a Major or a Minor Guild. A Guild leader has to 'balance' a Guild's energy so it takes an energetic of some power.

Haven—The space in the ether/dreamscape that an Ajna energetic creates for her or himself that is 'safe'.

Healer—The Healer may be someone who helps others recover from physical, emotional or mental health issues. Their affinity with the air element means they are able to draw on aspects of the weather like winds and storms. They are likely to use their empathy and intuition to read others' emotions and feelings and are highly sensitive. Strong Anahata energetics may be able to use air to lift and move objects (including themselves), or change the composition of the air into different types of gases.

Leech—An energetic who has turned into a Rogue, and is draining other energetics of their energy (not all Rogues are leeches).

Major Guilds—The six Chakras have one Guild each (e.g. Muladhara, Svadisthana, etc.).

Major Circle—The Major Circle is the highest form of government with one powerful energetic representing each Major Guild, making decisions on behalf of the race.

Manipura—The Navel Chakra, associated with the element of Fire and the color yellow. The energy of the individual; of confidence, of proactivity and of drive and passion. Playful and proud.

Master—If an energetic passes a Chakra trial at the end of their Practitioner training, they become a Master energetic, and receive a third thin black band around the top of their arm (left arm for females, right arm for males).

Maven—This is the name for those energetics who take on an Adherent to train in an energy. An energetic has to be at Master level to become a Maven, but Mavens are outside the power structure. Their symbol is an owl on their robes. A Maven can either take on an Adherent only once in a lifetime, or can take on several Adherents consecutively.

Minor Guilds—There are thirty Minor Guilds representing each combination (for example, Manipura-Ajna is a separate Guild from Ajna-Manipura).

Minor Circle—The Minor Circle is the energetics' second tier of government, and is made up of the thirty energetics who lead the Minor Guilds.

Muladhara—The Root Chakra, associated with the element of Earth and the color red. The energy of nourishment and home, family and safety.

Practitioner—Once an energetic has passed a Chakra trial, they are a Practitioner, and receive a second thin black band around the top of their arm (left arm for females, right arm for males). This is the most common level of power for energetics.

Protector—The Protector may be a great tracker, or a great hunter, able to find and capture Rogue energetics. Their affinity with the earth element means they can draw on the power of nature: flora, fauna, or in rare instances, both. They are likely to find working or creating with their hands comfortable and natural, for example, cooking, gardening, building, etc. Strong Muladhara energetics can shake the earth, manipulate plants or trees, or even communicate with animals.

Remnant Stone—A stone that can store the energy of an energetic who has been drained to the point of death.

Rogue—An energetic whose energy has 'twisted' into the negative version of the Chakra.

Sage—The Sage may be someone who is a great teacher and makes wise decisions, with the ability to retain a great deal of detail about a situation. Their affinity with the element of the mind means they have a strong memory, a thirst for knowledge, and may be able to mind-speak (telepathy). Strong Ajna energetics may be able to make true prophecies about their own or others' future, dreamwalk on the etheric plane, or manipulate others' minds.

Sahasara—The Crown Chakra, not associated with an element. The purest of all the energies. Only experienced through the Grace of the Source (the energetics' name for the creator, the divine).

Svadisthana—The Sacral Chakra, associated with the element of Water and the color orange. Fluid and adaptable, the energy of movement and connection, of practical and physical creativity. The energy of pleasure, sexuality and sensation, and emotions.

Vishudha—The Throat Chakra, associated with the element of Ether (Space) and the color blue. The energy of communication, of conceptual creativity, and of truth. Of expression, and of listening.

Warrior—The Warrior may be someone who courageously defends others physically or verbally. Their affinity with the fire element means they are able to draw on the power of light and heat. They are likely to be able to use their drive to make things happen, and if they go after a goal, they rarely fail. Strong Manipura energetics are able to use fire offensively (such as fire balls or bullets) and defensively (such as fire shields). In rare cases they can call lightning or use electricity.

The Guilds and Circles

The energetics' power structure is Guild based.

There are six Major Guilds, one for each of the six Chakras:

- **Muladhara** (The Root Chakra—Earth Element)
- **Svadisthana** (The Sacral Chakra—Water Element)
- **Manipura** (The Navel Chakra—Fire Element)
- **Anahata** (The Heart Chakra—Air Element)
- **Vishudha** (The Throat Chakra—Ether (Space) Element)
- **Ajna** (The Third Eye—The Mind)

  (Sahasara, the Crown Chakra, does not have a Guild.)

Each energetic has two activated Chakras, one dominant and one auxiliary, and it is the combination of these that influences their power, and to some degree, their personality.

Because of the huge differences between an energetic like Blaize, who combines her Manipura dominant with Ajna auxiliary, and one like Fintan, who combines Manipura dominant with Anahata auxiliary, a system of Minor Guilds also developed. There are thirty

Minor Guilds representing each combination of powers (for example, Manipura-Ajna is a separate Guild from Ajna-Manipura).

Each individual energetic therefore belongs to two Major Guilds, and one Minor Guild.

For example: Cuinn has Ajna dominant, and Muladhara auxiliary. He therefore belongs to the Ajna Major Guild, the Muladhara Major Guild, and the Ajna-Muladhara Minor Guild.

The Major Circle is the highest form of government with one powerful energetic representing each Major Guild, making decisions on behalf of the race. The Minor Circle, the second tier of government, is made up of the thirty energetics who lead each of the Minor Guilds.

- Muladhara-Svadisthana
- Muladhara-Manipura
- Muladhara-Anahata
- Muladhara-Vishudha
- Muladhara-Ajna
- Svadisthana-Muladhara
- Svadisthana-Manipura
- Svadisthana-Anahata
- Svadisthana-Vishudha
- Svadisthana-Ajna
- Manipura-Muladhara
- Manipura-Svadisthana
- Manipura-Anahata
- Manipura-Vishudha
- Manipura-Ajna
- Anahata-Muladhara
- Anahata-Svadisthana
- Anahata-Manipura

- Anahata-Vishudha
- Anahata-Ajna
- Vishudha-Muladhara
- Vishudha-Svadisthana
- Vishudha-Manipura
- Vishudha-Anahata
- Vishudha-Ajna
- Ajna-Muladhara
- Ajna-Svadisthana
- Ajna-Manipura
- Ajna-Anahata
- Ajna-Vishudha

Want More?

The story of the energetics continues in Phoebe's story, **Phoebe and the Artist**.

To get it now, visit my website where you can also receive updates, giveaways and inside information:
EllenBardAuthor.com/sign-up

Discover Your Energetic Profile!
Want to know what your Dominant Chakra would be?
Which Guild you would belong to? What your archetype is?

Take the Chakra Quiz, and find out!
EllenBardAuthor.com/chakra-quiz

Make a Difference with a Review

If you have a few minutes, I would hugely appreciate it if you had time to leave a short review wherever you bought the book, and / or on goodreads. For instructions, go to the link below.

EllenBardAuthor.com/how-to-leave-a-review

Your review will help other readers discover the series, and is greatly appreciated in spreading the word. Authors like me rely on amazing readers like you to share their love of books with others.

Thank you!

About the Author

Ellen is an author who writes paranormal romance full of enchantment, intrigue and action. Her writing blends a background in psychology and her experiences traveling the world, with a love of magic, fantasy and a happy ending.

Alongside writing fiction (and non-fiction under Ellen M Bard), she's a Chartered Psychologist, and works as an international management consultant. Her work in more than 25 countries and her passion for other cultures help inform her writing, as does her desire to try new things—from riding a motorbike, or art classes, or Krav Maga, the self-defence system.

A passionate and dedicated reader, find her on goodreads to see what currently has her hooked.

Born in the UK, Ellen lives with her family in Bangkok, Thailand, and her books reflect her belief in the transformative power of love and personal growth—to heal, evolve, and conquer any challenge, no matter how supernatural.

Connect with Ellen:
Tiktok: tiktok.com/@ellenbard
Facebook: facebook.com/EllenBardAuthor
Goodreads: goodreads.com/ellenbard
Instagram: instagram.com/ellenbard

Acknowledgements

I am incredibly lucky to have a family that are so supportive. My mum, Mary Bard, and sister, Sarah Bard, use their English degrees, smarts and love of books to be my alpha readers, and give me super helpful suggestions and notes on the early, **very** rough drafts. They are instrumental in me getting my work out there and I am so grateful.

My Aunt Ellen (it's a family name!), puts her detail conscientiousness to good use and proofs the final copy to make sure nothing strange has slipped in—or more important, has slipped out—at the printer. I am thankful for her work and the supportive words she always has for me.

I appreciate my editor, Heather Osbourn for all her suggestions, and my fantastic cover designer Erin Dameron-Hill for ensuring my book is something I am proud to share.

I have several brilliant beta readers who invest time and energy giving me feedback, including Katie Craddock and Eleonore King. Their feedback helps me understand how readers react to my work, and lets me tweak it to ensure I'm getting the characters of Archer and Cara across, as well as ther story.

Friends Tracy, Graham, Anna and Lisa are there when I need a pep talk, remind me to follow my own advice and take care of myself, and provide much needed love and support outside the book.

BookTok has been a new source of fun and encouragement for this book. If you follow me there, thank you!

To my partner, Fox, and our 'jeune homme'. You two are my heart, and I've loved talking magic systems over the dinner table, visiting far flung locations in Thailand that inspire me, and all the tiny day-to-day moments that keep me going.

And finally, if you're 'just' a regular reader, and you picked this up somewhere, and then you not only read the whole book, but you're reading these acknowledgements, hear this: I appreciate you. When you read an indie author's book, you give them the gift of your time and attention, and I am so thankful to each and every one of you. I wish you magic and sparkles every day of your life.